Island on Fire

Island on Fire

A True Saga

by JOSEPH HAYES

Publishers · GROSSET & DUNLAP · New York
A FILMWAYS COMPANY

This book is dedicated, as all others, to my wife Marrijane, with love and with gratitude for her patience and devotion, often ill-deserved by me.

And with a sidelong nod of thanks to James Oliver Brown and to Martha and Foster Harmon, all of whom helped in various ways.

PRONUNCIATION

It would be impossible to give English pronunciations for all the names in the book, but here are three very rough approximations of:

Heimaey (the island)   HAY-may

Vestmannaeyjar (the town)   VEST-mun-ayer

Kirkjufell (the volcano)   KIRK-yu-fell

This is a novel based on fact.
The eruption and the struggle to save this town actually occurred. The means used to fight the volcano are the ones described here.
Liberties have been taken as this is not a documentary account, but the story of people caught up in catastrophe. It is a story of human reactions, changes in character, and the interlocking fates of townspeople and strangers.
The characters are fictional and are not intended to represent any individuals.

ONE

AT THE END of the last Ice Age, approximately fifteen thousand years ago, south of the mainland of Iceland in the North Atlantic, where a finger of the warmer Gulf Stream joins the subarctic waters of the North, volcanic violence on the floor of the sea erupted and, rising from the depths like monsters seeking light and air, or escape from the chaos below, islands appeared—a cluster of fifteen rocks in blueness, dark and jagged, rimmed with white lines of surf.

The islands are of tuff, or volcanic dust and ash hardened into rock, and lava petrified by cold. Their landscape is at once majestic and stark, harsh but magnificent, with steep, furrowed cliffs standing high and crowned with flat, flower-strewn roofs of emerald green. Like these plateaus atop the bluffs, the lowlands are covered by a thin crust of soil that time has miraculously rendered verdant, although it is a soil not deep enough to nourish trees or, except on the island of Heimaey, yield tillable crops. Green mosslike grasses and reeds abound, and in summer the cliffsides are yellow with blossoms.

Peaceful and idyllic as they now seem—like the mystic isles of dreams or childhood fancies, encircled by the glittering sea breaking white against high, precipitous headlands—the history of the Vestmann Islands is perhaps even more bloody and barbaric than most. Legend has it that, before the settlement of Iceland by Norsemen around

1

the year 900, two Viking brothers, having raided and looted
and ravaged Irish villages, brought with them to the mainland of Iceland ten captured Irishmen as thralls, or slaves,
and that these Irishmen, rising up in fury, killed one of the
brothers and all his men and then took all the women as well
as one of the sweetly curved, eggshell-thin, high-masted
ships to an island they saw lying some miles offshore. The
other Viking brother, true to the Norse code of honor and
revenge, pursued them with his men, searched them out in
crag and cave, and mercilessly butchered them all. Because
in those times all people living in Europe to the west of
Norway were known as westmen, the islands have ever since
borne the name: the islands of the men of the west.

The ten centuries between that time and the present
have been cursed by invasions, piracy, plundering, pillaging,
carnage—and in 1402 by the Black Death, or plague, which
killed off two-thirds of the entire population of Iceland. But
in recent times, probably no more tranquil—or healthy—
place could be found on the map, nor a people more gentle.

Since there is scarcely any lowland on the other islands,
Heimaey is the only one occupied: a volcanic knob four miles
north to south and less than two miles wide. Heimaey itself
was formed five thousand years ago by the last outburst of a
volcano which joined two islets into one. Ever since, looming
and brooding over Heimaey, is the elegant cone of that volcano, Helgafell, rising almost seven hundred feet above rolling, flowered hills and surmounted by a delicate cone of
tephra.

At the beginning of the year 1973, on the northern tip
of Heimaey and rising clean and bright to the flanks of the
ancient volcano, reposed the quiet fishing village of Vestmannaeyjar, which appeared to have taken root on the lava
crust as positively and firmly as on any verdant plain or
valley meadow. Snugly perched on a low terraced hillside
over its own harbor—itself embraced and sheltered from the
sea's wildness by a curving configuration of immense cliffs
rising from the water and therefore known as Peace
Harbor—the town fanned out from the higher warehouses

and plants at wharfside to streets of gray lava cobbles and red lava gravel. The masonry stores and houses, built close together—roofs and walls painted white and yellow, chocolate and various shades of blue and green, pastel pinks and burnt orange—looked solid and neat, permanent, as if fixed in the basaltic rock, and unassailable. Yet there was something playful and gay about the village, too—as if its people over the generations had decided that the mingling of all those colors might provide some human defiance and inner protection against the gloom and darkness of nature during the bleak and endless winters. Surrounded by the deep, eternal sea, which is never so calm that its surface, whether brilliant blue or stygian black, is not adorned by rippling silver crescents, the town appeared to possess a vivid vitality, as if it had sprung up quite by chance on some atoll in the Caribbean or Mediterranean.

In those twelve hundred homes, greeting the New Year of 1973, none of the five thousand islanders gave any thought to that mound, lovely and sinister, which they had seen all their lives towering over the rooftops to the east. Indications were strong and hopes were high for the best cod season in a decade. By the end of January, normally the month when the sea gives up its richest yield, only three hundred and eleven human beings, many of them strangers, were on the island. And none could be certain that the town would ever again return to life.

Margret Magnusdottir, wife of Arni Loftsson, the school teacher, had fair skin like most of the other women, but she also, unlike them, had a fine and delicate-boned face and lush, dark hair with a raven sheen to it, and this difference in appearance—in contrast to the blond girls and women with whom she had spent her entire life here in Vestmannaeyjar—had been a source of disturbance to her. When a girl is young, she must be like the others. But now, at twenty-four, she had come not only to an acceptance of her appearance but to an áwareness that, because of this difference, she possessed a certain exotic beauty here, and she had come to take a certain pride in this. She had read, as a matter of course and without taking them as seriously as Arni seemed to, the histories and the Eddic poems and the Icelandic sagas, as had anyone passing through the schools, and she knew that the Vikings who had settled Iceland had brought thralls from Ireland with them and that, in time, the Celtic strain had mingled with the Scandinavian; she knew, too, that in years long gone, a freed slave, with the dark mottled mark of iron still showing round his neck, was treated as someone less than human and that his family, for a generation or two, was looked down upon. But this was 1973—January, a whole new year beginning really—and all those sad and miserable and cruel days lay in the past and were no part of her. Still, she sometimes wondered whether, if she had been light-haired, like most of the others, or even red-haired, like a few, Arni would have loved her more. Whenever such thoughts drifted across her mind, as they were doing as she lifted the tray of fried crullers, cold now, from the broadshelf to place them in the cabinet, she had to remind herself how very much Arni did really love her.

It was only the drink. Yes.

She had worked hard on the crullers earlier. In the well-lighted kitchen—the darkness outside, and down the street the lamps still burning since yesterday's dusk at half-after three, glowing and swaying high in a freshened breeze that, even as she measured out the cardamon and flour and sugar, had turned into a whistling wind, and while she had rolled out the dough and cut it into strips and fried them in the hot fat that steamed the kitchen pleasantly—she had known only joy: Arni's favorite breakfast. But he had not eaten. Again. He had gone out into the plaintively crying darkness without so much as a sip of the black coffee that he had always loved.

And then the fear had set in.

Again.

It was with her still. Beyond the windows the darkness, now a faint gray, showed dimly. Margret really didn't mind the dark. Unlike many others whom she knew, she had accepted it from the beginning. Even as a child, the daylight coming and going while she was imprisoned in the classroom—as well, as well, so it was. But there were those who felt differently. Many. And, like Arni, they turned to drink. Small wonder then at the rules governing alcohol in all of Iceland or that the temperance movement should be so widespread and influential. Nevertheless, if he wanted to drink, Arni would find the *brennivan*—aptly called Black Death. And there was always wine and rum on the foreign ships in the harbor. Arni always found a way.

And he had not appeared at the school three days last week. Did he think she did not know? Did he care?

It was by now that time of morning when, normally, a neighbor might come in for coffee or when, routinely, she might go to her sister's or to a friend's. Always for coffee. And a talk. A way to break the monotony, to take advantage of the brief time of daylight.

Margret felt a faint flutter of panic inside and fought it down. She really didn't feel like talking with anyone now. Especially not with her sister. Strange, she often thought, that she and Hana, parents long dead now, were not closer. But loneliness was streaming through her. And, yes, fear as well. Was Arni in his classroom teaching? And when he did come home—he always came home—should she tell him her secret?

She could not tell him certainly, unless he was himself—unless he was sober. But she had come to wonder which of the two men was really himself: the wild, cruel, accusing stranger, eyes frantic and tormented by suspicion and doubt, or the handsome, young, and vital man she had fallen in love with three summers ago at the summer festival.

She could not think of that now. She dared not remember.

She put on her wool cardigan, white with the brown and black design, wide and intricate around the neck, and then drew on her dark brown lambskin coat and her white knitted beret with pompon and matching mittens and went outside into the dimness, which was punctuated by the lights in windows and the rows of streetlamps running along both sides of pink gravel streets and meeting other similar rows at the corners. The wind surprised her: she had heard it from inside the house, yes, but it was quite strong really, harsh against her face.

And the thoughts of summer returned: the days that never ended, the light twenty-four hours, the sun, the enchantment. In the harbor, the many gull-shaped fishing boats, their hulls painted in primitive blues, greens, reds, yellows, the colors subdued and mellowed by sea and salt and sun, their radio masts swaying like pendulums, and the birds everywhere, in the cliffs and on the sea, a gentle drone always, and the sound of wings: the memories of the summer became a longing, an ache inside. And the festival, celebrated every year in Herjolfsdalur, named for the first settler, a lush and lovely valley some distance from town, aeons ago a volcanic crater but now a lake of green, green grass under the encircling precipice of Aegisdyr, where at the beginning of August a canvas city grows, as most of the town dwellers and many from the mainland move there for three days of festivities—games, music, dancing, laughter and the beautifully decorated valley takes on the magical aspect of a fairy tale. Oh, how the faces look then: lighted, carefree, eyes bright, so unlike the grave and solemn faces of winter. And the singing and the bonfire at midnight of the first day, the flickering flames playing on the green slopes, brown rocks, and colorful tents, lifted voices blending and echoing in crag and sky, the struggle of the stormy seas forgotten for a time.

And Arni. Who had come from Reykjavik to live here. She had not known love until then, three years ago. It had been his gaiety even more than his blond and Viking-handsome masculinity—the lean, tall strength of his body, the color high on his cheeks, the intense and burning blue of his eyes, and the wide slash of mouth that seemed then always to be smiling—yes, it had been his joyful and exultant spirit that had brought her to a new and quivering life.

And now.

Margret realized where she was going. It was a place to which, since childhood, she had retreated whenever she needed tranquility. Foolish, perhaps—childish, yes. She was moving now down a slight incline, hardly a hill, past the hotel, with the lights of the harbor glittering at the end of the street. And on her left, just beyond the fire station, was a low square building with a mural of birds and fish painted on its façade: the aquarium. And inside, how well she knew, the many fish gliding serenely behind glass, and the birds and small animals of the area in glass cases looked alive still. Already, as she approached, she began to feel more relaxed, not at peace, but hopeful of a few minutes, perhaps hours, of quiet. And a temporary escape from the questions haunting her mind—questions which she could not force into focus. Why did she hesitate to tell Arni of the child? *Why?*

Shivering, she turned and walked through the familiar and welcoming doors, and warmth reached out to embrace her.

In the year 1627 there were thirteen moons instead of twelve. It was the year of the Turks.

Actually the pirates, who raided and pillaged the island in that year, were men of many nations; the ship itself was from Morocco, and their leader was a Dutchman—a religious fanatic who went under the name of Rais Murad. He had raided the mainland earlier, robbing and ravaging. The islanders were defenseless. The invaders, three hundred strong, indulged every barbarism: they cut the elderly in half or burned them alive, snapped infants' necks, murdered one of the two priests under the eyes of his wife and children, razed farms, the church, and the Danish houses, raped the women, and then combed the islands for those who had hidden in caves and holes. These they drove to the three ships, hacking to pieces anyone who moved too slowly. By the time they left, they had killed thirty-six people and had taken along, to be sold to the slave markets and to die under the scorching African sun, two hundred and forty-two men, women and children. It was a devastating blow. All that remained was a village in ruins, with scattered, burnt, and broken bodies and a handful of survivors who had escaped to the cliffs and were now utterly overwhelmed by grief.

Every islander knows the story from childhood, and even today parents sometimes threaten unruly children with the "Turks."

More than most people in Vestmannaeyjar, Hulda Palmadottir was aware of the story in all its horror. The past was alive in her mind, not only her own past, all eighty-three years of it, but the past of the island. And the legends. For instance, when Hulda heard the wind grow from a whistling to a low mournful wail outside the walls of the home for the elderly, she was reminded of the Turks. Why? Because, she knew, the Turks were not only pirates. The Turks meant disaster, catastrophe of any sort. It could be a storm, one of those North Atlantic gales that she had survived many times. True, high winds were common on Heimaey, but since there would be a full moon at the beginning and one at the end of June, this was again the year of the thirteen moons. And further: the town had expanded beyond the upthrust stone that nature had set as its westernmost boundary, and the parson in the church was the son of a bishop. Had it not been foretold that when all this came about in the same year, the Turks would return? Hulda had not spoken of any of this to anyone; she knew what folk thought of the forebodings of old women. The elderly, she understood, were cared for here—their physical needs anyway—but let them chatter among themselves: the old always take delight in conjuring up bad omens.

Hulda Palmadottir was not bitter, or resentful. A large, big-boned woman, wide-shouldered, with thick white hair and a small but strong-chinned face, cobwebbed with wrinkles, with eyes pale and rheumy that had once been dark blue and clear, she sat deep in her favorite chair in the parlor listening to the wind mount in violence and gazing out at the dust being driven along the narrow, curving street in gusts.

Storms. Death. They went together. First, her husband: his vessel driven against the rocks, his body never recovered. Then, years later, her son: washed overboard into the arctic waters. Years ago. Many years ago. How long? How old was she? She sometimes had to stop and think hard in order to remember. And sometimes she was wrong at that. But they had found his body, her son's. It had washed up on the island itself, stiff and unreal, and he had been buried in the cemetery in the churchyard. But before that, the night she sat alone with him, she would never forget, she didn't care whether anyone believed it had happened: he had moved, he had sat up, he had whispered to her. She couldn't remember now what he had said, but it had happened. Why shouldn't people believe? They read these things in the sagas: those stories were filled with ghosts, with people coming back from death, speaking, predicting. Yes, now she remembered: her son had told her she would live long, before she came to the happy place where he resided. Yes. Even the gods can't sever the threads of destiny spun by the Norns at a person's birth. As the spinstress spinneth, so shall it be.

How many had she known who, during the long, dark night of winter, unable to bear more, had walked into the sea? Yes, and some from this very house. How many times had she herself been tempted? Loneliness is a heavy burden, yes, heavy, heavy. Her widowed daughter had married a mainlander and moved to Reykjavik. What was the girl's name? She no longer came to the island, even to visit. She would not be a girl now, a woman, with her own children perhaps or grandchildren even. What year was it now? January: she knew that. Oh, her mind might wander but Hulda Palmadottir knew a few things. When she was younger, she had been sharp-witted enough. A woman with her own will and stubborn as well, tart-tongued perhaps. But she had stood tall as Valkyrie.

But now, forsaken here, the gale rising, looking down the months toward the April sun and the June crystal brilliance, she gave in to her feeling of utter worthlessness, waste, waiting only to . . .

Why didn't she then walk into the sea? She could still walk, straight and firm. Yes, there would be a dignity in that.

Since Agnar, because of the weather, had not been able to take out his boat, the *Njord,* named for the ancient god of navigation, his wife, Ruth, had prepared the salt lamb and yellow-pea soup that in the twenty years of their marriage Agnar had come to anticipate on those days when he could not fish. She had taken pleasure in mincing the onion, cutting the rutabagas into chunks, and slicing the carrots; she had taken even more pleasure in watching the satisfaction on Agnar's heavy, deep-lined, leather-fleshed face as his thick muscular hands lifted the spoon to his mouth. A traditional dish, which both she and Agnar had known since childhood, was one of the compensations for Agnar on those days when he was imprisoned in the house, or at least in the town, the sea raging.

After the meal, Agnar had telephoned Jonas at the radio center for the third time that day. There was no definite prediction, although Jonas personally expected the wind to drop by nightfall. Then he had gone, restless, walking with his own heavy grace and vigor, into the living room, and she knew that he was now smoking his pipe and reading. A woman thinks that a man, given a day's freedom, would savor it, but no, a man like Agnar, no. And particularly not at the beginning of the cod season.

The wind was worse, oh much worse now: like some

frantic god on a rampage, Thor perhaps, whose chariot wheels made the thunder—although there was no thunder today, only the gray threat of rain. Ruth cleaned and waxed and polished, humming. With Agnar safe in the next room, the blow was not her enemy. There were other days, other times, when he was *not* in the next room but at a place reckoned only in longitude and latitude—och, then it was a different matter.

She heard him stirring and then Agnar appeared, drawing on his heavy coat with the faded sheepskin collar. The strong, rough smell of smoke came with him, and, as always, he bent forward slightly passing through the door, although there was no need—the lifelong habit of a tall man stooping in hatchways and companionways.

"Out into this?" she asked, pushing back from her high forehead a strand of hair that, while still fair, seemed to her fingers stiffened and coarsened by the years.

"I've seen worse," Agnar said, placing the black, years-crumpled captain's cap over his thick, brown hair. "If it settles—and it's my reckoning it will—I'll take the *Njord* out around midnight. Meanwhile, I'll look in on Axel for coffee."

"It's roast lamb for supper." It was almost always lamb and always meat—imagine a fish skipper who would never eat fish. "Rosa will not be working, so she'll be with us."

Agnar smiled faintly, probably picturing their blond-haired, brown-eyed daughter who, clerking now at the tiny Icelandic Airlines office in town, seemed, at nineteen, still an impish child, for all her slim height that dwarfed her mother's and almost matched her father's. Then Agnar's face sobered. "And Rolf?" he asked, shoving his pipe into his pocket.

What could she say? "I do hope," she said.

He nodded. Then he stepped closer and his face cleared. "And after the roast lamb," he said in quite a different tone, "and to hell with the American cowboys on television—the two of us, before I go out with the crew." He grinned. "I'll need warming after my lazy day and the long walking in the blow. Do I speak true?"

Ruth's body went warm, then hot, and she could feel a

familiar and an altogether exciting emptiness all through her. The man could still do this to her. "You speak true," she said in a whisper, wishing it were night again.

And Agnar, changing as he always did, laughed—a husky burst of warm delight to match her own eagerness and anticipation. He leaned and kissed her forehead. No more. Enough. He went out. The wind swept like a howl into the kitchen before he shut it out with his strength. Time's roughening of her once-silken hair was forgotten now, and the years fell away, even as she chided herself, returning to the scouring.

He would walk today, stiff and tall against the storm, and he would have coffee with Axel, one of his crewmen who, three years ago, had been washed overboard and hurled against the jagged rocks of the island of Geirfuglasker. Dr. Pall, who had also saved her son Rolf's life during his second attack of pneumonia, had amputated Axel's leg well above the knee, and the poor man had survived and now entertained at parties by jigging on his wooden leg. It was Agnar's way to take him tobacco as often as possible and, Ruth suspected, a bottle of *brennivan* to lift the spirits. Agnar enjoyed his cups, like the others, but he had not become its victim, any more than he had ever become the victim of the dismal night.

Nor had she. The dark was even less her enemy than the fury blowing outside now. In a few months the days would lengthen and then, soon after, there would be the sun and the daylight through all the hours of the night. Meanwhile, she took more than comfort, a certain sweet and harmonious gladness in the cavelike comfort of her home. The furnace heated it well, and she knew that, in time, Vestmannaeyjar would find a way to pipe the natural heat of the mainland under the frigid water and into the houses of the island. Why, it was only a few years ago that the villagers had collected water from their roofs in tanks and, in a drought, water had to be transported in ships from the mainland. But then they had constructed an aqueduct running twenty-two kilometers from Merkurland to the coast and then under the sea; and someday they would enjoy the other conveniences of Reykjavik. But they would enjoy them here. Ruth had visited Reykjavik only a few times; it was not for her. This was her home, here, and had always been.

After coffee with Axel Sitfusson, Agnar would, she knew, find some pretext—perhaps buying her one of the new novels—to stop into the bookshop up the slight hill from the harbor on Heidarvegur where Rolf might be working today. If he was not there, helping Kristrun Egilsdottir, he would be at the tool and building-supply store around the corner, working for Kristrun's husband, Rudolph.

Rolf.

She paused in her labors and went into the living room to play her piano. It was not so much a shadow that fell across her mind as a puzzlement. Hers was not so deep or so intense as Agnar's, that she knew. For all his size and the hardness of his body, Agnar was a gentle man. And kind. And, afraid of nothing for himself, it seemed he was vulnerable and open to wounding where Rolf was concerned. His anger, quietly explosive on occasion—his face going dark and hard and his blue eyes burning—erupted out of anxiety, concern. It might flare like poison, but its source was love. No doubt whatever that he wished—no, longed—that Rolf would in time take over the *Njord*. But there was more, and Ruth knew there was more, more, oh so much more. Rolf's motorcycle, his staying away from home at all hours, his boyish brightness, recently dulling to a sullen contempt that could, at times, cause his father either to reply in fury or to leave the room in dismay, a man bewildered.

Something in her nature, Ruth realized, some natural cheer or optimism, would not allow her to give in to Agnar's fear. The boy was, after all, only seventeen. Her pain was in sensing Agnar's and, God help her, Rolf's as well. Wasn't the child truly as bewildered and perturbed as Agnar—possibly more so? Rolf saw every film shown at the only theater in town: all the far places, the handsome people, the violent, the cruel, the exciting. How was she to know what craving, what aching need, what hunger gnawed at him? He had once blurted out that the island was a dull and dreary hell on earth. How had he come to feel this? How *could* he?

Still . . . still, Arni Loftsson, the school teacher, had himself suggested—during the summer festival in Her-jolfsdalur when he had joined her in the dancing—that perhaps Vestmannaeyjar was not the place for Rolf. And what was it Agnar had said when she told him? That, while Arni Loftsson might think of himself as Odin, the all-wise god and patron of poetry, that young man might soon find himself without even a job if he continued drinking in his usual manner.

Ruth ran her fingers down the keys and stood. It was time to begin preparing supper. The saddle of lamb would take an hour; she would have oven-roasted potatoes with long beans and sweet-sour red cabbage. She only hoped Rolf would come home in time.

And Rosa would be coming in soon. What a joy that girl was. Smiling always. And the bright innocence of her open gaze.

Ah well, all would right itself, after all. The wind would die. The days would lengthen. Rolf would search and find. Agnar would come to accept, and with less and less anguish and foreboding. And, in time, Rosa would marry. Ruth knew all this. It was not something she had learned. It was, she decided, something deep in her whole being. And whatever came, that something would save her—as it always had.

The people of Vestmannaeyjar are a kindly folk. They do not like to use words that might wound or ring cruelly on the ear. They shun words such as retarded or demented or insane. If a person is different, he or she is simply that: not like other people. These individuals, whether child, man or woman, or senile or old, are accepted as manifestations of the

variety and mystery of life on earth. They do not treat such
human beings with condescension, only with gentleness, gen-
erosity. Like the long, black nights of winter and the long,
silver days of summer, they exist. And, existing, they are
treated with an attitude deeper and more humane than pity:
acceptance.

Josef Gunnarsson was different. He lived on a farm so
near the southwest edge of the island that, from the window
of his bedchamber, he could see the flashing beacon of the
lighthouse flaring even through the darkest night. He was
sixteen years old, although age and years meant little to him,
and he was a happy boy. He had a dog named Odin and,
together, they cared for his father's sheep. In the winters he
enjoyed the sky that throbbed with many colors in the distance to the north, welling up far away like the fire of life at
the edge of the world. The colors would ebb and flare and
throb and fade and then flare again. His father had once told
him that these were the Valkyries swooping down in icy
flames to fetch a hero to Valhalla; but Josef did not understand. He spent many hours absorbed, content, watching
until the northern lights dimmed out and the empty sky
arched above, quiet and black as death. The lights reminded
him of Surtsey, off in the opposite direction, although
Surtsey had been much closer, higher, brighter. His father
had told him it was a volcano from below the sea and was
named for Surtur, god of fire. But Surtsey had gone away. It
had been there and then it had gone away and he had felt
sad. His father explained that it had become another island.
But while it was flashing and burning, his mother and father
had talked of Surtsey in low tones and with a kind of fear in
their voices, his mother especially. But Josef had loved it; it
had been part of his life for a long time. He missed even the
dry, scorched smell that the wind had carried from time to
time and the ashfalls that had given the snow-covered fells
and cliffs a speckled black-white beauty in winter.

In the winters, too, he took pleasure in the snow when it
drifted down and spread its whiteness everywhere, with the
morning light, throwing glittering silver spears into the sky.

It was winter now. He knew, even though there was no snow. Only a terrible rain. It did not snow often, not often enough. He was in his cave, his own place, on a ledge high up on a headland of rock, peering into the downpour over the sea which, with the light almost completely gone now, looked dark with high white ridges; and he could hear the breakers surging and crashing against the jagged stone far down below. But in the rain and dark he could not see his seals in the water, and in winter he missed his birds: the continuous sounds crying, and shrieking from the cliffs and sky, soaring on winds and circling in a never-ending search for food and building their nests precariously close to the brink of the ledges and crags—he could watch them forever, with a great, engulfing calm inside, a low-keyed rapture. His favorite was the puffin, his most loved, with its dark, white-chested, clownlike body and its white-tufted head and red parrotlike beak. Long ago he had watched them hunt the puffins, throwing the bodies down from the cliffs to be gathered by men in small boats below, but now they hunted only the eggs, and he hunted the eggs himself in the summer. His puffins would not come back until the days were long again. He especially loved also the sandpiper with its loud, strange, tremulous song and the whimbrel whistling delightful airs that, at times, could cause Josef to laugh with his mouth as well as with the other soundless parts of him. His birds were as real and as immediate as his father and his mother and his three sisters.

Today, however, even the gulls had taken shelter. Only the gulls and the drake harlequin, with its bright, bold colors of white, black, rust and blue gray—only these few remained in winter. But now they were not to be seen or heard.

Suddenly uneasy himself, he reached to place a hand on Odin, who was curled next to him, warm and shaggy and close. The dog's flesh was quivering. No, his whole body was twitching, shuddering. And Josef recalled of a sudden how the cattle had refused to eat the hay only a short time ago and how they had bellowed in their stalls, how the pony, neighing and stamping, had tried to break down the door of the shed. He felt strangely disturbed. Animals were in many ways wiser than people. Animals sometimes knew things before people knew them.

But what?

Josef made up his mind to stay in the cave. It was not that he was reluctant to go to the house. His mother's sharp tongue and bright, angry eyes were never turned on him, only on his father or his sisters. His father, a giant of a man with a huge flat face and a square jaw, never grew angry, and his sisters dared not. But he was staying for some other reason. He didn't know what it was. He bent his lean, strong body over the dog's and began to murmur soft sounds, not words, of comfort and reassurance. But the quivering continued beneath the thin and bony chest.

Then in a few moments, with the rain closing them in like a curtain over the mouth of the cave, Odin drew away and stood and began to howl.

The navigational radio complex, situated in the post-office building, was the communications center, or pulsebeat, of Vestmannaeyjar. Here, two operators, working in shifts, relayed messages from the seventy-seven vessels of the fishing fleet at sea to the processing plants lining the harbor: the catches, their size, location of the vessel, and approximate arrival time in port. But the station did much more. It was in contact at all times with the weather centers at the University of Reykjavik and at the international airport and NATO base at Keflavik, as well as with the various other vessels, coast-patrol and foreign, reporting from the entire area. It served also as telegraph and cable-relay office. The transatlantic cable, connecting the United Kingdom with Iceland and running thence on to North America through Greenland, passed through a narrow defile of black sand on the southernmost end of the island. In the large, spare office of the center two teletype machines chattered almost continuously. And through a complex and extensive switchboard the crews of the fishing vessels at sea were connected, by radio and telephone, to their homes.

Since on this Monday all the boats were in harbor, because of a rough sea and a southeasterly gale, force twelve, the action at the center was slow. During the afternoon a report was received that the wind at sea had risen to seventy-six knots, hurricane strength. But weather, ferocious or mild, was accepted here by a people living as close to it—and as dependent on it—as this always had. The rain outside was heavy and wild. But Jonas Vigfusson, a heavyset dark-haired man in his thirties who was on duty today, paid the downpour no heed. He operated the teletypes, three telephones, typewriter, and the immense switchboard as usual. His wife Jonina often told their four sons, after visiting her husband at work, that he seemed to be working with seven hands and at least two brains—even though she and the boys knew that he really had only half a one. The boys would smile, or whoop, and Jonas would grin. When he was with his wife and the children, he was relaxed and happy. At work he was often harried, even nervous inside, but remained calm on the outside and always seemed to be in total control. His shift today was from noon to midnight; tomorrow it would be from noon to six in the evening. The vehemence of the North Atlantic gale outside did not disturb him.

It did not disturb him because the fishing fleet was in harbor, the trawlers securely moored, their gull-shaped hulls bobbing and their radio masts swaying. The street was deserted.

The fishery-protection vessels, each named for one of the ancient gods, were not at sea either, Jonas knew. It always stirred an anger in him to think of the amused and condescending way the world press reported the so-called "Cod War," as if it were some sort of musical-comedy sham. If the rammings, the cutting of hawser lines, and the firing of warning shots across the bows of the larger British warships by Icelandic gunboats—if this was sham, then Jonas himself did not understand. The harvests of herring and haddock and cod in these waters accounted for a sixth of Iceland's total catch, and Iceland as a whole depended on fishing for more than half its foreign currency earnings. Let the journalists scoff, let the world smile—it was a life-and-death conflict here.

There was a lull, a few moments of silence with no phones ringing, no red lights blinking, the teletypes quiet, and Jonas sat back in his swivel chair and considered phoning his wife. It was almost ten hours before he would be off duty, and, after all the harsh male voices that he had been listening to and would listen to until midnight, it would be such a pleasure to hear her soft and teasing tone.

But before the impulse became action, Arni Loftsson came in. When Arni entered a room, he made his presence felt at once. Standing well over six feet, with wide, spare shoulders, his eyes blue as any sea, he stood grinning at his friend. And Jonas realized again how this blond and handsome young man had managed to win the love of and marry the dark and lovely Margret Magnusdottir. But Arni should be at the school this time of day. His eyes were even brighter than usual, his tie was askew, the straight slash of mouth looked slightly slack, and he was soaked and dripping. Jonas pressed a button, summoning relief for ten minutes.

Then he and Arni moved together into a small adjoining room, which was filled day and night with the good bitter fragrance of coffee perking, and they sat across from each other at a table, Jonas knowing that it would be useless to ask questions or to make suggestions. Arni said little, drank three cups of coffee, mentioned the wind outside, comparing it to the keening of women after a death at sea. Politely he inquired of Jonas' wife and the boys, and then, impolitely, he stood up, towering and with puzzlement in his eyes, and lurched out, disappearing along the narrow hall and into the main room of the post office, as if he had no idea where he was going.

Jonas sat a long moment alone. He had never known Margret well, but he and Arni had become friends since Arni had come from Reykjavik to live, three or four years ago now. Although Arni had never explained, he had hinted, during their drinking bouts together, that he may have come to the island to escape life with his widowed mother, whom he had mentioned from time to time in a mockery that might have been fond but might also have been bitter. Lately, though, Jonas felt helpless in Arni's presence, and confused. Many men drank heavily, especially in the winter, but Arni, of late . . .

Empty and sad, Jonas uttered a curse and returned to the radio room. Forty minutes later he received a report from a fishing vessel, not of the Vestmannaeyjar fleet, which had been badly damaged in the furious sea. The captain gave his position and did not request assistance at this time. He would attempt to bring the craft into the harbor on Heimaey because it was the nearest port, but he might be obliged to call for help later. Jonas went into action, informing the government coast-guard station at Reykjavik and alerting the Vestmannaeyjar harbormaster, who swore loudly and at length—not, Jonas knew, because it might mean work, and dangerous work, for him and his men, but because he, like Jonas, could picture that lonely boat, rolling and pitching on the swells and beginning to flounder in that tumult of wind and wave twenty-two miles offshore. There was, they both knew, no loneliness more profound, no sense of desolation and abandonment and distress more abysmal.

Jonas managed a quick, quiet prayer and continued with his work. As, on that boat which he had never seen, the crew would continue theirs.

The rain had thinned, but it was still being swept into twisted sheets of silver under the streetlamps which now, in the murky twilight, had been turned on again and were sway-

ing above the sloping pavement of Heidarvegur. The howl
of the gale and the beating of the rain against the plate-glass
window of the bookshop only added to the deepening depression that Kristrun Egilsdottir was fighting. Should she close
the shop now, since there was small likelihood of a customer,
and venture out into that turbulence herself, drive to the
school in her small car and get Gudrid, or should she allow
Gudrid to wait for her at the school? The child, who was only
eleven, wouldn't be allowed to walk home on a day such as
this. But what if, for some reason, she should take it into her
mind to do so?

The thought of Gudrid stirred perplexity in her—a disquiet, almost a dread. Bafflement. Not at the child. Yes, at
her, at Gudrid herself! For being so stubbornly certain, so
quietly convinced. And convincing, too. At least she had convinced her father. How absurd, to give credence to the imaginings, or dreams, of a child that age, as if her active young
mind actually *could* have any foreknowledge. Nonsense,
foolishness and witchcraft—there were no sybils in today's
world.

What had she planned for supper? Oh God, would the
winter never end? Boiled haddock and roe and liver: that's
what she had decided upon in the morning. If there was no
haddock in the icebox, there was cod. And why should she
have this quivering inside?

The bell over the door tinkled and Captain Agnar
Ivarsson came in. He greeted her, as usual, his dark blue eyes
looking down directly into hers as he spoke her name politely, but there was a shyness about the man regardless. Then
he strolled along the shelves. He came only on days such as
this; on others he was out on his boat—she forgot its name,
some pagan god or other, of course—and he always bought a
book or two, one at least, a novel for his wife Ruth: whom
Kristrun knew only by name.

Her decision was made for her: now she could not close
the shop. It was a small relief. By January every year, but
with more intensity as she approached forty, her spirits had
descended into a quagmire of melancholy in which she had a

difficult time even keeping her thoughts in order. She, Kristrun, who had always prided herself on her clear and disci-
plined mind, who had received highest honors at the University of Reykjavik—all those years ago, all those bleak winters
ago, would she prefer to be in Reykjavik then? Yes, oh yes,
anywhere but here.

Agnar Ivarsson purchased his two books—one a new
novel, one a travel guide with photographs of the
Caribbean—and then he inquired whether his son was working in the shop today. Wondering whether this tall, wide-
shouldered man with the sea-beaten face was also thinking or
dreaming of bright, hot places—palm trees and blinding sun
and dazzling white beaches and the flesh soaking in heat and
salt air—she told him that Rolf was unpacking a new ship-
ment. He nodded, thanked her in his heavy voice, and then
strode to the door of the small storeroom in the rear.

While she wrapped the books, Kristrun wondered
further. Rolf was a strange and unpredictable young man—
only a boy really—for whom she had come to feel great
fondness. Much smaller than his father in every way and
darker, he seemed withdrawn most of the time, almost secre-
tive, but with flares of blue bitterness in his eyes on occasion.
One such occasion, she recalled, was an afternoon when she
had mentioned his father's boat: Rolf had said, with a twisting smile that puzzled and yet excited her interest: *It's his. Not
mine. His.* And no more. But enough. She thought she comprehended, at least to a degree. Although Rolf spoke seldom
when he was working here or in her husband's store around
the corner on Strandvegur, there had been other sufficient
hints. Kristrun had concluded that Rolf hated the island and
the town as much as she did, or perhaps, being younger,
more.

But it wasn't true: she didn't *hate* Vestmannaeyjar. It was
only in the winter. And, after all, Reykjavik was also dark in
winter, and the winters lasted as long. Yes, but there were
things to do there, places to go—galleries and many shops
and museums and theaters. The mood of desolation returned.

It was then that she thought of the summers. The sun
shining gold, sometimes for days on end, setting at midnight
often, the dark red cliffs shining as if with their own light.
And the sea glittering from azure, matching the sky, to jade
green streaked with white crests, to the deepest most mysterious blue again. And a softness in the air, the green
grasses exhaling fragrance, clouds like silver feathers in the
sky, while the puffins and the gulls and the thousand others
sailed and dipped. And the flowers, the gardens and the boxes
exploding with tulips, daffodils, roses of every hue. Girls
playing hopscotch in the streets, boys shouting and chasing or
dangling from ropes on the yellow-blossomed cliffsides,
boats gliding in the harbor, whistles sounding. And even at
night, the red sunshine sparkling in the windows of shops and
houses, and then the August moon rising like a pale second
sun from the clear sky over the sea. Oh how she longed for
summer—it was an ache in every fiber. Wretched now in the
settling darkness, she pictured herself as others saw her: a tall,
slim woman with a long chiseled face, fading yellow hair
pulled tight against her temples and twisted into a knot
above—she knew she gave the impression of cool content and
containment, the composure a part of her quiet movements
and voice as well. No one knew, no one would ever know. Not
even Rudolf or Gudrid . . .

Gudrid. As the English poet wrote: a bell tolling her
back. Would the child decide to walk home as usual? It would
be like her. With memories of summer and the thought of
Gudrid mingling, Kristrun recalled the Sunday afternoon in
late August when Rudolf decided that they should have their
last picnic until spring and had driven them to a spot where
the grassy meadows—colored the purple of beach pea, the
white and yellow of mountain avens, daisies, buttercups, and
dandelions—flowed to the base of the cone of Helgafell. A
golden plover ran crying ahead as they slipped and stumbled
up the lava cinders, which often tumbled down at the touch.
The crater was shallow. There was growth in it: grass and
moss campion in clusters of brilliant pink. On the rim a
black-and-white snow bunting sang his protest at their intru-

sion and the wind blew. From there they looked out over the island, tilled fields lined by the same burnt, eroded boulders on which they stood, and in the distance the other islands, stark and massive in the spumes of surf. They could see Surtsey to the south, swathed in its brown sand cloud, still smoking. To the north, nine miles across glittering water, the long coastline of the mainland, brown and green and with mountains of rising miles beyond, glinting in the sun. It was a sight and an experience that never failed to fill Kristrun with a sense of gratitude and a joy at being alive. Had Rudolf, knowing her winter glooms, arranged this memory to carry into the months ahead? It would be like the man, yes.

But Gudrid that day had grown more and more somber, and later, while they were eating the spiced meatroll sandwiches, she had begun to weep. Startled and then alarmed, Kristrun and Rudolf had tried to comfort her, but it was not until they were home that evening that she confessed why she had been, and remained, so distressed.

There's going to be a volcano, she had said.

But, her father told her with a fond smile on his upturned mouth in his pleasant, slightly round and mottled face, *but my child, Helgafell is a volcano. Or was. A very long time ago.*

Gudrid only shook her head, her long fair hair moving full on her shoulders. *I don't mean Helgafell. I mean where we were—another volcano.* And then, soberly, very softly, she added: *I'm frightened.*

Gudrid, Kristrun asked, *did you dream this?*

The blond hair moved again. *No.*

Then, Kristrun said with a small laugh, *then how do you know?*

I don't know how. Her voice was almost toneless and low. *But it's true.*

Rudolf's face had sobered somewhat, and this startled Kristrun even more. *It's time for bed,* Kristrun said then. *And let's hope you have pleasant dreams.*

I didn't dream it, Gudrid said as before. *It was not a dream.*

And after she had gone to her room, after Rudolf had lighted his cigar and settled into his chair, and after Kristrun had stowed away the picnic remains (Gudrid had not eaten), she and Rudolf sat together, as usual, hearing, as always, the shouts and cries of children who were allowed to play in the streets until any hour during the day-lit summer nights.

She herself had gone to bed angry that night, she recalled now as Agnar Ivarsson emerged from the storeroom, his face grave, his jaw clenched, nodding his good day. He stepped out and into the wind which, Kristrun realized now, seemed to have lost some of its howl. No, she had not been angry; she had gone to bed that night perplexed and filled with an incredulity that, while she had felt it before, had never been quite so personal. For Rudolf, during that evening, had suggested that what Gudrid had said might not be so far-fetched after all. His grandmother, he said, his grandmother on his father's side, had had the power to foresee. In the family, when he was growing up, she had been thought of as a sibyl. Kristrun, despite her summer mood, had been shocked. Soothsaying, auguring from omens, the gift of prophecy— was it possible in this modern world that a man as well read and as intelligent as Rudolf could give even the slightest credence to the idea? Kristrun had then recalled that more books were published per capita in Iceland than in any country in the world, and every home, no matter how humble, contained great quantities of them. And the country as a whole knew no illiteracy. Yet . . . yet here was her own husband, whom she loved, speaking as though his own child—*their* child—might be a seeress. It had been a strange and mystifying day and an unsettling evening, but when they awakened on that Monday morning next, they spoke of it not at all or ever again. But Kristrun, in her dark mood of winter now, was remembering, and her depression threatened to overwhelm her.

She prepared the shop for closing, working fast, shifting the displays and the window racks about for no reason, telling herself again that Gudrid had been reacting to her early childhood experiences, when day and night for three and a

half years she, like all the other islanders, had only to look
out her window to see the pillars of brilliant fire and the
scarlet-streaked black smoke from the volcano that had
erupted under the sea only thirteen miles to the southwest, a
heart-stopping scene to which all had become accustomed in
time. And during it, there had been the earthquake shocks
felt here on Heimaey. Two of them. Any child—although
Gudrid had been only one year old when the eruption began
and four and a half when it subsided—would react in some
way to this awesome spectacle. And when it was finally over,
a new island had been created where fishing banks had been:
the newest land on the face of the earth. All of it had been
discussed in school, as it was still discussed by adults now, ten
years later. Children reacted in different ways. That
explained Gudrid's fears, crystallized into a terrible foreboding on that Sunday in August. Only that. She had not mentioned it since. And she had been as happy and carefree as
before.

Kristrun stepped to the stockroom door and told Rolf,
who was as usual working hard and steadily, that she was
closing the shop for the day so that Gudrid would not have to
walk home from school in the rain. Rolf nodded, saying he
would then go around the corner to the construction-supply
store.

Kristrun pulled on her fur-lined coat and tied a woolen
scarf over her head. She really liked that boy—and in some
strange way felt sorry for him. He did not seem to belong
here; or had not yet discovered a way to belong. Odd that,
because unlike her, he had lived here all his life.

The bell sounded when she went out the door. Yes, the
violence had abated. It snarled rather than shrieked as she
hurried to her Swedish car at the curb. She started the
motor, flipped on the wipers—and realized that the rain had
stopped.

Even the island formed by the volcano off the coast had
been named for an ancient god—fire, destruction!—*Surtur.*
Who had fought the god Freyr in the battle that preceded
the end of the world in Norse mythology. *Surtur from the south*

comes with flickering flame. . . . The stony hills are dashed to-
gether, the sun darkens. . . . Men tread the path of Hell, and
heaven is cloven.

She sighed as she drove the shining wet street. Was she
living in the twentieth century, or was she not? Gloom
swirled in the lingering squall and night threatened. How
many hours to first light?

To those of scientific bent—like Doctor Pall who was
always cynical—Helgafell was only a reminder of how the
island had been formed, as he often said, three thousand
years before the Reverend Petur's Christ had even been
born. To Reverend Petur, parson of the only church in Vestmannaeyjar, the cone represented one of the wonders of a
nature that had been ordained by his Christian God, and for
reasons known only to Him. But when Helgafell's maroon
gray height is bathed in the light of day or glistens in the
darkness with snow—only occasionally, for snow is not common on the sea-bound island—most of the islanders think of
it, if at all, only as their own volcano, now extinct, a hill, part
of the landscape.

To a few, though, Helgafell is what its name clearly
states: Holy Mount. To them, in that year of 1973, it was one
of the sacred places of which there are many in Iceland.
Baldvin Einarsson, the painter, was among those who considered Helgafell hallowed ground. Along with others he had,
other means having failed to convince, participated in dem-
onstrations objecting to the extraction of ash and cinder
for use in construction: roadbeds, building blocks, the two
runways of the small airport lying at Helgafell's southern
base. Baldvin Einarsson was convinced, along with others,
that what they termed the *tampering with Helgafell* was a desecration, a dangerous one. Why dangerous? Baldwin had
mentioned this to no one but his wife Inga and to his friends
Doctor Pall and Reverend Petur, but it was his belief that
Helgafell would avenge itself on man for man's profanation.
Petur considered Baldvin more romantic than pagan: *You are*
attributing life to an inanimate thing. And Pall, who usually
smiled with amused skepticism at these discussions, consid-

ered the very concept of enchanted areas on the same intel-
lectual level as belief in magic, the walking dead, soothsaying: *All the vestigial residue of an outmoded mythology—sheer
superstition, unadulterated by reason.* The three men—artist,
physician, and minister—often talked lightly and pleasantly
of serious matters, for they were friends.

At around four-thirty in the afternoon, it was Baldvin's
habit to stop work and to have coffee with Inga. Inga was
from Copenhagen but had adopted the island life when she
married Baldvin, after they had met at a sculpture show in
Reykjavik fifteen years ago. Thin, shorter and more delicate
than most of the Icelandic women, with pale brown hair
instead of very blond, Inga had come to love her life on
Heimaey. When it was discovered by Doctor Pall that she
could not have children, this fact seemed to bring her even
closer to Baldvin, who had wanted a child as much as she
had—perhaps even more because the town here teemed with
children. Inga always smiled at the joke so old that it was no
longer a joke: that, with the winter so long and so dark, there
were only two things to do: drink and make children. This,
of course, was not true. Neither she nor Baldvin drank more
than one small glass of aquavit at any one time, and they
made love as often as, or more often than, those who produced the children—and in the summer time as well! Inga
and Baldvin had discovered very early in their marriage that
they enjoyed each other—in thousands of ways too subtle
and delicate even to try to describe in her own mind. Inga,
instead of being frustrated by her loss, gloried in her love
and in his. It may have been for this reason that, when her
rather wide mouth was not upcurled in a glowing smile, her
face possessed a serenity, contentment, an inner delight in
whatever she might be doing. Withal, her eyes were quick to
merriment always.

The wind had subsided enough about an hour ago so
that she could do her marketing, and she had then hurried
back to brew the coffee and to cook the paper-thin pancakes
served with berry preserves which Baldvin had relished since
childhood. Now, balancing the tray on one palm, she opened
the door of the studio.

There was a swift movement inside and, to her astonishment, Baldvin stood in her path. His broad head, totally bald, gleamed in the whiteness of the fluorescent brilliance overhead by which he worked in winter. His brown eyes were luminous with some secret excitement tinged with an elation that she had rarely glimpsed before. But he smiled, as he always smiled when he saw her.

"We'll have it in the living room today," he said and moved, so that she had to back away. He closed the door. "I'll show you when I have finished it," he said. "I'll *invite* you to the showing. You alone."

She led the way along a short passageway. The house was old and solid, large and comfortable. Like other painters—as well as writers and sculptors and other artists—Baldvin had been granted a government subsidy so that he could do his work. He might not be a great artist; his work might never be seen outside of Iceland, although she secretly hoped that it would someday; no matter, his satisfaction was in the doing. To Inga this was really all that mattered.

Over coffee by the window which looked out at the incline of lava rock leading to the base of Helgafell, less than a hundred meters away, now masked in darkness, they spoke of many things, mostly trivial, but not of the painting that he would, for the first time, not allow her to see until it was completed. The wind was only a faint keening sound outside now, and at half-after four, both knew, the air would be growing colder by the minute. But the room was warm, glowing, and . . .

"Delicious!" Baldvin exclaimed, as he always did, eating the last bite of pancake and draining his cup. He then stood up. "I may work late," he said. "Do you mind?"

"Why should I mind? Suppose we don't have dinner at all tonight? You know what Pall said."

"To hell with Pall! Why can't a man get fat in peace? My blood pressure's no higher than his. We can't all be wispy little reeds like you."

"You don't like my being a wispy little reed?"

"I'll show you how much I don't like it later. But now I

have work to do!" The ebullient intensity of his gaze was in his voice as well. "With good fortune, I'll finish it tonight."

After he had gone, a heavy-fleshed man walking with swift and easy grace, Inga sat back, tempted to smoke a cigarette. Baldvin's blood pressure, according to Pall, was not a matter to be taken frivolously. She decided against smoking the cigarette, recalling with a smile Pall's growl and scowl. And, as she stood up to draw the heavy curtains against the night outside, she experienced again that pang of longing that came back more and more often of late. Baldvin had always yearned to see the great paintings of the world: London, Paris, New York. He had never quite made friends with the certainty that, generous as the government might be in subsidizing his life and work, he would never to able to afford to travel.

Unless, of course, as she had begun secretly to hope, one of his paintings should strike the fancy of one of the collectors or curators who occasionally stopped over in Reykjavik en route from Europe to New York. Only by such good and unlikely fortune would Baldvin fulfill the deep and pervasive craving that he had voiced only in levity or once or twice in the quiet minutes, half-dozing, after they had made love, and while they waited together, really together, for sleep.

After a few tranquil hours in the aquarium, with the wind moaning and then only whining its lament outside, Margret had walked home, idly noting that the wind had now veered to the southwest. And while she had prepared the evening meal—frying the lamb cutlets and, for some perverse or conciliatory reason, going to the trouble of kneading and baking the flatbread that Arni enjoyed so much, when sober—she had felt the slow, familiar fear return. She remembered the way he had left the house in the morning without breakfast. And, again, she wondered whether he had gone near the schoolhouse today.

She also remembered now how stunned and incredulous she had been the first time Arni had grown violent with her—had struck her with his open palm so that she had stumbled sideways and all but fallen to the floor. The demons were wild in the burning blue of his eyes then. The cruel devils of jealousy, mistrust. At such times he was a man possessed. How had it come about? Here, where there was little infidelity, where any temptation toward it was more often than not squelched, if not by the one so tempted, then by the certainty of exposure and condemnation—Vestmannaeyjar was not Europe or the States or even Reykjavik. How could he imagine, even in the wildest torment of doubt, that she could have a lover—or several, as he sometimes accused—without the fact being known or guessed by others? But that had become part of his dread as well: that others knew and he did not. The fear became a hopelessness in her. She knew his torture: she saw it in his eyes and recognized it in his later apology and contrition. Tears and humility and, often, he was unable even to recall what he had said or done. And all the while she knew that behind it, in some odd, twisted way, was love. For her. Yes. Love and need as well.

It had been hours now since she had laid the table. She sat there still. The food was cold—ruined. She herself had nibbled at the flatbread, remembering what Doctor Pall had said about eating well and heartily now.

And it was then that the fear focused into an icicle point of panic in her mind.

What would Arni *do* when she told him about the baby?

She started to stand up and discovered she was unable.

This, then, was the reason, clear at last, that her tongue had refused to follow the dictates of her will.

What if Arni, his mind drugged with alcohol and poisoned by suspicion, decided that the child was not his?

I have never allowed another man to touch me! He had driven her to this, to shouting, screaming, in some foolish hope that she might reach him. Reach Arni Loftsson, the boy she loved, the handsome, blond Viking of the festival, who had been so gay and teasing and had made her feel free and alive and a woman more than a girl. Even now, he could be so gentle, so quiet. Even now he could make her feel . . .

She controlled these thoughts and stood up. No more of this. If he came in now, he would be drunk—no doubt, no doubt, yes. And when drunk . . .

She made up her mind. She would go to her sister's house. Her sister and her husband understood. Of late Hana had only contempt for Arni; and Hana's husband, who was an understanding man, treated him with cool politeness tinged with compassion. She drew on her lambskin coat again.

Would he change? If she told him—he had said he wanted a son—if she told him, would he make up his mind and take his destiny, and hers, into his hands?

Yes.

No.

Never.

He must.

She went outside. There was only a breeze. But with ice in it.

The fear became terror. Not of the streets. She had read of cities, even small towns, all over the world: stabbings, rapes, violence on the street. She had not even locked her door. Her dread was of a different sort.

Her concern was for the child inside. For ten days she had known, been certain, and in that time, she knew now, she had almost involuntarily shrunk from using the words that might ignite—what, *what?* She never knew what he might do. But she had to protect that unborn, unknowing yet living presence inside her. And also, also, she could not risk allowing him to destroy the single most important element of her life: her own love for him.

The streetlamps glimmered wet on the yellow and pink and green and blue pastels of the walls and roofs, and behind the windows now the lights were going out. Tomorrow was another workday, the sky would probably clear, the fleet would go out. Tomorrow was another workday and the people needed their sleep. In only a few windows was there the bluish glow of the television—from the U.S. transmitter in Keflavik—and the pictures would soon be off the air until tomorrow evening. Behind the roofs, only the shadow of Helgafell was visible, and Margret did not lift her eyes toward it or even notice it.

When Arni did come home, in whatever state of consciousness, would he surmise that, for some reason, she had gone to Hana's house? Or would he, suspicion triggering rage, pain flaring hot in him, decide that she had gone to her lover, or one of them?

Oh God, how had they come to this? How much longer could she find in herself the forebearance, the understanding, the charity, and *love* to go on?

For sometimes she hated. Yes, sometimes she hated with such a consuming violence that it outstripped even his physical cruelty—and appalled her.

She passed the cemetery, arched entrance of white stone with the cross atop it gleaming in the dark. And then, seeing the church, also white—wide, graceful steeple and dark-red, steeply slanting roof—she was tempted to go inside. She knew that Reverend Petur was away, but she also knew that the doors were always unlocked. Would God be willing to listen? Would he, because of her plea, alter a human heart, restore it to its own true way? Could even God prevail against the malicious spirits that were gnawing and harrowing poor Arni's soul?

She continued walking, alone on the damp and empty street, realizing now her loneliness in all its awful portent: the future held more of the same. And more. And more. She saw the years stretching ahead: anxiety and alarms and a constant dread that would in time devour her. Until, in some future year, she would look into a mirror and see, not the lovely, fair-faced, dark-haired girl she now was, but some sad and bitter stranger with *another* expression in the unrecognizable blue eyes: bitter, defeated, lost.

She loved this place. Had always loved it. Not only the

bright days and dim nights of summer, as everyone did, but also the eerie beauty of winter, the stars shining and lovely, and, at times, the northern sky pulsating and quivering with the silver light that sometimes flared into icy flames of distant color. But she knew that happiness was not a place. It was love. It was a sense of purpose.

Was she losing both?

And if so, why? What had she done, what sin committed that she be destined so? Or was there, after all, as some believed, a fate from which no human innocence can protect you?

As she turned into the narrow paved walkway leading to the front door of her sister's house, she was relieved that lights still glowed in the windows. It was then that she recalled, from nowhere, the odd way the catfish in their glass-faced tank at the aquarium had behaved while she was there: thrashing, twisting, and squirming violently, creating a turbulence in the water. The director of the aquarium, whom she had known all her life, had explained that many animals—white mice, crickets, salamanders—react visibly to changes in the magnetic field. She had stood there longing to comfort them somehow, to reassure them.

She tapped on the door, lightly, and walked into the small entry. But when she heard the cheerful voices of the two children, she felt lonelier than ever. She wondered whether she should have come. And again, what Arni would do when he found the house empty.

As he lifted each photograph from the developing tray, Owen Llewellyn was relieved, gratified but, as usual, not excited. He had been concerned that the odd light of midwinter in northern Iceland might have betrayed him—and possibly have ruined the hard work of the last three weeks.

Instead, though, that light gave an eerie quality to the pictures, so that the inland ice sheet, the frozen waterfalls, the fabulous mountain of black volcanic glass all emerged in their grotesque and fantastic beauty (or ugliness—or both together), touched with an almost mystical grandeur. Studying each in turn, his satisfaction was, he knew, the impersonal pride of a professional craftsman not artist. There was the icy blue and storm-lashed lake of Askja, luminous sulphur smoke rising above its milky gray bubbling water; the lava desert, surrounding the brown crater of Viti (meaning Hell), a lunar landscape of black dunes. One by one the pictures took shape and form and color: the red, white, and yellow deposits, crystalline and weird; the deathly solitude of the so-called "Living Desert" covered with lustrous green moss; the boiling mud pots, sulphur fields, and shooting geysers. Even on paper the glittering glaciers dazzled the eye, blinding. Yes, he had done his job, and well—what more could a man ask of himself?

Todd's voice said into his ear: "Now, by God, I bet you're glad you came."

The whole thing was a fluke, really. He had been leafing through books in a shop on Fifth Avenue and had come across some photographs of Iceland, which had made him wonder whether the photographer had done justice to the subject, and then he had made the decision to go to Iceland himself, possibly because he was restless anyway and had no assignments, and then, after traveling the north alone, he had returned to Reykjavik and, on impulse again, had telephoned Todd Squier, the only person he knew living here. He had felt an odd hunger for companionship—something strange, something most unusual for Owen Llewellyn—and when Todd insisted that he come visit, he had found himself acquiescing; after all, his plane did not leave for New York until morning. And in the twenty miles between the city and this farmhouse in the bleak but somehow lovely country, he discovered that Todd, probably because he had adopted the country as home, knew more about it than some natives and took zestful pleasure in boasting about it: crime rate incredi-

ble, less than one murder a year, only a hundred law-
enforcement officers in the whole nation, most arrests for
drunkenness, no slums, no unemployment, no pollution!
Todd seemed more exuberant than Owen recalled his being
and, as the four-wheel Landrover moved through the rain
that was turning to snow, Owen found himself relaxing and
remembering that in New York Todd had once been like
him: a loner, detached. But with a difference: *I've been cursed,*
Todd had once said, *with a small inheritance and too many expen-
sive interests.* Owen had no inheritance, and if he didn't sell
the pictures, he'd be broke. Again. And to hell with it. He'd
been broke before.

They sat at a trestle table during the long dinner of
sautéed ptarmigan, a fowl he had not before tasted. Todd
said he built the table with his own two hands. It was a meal
punctuated by the laughter of Todd's teen-aged son and
daughter and gracefully served by his wife—Malfrour, called
Mal—a tall, square-shouldered woman with very light hair
tight to her head, who spoke in halting English. When she
smiled, it was a burst of brightness in her usually serene,
not-quite-grave face. The boy and girl spoke perfect English
and lapsed into Icelandic as easily when talking with their
mother. They struck Owen as quite different from the sons
and daughters of his friends at home: there was an innocence about them, a naïveté in their direct ingenuous eyes
and quick smiles. After the meal, the adults drank a pale red
wine which Mal had made, although, she hastily added, all
had picked the berries. Then there was chess, the figures
chiseled of soapstone, scoured smooth and carved with great
delicacy—by, of all people, Todd. The house, of concrete,
was tight and warm and heated by water piped from hot
springs. Even though Owen slowly began to feel that he had
stumbled by chance across a refuge, a haven of warmth, he
remained remote. The outsider. Detached. At the age of
thirty-one, he had not only come to recognize this fact about
himself, but to accept it. Even, he often suspected, to relish
the feeling. Even, he admitted, to nourish it in some strange
way.

Suddenly then, in the middle of a sentence about Icelanders copying manuscripts of literary treasures ages before Gutenberg invented his press, Todd had snapped his fingers and stood up. *How would you like to develop your photographs tonight?*

Owen had been startled. He ran a hand through his thick, red hair and down over the unfamiliar beard. *Tonight? Where?*

Here! I have everything here. Wheels and ovens for pottery, clay and lava for sculpting, ancient tools you've never seen before. Follow, come!

And even then, following Todd along a passageway lined with books, Owen had realized that his anticipation was less a deep and vital caring than a professional curiosity. Then, seeing the familiar equipment and smelling the familiar odors of his trade, he had felt some of that sense of detachment and isolation fade. Knowing, of course, that it would return. It always returned.

And now that the pictures were hanging along the wall in clips, now that he really knew what he had accomplished in those three weeks, he followed along the passageway again, hearing Todd call into a bedroom something in Icelandic, then translating: "The boy will play the radio all night if I don't say the same thing every time he goes to bed. And then I suspect he does it anyway."

Malfrour, having heard their approach, was in the living room pouring coffee, which held a hot and pleasantly bitter smell. Icelanders, Owen had discovered, drink coffee all day long and, presumably, during any part of the night that they are awake. Todd kissed her swiftly on the cheek and she, smiling, turned away, like a young girl embarrassed.

"Damned if I can believe you'd even survive up there by yourself," Todd said, sinking onto the couch, his mug cupped in his hands. "You don't seem to have missed much." He was staring at Owen. "You must be more rugged than you look."

It was true. Owen knew it. He was not a large man, neither tall nor heavy-boned nor fleshy, but his body had a wiry strength in which he took pride. "Let's say I finally know what winter means."

"Winters really get to some people here," Todd said. "High rate of suicide—more women than men for some reason."

"We are weaker," Malfrour said, sipping, the gravity of her eyes over the cup rim lighted by a mockery.

"Like hell," Todd said. "Look at her, Owen. Did you know that every Dane worth his salt brought Irish slaves here—and captured Irish princesses! Listen to the language—not as guttural, but it sounds almost Germanic. Only with a lilt in it." Then he was off: the Icelandic tongue is Old Norse, as spoken by the Scandinavian people before the tenth century, with a singing cadence that falls softly on the ear . . .

But Owen was not really listening. It was as if all this were happening to someone else. As if he were only an observer—and of himself as well. It was a familiar sensation, always a trifle bewildering, but never deeply disturbing. He had come to wonder what, if anything, *could* be deeply disturbing—or, for that matter, wildly exhilarating.

Todd was speaking now of the pervasive sense of easy relaxation in the country. There is no hurry, no urgency, or stress. Owen had found this true. No one is really a stranger. People speak with each other freely, openly. An outsider asks directions; he makes a friend. He inquires as to a food shop or restaurant and he is invited to dinner.

". . . perhaps because the people here live closer to a time most of us have forgotten, or never really knew, but still somehow remember, or yearn for—"

When Todd's voice drifted off, Malfrour spoke in Icelandic, and then Todd replied, nodding. "Mal," he said to Owen, "has just reminded me of another part of our life here. Hekla, for instance. You seem to have slighted our most famous volcano in your photographs."

"True. Perhaps if Hekla had been kind enough to erupt for me . . ." He broke off, instantly aware of the abashed glances.

Malfrour set down her cup. Todd stiffened almost imperceptibly, his face having lost all expression.

Hastily, Owen then said: "I didn't mean it quite that way."

"No," Malfrour said, softly. "I'm certain not."

"I did get at least one good shot of the cloud hanging over the summit, I think."

"Cowled Cloak," Todd said. "What the name really means. Some call Hekla the abode of the damned. Wiped out a whole settlement in about 1100. Poisoned water and buried fields for hundreds of miles. Covered more than half the entire country with ash."

And then, with an odd awe in her tone, Malfrour seemed to be quoting: "No man knew whether it was day or night, inside or out."

"Two hundred years later," Todd said, "another eruption lasted a whole year, and about the time of the American Revolution one lasted for more than two years."

"When I was four years old," Malfrour said as before, "the upper winds carried the ash over England and Wales and all the way to Helsinki. Even into Russia."

"That one," Todd said, "they estimate that one exploded with ten thousand times the force of the bomb dropped on Hiroshima."

Then there was silence. Owen could see the snow falling heavily outside the windows now. He cursed himself silently. Malfrour stood and took the ceramic coffee container into the kitchen. Christ, what an insensitive clod he had become.

"If you'd like to see one that's quieted down only recently," Todd said, his normal tone returning, "there's Surtsey. It's still smoking. I know it's been shot by everyone, but the way you . . ." Then he twisted his head and lifted his voice, speaking in Icelandic. Malfrour's voice responded. Then Todd nodded, facing Owen again. "You could fly to an island called Heimaey. Mal thinks you could charter a small boat from there, if there are no excursions this time of year. Look, Owen, you simply can't leave without getting some shots of Surtsey."

Malfrour returned. She extended her hand. "I must say good night." As Owen stood and took her hand she smiled again. "It is good of you. To come. Todd . . . *we* see few people. If you decide to go to Heimaey, I have a cousin living in Vestmannaeyjar."

"An Irish princess," Todd said, as he stood. "Like mine, only with black hair." He stepped to Malfrour. They kissed. Her body seemed to melt against Todd's this time.

And then, without embarrassment, all grave, pleasant dignity again, she turned to Owen. "Good night, Owen."

"Good night, Mal. May I apologize?"

She arched her fair brows. "For what? You are scarcely responsible for what Hekla does, are you?"

She was gone.

"I've lived so long alone," Owen said to Todd lamely.

"Forget it. How could you know? It took me years to learn. A volcano in these parts . . ." He shrugged, shook his head. "Would you like a nightcap? I have whiskey."

"No, thanks."

Todd sat again. "Last time I saw you, you were a wreck."

"You can't go on being a wreck forever."

"I thought she'd taken the life right out of you."

"That's over. Except for the alimony."

"Alimony? After what she . . ."

Owen stopped him: "I don't like to fight, Todd. I did a little boxing in college and decided I didn't like winning any more than losing. Yes, I could have won against her, but it would have been messy. I prefer to pay the alimony."

Todd nodded. "Yes—you would." He took a deep breath and stood. "Well, there are a lot of lovely women here. Why don't you stay a while?"

Owen shook his head. "There are a lot of lovely women everywhere. I had one once." He rose, stifling a yawn. "Many thanks for the thought, though."

"Owen . . . I'm sorry. About you and her. I always meant to say that in New York. Here, you do say it."

In the small bedroom that was his for the night, Owen wished he had accepted the nightcap. The snowfall had

changed. It drifted lightly now, and peering through its thin
veil, he could see the lights low in the northern sky: subdued
here, much less colorful and vivid than they appeared from
the wastelands up there. He was remembering a small lake at
the foot of a dazzling glacier and the icebergs on it, frozen in
place, luminous blue.

Overall it had been a quiet and satisfactory day. The
photographs were more than he had hoped, and he'd be able
to sell enough of them to finance the trip anyway, or almost.
Still, he was left with a sense of loss. Well, Todd—who had
always seemed at loose ends and a trifle frenzied around
New York—had found a place for himself in a world that,
for the Todds and Owens in it, rarely offered such. Is that
why he felt this odd disquiet? How can a man feel loss for
something he has never known?

In bed he thought again of the three-year disaster that
had been a marriage: a thing of beauty twisted to bitterness
and regret—the beauty itself finally recognized as illusion. A
trick almost unconsciously perpetrated by a girl who did not
know how to be honest, even to herself. And to hell with it.

He did not look forward to flying out to New York tomorrow. Or to the small rustic retreat deep in the woods of
Connecticut, pond, darkroom, and all. The picture in his
mind did not draw him home. It was only a place. He had no
home.

Rocketing up and down in the Landrover through lava
fields, twisting and turning between twenty-foot boulders,
through chasms and gullies, around crags and holes and
craters until the vehicle felt like a small boat being tossed in
an Atlantic gale, like the one that had blown this
afternoon—strange, he already missed the bleak and terrible
grandeur he had left: the infinite silence, the bareness and
austerity and, yes, damn it, the majesty of it all. Alone there,
he had not known loneliness.

But here . . .

While most of the people in Vestmannaeyjar slept—all
windows dark, only the streetlights burning now—a small
man of thirty-three years, wearing a dark knitted seaman's
cap and a heavy, faded pea jacket, was walking along
Heidarvegur, aching with nostalgia and another pain that
was deeper and more virulent. Downhill, at the end of the
street, lay the harbor; he could see the lights. He was passing
the hotel now, where earlier in the day, during the high
brutal wind, the manager had asked him, politely but with
firmness, to leave. Olaf Jonsson had been insulted. He
prided himself on being a peaceful man, sober or not, but,
not sober then, he had complied. And he had been walking
since, walking and stopping to rest and to have another swig
of the brennivan he carried in his hip pocket.

He had been drinking steadily, alone, since late afternoon, when he had seen her. The child. She had been strolling, head upright against the fierce wind, with two others at
dusk as the streetlamps came on. And he had recognized her
at once. Because she looked so much like her mother, and
because, under the swaying light, her red hair had been
streaming out behind her head, wild and lovely, and his
whole being had gone hollow, as if he had been hit a powerful blow in the gut. She had not seen him across the narrow
street, and if she had, she would have seen only another
seaman whom she did not recognize. Why should she? She
was not his child. She was the daughter of Juliana and her
husband, Halldor Danielson. She was eight years old. Yes, he
had shipped out nine years ago, when Juliana married, so
the girl, whose name he did not know, would be seven or
eight by now. No mistaking her, though: the same fair and
(he knew) freckled face, the same quick but graceful way of
using her hands as she spoke, even the same heart-clenching
tilt to her head. He had stood quite still, with his flesh hot

and the gnawing emptiness inside becoming more unendurable, and watched until she had turned a corner and passed out of sight.

Then he had begun to drink. Not that Olaf Jonsson needed an excuse. Nine years at sea now, shipping out anywhere, from any port, to whatever hell-hole a job would carry him. A first-class seaman, and so recognized, with papers to prove it. The wind had been high all day, reminding him of that island in the Azores when the hurricane struck. No, the Caribbean, somewhere. The tile roofs of houses torn away and shattered, the straw shacks turned to rubbish, dead bodies in the streets.

He was walking past the darkened window of the bookshop now, and the outlines of the harbor ahead were more clear: in the foreground, the wharves, abutted by the precise, rectangular buildings along Strandvegur—the freezing and processing plants, the net stores, shipyards, machine shops, and liver-oil plants. High and neat and clean. Olaf turned from the street and walked along the quay, conscious of the shrieks and screams and calls of the birds, which could, after the wind, be heard again, and pictured in his mind some of the waterfronts he had seen: filthy, crawling with rats and human vermin, raucous and ugly. Why had he left this place?

But of course he knew why.

It was then that he saw the lights of a fishing vessel, its shadowy hulk moving and tilting and plowing slowly through the narrow mouth into the safety of the harbor, which lay in the embrace of the curving, dark-shrouded headlands. Drinking at the hotel earlier, he had overheard, and now vaguely recalled, a discussion of a radio report that had said that a fishing boat from the mainland port of Thorlakshofn was in trouble somewhere but had not requested aid. Now he watched it limping into port, having somehow survived the weather that had kept the Vestmannaeyjar fleet from venturing out.

He had no place to go. His parents dead so long ago that he had no memory of either of them, he had been brought up by an uncle, a fisherman, a kind and loving man who had taught him all he knew of the sea. Uncle Lars had suffered a stroke and was now in the hospital where, when Olaf had visited him in the morning, he may or may not have recognized his nephew. The brawny man had gone frail and white and he could move and walk but could not speak. And, filled with a deepening sadness and sense of loss, Olaf had begun to wander the strange but familiar streets. Having no place to go. Having no one to see.

He had been alone. He was still alone.

He turned and retraced his steps, his small frame bent forward as he went up the slight hill, the town, his town, lying ahead of him. His arm had begun its familiar torture— the one he had almost lost, crushed by boots, in that violent and pointless barroom brawl in Marseilles. If the pain became too intense, he had the medicine in his pocket, the pills that brought on that feeling of distance and detachment while the pain faded into only a tormenting ache. But, even though the emptiness remained inside now, he did not take another drink, either. There was only an inch or so of *brennivan* left in the bottle. Earlier, he had considered trying to locate old friends. (On the streets there were so many who were now strangers.) But all his friends would be married now, and, while they might be pleased to welcome him, to hear of his travels, he had felt only reluctance, a slow dread. The sweet and cruel past lay about him like a pall that he could not throw off and did not altogether wish to.

It was then that he felt or imagined, a shaking beneath his feet. He did not halt. He was drunk: he knew that. And earth tremors, he recalled now, were not uncommon here. He had forgotten that. Imagine.

Nevertheless, he remembered his old uncle's description of *fylgjur*. Guardian spirits. A person who sees his own *fylgja* is death-doomed.

Olaf Jonsson had always smiled at the old beliefs. Yet he had found their counterpart in almost every country he had seen: voodoo, sorcery, shamanism, witchcraft, miracles. He did not smile now. He did not care now.

He did not care about anything. If he were to see his own *fylgja,* so much the better. And the sooner the better, too.

Hands shoved into the high slit pockets of his jacket, he continued his aimless walk, the pain reaching and probing into his neck, his chest, his head—his soul. And he remembered nights such as this, in ports thousands of miles from here, long nights of agony and despair, during which—how many times, how often—he wished he were no longer alive.

There was a jolting under his feet. A hard single shake at first, and for a moment he felt that he might lose balance. He stopped. Waiting. But it did not come again.

Then, down the street, a light came on in the window of a house.

TWO

AT THE CORE of the planet there is a seething violence. There, perhaps a billion years ago, cosmic gases consolidated and, by the newly created nuclear fission, matter was transformed into radiant energy. Why? By whose command, whose whim?

Thousands of miles above this hot cosmic turbulence, the crust is not the fixed and solid rock that the eye perceives. It is, rather, brittle and cracked—precarious. And it is in constant movement so that huge, irregularly shaped plates are forever shifting, grinding against each other. The Pyramid of Cheops is now two and a half miles south of where it was erected. The Strait of Gibraltar is three miles wider today than when it was known as the Pillars of Hercules. Rome is shifting toward the equator, and Australia is approaching the South Pole. America, too, is shifting westward, the distance between New York and Cherbourg expanding one twenty-fifth of an inch every day. Great continents drift around like lazy rafts on the broken crusts, not anchored in place at all.

And when the edges of these enormous plates make contact, rub together, compete for space, weak zones are created—and stupendous, unimaginable energy. Then, when any small part of the subterranean heat escapes, the land heaves, shatters, the earth quakes, fire erupts.

Unseen by any human eye, a strip of land east of the

cone of Helgafell and on the eastern edge of the village of Vestmannaeyjar began, in the darkness of the arctic night, to bulge with a quivering sigh, like a man sleeping. Then it began to heave. Pebbles lifted from the surface, as if they had been lying on a taut skin which had been struck lightly; then they bounced down, only to be hurled up again, as the swelling increased, and the ground began to crack. Then, as if a sharp knife had been drawn over the shuddering flesh to allow poisons to escape, the distended membrane cracked open in a long slit, and fire and embers and black smoke began to spurt from the incision, which, in an instant, was more than three yards wide. Then from the wound came the lava, welling out like heavy blood, glowing hot. The fissure became a row of fiery fountains, spewing molten pumice and red embers, magma from the depths of the planet itself, more than a hundred yards high into the winter darkness.

The night caught fire.

The clock on the town hall stopped at 1:55. No one observed that, either.

By sheer chance the person who first saw the eruption was Jonas Vigfusson. He had left the radio communications center a few minutes after midnight, on schedule, when his partner came on duty to relieve him. Although it had been a relatively quiet day since the fleet was in harbor, it had been a long one: twelve full hours and not enough to keep a man busy. In spite of the southeasterly gale, force twelve—which had now tapered off to force four and had veered to southwest—only one vessel had reported distress and, less than half an hour ago now, had limped into port on its own. Jonas left the post-office building tired and relieved to escape the clatter and the sound of his own voice repeating the weather advisories. (Was there a more disgruntled creature on earth than a fisherman kept from his fishing?) He looked forward to walking home slowly and to stretching out beneath the warm *dyna* and giving in to the luxury of his tiredness. But tonight Arni Loftsson had been waiting—as, after the schoolteacher's visit during the afternoon and in view of his condition then, Jonas realized he should have anticipated. This changed his plans, partly because he wanted a drink himself, but largely because he felt again that pang of compassion combined with annoyance that Arni caused in him. He promised Arni—and himself as well—that he would have only one, so he had two, of course, joking with Arni as to why a man with a wife as lovely as Margret should want to stay out this time of night. For some reason Arni's handsome face and intense blue eyes, already somewhat hazy with the *brennivan,* had clouded, become puzzled and angry. So Jonas, confused once again by his feelings towards the tall young man, had begged off and had gone for a walk alone.

The wind had subsided even more and was now only a pleasant freshness against his face. Some of his energy restored by the drinks, he was strolling the deserted street when he became aware of a sound besides his echoing footsteps—like a groaning or a low distant thunder. Then he saw the glow in the sky. His step faltered and he halted, staring. At first he thought that a house to the east of town was burning: he saw flames leaping up about a quarter of a mile ahead. Flames and sparks and billowing smoke.

He began to run and then he stopped again, staring. He was struck now by a new and deeper incredulity. He stood rooted in astonishment. He remembered, in a rush, what he had heard so often about Helgafell: many people, himself not among them, believed that the old volcano would have its revenge. But the old crater was dark, its cone outlined by a line of fire beyond. He ran again—until he saw the gash, a long curving line which at first appeared to be a wall of flame but which, he realized, was in reality a vivid red opening, shooting fountains of lemon yellow fire and red ash up to a height of perhaps a hundred and fifty meters, fiery smoke churning even higher. Dumbfounded, aghast, he wondered

for a second whether he was in shock. Fleetingly it occurred
to him that he may have had too much to drink. His mind
rejected the idea with reluctance. He knew. He knew, oddly
enough, with an overpowering sense of inevitability—as if,
somehow, he had always known in his blood that this would
happen.

He turned from the furious chimneys and faced a decision even as he moved, running again, this time toward the
town center. There were at least seventy-seven boats in the
harbor, stalwart, seaworthy: he had to alert the town. There
was, after all, only one action for them to take. By now Jonas
was convinced that the ash and fire and lava would engulf
the entire village. Nevertheless, he changed his path, turning
a corner toward his own house, as he became conscious for
the first time of a trembling underfoot and, at the same
moment, of the sound on all sides—as if the air itself were
throbbing—and of lights coming on behind windows. First
things first, God help us all. He was almost to his own door
before he recalled his wife's dream. How long ago had it
been—weeks? months?—since that night when she had
awakened crying, almost screaming, to tell him, trembling in
his arms, that she had dreamed of Helgafell erupting? He
had, whispering, tried to reassure her: how improbable, how
really unimaginable. And, while he had now been proved
correct, so in a way had she. She had not mentioned the
nightmare since; nor had he. And now he must waken her
back into it—no longer nightmare, reality.

He did this as quietly, as gently as possible, in a muted,
level tone, the urgency carefully controlled. And then, fully
awake, she stared into his eyes, comprehending at once,
standing up from the bed, not going to the window to confirm what she knew was true because he had said it was true,
and then she went in to the children while he telephoned.

His voice, which sounded strange to his own ear, low
and tense, did not convince his partner, who yawned audibly.

"Eruption? Och. Jonas, have another drink. For me."

It took a full minute to persuade him, shouting angrily,
that a volcanic split, two thousand meters long, had opened

and that Jonas was taking his family to the harbor, before returning to the communications center. It was not until the other man heard the windows of the post-office building rattling, that he agréed to put out the alarm.

"Mayday?" he asked Jonas.

"Mayday," Jonas said.

In the small, white police station the officer in charge, who was very young and unmarried and who rather enjoyed the stillness and solitude of night duty, had been wondering whether the gale of the afternoon and early evening might not be returning: the windows seemed to be shaking in their frames, and he had had the sensation several times in the last minutes that the whole structure was swaying slightly. When he received the Mayday alarm, his first impulse was to run outside and to look. Instead, though, knowing his duty, he telephoned the chief at home while his mind reeled with visions of panic and disaster. The isolation of the island struck him for the first time in a life spent on it, and he was thinking of what he had read of Pompeii—the fearful cloud rising from the towering volcano's peak, snuffing out the sun, and then the mountaintop cracking open, the rain of death beginning. And he remembered photographs of the hardened mud molds that had preserved the victims' final postures of terror and attempted flight for sixteen centuries. Hadn't that convulsion killed almost two thousand people and hadn't it transformed a thriving port into a huge burial vault? Just before he heard the chief's sleep-filled voice, he began to quiver inside and wondered whether he himself was going to panic.

The chief who, unlike most men on the island had no children of his own, always treated his younger officers with a gruff warmth tinged with a fatherly condescension, and

now he was growling at being awakened. But the sound of
his voice somehow dissipated the incipient hysteria in the
younger man. In spite of the sleepiness blurring his words,
the chief inquired in an amused tone whether there had
been a murder in town. Since the town had never had a
murder—at least in recent times—this was his own small
joke, often repeated, sometimes to put his subordinates at
ease and to put minor violations, such as they were, into
proper perspective. When the young officer reported that an
eruption had started a short distance above and east of
Kirkjubaer, the church farm, there was a silence at the end of
the line, during which, perhaps because of the almost giddy
excitement that he had now begun to feel in place of the fear,
the young man recalled that *simi*, Icelandic for telephone,
translates into English as "the thread that talks."

Then the chief was speaking, giving orders in a quiet,
firm voice: he himself would contact the mayor, who would
have to issue the order that the island should be evacuated,
while the officer on duty was to inform the civil defense and
the Reykjavik authorities and to summon all police officers.
"Also," he said, "alert the hospital and put both patrol cars
on the streets, with lights and sirens. Advise everyone to go
to the harbor, although they'll probably do that of their own
will. Explain that this is not an order. Not yet anyway. And
sound the fire siren. I'll be there in a few minutes."

"Yes, sir," the young officer said, and his giddiness fell
away. Suddenly he felt, instead of the unstable recklessness
and fear, a deep and unshakable calm: there was work to be
done.

He quickly arranged the priorities in his mind, and,
speaking in a voice that reflected the cool self-possession of
the one he had just heard, he followed the chief's instructions, hearing now for the first time a low grumbling in the
distance, as of some gigantic beast stirring.

She slept lightly, waking over and over. After she and Agnar, alone in the house, had had their private time together, he had gone to sleep early with good intentions, asking her to waken him so that he could telephone the crew and take the *Njord* out before midnight; but it was past two now, she sensed, and each time she shook him gently awake, he would grin, half-asleep still, and whisper, "Later, later, in half an hour perhaps." Perhaps—och, he would not go out till first light now. And what matter really? His slow and sonorous snoring was reassuring as he lay there beside her, heavy and warm and so alive even in sleep. And she herself would have slept soundly, deeply, as she had done all her life, were it not for Rolf. Rosa was in her bed, as usual, but her mother lay half-awake, and had done so for hours, tensed for the sound of Rolf's motorcycle. For a boy of seventeen to be out this time of night—hadn't the police complained to his father already? Oh, not that Agnar would tell her that, or anything like it, but a mother knows. She still could not really believe—how life fools, confounds!—that little Rolf had become what her own father, may his spirit never roam, had always called a "wild bird." Rolf with his dark hair and pale blue and tender eyes that of late had come to seem masklike, as if the boy were concealing something in himself that he feared others would glimpse. Even his mother. And most especially his father. The old turmoil inside kept her awake. Again. And no cycle engine spluttering along the sleeping street. Not yet.

She opened her eyes. There seemed to be a faint pink glow beyond the window, which faced east. Or did she, in her torpid half sleep, imagine it? She was thinking, of course, of where Rolf might be. Och, what men knew and what men imagined, or hoped, that women, protected, did *not* know. Women knew even more than the menfolk, if it came to that.

If it came to a woman like the French one. Who had arrived three years ago, married to a Dutchman who was seeking, so they said, a quiet place where he could write his novels. But the poor man had not survived one winter, leaving, so they said, the unfinished manuscript of a book describing the way of life here. As if a foreigner like him, who had not been able even to master the language, as if a man like so could write about life here in Vestmannaeyjar. And then, the man buried in the cemetery alongside the church, among strangers, the woman had stayed. No one understood. It was said she had no money. It was said she had come to enjoy her life in that old farmhouse on the cliff above the sea, far south of town. Well, if the lonely woman had come to love life here, that Ruth could understand, for hadn't she loved it herself for more than forty years now? Yes, yes. But the French woman remained a mystery, tall and dark in her foreign-looking bright peasant skirts, walking into the village to market, olive-skinned face, slim and solemn and composed always. A beauty by some standards, no doubt of it. And different here. And some there were, uncharitable at that, who said she had brought vice and corruption to the island—didn't she entertain the young people, mostly the young men, into all hours? And what was it they found so attractive out there, so appealing that, when all decent people were abed with the lights off, music (some said) still flowed out across the craggy, barren fields from the old thick-walled house that had been abandoned for years—what was her mesmerizing allure?

There seemed to be a rustling in the house now. In the walls and beneath the floor—as of voices whispering. A strange sound, really, not disturbing, only puzzling. Ruth could hear it, even above Agnar's peaceful snoring.

If only Rolf would come in! She had a single abiding fear that, having had too much *brennivan*—or whatever they drank or smoked, today—Rolf would drive his cycle raging along and across the dock into the harbor or off some headland into the cold, dark sea itself. She struggled to control her imaginings, and could always control them—except at times such as this. A man could not survive in the arctic waters for many minutes before going helplessly into shock. How many fine men had perished so! And if the boy's mind were sluggish, his muscles feeble with drink or drug—she reached and placed a hand on Agnar's brawny chest.

The pink luster remained beyond the windows, mystifying, and the strange whispering seemed to become a crackling in the walls, somber creakings, furtive and vague, under the floor. Then she heard the fire siren. There was a fire in town. And close, too. Then it was not in the plants at the harbor.

Agnar wakened even as her hand began to shake the long hard muscular body. At first he mumbled something about waiting till light, but then he heard the siren, too, which was distant but distinct. He rolled out of the bed and stepped heavily to the window, where his tall, thick profile was now hazily outlined against the odd hue beyond. Then he turned and, in a voice so low and so gentle that she could barely hear it, he said: "Wake Rosa and Rolf."

She stood up. "Yes. Is it a fire?"

"No." That same voice. "It is not a fire, Ruth."

Then she knew. If she had not known all along, evading the possibility, the stunning inconceivability. "Helgafell?" she heard herself ask.

"I do not know."

"Then?"

"Wake the children. We'll take them to the *Njord.*"

And, standing there, chilled and still incredulous, but not trembling, she had to tell him: "Rolf is not here."

She heard him utter a low curse, lost in the distant repetitious wailing of the siren. Then he was moving—no need for instructions now. She went out and along the short passage and into her daughter's chamber. Rosa still slept. Her mother bent down and spoke in a whisper, and the blond-fringed blue eyes opened; then, when the girl understood, she did not speak, only nodded and threw back the *dyna.* Ruth explained that Rosa's brother had not come home, and, even at such a time, the tall, frail girl murmured her lack of surprise, and Ruth, moving from the room, telling the daughter to dress warmly and to take something for the head by all means, realized that Rosa's quiet acceptance, her sweet basic goodness of nature, would again go unremarked, lost in the concern that her brother always stirred, demanded. How unfair that the gentle and submissive one should receive so little of the human heart's concentration. On impulse then, with wild imaginings of Rolf threatening her mind again, Ruth turned, retraced her steps and, for a brief moment, held the slender, lithe body in her arms, before turning away to perform the chores that she knew had to be performed.

She could hear Agnar's voice on the telephone in the living room and then, lifted, it called: "Not Helgafell, Ruth."

But there was no relief in the tone and none in her.

Agnar took over then: he had already phoned his first mate, who would inform the crew. They and their families would go to the harbor. He would drive Ruth and Rosa to the *Njord,* and then he would go in search of Rolf. If he was not permitted to drive through the streets, he would walk. Did he know where Rolf might be? Their eyes met. He did not answer her question. By the time the *Njord* was loaded, he would come with Rolf and with Alex, who could get to the dock on his wooden leg but should not have to. They would all go to Thorlakshofn, the closest port on the mainland.

And after that? They did not discuss the matter. There was too much to do. Ruth thought of a hundred things she wanted to take along, especially her old piano; she took only a few clothes. And Rosa, in silence and without being told, did the same. Agnar, whose face was fixed in concentration but no longer grim, only determined, smiled approval once, just before they went out the door. They did not look back.

The sky had a deeper, ruddier glow now, the siren seemed louder, more than one now, there were others on the street, moving shadows, the air seemed strangely warm, and from faraway across the town came a sound, not loud, as of distant thunder moving closer.

At first he did not know why he had wakened. Then he heard a sound and decided the storm was returning. The storm was the reason he felt tired: all those minor injuries that he had had to treat in his office at the hospital. Not a single bruise or fracture or chill that couldn't have been prevented if people weren't such damn fools. Thinking they could challenge the wet and cold and wind. Like the wisp of an old lady when he asked her why she would go out in a blow like that: *I have been in winds before, Doctor Pall.* He could only shake his head and set her fractured hip. And now, that memory fading, he became conscious, as he did every time he woke from sleep, of the emptiness in the bed beside him. He would never accept it. The actuality of his wife's death reached him in small and sometimes trivial ways, as all deaths really do. He knew, because he had seen his share, more than his share. First, the shock, sharp, but then slowly, slowly the realization, cruel and insistent. Time's passing—could it really be almost six years?—had only intensified his sense of aloneness in the small house. And slowly, too, the tiredness: how gradually it came upon him through the day, how inevitably. Today's work had nothing to do with how he felt now: he knew, he knew. A large man, and heavy, he moved through the days with a robust vigor, bluff and often scowling—some patients were amused, others irritated, but he noticed they all were damn-well reassured. Many knew of his wife, but none knew of the emptiness that he carried like a malignancy through his whole being. Only Odette sensed it. When he visited her in the farmhouse on the cliff above the sea, he felt free to give himself over to any mood that threatened. She asked few questions, made no demands. *But you never sleep afterwards,* she had said once. And he had answered: *No.* Because he would never waken again with anyone next to him in bed—ever. Even someone as lovely and lonely as Odette. They shared a respect one for the other—for the loss inside that the satisfying of their healthy physical appetites appeased only temporarily.

Then he heard it and knew what had roused him from sleep: a distinct cannonade, not thunder. He rose and, body hunched bearlike, he went to the window and drew back the curtain. There was a lurid glare in the sky from the east.

He was only mildly surprised, not shocked, and his first thought was that Baldvin's prediction had been fulfilled: Helgafell was avenging its desecration. The idea brought a bitter taste to his tongue, but he had no time now for thought or conjecture. He dressed swiftly in the dim chill, then telephoned the hospital, gave instructions that all patients were to be prepared for evacuation, and learned that the two other doctors in town had not appeared or reported. Just like those young ones: they'd leave it all to him. But . . . but they did have wives, children—what would he do if his wife were still alive? Or the child whose death in birth had killed her? At least *they* would not have to suffer through whatever lay ahead now.

He wasted no time in indecision: the ill and the elderly were his people, and he had no choice but to do what he was now doing: driving his small car in the direction of the hospital. Would they be warm enough on the fishing boats? What of the airfield? It offered, he decided, little hope: its single crisscross of runways lay at the very foot of Helgafell. He was not sure that there was, in fact, any hope whatever. He thought fleetingly of Petur's description of his Christian God: compassion and love. Well, he was a God of wrath tonight—but what had these people done to deserve it?

If they shared his bleak foreboding—and some most certainly did—there was no evidence in action or demeanor on the streets. A few cars, headlights glowing dimly in the faint red radiance that was everywhere now, moved in line, no passing, no sounding of horns, and those walking, all in the direction of the waterfront—adults with intent and sober faces, not grim, and children straggling and twisting their heads as if hypnotized, even lured, by the furious iridescence from which deep rasping coughs now sounded—all moved with quiet dignity and fixed determination. Some held hands, some carried travel bags and loose clothing and toys and infants; one woman held aloft a fringed lampshade, an old man, walking with a cane, grasped a framed picture or photograph. Like the frail old lady now in hospital, they had all been in winds before. But none had ever been in anything like this.

Behind the lighted windows of a few houses shadows moved, and he could see figures sitting over coffee. If the world came to an end, these people, his people, would have their magical brew first, if possible. He cursed them: his people were as stupid as any other!

Then, suddenly, a deafening cannonlike blast split the night and the sky brightened, with sparks spluttering and cascading down—but not into the town, not yet. He heard a murmuring ripple through the crowd, but only a few hesitated, and fewer still halted.

He turned a corner and moved against the tide of humanity flowing to the harbor on Kirkjuvegur, passed the bank and approached the hospital, the familiar sculptured giant beside it looking grotesque, even sinister, in the eerie light. Then he saw the eruption. Not Helgafell, after all. A row of immense and furious chimneys stretching as far as the eye could travel to the north and disappearing behind the illuminated but stolid cone that he had known since birth. Not Helgafell. He thought of Baldvin: his house must be as close to that riotous wall of flame as any. But if not Helgafell, then was there hope? Could one or both of the two airstrips be used then? Was anyone doing anything about all this? They would need aircraft—what was being done?

He brought his car to a halt and hesitated, staring but now not really seeing, because he had gone faint, struggling against a memory yet trying to get it into focus. He knew he should move, but then it came to him: the dream. In the years since her death, she had haunted his waking hours, but he had dreamed of her only once. She had simply appeared—as he knew her, as he loved her. But she was struggling to speak and could not, and her face was ravaged with the effort, and he saw her lips moving without sound, cold fright and desperation in those eyes that looked alive again; she was trying to warn him of something but could not, and he had wakened distraught and quivering with a hunger to return to the dream, to see her once again, to reassure her. Could she have been trying to warn him of this night? No, damn it, no.

He stepped out and into the cold that swept down across the sea from the glaciers and tundra to the north, probing his clothes at once; yet the flesh of his face felt dry and warm, as if heated by the flare from the east. He strode to the steps of the hospital entrance, seeing the lights in every window. But his mind stayed with the dream, that single dream. He was a man of science. He was not one of those superstitious fools who believed in omens, ancient gods, auguries and premonitions. He was a man of science, and he also did not believe in the resurrection and the light and salvation and hellfire and his friend Petur's omniscient Creator. If there was a Creator, He had botched the job—and tonight was proof enough. Nothing, not even his own precious dream, was enough to persuade him that dreams were anything but the unconscious conjuring up of longings and fears, not yet comprehended by science, creations of the dreamer's mind, not ghosts, not separate animate entities. Spirits do not exist in reality.

Faced now with the chaos of uncertainty, this small community within a community, occupied by helpless human beings who must somehow be helped, he put aside all conjecture, all extraneous wondering, as he went inside. He removed his hat and ran his hand over his very short gray hair and then over his black shaggy brows and down over his big-boned face, as if this would clear his mind for the job ahead. It was, he suspected, a hopeless task, but one that, being hopeless, had to be faced with hope. He had, regardless, returned to that small world that, since his wife's death on the third floor above, had become the only place where he felt completely at home. What would become of it now?

The lighthouse beacon, perched on the headlands forming a huge peninsula four miles southwest of town, continued to emit its forlorn warning across the North Atlantic
to the west, but its flash was somewhat dimmed now by the
raw brilliance northeast of it.

Gunnar Axelson, who even on an island of large men
was as huge as the god Aegir himself, a raw-boned giant with
wide square shoulders, enormous gnarled hands and a flat
face with a boxlike jaw, was riding one of the tough little
Icelandic ponies from his farm toward the village. His long
thick legs all but dragged the surface of the road. The lighthouse lay behind him—as did his wife Svana. And his three
daughters, all of whom were afraid to risk their mother's
wrath by leaving. From the time Josef had come roaring into
the bedroom to shout with wild delight that there was
another Surtsey, their own Surtsey now, here, here on
Heimaey, the woman had been adamant, mulish as any hag
in hell, thin face clenched, fierce eyes turned, not on Josef,
never on the boy, thank God, but on him, Gunnar, and on
their daughters, on the world itself: if everyone else was
terrified, they could go without her! She, Svana Hannesdot-
tir, she was made of a different clay! And the daughters
cowered, while he—he, Gunnar—begged, cajoled in un-
manly fashion, feigning more alarm than he felt, yes the
woman could bring a man to that, had often done so. And
what had Josef done? The boy had disappeared. With his
dog Odin. Had vanished from the house, the fells, the cow
shed. Gunnar, discovering, had cursed, unleashing a rage he
had controlled for more than twenty years, had faced the
woman, seeing her reckless courage now for what it was: the
evil that had all but destroyed their life together—her selfish
unreason, her whim the only reality, her quick wilfulness the

only decision possible. The sagas, he knew, were filled with such violent women.

But Josef was his father's son. And now his father would find him and save him from himself. Yes, from himself—for in his gentle way, he was as untamable as his mother. Fifteen now, but still so light-minded, hadn't he gone running off without seeing to the few cattle, the many sheep? The girls were out now, in the cold, at his order, trying to gather the ewes together, to locate the three rams. Their mother was fuming and frothing in the house, like one berserk. While the boy . . .

He had not gone to his cave in the cliffs. Gunnar had hurried there first. Then where?

Seeing the ruddy incandescence ahead, the straggling houses of the village outskirts only silhouetted, Gunnar felt his confusion and vexation mellow into a concern so deep and harrowing that he had to cling to the pony's sides with his legs to keep from toppling. The boy might do anything. Not knowing fear, he could even be so foolhardy as to dash toward the blaze, to . . .

He urged the pony forward, feeling the animal's shudders between his legs, sensing the small beast's inborn animal reluctance, and, at the same time, sensing something else in the horse, as well as in himself: a panic that, instead of sending it stampeding away, seemed to impel it, in terror but in fascination as well, in the direction of the holocaust itself. Gunnar did not believe it—in the beast or in himself. Could not.

He passed the school and arrived at the church. His eyes searched the group that had gathered there near the police van parked at the arched entrance to the churchyard, its blue dome light slowly spinning. The white church was no longer white, but pink, its red-roofed steeple framed sharply against the flare beyond. The air itself was thunder here, with sporadic booms and abrupt explosions that seemed to send the fire higher against the ugly, black billowing above. Gunnar slid from the pony and, standing, felt the ground beneath his feet shudder. It took him a long moment to achieve balance. He recognized none of the faces. Most were grim, some stunned, a few almost angry. There were two young couples passing a bottle of brandy back and forth, their mouths opening in shouts and laughter, but all unheard against the detonation. Josef was not there.

Gunnar approached the young police officer, who nodded as if he had answered every imaginable question tonight. No one was allowed to go closer, he shouted against the crackling din and gestured: no one, unless he lived up there; most people were going to the harbor. But Gunnar shook his head and inquired, his normally soft and husky tone a bellow, whether the man had seen his son, describing him in such a way that the young officer lifted his brows and spoke the boy's name as if he knew him, yes, but no, he had not seen him, not here. He was, his eyes said, sorry, very sorry, and his lips said he would take care to look for the boy.

Helplessness chilling his blood, feeling the heat on the flesh of his face, the towering hulk of man turned away and glanced about, pale and gentle blue eyes baffled, as if someone *had* to offer help, anyone, somehow, anyone. He turned to the church again. His parents, both, were buried there in the churchyard—what would happen to *them?* And then he was tempted to go into the church, momentarily imagining how surprised the Reverend Petur would be, and then he remembered that the parson, who sometimes called him Aevar and sometimes Josef, but never Gunnar, was not on the island because of illness in his family. Where then could he turn, to whom, and what could he . . .

Abruptly the sky seemed to shatter with a blast that thrust rockets of fire skyward, that intensified in a split second the warmth on their bodies and faces, that shook the earth beneath them so that it felt as if it might crack open and engulf them where they stood. They only stared, all of them, young and old, no drinking now, no mouths opened in laughter, and there was a movement away, in the direction of the town center, away from the church and the inferno behind it, away from the silent dark cone of Helgafell, which seemed only to stand by passively, itself illuminated, no longer brooding in menace, only stolid and observant, detached.

The pony reared on its hind legs, teeth bared, eyes gone savage and frantic, and then it rushed headlong, its stride becoming a gallop in an instant, in the direction of the fire not away from it. The police officer took a few futile steps, then stood watching as the small body mounted the incline of roadway. Gunnar saw all this with something less than surprise, as if somehow he understood, or might at least have anticipated, that the animal would become victim of an impulse that seemed by reason to contradict instinct and that Gunnar, having shared the urge, comprehended.

Now where could he go? Would Josef, like the pony, plunge witlessly toward the peril rather than, like the others, flee in the opposite direction? Gunnar knew that he could not predict what his son might take it into his strange and disordered brain to do.

Gunnar's impulse to go into the church was gone now, and the thought came to him, moving away, that, with such mighty things happening, God would not have time to listen to one small man's plea—a farmer like himself. No. He would not bother Him now. He would do alone what had to be done. And, walking between rows of houses—where doors stood ajar, where an occasional figure moved behind a window, where cats ran or cowered, deserted, where strangers moved—Gunnar realized where he was going next. Not to the boats, not yet—first, Josef. Josef, whom he loved. Whom he understood if anyone did, understood enough to guess where the boy would go—where he might feel safe.

With mounting certainty and with triumph in his mammoth stride, Gunnar realized that he had already turned off Kirkjuvegur, which led in a curve to the harbor, and into the direction of Heidarvegur, which also led there but which, on the way, ran in front of the aquarium building, the only place in town that Josef ever asked to visit.

Rolf had come to like the wine that Odette offered him. Not him alone, but any who came to while away the long evenings with the sea washing and breaking far down against the cliff and the gulls railing, even at night. During one of the long silences that often fell across the company, the birds and the waves could often be heard even through the meter-thick walls of the ancient farmhouse and above the soft sound of music that seemed always to be playing here. To-night, as often, the company had narrowed down to only the two of them: Odette and Rolf. And these were the times that Rolf most savored and remembered. He knew the rumors that the village secretly enjoyed: that this old place, reno-vated into a haven of paintings and books and cushions on the floor and colorful silken hangings and pictures on the walls, had been converted into some sort of cave of vice and depravity. Well, his parents were always saying he was a man now, weren't they? What they meant was that he must pre-pare himself for the town; that the island's limits were the limits to life itself; and that someday he would take over the *Njord* and, like all his family, become a fisherman, the years streaming endlessly into years, until he himself would be old and smoking his pipe on the wharf and watching for the return of the *Njord* skippered then by *his* son. Caged and defeated and growing angrier month by month, he had dis-covered refuge with Odette and in Odette's house. Here he dared to speak freely. Here was talk of Paris and London and Amsterdam and even of New York—Odette had been everywhere. Here, for him, was deliverance from his melan-choly and from the ways that they—his parents, the town life—were shaping him.

Odette was yawning now, she was telling him in her low voice and curious accent that it was much too late, she was leading him to the door. And he thought at once of Doctor

Pall. Late as it was now, would Doctor Pall come? He felt a knife stab of resentment, sharp jealousy. Was Doctor Pall the reason she . . .

"The sky," she said. "See."

He looked. Beyond the rooftops, which he could not see from this distance, there was a fiery cloud with black above it, but it was not Helgafell, because the familiar cone was silhouetted against the incandescence beyond. He thought of Surtsey but that was in the opposite direction and over the water.

He would know soon. But first . . .

"Are you frightened?" he asked.

Odette was in shadow; the slightly mocking smile was in her voice. "Should I be?"

He didn't know. He couldn't be certain. "No," he lied, an excitement kindling in him. "If there's danger, I'll come for you." He was in the seat of the motorcycle now, kicking at the controls. It was a stupid thing to say, something out of a children's version of the ancient sagas. But he had no time now to feel foolish. He was on his way, every nerve and muscle quickened into life, the salt air wet and stinging cold against his face, the road pockmarked and thudding under his wheels, motor roaring, eyes on the straight narrow beam ahead. He thought, incongruously, of the police, of the complaints lodged with his father. Excessive speed, engine too loud, disturbance of the peace. He recalled his father in the storeroom of the bookshop during the wind of the afternoon: tall, forever towering above his own slightness and shortness—of which he had always been painfully aware—the older man solid as a pillar, the rudely hewn face like leather or stone, the kindly eyes growing stern with warnings, and finally the jutting chin of anger as he withdrew, the gentle eyes gone furious. More than anyone else, his father, with whom he had once been friends, and whose friendship he achingly missed, had come to epitomize his captivity here. How could you please a man, if the man could not understand what you were saying—what you were longing for? Because that man had never himself known such longing.

He did not go toward the town center but took Kirkjuvegur and, long before he arrived at the church, which was profiled by the flame beyond it, he could see a high wall of fire, yellow below and rising to jagged peaks of livid red hundreds of meters high. And the heat was so intense, even at this distance, that his face had begun to sweat. He became aware of a low barrage with occasional coughs and convulsions and, fascinated more than dismayed, he saw black pumice, ash and large clinkers of lava flowing along the entire stretch. But, to his astonishment, there was no cone, no suggestion of a volcano as such. For a long moment Rolf had the impression that he was trapped in a dream of some sort, that all of this was unreal, perhaps imagined.

A particularly violent blast shattered the night. The fiery rampart itself seemed to explode. High plumes shot upwards along the entire stretch, higher than any before, scarlet, reaching for the sky. And he could picture the thick, black lava boiling up from the long trench that he could not see.

And then he knew.

The town would be destroyed.

But instead of a fear, a wild exultation took over. Something destructive and terrible sparked to vivid life in him. Let the cataclysm take over. Devastation. Holocaust. Let the fire and lava leave the town, the whole island, a bleak and barren waste!

He was not afraid. Not himself personally.

Imagine that.

Instead, he felt exalted, caught up in a paroxysm of sheer joy.

He turned the cycle in the direction of the town center, speeding past the church, the school, the hospital, the bank, and town hall.

He should be appalled at himself.

He was not.

He saw a police van, heard the raucous blare of a loudspeaker, sirens crying. Only a few people were straggling toward the harbor. In fear—probably shaking with terror.

But no.

They were walking, in groups, children as well, only walking, heads held straight, eyes forward. Fear? Terror?

He was bewildered. Everything was baffling. Himself included. He realized that he was going toward the docks himself. For what purpose? To get his own small boat, not to join the others, to go alone out into the harbor and to sit and look back, to watch it all happen.

But shouldn't he go home?

No. No need to warn his mother, his father. Agnar would see; he would know what to do; he would act at once, and wisely. Trust Captain Agnar. Father knows all. Father will take care of all.

From the wharves, dismounted, he could look back in a southeasterly direction and see the inferno above the roof-tops. There were no tremors here. But the blaze, farther away now, nevertheless put a shimmer on the water, a moving rose-tinted glaze, that was at once dreamlike and horrible, hallucinatory in its beauty.

But still he was not frightened.

Then what was that faintness all through him? Why then that chill along his spine, in his marrow, in spite of the heat on his face and the sweat in his clothes?

He didn't want to die.

He hadn't yet lived!

He couldn't die now.

Then he *was* afraid?

Yes.

Wasn't everyone? Only a fool . . .

He looked at the fishing boats, huddled together against the moorings, people climbing aboard. He could not see the *Njord* from here. All the boats, of various colors, usually dull and pale from salt and sea, now gave back a blinding and coruscating glitter.

There was a tremendous bellow and he turned; the earth seemed to be disemboweling itself, spewing crimson streaked with gold, the whole turning into black and then showering sparks over a wide area. Yes, the town was doomed.

And was he doomed?

Swiftly he went into the boathouse where he kept his own fifteen-foot boat, knowing, even as he stepped toward it, that he might not be able to get it into the water alone. But he couldn't wait. A grinding urgency drove him now. If he could somehow get it into the harbor, and if he could then look back—then what? Would he exult as he watched, or would he only sit out there and shake with fear, wondering whether the fire would somehow reach him across the water?

He looked around the boathouse for the rollers. There were four other weathered boats and one, a twenty-foot hull, still raw, half-constructed, its ribs still bare.

Then he saw a movement and, in spite of all the activity outside and the fulmination in the distance, he heard a sound. The sound, unmistakable, of a human voice. Startled, he shouted. And heard an answer. He stepped to the unfinished hull and looked in.

Curled like a human fetus lay a form—the form of a man. His hands were jammed, as if cold, into the pockets of a blue pea jacket and his knitted cap covered only half of his small head. In the dim light the face was obscure at first, but the voice was clear enough. It asked for help. Rolf bent his short, lean body down—and recognized the man. He didn't know him. He had met him only once, this afternoon on the street, when the man, whose name—Rolf remembered now—was Olaf, asked him if he knew where Halldor Danielsson lived. The man had been drunk then, and he was drunker still now. Rolf recalled that the man had tried to describe Halldor Danielsson's wife, and that he had mentioned her hair several times: it was red, a beautiful red. And then they had had one quick drink together, during which Olaf had spoken of the foreign ports he had visited in his travels as a seaman. That had been hours ago, and by now the man's red-streaked eyes, above his short but thick brown beard, had gone dim and out of focus.

No point in telling the man what was happening. Yet Rolf couldn't leave him here—walk away and allow to happen to him whatever would happen. Why not? Hadn't he been ecstatic only a few minutes past to think of the whole village going up in flames, being smothered by lava and ash?

"Can you stand up?" he asked.

"I don't know," Olaf replied.

"Will you try?"

"If you got *brennivan*."

"I got *brennivan*," Rolf lied. "Now I need help with my boat."

"Boats. I know all about boats. Ships, too."

But when they were out in the harbor, Rolf rowing, he felt a slow paralysis take over body and mind. He was distantly conscious of the bearded seaman demanding something, begging, then threatening. Rolf pulled at the oars, the small craft bobbing in the wakes of the much larger vessels making for the harbor entrance—but he was too weak, he was weak all over. Across the sheen of water he could see the town outlined against that ferocious wall of blaze. Soon, very soon now, that fire, with its rock and ash and flow, would rake the town. Would raze it to black ash. Might even cover it completely.

And he . . . he was going to die.

No. He was here, away from it, safe.

It would reach him, though. It would reach him somehow and he would die.

The boat was drifting, tilting. Why wasn't he rowing?

Because it would do no good.

But he didn't want to die. He couldn't die. He was only seventeen. Oh God, please don't let him die. He hadn't even lived.

Then he was cursing himself, inside, for the coward he now knew himself to be. But still he could not force his body to stir, his arms to pull, the boat to move. He could only sit, bloodless and empty, and watch it happen over there.

And while he sat so, limp and palsied, his hatred of the village turned slowly and cruelly onto himself.

A city was quickening to life. Located in southwest Iceland, Reykjavik is the most northerly metropolis in the
world: very modern yet old-world in atmosphere with narrow, winding streets and a large, beautiful lake, frozen over
now, in the town center. Lights were coming on in houses
and on the few vessels in the harbor and in the eighteenth-
century government building and even in the Parliament
House. Buses and cars were moving, telephones sounding,
hope rising against fear, shock subdued by activity. Having
experienced so many, the country was prepared for disaster.

The Civil Defense Committee was convening at the main
police station in an underground bunker constructed to provide protection against nuclear devastation; its thick steel
walls would have been useful under the cascade of magma
and fire seventy miles to the southeast. Nine men faced a
magnitude of problems. Transportation had priority. Vessels on the island, with passengers, were even now putting
out to sea. It was decided that they would dock at the mainland port of Thorlakshofn, which was the port closest to
Heimaey. But Thorlakshofn was a forty-five-minute drive
from Reykjavik, and there were more than five thousand
people on Heimaey—could sufficient overland conveyance
be provided? All city buses were officially appropriated and,
with the announcement of the eruption already on the radio,
it was safe to assume that relatives and friends of the islanders
would offer not only transportation, but housing. Living
space, though, was limited—how could five thousand people
possibly be accommodated in a city of only eighty thousand? It
had to be done.

It would, they decided, be done.

From his office he could hear the vessels streaming out of the harbor, engines churning and whistles bleating against the distant bombardment, and his concern was that sooner or later the last one would be gone and Elin would not be aboard. The office above the freezing plant was far from comfortable, furnished in spartan essentials only, as it had been when Elin's father sat in the chair that Thurbjorn Herjolfsson now occupied behind the bare desk. Looking at his wife who was staring down upon, but probably not seeing, the activity below, Thurbjorn remained stunned. Not so much by the eruption now, as by the transformation in Elin that he had witnessed in the two hours since he had awakened to the wail of sirens and had discovered that the bed was quivering.

He had somehow known on the instant what had occurred—was occurring. He sat up in the dimness and Elin moved. He told her. Thurbjorn was prepared for—and even somewhat gratified by—what followed: Elin, who also seemed to comprehend at once, begged him in a breathless whisper to take care of her. He reached, touched her face, then rose and turned on a light. Elin was cowering on the bed, her lovely small-boned body trembling like that of a frightened bird. She had always been a pale creature, delicate of face and feature, with innocent eager-to-please gray eyes and hair so fair and fine, that it seemed almost transparent.

While he dressed, he reassured her: Brekkagata was on the extreme west of town, some distance from the eruption—which he had at once assumed to be Helgafell's fury finally unleashed—and he would take her to the boats, but hurry, please, please hurry now, take whatever can be carried.

"What," Elin asked, "are you going to do?"

"I might be needed," he said, "at the plant. We'll see how bad it is, and then I'll decide what I should do."

Then had Elin changed; she leaped from the bed, soft eyes hardening into bright dark points, and her normally high, thin voice took on a deep harsh passion that he had never heard before: *The plant! Is that all you can think about, even now? What about me?*

You can go to your father's, he told her, the gnawing urgency overcoming his surprise. *There'll be boats to the mainland. Now dress yourself; it'll be cold on the water.*

Your job, she cried, *is to care for me. It's your duty! What will I do on a strange fishing boat, with strangers?*

Her unreason unnerved him; his own anger surprised him. *No one on Heimaey is really a stranger, Elin. You've lived all your life with these people.*

They all hate me. They envy me! They always have. Then her tone became rigid and low: *I'll go with you. Wherever you go.*

His anger had receded then. For he had recognized her panic. He understood her terror, and he was sorry. Because of this he had brought her here to his office, where she had continued to ignore all his pleas and then demands that she get hold of herself. And all his explanations: if either the water pipes or the electric lines running underwater from the mainland were to break, the plant would not be able to function, there would be a tremendous financial loss and her father would hold him responsible. But even as his own words echoed in the room and in his mind, he had known what she would say, and she did: *And what could you possibly do here if that should happen, please tell me.* This logic, in a world gone awry with unreason, only brought back his anger. Was he the one being unreasonable then? And if so why?

"You're a coward," she said now, but quietly. "You imagine you're being brave—to stay." She turned from the window. "But you're afraid of what people will say if you leave. What are you trying to prove—that you're a man?" Before he could answer, she came closer, giving in utterly to the storm inside, fright exhuming venom, her small face deformed now. "You're not a man!" He heard her screaming above the sounds of the deep bass concussion in the distance, above the motors in the freezing area below, and the whistles hooting in the harbor. "You've never been a man, really! It's all been pretense!"

Shocked, incredulous, he did not shout the words that leaped into his mind: that no man, no number of various men, could ever satisfy the insatiable sexual demands that tormented her; that for some reason, some tangle of reasons he had long ago stopped trying to discover or to unravel, she could never reach the satisfaction that other women, he knew, were happily capable of and took pleasure in. His rage plumbing hot fathoms in him, he stood up and heard his own voice bellowing: she would go down the stairs and onto one of the waiting vessels, or he would pick her up and carry her down!

She became a raging savage, so violent that she now leaned over the desk, small sharp teeth bared, and screeched that he would do what she insisted he do, or she would stay here, right here, in this office until it was swept into the harbor by the lava! With some reasonable part of his mind recognizing the insane contradiction of demanding to be saved by threatening to be destroyed, he was on the verge of giving in to what must be, he knew even now, a need for him that he had never recognized, but then he heard her scream: "You don't love me. You never have!" And he saw her for what she had become: not the girl he had always thought her, but a ferocious shrew—stranger, harridan. And all the rabid turbulence in her had turned, not on that sinister accident of nature out there, but on him. In his rage and astonishment, he could not speak.

Then, in a voice that sounded forlorn and distant, she said: "You only married me for Father's business."

She had never said this before. How long had she believed it, felt it? And was it, to some extent at least, true?

There was an expression on her face he had not seen before: a smirk of triumph, almost a sneer.

He discovered that he hated her.

He saw her reach for the telephone, knew the number

she was dialing, hoped the line to the mainland had been severed, and sat breathless and listened.

"Father?"

He did not hear what she said; he did not need to.

Then she extended the instrument across the desk, and he took it, feeling as he always did when he had to deal with the man. Her father's voice, over the crackling wire, sounded very quiet and calm and distant. He was to bring Elin to Reykjavik, to fly if possible, but to get his daughter off that island at any cost. His hatred for her father exploded then, a hatred he had managed to control for years, and he heard himself crying out, in a voice he scarcely recognized, that he was staying to take care of the plant, that was his job, Elin could leave now, he had been *begging* her to leave! The voice then spoke again, restrained as before: "I am not begging. I am giving you an order. Bring my daughter here without delay." Seeing Elin's eyes almost black now and glassy, fixed on him, he hurled down the telephone.

Her expression changed again—became sly and shrewd. "I know why you wanted me to go without you." The fragile face looked thin now, fixed and sharp-boned. "I know all about that French slut. Everyone knows. Do you imagine you had me fooled? The way Doctor Pall thinks he has the whole town fooled. If Father ever heard of it . . ."

Thurbjorn stood then, stood and listened to himself cursing her father in a long vituperative staccato of maledictions, blasphemies, and obscenities, all the bitter toxins of the years acrid in his mouth and thunderous, even against the detonation from the east.

But when, face swollen and every nerve quivering, he stopped, Elin spoke, very quietly: "Yes. You are only trying now to prove you are even a fraction of the man he is."

His mind flashed white with murder then, and his life came sharp and clear, and he saw her: self, self, always self, even her insistence that he go with her, that he care for her, self, and her insistent passion to possess him, self, and that need in her, that craving, only self, only to devour, not to love, only to gratify, to feed herself. After a long moment, he sat down again, not in his chair, but in the chair that would always be her father's, and he felt his body sag along with his mind. He was suddenly exhausted. Spent. As if Elin sensed this, she waited, her eyes animallike with hatred through slits, not fear, hate, not even panic, disgust, contempt. It was then that it came to him: he would allow her to win tonight, to imagine she had won, he would take her to her father's house, and then he would return. Why return? He had never touched another woman in the years of his marriage, he had never so much as spoken a word to the Frenchwoman named Odette, but he hoped now that, when he did come back to the island, Odette, or someone like her, anyone, would be here. He stood again, his legs strong and unquivering now, and he felt his face twist into a smile, the muscles only, and he nodded and said, "I will take care of you, Elin. That's a promise."

Huddled with the others on the desk, hugging her body with her arms while the whistling cold cut through her, Kristrun Egilsdottir kept her eyes from drifting back, as the others' seemed to do over and over, to the low kindling rim of fire. The image of Lot's wife flared in her mind—and the pillar of salt. The sea was rough and already some were sick. Other boats moved ahead and many others trailed behind—a procession of lights on the surface of the deep, frigid water. Every Icelander, she knew, prided himself on lofty indifference to discomfort. What's a little ache? What's rain, or snow, or hunger? This, tonight, was more than any of those, but the tradition, Kristrun realized, sustained them. She was reminded of the old sagas, which still sold in many editions in her bookshop, especially the one describing the voyage from Iceland to Greenland at the end of the tenth century—*Eirik's Saga*. The many weeks, the fearful storms, day after day without a glimmer of sun, only the gray sea, and the fogs rolling in, the intense cold; then one morning the voyagers awakening to flooding sunlight, chessboards appearing, sodden clothes and blankets spread to dry—a day to take a reckoning of location, to tell tales, to ease the torment of the salt sores; then another storm, always another, to slue the ship and lift the bow and shred the sail; and death always walked the small ship, the dwindling band of survivors tilting the board with its still burden, abandoning the loved one to the unloving sea, wondering whether the fiendish swell would surge over the gunwales and turn the gullshaped hull into one chill coffin for all. She recalled the exhaustion so vividly described and the hallucinations, those eerie visitations as the fog took form, ectoplasmic emanations of grief—a beloved white face peering forlornly into the ship, a woman keening or a man moaning in the wind. In time, the salt meat rancid and the dry, hard fish mildewed, they caught fish and devoured them raw—heads, eyes, guts, tails. Then, after months of days and nights fighting a violent sea, they saw the blue black mountains, rising sheer from the waves to an enormous height, sheathed in ice, and, beyond, the inland ice, the glacial crust glittering and blinding in the sun, sending shafts of silver skyward. The wretched voyage over, fifteen of the thirty were safely there at the start of winter, while fifteen would drift forever in the ocean, to return and be remembered in dreams and waking fantasies.

Kristrun sat on a narrow shelf running along the inner side of the gunwale, lips already cracked, mouth and skin briny, holding Gudrid, who slept, against her body. Her damp leather gloves made her hands shrink and shrivelled her fingers; and mingled with the raw cold spray of the water, through which the trawler punched and fought its way, was the stench of fish from the hold and from the floor of the deck and the smells of wet wool and of Gudrid's sweet breath against her face—but no longer that reek of sulphur fumes. A few slept. Most sat or stood with eyes closed and minds filled with dread and regret and gratitude for deliverance. The men had been asked to occupy the hold below, and a few had emerged pale and sick and ashamed of their weakness. Many of the children, like Gudrid, slept, some clutching toys, some snoring softly in peace, secure.

It's happening, Mother. Kristrun knew that if she lived to be the age of her own mother—who was standing at the rail staring back, her wrinkled parchment face revealing none of the thoughts or feelings that must possess the mind and heart of a woman leaving her home for the first time in ninety years of life—if Kristrun lived to be her mother's age, or longer, she would never be able to purge from her memory Gudrid's voice: *It's happening, Mother.* And only that.

Was it possible, was it even conceivable that, of all the people on the island, only Gudrid had awakened without surprise? She had not once—while dressing, while gravely selecting the stuffed giraffe she still held, while sitting upright and curious in the seat on her way to her grandmother's house, while Kristrun argued and pleaded against her mother's stolid determination to stay, at whatever cost or consequence, in the home where she had always lived, and while on the way then to the wharves and onto the boat—in all this time, Gudrid had not once reminded her mother or father of that Sunday picnic in July. *It will happen here,* she had said, at the foot of Helgafell. Nor, tonight, had Gudrid inquired where the upheaval had taken place. It was as if she knew. In the last three hours Kristrun had struggled not to consider this, but now she realized how her bafflement had intensified. Her defenses were shattered, her own preconceptions a bewildering blur, and she was filled with more awe and wonder than, she would venture, any of the others on board were now experiencing, as they left behind the devastation that visited them from the mysterious bowels of the mysterious earth.

The waves slapped the side of the boat and struck the prow with steady hammerlike thwacks as it plowed stubbornly on.

Kristrun's neck was stiff. She wondered about Rolf, who worked for her in the shop, and she thought of others whom she knew, and she looked across the blackness beyond where the few lights from the boats glistened faintly, and tried to imagine what lay ahead—not tonight only, but in the yawning future which had so abruptly become uncertain, empty. Inevitably then, her mind, tired, gave in to the one thought that, more than any other, she longed to escape: Rudolf.

Rudolf had decided to stay. Kristrun, who had read much, knew that in most places a shopkeeper like her husband would do so in order to protect his property. Not against the effects of the cataclysm, for that would be impossible, but against the maraudings of his neighbors. That thought, his wife knew, had never so much as entered Rudolf's consciousness. *Some of us,* he had said, *will be needed.* Only that. But enough. Kristrun, tempted, had not questioned his decision; and she had not known rejection, only chagrin and a harrowing concern for him that remained keen and terrible in her still.

There were times, not frequent, when Kristrun wished that she had not read quite so much as she had. Tonight, feeling the warmth of Rudolf's blood in his daughter flush against her, she wished that she did not know of Krakatoa, the Indonesian island that had been, not smothered in ash or innundated by molten lava, but blown apart completely by a titanic eruption toward the end of the last century. Where earth had been, there were now only the waters of the sea. The reverse of Surtsey. The sea giveth and the sea taketh away.

Rudolf.

And then, with hot shame flooding her in the wet chill, she remembered how she had felt, how she had behaved and thought during the last few dark months. As she always had in the dismal, sunless depths of winter. She thought of the shop, warm and light, and the books neat and inviting on their shelves; she thought of the house, snug and filled with light and as much heat as anyone would ever need; and she thought of the pattern of her days from rising to the good dreamless sleep, the warm *dyna* light but enfolding, and of Rudolf making love, his fine manly but unhandsome face enraptured. She recalled how she had ached for the summer, dispirited and forlorn, nursing her own melancholy, her own self-pity.

Those days. Those nights. Gudrid's shouts from outside. Rudolf's quiet nature, his cigar, the smell of its smoke, the rooms of the house, the familiar pattern of the streets—in all this, which now was gone, might be gone forever, she had dared, she had had the selfish arrogance to feel deprived!

"Are we there?" Gudrid's voice, hazy with sleep, asked.

"Not yet, dear."

There? Where? A new desolation moved in. Was all of that gone then, all that she had been too blind to realize?

Does anyone ever realize? Ever?

So all that was going on.

And now?

Now?

The pain in Olaf's arm had returned while he was helping to launch the small boat and, by the time he was afloat in it, staring back at the docks and lighted streets and whatever that dazzling red light was beyond, the pain was unbearable, and he realized that the boy had lied, he had no *brennivan*, he had tricked Olaf into helping. But where were they going? At first the boy had rowed as if he intended to leave the harbor at this time of night. To where? For what? Why?

Many times in the past, as he had done tonight, Olaf had taken the pain-deadening pills while he was drinking, recalling each time that the doctor in Liverpool had warned him against mixing the two—because, the old man had said in his clipped British accent, both were drugs, actually. Now he had no more of the pills, the boy had no *brennivan* or whisky or rum, maybe it was all in his mind, all this, because, look now, a sirocco was blowing, he was caught in a sirocco, and, even in the boat on the surface of the cold water, he was hot, and what was that fire in the distance and that sound, what was happening, or was it happening really, who was this boy staring so intently back at the land, resting on the oars now, fear in his face, and how had he, Olaf Jonsson, come here? Was that Vestmannaeyjar over there, if so, was it afire, was the whole town burning, if it was, he had to get to Juliana, he had to warn her, he'd kill the husband if need be, he'd almost killed a black in Capetown once, or was that Port of Spain, yes he'd kill Halldor Danielsson, he hated him enough, had hated him for nine years, a thousand centuries, in a hundred different places. He knew it was the medicine doing this to him, the water seemed to be burning, water doesn't burn. Oh God, oh Christ, if Juliana was that close after all these years, what was he doing out here, after all the dirt he'd seen, and those people, scum, evil, sucking the sailors dry then throwing them into the crawling cells with vermin and rats—the stench, oh God, the stench. And once he had walked the fields with Juliana through air like crystal, with Juliana through the winter snow, on the streets of home. Now what was that smell, the wind not more than ten knots southwesterly, the smell came from the flame that he was not sure was a flame anyway, the stink of sulphur, like solfataras, the steam from the hot springs and geysers on the mainland, he had it clear now, a volcano, a volcano on Heimaey, oh God they had to go back, he called to the boy. He heard himself calling, but the boy sat slouched and abstracted, still staring; he had to make the boy hear him, they had to go back, that was a volcano, listen to the thunder, Thor himself raving in rage, and soon, if the wind changed, if the wind turned easterly, and it was the time of year for the wind to prevail easterly, then the burning ash would fall on the town. He hoped it was all in his mind, but if it wasn't . . .

If it was real, his daughter would die. Be killed. Yes. His daughter, *his.* The girl he had seen on the street today, in the wind, red hair blowing, like Juliana's. He did not know the child's name, but she was his daughter. Not Halldor's—his. And he must get to her, to her and to Juliana now.

"What are you doing?" the boy demanded. "Sit down, sit down. Do you want to go overboard? Sit down!"

But he had to explain, he had to make the boy see. Couldn't he *see* what was happening over there? Couldn't the young fool *hear* it?

"If you don't sit down," the boy shouted, "then I'm going to knock you down. I swear it. That's what I'll do."

Olaf was too weak. He sat back. He had worn himself out launching the boat. If the boy struck him, he'd go over the gunwale. If he went into the water—which was arctic cold inches below the red luminous surface, he knew, he knew—then he would never be able to save them both. He sat back, blinking, feeling faint, his arm throbbing to the marrow, and had no way now to blank his mind, no way at all, except in time the pain would do it, the pain itself, his only enemy worse than loneliness.

He would wait his chance. The boat was drifting toward the cliffs. The wakes of the departing vessels were driving it there. If the boat cracked up on the rocks, if he did not take it over—Olaf Jonsson knew of such matters. And he knew the tricks. He would wait his chance, but damned if he would sit here and let the boat splinter on Heimaklettur.

It was then that he saw the boy take his gaze from the town and look up. In the distant rumble and the closer growl of the engines of the vessels as they streamed off, he had not heard it, but now he saw a small plane overhead, flying low, wing lights flashing.

From above the pilot could see a flotilla of lighted vessels passing through the narrow mouth of the harbor and then proceeding in a semicircle around the high flat-topped cliffs that formed it and then in a northwesterly direction. In the harbor, as he banked low, he saw more shadows of boats on a reddish glare of water and clusters of people on the docks. In the convulsion and turbulence flaring over the whole scene, he felt he was looking down on a world gone berserk. And what he began to feel, in addition to the excitement that had sustained him till now, was not fear but isolation: he was alone and then, down there, each one was alone, and desolation threatens every man always.

En route, in the plane of the directorate of Icelandic Airlines, he had remained trapped in his own resolute decision to land the craft regardless of warnings or risk. Conflicting reports had informed him that the fissure had split apart the east-west runway and that the north-south runway was too short to accommodate his craft; but the Vestmannaeyjar tower had assured him that, in spite of a downfall of sparks and some large chunks of pumice here and there, a fixed-wing plane, such as his, could set down safely from the east, provided the airstrip was approached with very great caution. He himself—middle-aged, experienced at scouting and rescue missions—knew that, eruption or no, it was always treacherous business to come in over the sea and into the narrow cleft between the high rocky bluffs of the eastern approach.

Crouching over the controls, every fiber of his being alive and quivering, the plane buffeted by whirlwinds and flaming clouds, he passed along the open fissure. When the opaque blackness cleared here and there, he could see the red molten lava roiling and could feel the ferocious heat rising from miles beneath the open wound. Yet he seemed to be drawn lower and lower, as if he had no will. It was as if some mysterious power had been loosed on the world, and he was at its source, and, like boiling quicksand, it was luring him closer. He banked east and upwards, almost in desperation, and then he was in the dark drift of cloud and circling, finding his glide path. The chaos seemed to lie ahead, and he seemed headed for it, but he corrected his speed and nosed the plane in a faster descent, aimed it with precision between the profiled upthrusts of crags, the tips of his wings seeming almost to brush them, the dimly outlined runway coming clearer, and then he felt the wheels touch. He was rolling in a shower of sparks and a hail of falling ash, black and red, which he could hear pinging on the metal. He came to a sharper halt than he had intended.

Then he sat a moment, alone. He had brought in the first plane. No one else. There was something in that for a man.

The phone was ringing. There was another sound as well, farther away—but could he be sure?—the phone in the parlor was definitely ringing.

He stood up from the bed, his long muscular legs wobbly and his mind faint; he groped his way, cold through his flesh, the cold that brings out the iron in a man, making the blood bound, warmth is for weaklings. What was that other sound? Possibly only the *brennivan* still in his veins. He answered the telephone.

"Arni?"

It was his mother. In Reykjavik. But at night? Now?

"What time is it?" he heard himself ask.

"Arni, listen to me now, listen." And then, while he pictured her face—the hooked nose, the bright and devastatingly sharp eyes, her outthrust chin—his mother told him that there had been a volcanic eruption on Heimaey. Where he lived. Where he now was. Was he listening? Didn't he hear her? Was he drunk again, again *was* he? *Listen!* She had received a phone message from a friend of hers, a woman whose son was a police officer on duty tonight in the main station in Reykjavik, and he had reported that the island of Heimaey was about to blow up. Was this true? What was Arni doing about it? Did Arni wish to come to her house? It was his house really, his home, it would always be. Well, did he?

It was all too much. His mind refused to grasp, to comprehend. It was perhaps a dream. But there was that sound—as if the storm were returning. Only during the afternoon there had been no thunder. And he realized that he could see the furniture in the room. There was a light at the window, an odd light, pale, fading, returning, rose-tinted, unreal.

"Arni, have you heard me? *Arni!*"

The hated voice. The demanding voice, always demanding. Now she was telling him what to do. Again. As if he were still a child. He stood up, aware of his weight and his height, the width of his shoulders. Drunk he may be still, drunk undoubtedly he was, but he was a true son of the North, let no one forget that, hot-tempered, bold, but shrewd, full of energy, practical. There was something to be done now. If only his mother's starchy voice would allow him to think.

"Yes, Mother," he said softly, the words and his tone a hateful echo of childhood. "I'll waken Margret and we'll come. Yes." Always yes. Always yes-mother. But when he went into the bedchamber to rouse Margret, even as he sat down on the edge of the bed, an ache of contrition and love settling into his mind, an old aching gentleness, he discovered that the *dyna* had not been turned back, no body lay in the bed beside the place where his had been.

Where was Margret?

Where had Margret gone?

He went to the window on legs gone more feeble still, his mind fluttering. And then he saw the eruption. For that's what it had to be. The flames reached upwards beyond the roofs, the other houses silhouetted, and now, for some reason, his eyes perceiving, he heard more clearly the thunder that was not thunder, a steady, low roar with a crackling within it, and saw the sky brilliant yellow with red above, then going into black and smoke, billowing, twisting, snarling above.

It had happened then.

He had never once so much as given the possibility a thought. Not in his three years here. Not once. Yet . . .

Where had Margret gone?

Now was the time for a man to act. Now, at last, after wasting himself teaching, now he had the opportunity, to-night, this minute, to behave as a man must behave. The warlike spirit of his ancestors had been bred into his bones. His blood stirred. His forebears had prowled the oceans in search of adventure, plunder. Was he any less a man? He had wished recently that he could take part in the attacks against the British fishing vessels invading his country's waters! Now, though, this was bigger than that. The heroic lays, the scaldic poems, the Icelandic sagas celebrating honor and bravery—all this was part of him, Arni Loftsson, the part of him called upon now.

But what he felt was anger. A depthless, inner rage. Toward her, toward Margret.

Realizing that he had not undressed, he gave himself over to fury and went into the kitchen. There was no *brennivan*. The violence inside seethed and simmered upwards, his breath and mouth going sour, his chest constricted. She had hidden or perhaps poured out his *brennivan*. Damn her: Damn the bitch!

No.

No, she was not a bitch. She was Margret, the girl with the fragile face and luminous raven hair, whom he had met at Summer Festival, had married and had then loved more.

And he needed her. Now. Where was she, because he needed her!

He shouted her name.

She needed him, too. Who would take care of her?

He strode to the door and threw it open. There were shadows on the street, moving, and headlights, a spinning domelight, blue in the pink glare that seemed more livid now.

It was then that terror reached him. Its cold hands probed sharply into his vitals, clutched his heart, shredded his guts. He felt his flesh begin to quiver.

But Norsemen never knew fear.

He was one of them.

He was not, like Margret, descended from dark Celtic slaves.

Yet he could not seem to move.

And standing so, helpless, shaken, and faint, his fine young body gone sapless, he realized where Margret had gone.

To him.

Whoever he was.

To him.

And not for the first time.

At a time like this, too. To forsake him now, to place her body beneath the body of . . .

He recalled the softness of her. The dark beauty. The blue eyes intense or laughing. Her body smaller than the others he had known, her shoulders white, her supple, encircling arms. The infinite womanliness and warmth, warmth to drive a man to . . .

It would not be so. It could not be.

He vowed revenge. His mind focused now, and he vowed revenge, as his ancestors would have done, the ones who had crossed the immense, boundless, raging sea in barks too frail and small. A friend to a friend always, as the Edda had it, but ruthless to a foe and faithful to his word to both.

The man, whoever he was, the man had his word now. A Norseman has the sacred and inalienable right—no, not right, *duty*—of blood revenge. The man had his word, and so did Margret.

Margret.

Volcano or no, let the others flee, let them all run frightened to the docks, to the mainland, he, Arni Loftsson, had something to do first. Something more important.

He could feel the blood beginning to hammer through his veins again. His tall, cold body kindled to warmth again, then went scalding hot. And he recalled where he had hidden a half-bottle of *brennivan* against such an occasion.

Well, not such an occasion as this—because he had never imagined a night like this. Nor had he ever imagined that he would wish harm, any harm, ever to come to Margret. The bottle was where he had concealed it.

Like many others in the town, Agnar Ivarsson had had
to weigh his responsibilities, had had to consider the complex
and contradictory elements that he faced, and had then to
take action. His wife and daughter were now on board the
Njord, along with many others, including Alex Sitfusson—
whom he himself had taken there because of the man's missing leg—and the families of his crew who went aboard,
without being asked, as soon as they arrived at the dock, and,
although the vessel was now almost full, and although other
boats, when loaded, were pulling away, here was the skipper
driving his car uphill and away. Decision made, right or
wrong, for good or ill.

Although he had heard no official report of any kind,
Agnar knew that the lava must be flowing, and he knew as
well that it had to be moving downhill toward the town itself.

In his mind, as he drove south, he was tempted to raise
his fist and to shake it at that red glowering over there on his
left, having long ago now put from his mind the predictions
that the winter was expected to be the best fishing season in
many years, his mind now envisioning buried houses and
streets and the streetlamps dead forever beneath the black
tidal wave. He had to fight the picture of even more terrible
possibilities: the island itself exploding like one mighty
bomb, convulsive and shattering, even its parts disappearing
forever beneath the vast, uncaring waters of the ocean that
stretched eternal and heedless, forever taking life as it gave
it. It could happen, yes. If the island of Surtsey could be
created, the island of Heimaey could be annihilated. And at
any moment now.

He could feel the urgency in the engine, vibrating and
straining as if in rage. Past the last few houses, empty shells
standing, waiting, and then between the sparse, dark fields,
only palely tinted at this distance from the fuming corusca-
tion. He was not thinking of his son Rolf now or of where he
was going or why. He was lost again in a sensation that had
been returning over and over since the moment he had been
awakened to the sound of sirens by Ruth's gentle touch: the
impression that all of this had happened before. More: that

he himself had done all this before, perhaps in some other life or time or place. There was a phrase for it, he knew, but his mind had no time to search it out—some foreign-language phrase, not Icelandic. But what?

The ancient farmhouse, built centuries ago by some fool in defiance of the west wind, crouched low and stark and dim on the rim of the headland with darkness over the sea beyond. A single light glowed dimly golden in one narrow window. When the beams of his headlamps raked the area as he turned in, he did not see Rolf's motorcycle.

If the boy was not here, then where? All the apprehension of the night seemed to focus now on his son. But should this be so? The *Njord* was still moored, when it should be miles away by now. Yet he knew that Ruth understood: it would be unthinkable to leave the island without their son. But Ruth, naturally, knew nothing of this woman. He had kept the goings-on here, whatever they were, secret from the boy's mother and sister. Men may not understand more—for himself, there was no approval in him, only puzzlement and the anger that puzzlement fed—but a man's duty is to protect a woman from such. Striding toward the door, he could hear the breakers smashing below, and he noted that the wind, praise God, stayed south-southwest—they would all need God's mercy if it changed to easterly across the blaze back there before they were gone. As he knocked, he wondered again what exactly it was that the woman here offered the young men. Was it more than the wine, more than the marijuana that, it was suggested, she gave them or sold them? Her body then? Or more? Could it be something that, even if he could define it, he would not be able to fathom or to accept?

Her body in the doorway, against the dim bluish light from an oil lamp behind, was slim and tall; her voice, which he had never actually heard before, was deep-throated, the words accented, not only by her recent acquisition of the language, but by a strange mockery of tone.

"You have come for me?" She stepped away. "Enter please."

Agnar felt clumsy and foolish as he looked around the low-ceilinged room. It possessed an exotic quality that seemed, at once, inviting, even charming in its individual way, but foreign, oddly disquieting. Sheepskin rugs spread over the floor, and there was a gleam of natural blond on the furniture that her Dutch husband must have carpentered himself before his death.

"You have come to take me in your car, yes?" she asked as if amused. "And what if I should prefer to stay?"

"My name," he heard himself say heavily, for he was ill at ease, "is Agnar Ivarsson. You know my son, I think."

She was smiling then, a faint smile that did not deride but glittered in her jet black eyes in friendly fashion. "Rolf I know, yes. So you have not come to take me to safety? Listen, hear the old beams? They have begun to sigh like the timbers on a ship, you hear? Rolf, he is no longer here." Then she took a single step, all smiles vanishing. "I am sorry." The sincerity and gravity in her tone were startling. "He was here, yes, but no longer."

It was then that Agnar, struggling with the dismay and the appalling anxiety throbbing in him, made another decision, but spoke the truth: "I did not come to fetch you, but I think you should come."

But she remained still, the only movement a tilting of her slender head on which the black hair, pulled taut and tight, glistened softly. "Would it be . . . advisable for you to take me?"

He considered. The thought behind the words was kind. The woman knew her reputation, but she did not know him, Agnar Ivarsson. "It would be bad if I left you here." He did not mention his forebodings, but the urgency, renewed, caused him to turn to the door. "If there's anything you would care to bring along . . ."

She took a sweeping glance round, as if wondering—the same glance so many must have taken in the last three hours—and then she took up only a knitted wool poncho with a hood, slid it over her head and shoulders and walked to the door. She did not stop to look at the glare on the east horizon but, he knew, she could not help but feel the quivering beneath her step.

Beside him in the seat, she was silent, and he was hesitant to intrude on her'thoughts. But, with his own mind trying to imagine where he could now search and to decide whether such further search was wise—after all, Rolf might be on the *Njord* by now or on one of the other vessels—Agnar was astonished to hear himself asking questions. There was a phrase, it might be French, he thought, perhaps she could tell him: it was as if all that was happening now had happened before.

She spoke from the dimness: *"Déjà vu,* yes. It comes to me often. To you?"

"Now," he said.

"Que c'est étrange," she murmured. "At a time like this. *Très étrange."*

Then he remembered. Years ago—how many, how long ago now—he had had a dream. He had been living with his aunt in Reykjavik then because he was attending navigational school, and he had told her, that kindly old lady, of his dream, and she had explained that he had been reading too many accounts of the floods in the Netherlands that year, but no—odd how he recalled it quite clearly now—he had insisted that no, he had dreamed, not of a flood, but of a volcano, he had seen it quite clearly in the dream and it had filled him with a terrible dread that had remained with him for several days and nights.

Staying west, they passed a house on Illugata in which a party seemed to be taking place. One young couple stood on the lawn, the boy lifting a brandy glass in toast in the direction of the east, the girl, probably his young wife, laughing and clinging to his arm. Another couple came out to join them, the four waving and shouting at the passing car. They looked young and drunk and happy, and Agnar was stabbed with a quick, sharp solicitude. The young fools, the young vulnerable fools—what would happen to them?

And then, as he turned onto Hosteleinsvegur, he knew what he must do now. All choice gone, time draining away faster and faster, he must abandon the one for the many. He had no right—he, Agnar, had no such privilege—to hold fifty or sixty people in peril on his boat, while he went searching for one. Even if the one were his son, whom he loved? Yes, even so. Even if the death of that son, if it came to that, would destroy the woman he loved and cherished, even if such a loss would destroy him too? Yes, even so.

As if she had divined his thought in the air between them the woman said: "Rolf will care for himself. Possibly . . . possibly he is more of a man than you can allow yourself to think him."

Anger possessed him then. Rage. At her—what rude audacity, what boldness and shamelessness in this strange, foreign woman to take it upon herself to comment on him, on his relationship with his son. And rage also at Rolf, although even as it choked him now, he knew it for what it was: love and helplessness and defeat. Where had the boy gone? What was he doing now? Was he safe?

At the quayside, where cars were parked in disorderly fashion, deserted, he was forced to pull up at least twenty meters from where the *Njord* was moored beyond the ice-packing plant. There was a faint smell of sulphur in the night, reminding him of the deadly gases that were often emitted by a full eruption, but the wind, perhaps freshening a knot or two, remained southwesterly and might have veered a degree or so farther west, so that the fumes, like the other ejecta, were being carried off to sea. The rumble echoed back from the cliffs hemming in the harbor. On the wharves the townspeople waited—no crowding, no jostling for position—and he felt a flash of pride. In the nightmare light, glittering metallic on the water, the flare was reflected, and over the rooftops the flame was an intense white rising to a terrible yellow, the ruddy red and jagged edge above turning into black billows, folding in upon themselves like soft claws and darkening the sky. There was about the entire scene an atmosphere of the spectral, the ominous, and the utterly unreal that, Agnar knew, if he lived, he would remember forever.

Vessels were proceeding with caution, slowly, to the narrow mouth of harbor and then disappearing in the vastness beyond. In the time he had been away, the line of fire had extended itself to the water's edge. If the lava was moving as well, if the harbor entrance, that single aperture between stones, should be obstructed, they would be imprisoned here. The airfield at the foot of Helgafell, where the inferno seemed to be most concentrated now, was small. Even if accessible, he doubted that that single crisscross of runways could accommodate planes large enough to remove even the number of passengers now crowded together on his *Njord.*

Walking along the dock next to the tall woman, whose name he knew was Odette, although he had not spoken it on the ride into town, Agnar passed the low boat-construction shop. Rolf's motorcycle stood against its wall. Agnar felt rather than saw the woman's head turn. He stepped to the wide doorway which was open. In the flickering dimness it was clear that Rolf's boat was not there.

Stunned a moment, the father stood motionless. He had to thrust from his mind the idea that his son might, terror-stricken, have tried to make his own escape. Perhaps by attaching a motor to his small craft. No. The boy knew the waters too well, he was no fool! Then, rage engulfing him because of the alarm that surged hotly in his blood, he strode to the *Njord,* which was already crowded; he stood back to allow the woman to move up the short gangplank which he and his crew rarely used. He glanced about at the many faces, most of them familiar, a few heads nodding. Ruth's face was framed in the window of the wheelhouse. His eyes met hers. Her face was sober—beautiful, beautiful! And, even at the distance of several meters, he could see the love and concern in her eyes, and again he had the sensation all through him not only that all of this had happened before, in some mysterious other time or place, but that this woman's spirit was what warmed and lighted his life. He ignored the questions in her eyes and climbed the steps into the wheelhouse.

"Away?" His mate was there, waiting, his beefy hand

already reaching to the controls, his other lifting to give the signal to the crewmen who were, the skipper knew, stationed on the pier ready to lift the hawsers from the bollards.

"Not yet," Agnar said and took up his old but powerful binoculars, turning away, conscious of Ruth's presence and of her hand touching his shoulder.

Through the glasses the surface of the water gave back a tinted shimmering refulgence, and as he scanned the churning harbor, his view moving past and between the trawlers and their human cargo, he reminded himself again that Rolf was too sea-wise to imagine that he could make it to the mainland in that small craft. Then why was he looking for it now? What if the boy were drunk or had smoked too much pot? The fool, oh the young idiot, the boy, the damned child! Choked with love, cold himself now, Agnar shifted his gaze to the base of the high, steep cliffs rising in the distance, scanned the water, which was darker there, and then he saw the boat: the glasses, freezing in his two hands, moved beyond for a split second, then returned. With quick precision he fixed the focus. Rolf's boat? Rolf? His heart was still. He was not breathing. And he did not speak to Ruth behind him.

Two figures, visible but obscure, were in the small boat. The binoculars were not strong enough, in this light, to reveal either face. They were not large men, either of them, and the boat was the size of Rolf's. And it was adrift, bobbing. The two figures faced each other, one standing, one seated at the oars. And Agnar realized that their attitudes were hostile. Why would a man stand up in a boat like that? If he toppled into that water, he would freeze in the instant, drown in less than two minutes. And why wasn't the one at the oars—was it Rolf, was it really Rolf?—why wasn't he bringing that damned little craft to the docks before it washed against the cliffs and splintered? Then the upright figure took a step, the boat tilting, the figure spreading its arms for balance. Then one arm went wider still, swinging, and it appeared, at the distance, as if he had landed a blow against the side of the head of the sitting figure. The small craft

rocked precariously, so low on both sides that Agnar knew
that water was rushing over the gunwales and that it would be
swamped completely and would capsize unless . . .

Now the seated figure rose up and both stood upright in
the rolling hull facing each other, and then Agnar realized
that the one who had been sitting held an oar in his hand.
When the other figure moved again, tottering but threatening, the one with the oar stepped backwards not so much in
retreat but as if to maintain or to gain balance and to be able
to move. It was then that Agnar knew what the man intended. He lifted the oar overhead and, careful to bring it
down from above and not from the side so that his attacker
would not go overboard, he bashed it in a straight-down
stroke onto the skull of the other man, who for a moment or
two appeared as if he might tumble overboard regardless,
but who, instead, crumpled and all but disappeared below
the gunwales. Unable to move, again struggling to focus the
glasses that would not provide more power than they
mechanically possessed, Agnar still watched. He saw the figure with the oar resume his seat, insert the oar into its lock,
and then—as if the action had somehow brought him to a
decision—he placed the two blades in the water and leaned
into the oars. That boat began to turn in the water, and then
its prow was directed toward the docks, the back of the
oarsman's head and his pumping shoulders visible above the
sharp beak of the boat whitely knifing the dark water.

The captain lowered the glasses and looked across the
heads of his passengers on the deck. In spite of everything he
felt a deep relief: if that was Rolf, he was on his way. But how
could he be certain it was his son? And if certain, did he now
have the right to keep these others here waiting when at any
moment . . .

Ruth behind him remained silent.

He did not have that right. But he would wait regardless. He hoped God would forgive him. He hoped that the
explosion that would either close the harbor or reduce the
whole island to rubble would not occur until his son, if it was
his son, had reached the quay. He returned to Ruth and felt

the stiff flesh of his face smile. He saw the questions in her
eyes fade away.

He heard the short blasts of whistles on the water, and
he could only hope that he had made the wise decision—if in
fact it had been a decision at all. How much time did they
have left?

"Away?" his mate asked again.

And again he answered: "Not yet."

Less than one hundred meters from the base of Helgafell, Baldvin Einarsson's house was closer to the fissure
than almost any other and was, therefore, his wife Inga
knew, doomed from the beginning. From the time, several
long and unreal hours ago now, that the large house had
begun to sway as if it were on a string, through the time that
the ground exploded and belched fire and then red ash,
until now when that ash, in chunks and pebbles of all sizes,
was battering the roof, the flame seeming to envelope the air
on all sides, Inga had known that they must abandon all this
and take flight. But she had been unable to reason with her
husband. From the very start Baldvin had been like a man
gone mad, a stranger, his eyes aglitter with a strange unreason and triumph—and it was this that terrified her more
than the trembling, that had now become a quaking under
the floors and foundation. If she had not been born in and
had not lived most of her life in Copenhagen rather than
here, might she have been able to comprehend?

Now Baldvin had gone out of the house again. She had a
mental image of him, heavy and intent, shoulders hunched
forward, making his way to the hot fringe of the inferno, his
bald head protected only by a knit cap from the falling

pumice or hot volcanic glass and the rain of cinders, his mind in a turmoil of satisfaction that left no room in it for fear, for so much as an acknowledgment of danger. She was alone in the quivering, rattling house, remembering his exultant voice: *They wouldn't listen! No one would believe!* She had known then what he meant: hadn't he, and others, predicted that Helgafell, the Holy Mount, long quiescent, would somehow avenge its desecration by foolish, blind men who dared tamper with it? Until now Inga had viewed the argument as amusing: didn't all men have some quirk, some twist of mind that set them apart from others? But now . . .

She did not know whether to gather together a few possessions—which ones, what could be saved?—or simply to take the car and leave on her own or to wait. If the house had to go, need they perish with it? But she could not leave Baldvin. She could not make him listen, she could not convince him, and she could not leave him. His face had been flushed from the start—the color too bright, too high, dangerous—and although she had mentioned his blood pressure, had tried to calm him and to induce him to swallow the pills that his friend Pall had prescribed for moments of intense excitement, Baldvin had been deaf to her, hearing only some inner cry of triumph and the terrible stentorian tumult that engulfed them and drowned out her shouted appeals, her frantic pleas. The fortissimo dissonance, harsh and deep, seemed to have penetrated her entire being, and now she knew that, instead of the merriment in her eyes that Baldvin had always loved, there could only be bafflement and a horror-stricken desperation. Over and over the calm voice on the radio, which was turned full-volume yet emitted only a crackling mutter against the wildness of sound shuddering in the air around her, urged everyone to go to the harbor, where boats were waiting to transport them to the mainland.

Inga, who was not religious either in Baldvin's way or in the way in which she had been trained as a child, found herself, as she wandered from room to room, wishing that she could pray now. Alone and abandoned, she felt herself in full retreat—from everything, everyone, herself as well, all her beliefs and convictions. She wished Petur was here now, although she knew he was far away in some town in the north where his wife's father was slowly dying. Would the cleric have been able, if here, to give her the comfort, the strength she now needed? Feeble, emotional, faint of heart, she felt herself collapsing inside and reached, in her mind, for some thought, some memory, some trivial picture that might sustain her. What came to mind was the Reverend Petur, tall and dark and lean, striding the streets while old men lifted their hats and mumbled greetings and children solemnly nodded, and she wondered, in an uprush of giddiness, whether Petur himself knew that he almost invariably greeted them by their wrong names. No, Petur could no more convince Baldvin to do the reasonable thing now than he had ever convinced him, in those amusing discussions, that there was one god only, that all else was heathen superstition. And suddenly, in the kitchen at the broadshelf, trying to pour coffee into a cup that would not stop jiggling and clattering, she realized that she had come all this way to the Vestmann Islands to live amid a people who, in their deepest hearts and minds, believed in demonology, necromancy, cruel gods, fate! Here in this centuries-old town, haunted by old ghosts, old tales, ancient myths, and surrounded by the ageless sea, from which this very earth had risen with fire and from fire, here she had chosen to come and to live her life. And until now she had been happy. (Was it possible to be too happy? Was there, after all, punishment for that, too?) Until now, she had been a cheerful woman of smiles. Until now, she had had only one regret: her childlessness.

The rumbling tumult outside, which seemed a part of the house itself now, gave forth a series of deep, rasping coughs, like those of some gigantic sea creature of prehistoric time and then, *POOM*, a cannonlike blast that shook her bones and sent china and glasses crashing and splintering. In the same instant the house lit up like a torch, as if lightning had struck, and she found herself cowering and running, crying his name, crying Baldvin's name, her voice lost in the profound, deafening cacophony in which she was about to become submerged forever!

She found herself in the studio. From the high, peaked ceiling fell the fluorescence by which he worked, summer and winter, the bluish light, dimmed now in the glare from the high windows, mingling with the flashing reds and oranges outside, giving the large room an unearthly strangeness. One window glass glittered with a sharp-edged zigzag crack. She turned to leave, to escape—but where, *where?*—when her eyes fell upon the oil painting on the easel. And vaguely she remembered that this was the one that he had not wanted her to see until he had completed his work on it. But she could not take her eyes from it. It was of two volcanic cones, one beside the other, neither in eruption, the one on the right an exact replica of the long dormant Helgafell, but the cone on the left, almost identical in height, was one she had never before seen. It did not exist in reality. Even now, outside, the new eruption was a long slit with fountains of fire, not a mound or mountain. Nevertheless, the painting as a whole held a brooding menace, the brown serenity of the two cones side by side even more sinister, somehow, than the real and immediate fury surrounding her. She stood transfixed. And even though heat bore down on the house, clogged her pores and seemed to singe her flesh and to carbonize the very air, although the walls seemed to exhale it, and she could not breathe, she began to shiver as from cold. And in a second's time her whole body was shuddering.

Then, not hearing because hearing was impossible, she felt his presence in the room behind her. She did hear his voice then, the words distorted and unclear—something about the lava moving—and then he was standing in front of her, close, his familiar face feverish and bewildered, but the triumph still glinting in his brown eyes. When his voice became more clear—a shout—his tone was vibrant, not with the earlier satisfaction and wild glee, but with a solicitude and tenderness and anxiety that went deeper than love. "What have I done to you?" he asked, stricken, appalled.

She strained to say it didn't matter now; she longed to

say it didn't matter now because he had come back, himself again, the man she knew; but her throat and tongue would not at first respond to the urging of her emotions. And then, when she was at last able to answer, it was to say: "Take the painting, Baldvin."

He did. And as he clasped the stiff canvas, she saw his fingers dig into the glistening oil, the still-wet paint along the top, above the crater-mouths of the two volcano cones standing side by side.

As a schoolgirl Odette Haanstra, née Descourd, had studied French history. Mount Pélée, on the Caribbean island of Martinique, exploded in 1902 (she even recalled the year) and shot out of its flank a broadside of compressed air, followed by a wall of fire roaring toward the sea at five hundred kilometers an hour. In only seconds the town of Saint Pierre, nine kilometers away, was totally annihilated, all but one of its thirty thousand inhabitants dead. A thick deposit of ash left the area a vast wasteland. But Odette, huddled now on the deck of the fishing vessel owned by the so kind Captain Agnar, was not thinking of what such a catastrophe might portend here so much as she was thinking of the people around her: the sober, quiet faces, the incredible patience and calm of all of them. No crying out or wailing, no demands to be taken aboard or for the boat to push off. Only a pervasive, stolid quiet that seemed to Odette to border on the unnatural. To her Gallic temperament, such restraint in the face of such peril and loss was beyond belief. She would have been made more easy by the sight of a tear, the sound of weeping, or a snarl of protest. Yet, her admiration for these people, with whom she had never come to feel at home, deepened as they waited—was it too late now to become one of them?

She had overheard a single conversation, straining to

translate. One elderly raw-boned woman with stricken eyes had asked a very tall fair-haired girl why the boat was not leaving like the others, and the girl had replied that her father was waiting for her brother to come aboard. The older woman had nodded, as if this simple explanation were sufficient and immediately understandable: what was more natural than that they should all wait patiently for the captain's son? The strangeness of it all was one with the weird light that played over the entire scene. *Incroyable.*

And now she thought again of Pall. Did she wish he was with her? Yes. But she knew, too, where he would be now: at the hospital, *naturellement.* He did not have need of her now. He came to her with one need, a desire which she gratified always and which also satisfied her physically, but never left her feeling truly fulfilled. As Pall was not. As they both knew. In the reaching out, they had never really touched, except physically—and the longing that she had always felt with Maarten, with every man all her life, had not been assuaged in any but the most superficial, although exciting, way. Now, she was leaving Maarten, too. She thought of the cemetery alongside the church. Would the volcano spew its fire and ash and cinders and lava as far as the churchyard? If alive now, could Maarten have survived this? One bitter winter here had been too much for his lungs, already withered. But if he were here now, if he had not died that lingering death, her knowledge of him might have remained the illusion that she had nurtured rather than the reality she had come to experience. Seeing these people around her, she knew that it was not necessary to die poisoned, poisoning yourself the very air for which you gasped. He had killed her love before he had killed himself by his own frustrations and self-knowledge, his own failure as a writer and as a man. *Adieu, Maarten, adieu.* A phrase from her Catholic childhood in Lyon returned: *Requiescat in pace.*

Then she saw Rolf. He was approaching along the wharves with his father and another man, bearded, wearing seaman's clothes, his body swaying so that Rolf had to put out a hand every so often to steady him. When they reached the gangplank, the stranger halted, staring at the boat, then stepped away in an attitude of defiance. She heard Rolf's voice then, raised but somewhat obscured by the distant booming accompaniment to all other sound. Rolf was saying, Odette thought, that he was sorry, he had not meant to injure the man, he had done it (whatever it was) only to make him sit down and to keep him from drowning. The man, who was almost as small as Rolf himself, swiveled away, and she caught in the weathered face, at a distance of only two meters, an expression of pain and bewilderment so profound that her heart writhed in slow compassion. Rolf reached again and the seaman twisted away, shaking his head, his own hand reaching across his chest to clasp his other arm, as if here were the root of his pain. Mystified, she watched as the seaman, looking miserable but determined, started off and away, shouting now. She could make out only a few words: ". . . Juliana . . . daughter . . . save them . . . *my* daughter!" And then he was lunging with a sideways stagger along the quay toward the empty streets and deserted houses of the town. The captain and Rolf stared after him. Then Rolf took a single step as if to follow, his father spoke, gently, so softly that she could not hear the word, and Rolf swung about to face his father. What she saw then startled her still more: his boyish face, which she had seen in many moods, contorted, his eyes blazed in the eerie radiance, and his small-boned body stiffened. He said nothing, only stared into his father's face and Odette saw reflected in the son's attitude now all the rebellion and repression and sullen resentment that she had sensed in him over the months he had been coming to her house. Could it be actual hatred toward a man as good and strong as the one who had brought her here? Baffled, she waited. And Agnar Ivarsson waited. Was Rolf's mother the woman above in the wheelhouse window? Was she also watching?

Rolf nodded his narrow head. Once. Then he turned, without a glance in the direction the unknown seaman had taken, and he came up the sloping plank and onto the boat.

The skipper lifted his arm in the direction of the

wheelhouse and then came aboard. A single bell clanged, once. There was action. Lines slipped from posts, the gangplank was drawn up, the engine ground to life and muttered.

The captain, Odette realized, had decided: they had waited for his son, they would not wait for this stranger who refused to come aboard anyway. The time was now.

The *Njord* slid from its mooring and turned its nose out into the glistening harbor. In a few moments it was moving closer to the blaze, which was low to starboard, its flames licking at the cold water and plunging beneath where they seemed still to burn, a red radiance beneath the surface. The odor of sulphur mixed with the fish smell from the hold and decks and with the cold salt air. Beyond the narrow harbor opening stretched the night darkness of the sea. And what beyond?

Odette was leaving still another home—for what? Where?

One may as well do something, so Hulda Palmadottir knitted. She was terribly tired and confused and had been ever since they had wakened her and told her to dress. They never explained anything here—let the old folk do what they're told, no questions asked. She was chilled and tired, bone-weary from doing nothing at all, as usual. But she had not been frightened from the first, and now she was more curious than reluctant: what would it be like somewhere else? Would they take her to Reykjavik? She had never been to Reykjavik. She certainly wasn't going to behave like some of those around her here in the parlor where they'd been asked to gather. No one had told them what was happening, but most of them knew. One woman, whose name Hulda could not remember—although she had known most of these people for more than eighty years, their names would not come easily to her mind—one old woman was hysterical, now crying, then screaming, then moaning. Such terror Hulda understood, yes, but she did not approve: it was not the way to behave now, at a time like this. Others found the idea of death unfrightening: one frail old woman with a face of cracked dry leather sat quiet and serene, with an expression of peace in her watery eyes, almost anticipation, as if she were looking forward to relief or perhaps to seeing those whom she had once known and loved, whose spirits, she knew, were awaiting her. But one man, whose name Hulda did know because she played chess with him almost every day, but whose name she could not, in all this weird confusion tonight, bring to mind—he who had always seemed so courtly, so kindly and gentle—was now standing, not tottering as he sometimes did, but firm and stiff, and he was crying out that this was the wrath of God, the promised retribution, the just punishment! No one, including Hulda, who did not agree that her village, her island, deserved the vengeance of his god or of Thor, no one appeared to be listening. Yet her mind did struggle to find some meaning in the scourging that was being inflicted upon all of them.

She must have gone back to sleep: the hot drooling of her saliva wakened her, and, for a while, the large room had no semblance to any room. It was only space in which there was sound, a whooshing and booming outside, like the hollow breaking of heavy surf, and closer, voices and a weeping somewhere, and there were figures around her, shadows really, and then a man's voice urging her to stand up, to come. But no, he was not speaking to her. He was addressing the woman sitting beside her. And the woman—her face wrinkle-hatched, eyes sharp and rheumy, jaw stubbornly set—was refusing to move. And her voice, shockingly crisp and clear, youthful even, was saying that if the island was to perish, she would perish with it. Then the man, who was young and strong but very tender, was lifting the brittle-boned and doll-like body into his arms, and Hulda knew that it was time. She would go wherever they were taking her, but

she knew that it would be unavailing. The Turks had returned, hadn't they? And wherever one hid, in the cliffs, in
the crags, huddled along the breakers, the Turks would find
you. They would find you and they would slay you. There
was no use in hiding. The Turks had returned after all these
years.

She went outside, where she could feel the heat on her
face, but where, in spite of her many skirts and sweaters and
the long coat that made her feel cumbersome—she did not
want to catch a cold, of course—and in spite of the lamb's-
wool shawl wrapping her head, she still felt the January cold,
for it *was* January, wasn't it, she couldn't remember now just
what year, but past her eightieth, she did know that. She was
seated in a large bus—how long it had been since she had
ridden in one—an empty space beside her, and now she
became conscious of the pinkish luster falling over the
streets. Why, the streetlamps looked like huge roses swaying
above, roses, imagine, she had always loved flowers. The
vehicle turned, bouncing and swaying, and she recognized
the street: Kirkjuvegur, where she had walked so many
thousands of times, where someone she once knew had lived.
Could it have been—yes, she had it now: her husband's
mother who, when she heard of her son's death, had waited
for the sea to give back his body, which it had never done. All
that seemed so long ago, so many centuries ago, that it may
as well have been in another place altogether, in someone
else's life. More and more Hulda had begun to feel that all
her memories were tales and incidents in which she herself
had had no part. Behind her someone was sobbing and
another voice was speaking comfort. And up front the man
who had been raising such a hue about God's punishment
and vengeance, was now sunk deep in his seat and silent, his
bare head down, the thin white hair not covering his
baldness—oh why would anybody come out in weather like
this without a headcovering? She would offer him her shawl
now, but she knew that in the jouncing bus she would not be
able to walk the aisle; better to wait till they arrived at wherever they were being taken. In the seat in front of her a

woman named Freydis—yes, she knew Freydis, they had been neighbors once—was sitting stiffly upright. Poor Freydis: strangers visited her at night making threats and stealing her needles, her thread, the tiny razor she needed for the bristles on her chin. She lived in fear, with shadows, not spirits, and she accused those around her of theft, of wishing evil on her, of conspiring to injure her. Poor Freydis: she was past ninety years and often wished aloud for death. Was she wishing so now?

Then Hulda became aware of the intense glare on her left—flames, really. And she became conscious, too, of the surf-sound again, but it was not surf, although she knew her hearing was not now what it had once been. So that was where it was happening. Not a volcano at all—why had someone said eruption? It was more like a burning wall over there, only that. And beautiful, too. Nothing to fear regardless; why should one fear dying anyway? Dying was only a passing, a part of nature, no cause for alarm certainly or sadness or the hysteria that, in the bus, had now quieted to a low keening sound behind her.

They passed the bank on the left, her eyes could not make out the time on the clock, and then the cumbersome vehicle lumbered to a halt. The hospital, she knew where she was, the new hospital on Kirkjuvegur, which she had never seen before. So that was where they were taking her. But, about to summon the energy to rise, she caught sight of several people emerging from the hospital doors, being led down the steps by women wearing white caps, and then the other seats were filling. A man sat down beside her: old, very old, feeble and pale, his whiteness startling. His eyes seemed to see nothing. He did not speak. The motor, which had continued, now grew louder and the bus eased forward again. She recognized the man beside her, but, again, no name came to her mind. All she could remember, as the blaze on the left, unobstructed by buildings, became more visible, all she could remember about the man was that he had been one of the fishermen with whom her son had worked—would her son have looked this old if he had survived?—and that the man had raised a boy, not his son, his nephew, yes, his sister's son, who had often walked past the resthome windows holding hands with a red-haired girl, their faces sometimes lighted by laughter, sometimes sweetly grave, but always stirring in Hulda a nostalgia that was not quite a yearning for her own youth but more a sense of loss combined with excitement and hope, hope for them, for all the young people of the world whose lives stretched ahead with such bright and beckoning promise. She was about to inquire of the man whether his nephew had ever married the red-haired girl when she recalled something else: the boy had gone to sea, one of the few from Vestmannaeyjar. But the old man seemed unaware of her presence, and she had the impression then, as they passed the church, with the cemetery where so many of her friends and relatives now rested, that the man had no sense of where he was. Lars. His name came to her, the way names did once in a while, out of nowhere. She turned to him to speak, seeing his lined and sea-weathered face withdrawn turtlelike in his sweaters, but she did not. She was not sure why her tongue did not move, her lips did not open. But the way he sat, not so much as glancing at the conflagration out the windows, stirred a suspicion in her that became at once a certainty: the poor man was paralyzed, probably deaf, certainly mute. The poor, poor man. Even now, even here, the awful fact of his personal isolation stirred her compassion, and she wished that somehow she could reach out, could at least explain what was happening.

The familiar cone of Helgafell loomed on the left now, lighted by falling sparks and flashes, and Hulda realized where they were being taken. To the airfield. She twisted to look out the window and into the sky: swirling black smoke and twisting clouds, red and gold, ugly and beautiful at the same time. And ahead, up the hill, in the flickering incandescence, she could make out a beacon, blue and dim, the tower silhouetted and fragile, and then she saw a kind of airplane she had never seen before: it seemed to lift straight upwards, with blades spinning above it, and then it veered off and was lost in distance.

Her heart seemed to lift with it. She had never been off Heimaey in all her years, except on her husband's fishing vessel: and even on that—she had forgotten its name, no she had not, it was *Hulda,* it was *her* name—even on the *Hulda,* though, she had never crossed to any other town, only the off islands where no one lived. Not that she had desired to go anywhere else. And she had never flown in an airplane, not of any variety. Now she was about to go to a place she had never seen, and on a craft that would carry her magically above the world. And at her age, imagine.

She was still alive. Yes, after all the depressions and all the thoughts of walking into the sea because she was no longer of any worldly use to anyone—after all that, she was still alive.

And grateful to be so. They should all be grateful.

It was the year of the thirteen moons and the cursed Turks had returned in different guise, but Hulda Palmadottir would escape them, after all.

Nothing would ever make her warm again. Bundled like the others in sheepskin and wool, only her pale Celtic face exposed, its flesh so frigid that the sensation was of burning, Margret leaned back against the gunwale, closed her eyes and listened to the savage sea. Against such dark and angry power crashing and surging, the trawler seemed somehow fragile and palsied as it rocked and rose and fell and tilted. The spray and spumes had drenched all on deck, the glacial dampness penetrating the most closely knit of cloaks and sweaters. If it was true, as she had learned, that the Gulf Stream curved west here, none of its equatorial warmth rose to the air. Someone had whispered that the trip would take four hours, but she had lost all sense of time since that cockscomb of light with its wavering crest of fire had faded from view. Across the stretch of arctic water she could see several of the other vessels, only lights flickering and trembling on the rolling surface.

In order not to think of the cold that had invaded her marrow or to ponder what lay ahead now, Margret closed her eyes. She thought of the Viking ships of the distant past. In those single-masted vessels the planks were secured to the ribs only by lashings of roots, and in a turbulent sea such as this, the whole hull worked, the bottom rising as much as several inches, and the gunwales would twist half a foot out of line. Arni had told her that. The past, those ancient times meant too much to Arni still.

She could not think of Arni. Dared not. Why was he as he was? How had he become so? If only she had some hint or inkling as to the roots of his sick suspicions and jealousy. No, she would not think of Arni now. She opened her eyes.

The scene was as before. Some stood; some slept sitting up or curled on the deck planks. Many stared blankly ahead, as if wondering. Most had their eyes shut against the briny splash and mist she could taste salt-bitter on her lips. A few looked back—across the bleak and desolate water toward the island, now only a faint glow in the vastness. Heimaey—island of home. Tonight that word's meaning held a bitter irony. It came to her then that these people, her friends and neighbors, were refugees—yes, like all those through history that one reads about without comprehending—leaving behind homes, businesses, all possessions, even livelihood and sustenance itself. Yet there was quiet here, as there had been on the wharves. The faces bore a look of stoic self-possession—acceptance without resignation or defeat. This in no way surprised her. What had happened, no one had caused and no one could control; it had only to be endured. She wondered how many of those crowded around her found solace as well in the passive faith of generations past: he who is not death-fated will escape, survive. How many felt secure in the belief in an inevitability woven by the gods? How many here were blessed—or cursed—by such ancient blood-born certainty?

Not she. No. The coldness in her sharpened, as if a

pointed wind off the northern glacier had stabbed down across the mainland that lay ahead and had found its target in her heart.

Feeling the need, hunger, for human contact, she turned to the girl sitting beside her. The child, with the kitten under her coat, still looked back, as she had from the beginning. Both she and her brother, after the first shock, had been enthralled, mesmerized, as if the color and the elemental violence possessed some primordial magic that, like a magnet, beckoned both children, hypnotized them, held some mysterious promise for them that no adult could comprehend. Margret, bewildered, wondered whether the young ones were not, in some depth beyond words, reluctant to leave. She shuddered.

And remembered. Her fitful rest had been shattered by the sound of one of the children screaming. Alone in the strange bed, Margret had had to think a moment: she was at her sister's house, and so it was then one of Hana's two children shrieking—but why? Her sister's voice called her name. She heard the word *eruption* and heard activity in the other chambers, cupboard doors opening and closing, closet doors, her sister's husband answering questions in his quiet husky voice, Hana herself demanding clearly: *Why? Why should this happen to me?* And later, while Margret dressed: *It's not fair. What have I done to deserve it?* A siren's repeated wail seemed somehow more appalling and terrifying than the resonance, that distant detonation that she knew came from the depths of the earth itself, throbbing, then barking, then returning to that steady low and terrible concussion that seemed filled with wind. Margret had been astonished at her own calm. She knew she should not have been here and regretted her decision, made earlier out of a fear that had been more intense and personal than what she now felt. She telephoned. No voice answered. What if Arni had come home, had gone to sleep in a stupor, and what if he were lying there now unconscious? Hana had refused to leave. Ponderous and still, she sat and said, flabby chin lifted, *It's only Helgafell.* Her husband, a thin, small man with hair so blond that it was almost white, had pleaded at first and then, provoked and desperate, had threatened to take the children and go. *Hana, you must think of the children now.* Hana only shook her head. Panic? Or the same blind unreasonable self-absorption that had always run like a current of rancor and indignation in her mind? Margret had found the way to reach her: *I know what I must do. You see, Hana, I'm pregnant.* There followed a silence that seemed to shut out the sounds of the cars moving on the street and the doleful whine of the siren. Then, as if something invisible deep inside had collapsed, Hana had stood, her puffy face going awry, then firming, and she began to speak: they must hurry, what was everyone standing about for, bundle up, children, and be sure to cover your heads, it's cold on the water, where were her fur mittens, someone had removed her mittens from the closet, someone was always mishandling her things, her hands would freeze on the boat. It had been then that Margret had walked home, found the house empty, had written a note for Arni, in the unlikely event that he did come in, and had then rejoined the others on the dock, where she had found Hana scowling at her husband, who was kissing the children. Hana was stiff, eyes injured: how could he think of deserting them all now when she needed him most? No she would not kiss him, no, his place was with her, and if he did not love her enough, what of the children, he had always loved the children more than he loved her anyway. And her husband had then taken her thick arms in his hands and had shaken her once, hard, and in a level, thin tone that was new to him and said: *You are the one who must think of them now. You must act as you wish them to act.* And at this her sister had subsided into a state of lassitude that had carried her aboard, almost somnolent, and had held her so ever since.

Margret looked past the girl, sleeping now, and at her sister's thick and pudgy face. Her glazed eyes stared straight ahead—at nothing. Should she be stirred? Would that be kindness or cruelty? Her sister had always lived in a world foreign to Margret, and tonight she seemed to have withdrawn even farther into recesses that Margret could not comprehend. Tonight Hana, she knew, continued in her mind to interpret even this massive and horrendous cataclysm as only another attack on her, on her alone. And because of this turn of mind, or distortion of soul, was she then cursed, destined always to suffer more than others?

Margret turned away to the boy sitting in silence on her other side, stiffly alert, eyes bright but baffled. When his eyes met hers, he smiled—as if to reassure *her*.

And then a familiar yearning was rekindled. And it warmed her. She thought of the new life she carried within. That yearning would be fulfilled, regardless of tonight's holocaust and regardless of Arni.

Arni. Maybe now he would never know. Would he read her note? And then what? He often could not remember. Even when he shouted and struck her, he could often not recall it the next day. At first, she had imagined that he was feigning lapse of memory because of shame, remorse that he could not face. But no: it was the *brennivan*.

Where was he now?

But she realized, and admitted, that what she felt was not the hot and pressing concern that, God forgive, she knew she should feel. If Arni did not care enough for her to be with her now, then she no longer cared! But, feeling shamed herself now and growing colder still, she reproached herself: she was not her sister. This was no time, no place, for petty hurts and selfish vengeances—she knew, please God help, that she still cared. Still loved. And a picture in her mind returned to haunt her, a familiar image: Arni's long hard body stretched slackly out along a street curb, his handsome Viking face skyward, eyes closed, his mind blanked by alcohol—the ultimate degradation, his self debased, the fine pride humiliated beyond redemption. What if that inevitable state, which she had always feared, should occur tonight of all nights, and the molten lava should flow from the ghastly pyre into the streets of the town? In that state he would not hear, would not know, would never know . . .

She could not give her mind rein to conjure such a dark and unlikely spectacle. She was doing what she had to do.

She was carrying this new life within her to safety. Arni, for all his cruel and implausible but painful imaginings, would have to understand.

To fight the gnawing panic—the welter of thoughts and emotions that she could not bring into focus here, now—she looked around the deck and realized that the lurching had stopped and that the billows had become only choppy waves that hammered the hull in a staccato of sound. The vibrations underfoot seemed to increase and she could again smell the engine fumes. In the distance now she saw lights that did not totter and wobble on the heaving surface but remained fixed and yellow—not the other boats, but land itself.

No voice spoke, but there was a movement on the deck, as if all had seen or sensed it—no cries of relief or joy, but a quiet jostling and turning of many bodies. Then, after a moment, a single word was spoken, loudly, with excitement in it: "Look!" She glanced in the direction of the voice and saw the boy who had uttered the word and recognized him. His name was Josef and he lived on a farm out of the village. She had seen him many times over the years, always with the dog that now stood at his side and always with a huge and powerful-looking man, whose broad, flat face, like the boy's, held a gentleness. The man was not among those on deck; he might be with the other men in the hold below, but he had probably remained on the farm to salvage what he might— but how, how? On the boy's face was an expression of joy, almost ecstasy, and Margret wondered suddenly what would happen to such a person now, away from the safety of the farm and the kindly acceptance of the townspeople? Surrounding him were three girls—his sisters?—whose faces looked blank and somewhat sullen. An ageless woman stood somewhat apart: sharp-boned, face carved in stone, eyes that glittered even in the dimness, not with relief or with Josef's rapture, but from some inner fire or discontent or wrath that gave her whole countenance a cast of such ferocity that Margret was reminded of the women in the sagas. And of Arni's mother.

Was that where she was going now? To *her?* The huge

woman with the devastatingly sharp eyes, living alone in that large house across the street from the lake in the center of Reykjavik. No. There was no peace between them, ever, never had been, and it was the older woman's doing, not Margret's. The jutting chin and cunning eyes and knife-edged tongue: no. Whatever else, no.

Margret turned her mind away from the thought. Where was the girl she had seen boarding one of the other vessels?—her body huge with child, her young face beatific—had she reached Thorlakshofn, or had she given birth at sea? Would Margret ever know? She had then the overwhelming presentiment that, once the boats docked on the mainland, the town of Vestmannaeyjar, regardless of what happened to it physically, would cease to exist. Its people would move off and away in various directions and be lost to each other forever.

As for herself?

She did not know.

The port ahead seemed ablaze with lights, and these stretched not only along the quay, where other vessels were docked and unloading, but along the streets and out into the countryside, strings of lights, as from vehicles waiting. They were being met. She relaxed slightly. Iceland takes care of its own—how many times had she heard it in her childhood? Iceland takes care of its own.

But then, as a murmuring broke out when the engine slowed and its pumping growl subsided somewhat, she knew that she really had no choice. She must go to Arni's mother. The great hooked nose, the fixed chin that, like her eyes, never reflected a moment's wavering of mind. And as the picture invaded her mind, all Margret's resolutions—never to allow herself to be victimized by the woman's will, never to become herself embroiled in whatever mysterious and complex conflict smoldered between the woman and her son—all her fine, brave resolutions now dissolved in the cruel kettle of necessity. Her only relative on the mainland was a cousin of whom she was fond, but Malfrour had married a man from the States and was now living in the country: Margret could not think of intruding. Her other alternative was to take whatever refuge the authorities could offer—and what of the child in her under those uncertain and probably crowded circumstances? The boat was in the harbor now, edging toward a pier where strangers and vehicles waited. If Arni came, he would go to his mother's. He would expect to find her there. And Arni was the child's father. Whether he would ever believe that or not—oh God, what if he did not, would not, could not, oh God!

The boat hugged the pilings, which sighed against the hull. The cold went deeper still; she was shuddering, her flesh was quivering, fear and panic shook her mind. There was sound on all sides now, voices at last. Movement. And reluctance held her rigid and still against the rail.

On either side a child stood. She heard her sister's thin voice edged with complaint. She saw the boy Josef and his mother and sister move to disembark.

She was not one of them.

She was alone.

She had never been so alone.

Far below, but streaming in the opposite direction of the plane, lights moved like dancing dots on a depthless void. Fishing boats, the pilot had told him, evacuating the island toward which the plane was headed. A single word occurred to Owen Llewellyn: exodus. Beefy-faced, middle-aged, the American pilot chewed a cigar and muttered obscene reports into the radio, all the while hunched forward staring at the reddish smudge in the distance that kept disappearing behind heavy clouds. After sneering at Owen's rusty red beard, the pilot had agreed to take him and his camera gear aboard, but he was damned if he knew how Owen would get back because this crate would be packed to the gills with who-the-fuck-knew what when it returned—got me? Gotcha. And if anyone asked how Owen got there, he would say he swam, got me? Gotcha, Major.

Once aloft, the copilot, blurred eyes and hangover stench, had retreated to the passenger area and had gone noisily to sleep across two seats, leaving Owen to join the pilot in the cramped cockpit. The reappearing splotch in the distance had to be the eruption, but the pilot was more interested in the plane: a modified DC-3, twin-engined workhorse of World War II, never mind the goddamn vibrations, it rode angry but it got there, and headquarters still didn't know for sure how large a crate you could bring down on that two-bit airfield they got out there. Owen had flown DC-3s in Burma and South America and Canada, and he knew of the love affair between the plane and most pilots, but he found himself only half-listening, as usual.

If Todd Squier's son had followed his father's order and had not been playing his shortwave radio in his room after the others had retired, Owen would not have learned of the volcanic upheaval until morning, and by then he might have been on quite another plane on his way back to New York and Connecticut. At first he had felt a certain selfish relief—an excuse not to go home—but then, seeing the stricken faces of Todd and his wife Malfrour, he had remembered the evening and how they had reacted to his callous comment about Hekla. What a bastard. What a bastard to feel only professional curiosity when thousands of people were struggling to escape utter annihilation less than a hundred miles away. The loneliness and sense of isolation had returned, together with a familiar self-disgust. Owen often wondered whether that detached-observer part of his nature was a curse or a blessing. Could it be the part of him that made him such a damn fine photographer—and that served as his armor against intimacies and involvements that he really no longer desired? Malfrour had suggested that, after taking Owen to the Keflavik base, Todd drive to Thorlakshofn to meet her cousin and family if they docked there and to bring them to the house if they had not made other arrangements.

In the DC-3 now, Owen was gazing down: could it be

that the cousin—whom Todd had described as an Irish princess last night—was aboard one of those boats below?

While he and Todd were moving ghostily along on roads radiant with new snow, Todd had said that no one ever becomes acclimatized to the idea of volcanic eruptions, even though, in this century alone, there had been an average of one every five years in Iceland. Still, whenever one occurred, the shock was the same. How lucky Owen was, though, to be able to shoot one this early on. Yes, he was lucky, he supposed: he could probably sell the photographs worldwide, if there was enough interest in the incident; and later, who knows, he might be able to gather them into a book. But he was aware that there was something missing. Beyond the curiosity and anticipation that he had begun to feel, shouldn't there be more?

But what?

"There," the pilot said with a growl of satisfaction and alertness, as if an enemy craft had been sighted.

Feeling the sharp descent and veering, Owen was brought back to the moment. Ahead and below, pillars of light probed the darkness. Not red, not flamelike, but the color of salmon from this distance, at this height, with the clouds between. Not a single crater of spewing brilliance, as he had expected, but a row of thin towers, stalagmites rising from the floor of the cave of night. And Owen became conscious of a new sensation: a kindling of horror and awe as he stared at the sinister beauty, a black wonder drowning his mind—like his ancestors at once stricken by terror yet fascinated, mesmerized, by the sight of the first fire; like his contemporaries sick with horror, appalled yet marveling at films of the atomic mushroom cloud.

He counted the pillars—more than forty. And then he saw the black cone of Helgafell silhouetted against the wall of fire, which seemed to redden as the plane lowered and came closer, and then, below the blazing inferno, the town itself, cowering. Lights in windows, streetlamps flickering, streets deserted, slanted roofs all tinged with pink. Unreal. Incredible, like some brilliantly lighted scene from dream or nightmare. In the grip of feelings too complex and overpowering to sort out, Owen knew that he would never forget these moments. Never.

The pilot was barking into the radio, which crackled differently now, loudly, blurring the voices. But Owen became aware then of another sound as well, as of a barrage or bombardment. The plane was climbing again and passing over what appeared to be a harbor with cliffs half-encircling it, and Owen's sense of unreality, of incredulity, deepened into an abyss. What he saw below had to be an apparition, a fantasm of the mind, delirium. Across the water lights glittered, in patterns elongated and truncated and wildly confused, shimmering as if the water itself, tinted red, were struggling for breath, while across the sheen lay yellow and orange-colored glares, reflections from the docks and the buildings along them, through which boats with lighted masts were passing. These moved phantomlike, slowly, through the radiance, toward a space between rocks, and then into the sea beyond, circling beyond the cliffs to pass the island on the north. A floating city, lighted, tossing on a turbulent sea. His mind churned up a memory of photographs: the exodus from Dunkirk across the English Channel in World War II.

The plane passed over the jagged cliffs now—they seemed to be topped with a flat table—and it circled southward so that he was looking along the line of flame, which seemed to shoot up but also to explode in all directions, lemon-cored, violently crimson and reaching the edge of the water—no, plunging beneath the surface itself and continuing to burn with lesser but distorted brilliance even below the crust of water, as if the lava's fire were fighting to survive the cold, wet power of the sea itself. Meanwhile, the plane moved through the utter black spumes of smoke that surged skyward over the blaze.

Above the chaos, Owen knew that nothing—no photograph or report or story by anyone, anyone, not even Dante—nothing could have prepared his mind for the riot now taking place in it. He could see the vast uncaring sea stretching mile after mile, deep and cold, on all sides; he could see this small knob of earth standing alone above the water's surface, the village perched on it, and he knew then a sense of loneliness and isolation greater and deeper and more harrowing than any he had ever experienced before. Across those thousands of miles of sea, there were lands where calm people were asleep and at peace or going about their routine tasks all unknowing, mercifully blind, imagining themselves secure. What was happening in this tiny, remote and unknown area near the top rim of the planet— what meaning or portent could it have for them? His mind flooded with images of ruin, devastation, extinction. And his own feelings baffled him, tenderness streamed through him, and, for the first time in his thirty-one years, he felt such overpowering sympathy that, hovering now above the empty town while the pilot waited, muttering curses, for permission to land, he wondered whether he had lived there himself, had walked those streets, known these people, these strangers, yet *not* strangers in some deeper reality that made him now feel one of them. And as that knowledge came to him, as the plane's engine changed its harsh tune to a roar, while earth and sea reeled below in a kaleidoscopic blur of color and fire, a cry broke from somewhere in him and did not reach his throat—a silent bellow of pain and compassion and oneness with the people who should be *walking* those empty streets, *sleeping* in those empty houses.

The nose of the plane plunged between crags, its wingtips seeming to scrape the rock, its engine vibrating furiously, the dark, dead cone of the old volcano suddenly towering above the runway on his right, and life appeared before him in the brilliance: figures of people moving, shadows of other planes, trucks, ambulances with blue lights flashing ghostlike in the red, and all about a shower of falling sparks and burning cinders and coarse black ash, which he could hear pinging on the fuselage and wings as the pilot, himself uttering a grunt of satisfaction and triumph, brought the craft to a shuddering halt.

As Owen retrieved his knapsack and camera bags, he

knew that the expectancy he now was feeling had little to do with the photographs he hoped to take. Hell, it hadn't even occurred to him to take a shot from above. Excitement was running high in him, almost elation, a weird intoxication that would not allow him, for the first time that he could recall, to stand off and to observe himself like some cool and disengaged stranger. Astonished, he gave in to the sense of promise roiling in his blood, the expectation—no, the certainty—that something was about to happen to him at last, to him personally. And walking down the incline of the aisle, he realized that the mystery of that promise only intensified it.

Then, unaware that his flesh was stiff with cold, he stepped out and down and felt the heat envelop his body, while his mind, stunned, dazzled, struggled not to be overwhelmed. The stench of sulphur assaulted his nostrils. The low cannonade became deafening. Beneath his boots the runway, packed with black ash and already zigzagged by cracks, quavered, pulsating with the might that seemed to emanate as much from the night air, from the sky itself, as from the power ominously churning and raging below. Owen stood alone in chaos, sparks showering around him, and he was aghast. Yet solemnly exalted. No camera could ever capture this. And there were no words for this sinister splendor.

He wondered whether he had stepped over some mysterious line, or border, that lies invisibly between living and dying. Yet, even if he had moved into the deepest chasm of hell, he had never felt more quiveringly alive.

THREE

ON THE FRIGID AIRWAYS and through wires coated with ice, the news reached out across the mountains, glaciers, and high plateaus of the forty thousand square miles of the island that is Iceland. Lights came on in small villages, in the windows of farmhouses; prayers were uttered. And there was a sense of helplessness and kinship—and dread. A few were possessed by a feeling they could not bring into focus or put into words: a cold certainty that, however vast and mysterious the universe, we are huddled together on this planet for a short while only, each separate, yet each one with the other.

The news services—and therefore the most important papers around the world—reported that the volcano of Helgafell had erupted. But on Heimaey itself, because the fissure had cracked open a short distance above and to the east of Kirkjubaer, the farm at the easternmost edge of town which was the property of the church, the new volcano had been unofficially named Kirkjufell, or church volcano. Who first named it so? Did anyone? Or did the name simply occur to many during the night? Putting a word to such chaos was a first faltering step toward taming it or, at least, accepting it: the beginning of a way to face its unspeakable horror and then to deal with it. Somehow. But how?

Kirkjufell. The pastor of the only church on Heimaey, Reverend Petur Trygvasson, was not there, but in the small town of Isafjord, built on a spit of land on the northwest peninsula, itself almost an inaccessible island on the edge of

the Arctic Circle, where the sun shines only two months of
every year. When the telephone sounded, he hoped it would
not waken his wife in the next chamber with her father, who
was dying, so he picked it up as quickly as possible. It was his
own father, bishop in Akureyri, who had received a message
from the bishop in Reykjavik. He had, he said, bad news.
And while Petur listened, too numb for shock, he thought of
his friend Baldvin Einarsson who had repeatedly claimed
that Helgafell would have its revenge, and he thought, too,
of the legend about the year that the village would expand to
the south beyond a certain stone, the year when the priest
would be the son of a bishop, the year of the thirteen
moons—all nonsense, all mischievous and pagan foolishness,
more of the barbarism which forever surrounded him. He
thanked his father in a whisper and replaced the telephone.

He felt a bitter guilt stabbing: what was he doing here
when he belonged there? He stood. His duty was to reach
them, his people—how could they survive unless they accepted the will of God? And if they were to perish, it must be
with the faith that gives joy and affirmation to that inevitable
transition from a world known into a brighter, kinder world
unknown. But, urgency heating his blood in the chill room,
he did not move. Could not. He could leave the peninsula
only by air at this time of year. He pictured the narrow
one-way airstrip under the cliff wall: depending on the wind,
a plane could take off one way or not at all. He moved to the
window and looked out through the ice-encrusted pane: the
night was black. Was he frightened then? For himself?

The picture that he dreaded most returned to his mind:
himself, tall and thin and sallow, treading wraithlike through
the little streets of the village to which he had been assigned,
timid in the midst of his robust parishioners, often greeting
them by the wrong names, his lean, studious face out of
place, foreign, forever foreign to them all. He was trapped
now in a familiar indecision.

But he was needed. He could not stay now. How could
he dare, how could he *presume* to give in to his paltry personal
fear when they . . .

He turned and sank to his knees. He prayed. He did not

pray for courage (it could never be his) or for guidance (he knew what he should do), nor did he pray for himself. Vestmannaeyjar, as the Lord knew, was not Sodom or Gomorrah. He was not questioning God's will, but he knew that his people did not deserve chastisement or retribution. He knew, too, that what was happening down there was not, as his friend Doctor Pall would contend, accident, sheer happenstance—how could a man live believing that? Nor was that monstrous apocalypse fate—he rejected Baldvin's ideas as well: heathenism, superstition, heresy. No, he accepted it, because he knew that God had a plan beyond the reaches of his poor mortal mind and soul. But, please, God, please— mercy, mercy too . . .

Then he stood again, renewed, his mind decided. And grateful. The fear remained, but he would accept it as one of his own many weaknesses and, in so doing, would vanquish it in his own way.

From time to time the town shuddered, as if to shake off some unwelcome visitation. But the pain in his arm was gone.

There were lights burning behind a few of the small windows of the fish factories and freezing plants. Squatting atop a bollard on a pier, Olaf was staring across the tinted water of the harbor. Most of the larger vessels had gone. A coastal-protection cutter was entering, its forward beam sweeping the surface.

He was happy. Even the agony in his head was gone. Why had that boy tried to split open his skull with an oar? Poor boy must have been insane with fear. It didn't matter now. Nothing mattered really.

Euphoria possessed him.

Doctor Pall had given him the pills. He had taken most of them, and he knew that in a few hours he might wish he hadn't. But now he was drowsy and he was conscious of things as from a vast distance. He had also been drinking. He had simply walked into a house, which was lighted and empty, and had found a bottle on the broadshelf. Almost full, too. He had been warned, of course, not to mix the two, medicine and alcohol. But what did doctors know? If he could feel like this, what did anything matter?

Juliana. Yes, she mattered. And the child, his child.

Some time ago—he had no idea about time and that was part of the pleasure of it—the wind had changed, shifting suddenly to south-southeast, he knew his winds, and for a while, but not for long, ash had blown over the town. And hot chunks, not quite aflame, had fallen. But now the wind had veered again, and the tephra was once more being carried out to sea. But since then there had been the sound of sirens again. And the clanging of fire bells. Or had there? He may have imagined that.

He could hear the birds, although it was not yet light enough to see them. The gulls. And others. He knew about birds, too. At first, their screeching silenced by the explosion and the weird light, they had retreated inland or to the distant cliffs on other islands. But growing accustomed to the furious flames and the rumbling frenzy, which Olaf now ignored, they had returned to hover over the vacant harbor, searching for food. When the sky over Heimaklettur and the other bluffs grew lighter, he would cut up and throw them the fish they yearned for.

Olaf knew what it was to long for something, to hunger and need, and not be able to find.

Behind him, the sound of sirens whined, then faded. He thought of the fire apparatus charging along the street. It amused him. Who was there on the street to get into the path of the fire truck?

The house was appallingly empty. As he had known it would be, of course—hadn't he himself taken his four sons and his wife to the harbor? Nevertheless, Jonas Vigfusson stood staring at the familiarity of it, and his aloneness—his isolation from all that rooted him to life—was more horrendous even than the other threat flaring and booming in the distance. He decided that he could not spend whatever few hours he could allow himself for rest in this deserted and abandoned shell which contained at every glance some reminder or symbol of the years that, being happy ones, he had taken for granted here.

He went out and walked back toward the communications center. One house had gone in flames, ignited by a flaring cinder during the time, earlier, that the wind had shifted temporarily. The first—would it be the last?

He saw no one on the streets and recalled the crowding only a few hours ago. How few hours, yet an eternity. By now, he surmised, most of the vessels had probably reached Thorlakshofn. And here there were—how many?—perhaps a hundred men now. But he knew others would return: those who had chosen to accompany their families to the mainland, but who knew they would be needed here.

Needed for what? What the hell could a man, or any number of men, do against that vomiting gash that, he knew, had extended itself southward to reach the sea: it was not a full two thousand meters in length, if he was any judge. As he walked, an unfamiliar hopelessness moved in his blood, coldly. The island was doomed. He knew, because he had seen the devastation wreaked by volcanoes: miles of flourishing green fields turned into desolate wastelands. The heavier pumice was being carried out to sea again, but let that wind shift to its normal pattern, then the hot ash and cinders would be driven over the roofs and would fall on them and into the streets to burn or smother or crush to rubble. Even more tephra and finely pulverized lava was falling as he moved east. Molten lava was gurgling heavy and red over the lips of the three-meter-wide mouth of the open wound— would it, turning black but cooling only on the surface, reach the town?

And who could say for how long the eruption would go on? When Jonas was a small child, he had watched Hekla on the mainland exploding for more than a year, lighting the sky so that at night it could be seen here on Heimaey. And ten years ago Surtsey, much closer, had continued for three. Three *years*—there would be nothing left here, nothing.

He turned into the doors of the post office and crossed the high, empty room. He could hear the teletypes chattering and the radio crackling in the rear room. But he could not face it. Not now. After twelve hours duty and then no rest in the six or seven hours since he had discovered the fountains, he could curl up on the hard floor and pass out for hours. When the post office opened, some one would waken him. But the post office would not open. Nothing would open. All that was in the past. Forever in the past?

Yes, forever.

He went along the passage and into the radio room and received the message that the town council, of which he was a member, was being called into emergency session.

The young officer who had first received the news of the eruption came into the police station and saw the chief sitting behind his desk in his small office, the door open. The chief looked older somehow but in his eyes, which appeared tired and slightly reddened, there was an odd expression of amusement.

"Any looting?" he asked, his tone ironic.

"Looting?" The young officer was puzzled.

"The mayor just telephoned to call a meeting of the town council. He thinks there'll be ransacking and general filching. A man who's lived here all his life. So you tell the others to be on the lookout for pickpockets, understand?" Then he put his head back, his teeth glimmered, and he roared with laughter.

Laughter, now, at a time like this. "Would you like coffee, sir?"

"I'd like sleep. But to hell with it, I'll take coffee."

While the young officer prepared it, he realized that tonight, in the small concrete building that was shuddering slightly, he felt a kinship with his chief that he had never known before. So he told him about the pony. One of the wide-bodied and heavy-fleshed but very small Icelandic ponies, sturdy tough little creatures all, had run into a stream of red black lava, as if he really wanted to get to the fire. Then, confused and in terror, flesh flinching, he wheeled in circles, half-blind, whinnying, hair singed off his hide. The young officer, who wore a gun for the first time on duty tonight, had taken pity and shot the crazed animal. Even now he was suffering for it, though: he couldn't get the damn picture out of his mind.

His tone reflecting the possibility that he might have sensed this, the chief asked: "Do you know who he belonged to?"

"I think a farmer named Gunnar Axelson rode him into town. He was looking for his son."

"I know the man. And the boy. Well, it's the first casualty, let's hope it's the last."

He said it in such a way that the young officer knew the possibility was so slight that the chief hoped to strengthen it by putting it into words.

When he returned to the chief's office with the coffee, the man's heavy head, showing a circle of baldness at the crown, was resting atop the desk. He slept.

With all this going on—amazing. The officer decided to let the older man sleep for fifteen minutes. The station was not far from Town Hall and it would take the others longer to get to the meeting.

With the thought that he might be needed during what was left of the night, Doctor Pall had decided to stay at the hospital, even though this placed him closer to the turbulence. But once he had rolled a bed into the reception room adjoining his office, he began to wonder whether he, or any of the men left on the island, would ever learn to sleep in this tumult combined with the second-to-second threat of that wall of flame out there. Were it not for the need to stay alert, he might have swallowed one of the pills that he would have prescribed for anyone else. Such as that young seaman with the beard, poor fellow: the surgeon in Europe, whoever and wherever, had done a fine job on that arm, but there would always be the pain. What he had given him, though, would kill it and would also serve as a barbiturate. Lucky man.

Well, all of the ill and aged had been evacuated, thanks to Icelandic Airlines and the planes and 'copters from the U.S. Naval Air Station, Keflavik. This, he told himself with satisfaction, had been accomplished in orderly fashion. But what of that young wife who had insisted on going by boat because she was afraid of flying? He wouldn't be surprised to learn the headstrong young fool had had her baby on board one of those lurching, smelly things, probably at the hands of some midwife with fish scales under her nails!

Anyway, there had been only minor injuries, mostly burns. Now *there* was a miracle to report to his friend, holy Petur, who was off north somewhere with his wife, tending her ailing father. What would this prove to Petur? That his God was merciful? Hearing the spasmodic belches and steady whoosh and fuming, Doctor Pall wondered whether it wouldn't be as fair to conclude that such an all-powerful God was capriciously cruel, if not malicious.

If Odette were here, he would sleep. No—for he had never slept, actually slept, with Odette. And never would.

Then he thought, as always, of his wife and wished that he had the faith, Christian or pagan, whatever, that would promise his being with her again after his death. Which might be sooner now than he had ever imagined. And then he thought again of that dream he had had: could it be that this night was what she had been trying to warn him of? Were there really more things under the sun than were dreamed of in your philosophy, Horatio?

He had to learn to sleep. And he would learn. For no one—probably including Petur's God—knew what really lay ahead. Even sleeping, one could be annihilated by falling walls or fire or by the noxious gases which, sooner or later, would be swirling unseen, in the atmosphere. He would have to inquire about these: by first light the town would be swarming with scientific experts.

He was no closer to sleep than ever when the telephone sounded. He reached. He listened. "I'll be there," he said.

He walked in a thin, dark dust falling like dry rain. Out of habit he glanced up at the clock protruding from the corner of the two-story gray bank building: it had stopped at 1:55.

Going up the narrow stairway, he felt a shuddering through the whole structure, and in the meeting room the windows chattered in their frames, steadily except when one of the sporadic blasts threatened to crack and shatter them. To be heard above the din, voices had to be raised, and the meeting had already taken on the aspect of a shoutfest. The mayor, a balding, florid man with normally friendly eyes, did not look so friendly now as he stated with some heat that, not only did the chief of police not have the authority to issue an order for everyone to evacuate, but the issuance of such an order suggested total surrender—there was a matter of pride here, too, wasn't there? To which the chief, a bulky, gnarled-looking but usually gentle man, uttered an obscenity under his breath and reminded the mayor, *again*, that he had *not* given an order but had told his men only to suggest the obvious! Most citizens hadn't needed even the suggestion, but there were always boneheads and sentimentalists and reckless fools—such as the two young couples who had been soaking up brandy and had had to be forced aboard one of the vessels, and he for one hoped they were having a rocky voyage. Taking a chair, Doctor Pall recalled that the mayor and the chief, when young men, had both fancied the same girl—who had left the island to marry an American flier stationed at Keflavik during World War II.

Nodding around the table, Pall decided that they were a sorry-looking lot—except for the two middle-aged strangers assigned by the minister of defense, who reported, in a lull, that offers of aid were coming in from around the world already and that the government would provide whatever funds might be needed here: and the black-bearded young volcanologist from the University of Reykjavik, who informed them that although the eruption had calmed slightly and there were fewer fountains now, they were quite active still. That, the mayor said, was quite obvious to the untrained naked eye—why had there been no warnings? There had been, actually: two hundred mild shocks recorded on Sunday, very mild and in a large area, exact locations undeterminable; and ten more tremors on Monday, but the sharpest only 3.1 on the Richter scale, scarcely anything to alarm anyone in these parts. Then he tugged at his beard and sighed in a youthful voice: "For all our delicate instruments, mine is far from an exact science, gentlemen." He shrugged. "With volcanoes as with people . . ."

Pall understood. Men's tempers, flaring here in anxiety, might seem puny and insignificant in contrast to the wild titanic turbulence and the impending holocaust outside, but these small vanities, buried resentments of past and present, all these flimsy inconsistencies of man's nature, all were part of man—and so, being a part, worth saving if man was. There was no denying the acute torment of concern and the burning urgency that each brought with him to the table— otherwise, why stay when safety lay elsewhere?

Jonas Vigfusson entered. The young man seemed on the thin verge of collapse, and Pall wondered how long it had been since he had slept. If he had worked twelve hours before he discovered the eruption and had been aware since . . .

Jonas did not sit. He had, he said, smiling wanly, an announcement. He had just learned by radio from the vessel *Veida* that Vestmannaeyjar had a new citizen; a child had been born at sea; mother and infant both healthy, and the mother had already chosen a name: Oceana. A few male grins, pleased but abashed, and a tapping of palms on the table—the tension relieved for a moment. Pall himself was also relieved but annoyed: why, when the headstrong little idiot could have had all the advantages of a hospital delivery room and competent physicians if she had gone by plane? More human nature.

Jonas took a chair and answered questions: yes, the telephone was still functioning but no way of knowing for how long; the television transmitter had been uprooted, but the radio tower was still in operation. Pall did not like what he saw in Jonas' red-streaked eyes and heavy, bent shoulders or in the glum, grim faces all round.

The fire chief was not present, the mayor reported, because volcanic bombs had fallen into the church-farm complex, and at least three houses were burning. Earlier, as most of them knew, one house closer to the town center had been ignited by a fiery cinder and had been gutted in spite of all efforts to save it. That had occurred when the wind had shifted east for about ten minutes.

Jonas shook his head. "The wind is east again," he said. "Look at the windows."

All turned. Heavy black snow appeared to be falling now, thick and almost opaque.

Pall decided to turn their attention. He lifted his voice: "The first-aid station will be in the hospital. I've already treated four cases of second-degree burns—on the soles of the feet of damn fools. I'll have a hell of a lot more if grown men don't learn they can't walk on fire." A smile here, a snicker there. "My two confreres have deserted, and I think they're smarter than we are. So if anyone gets a bellyache or can't sleep in all this silence you're listening to, you'll have to come to me whether you like it or not."

"God help us all," the chief of police said, grinning himself now.

Pall stood and lumbered to the windows, wondering why he wasn't as tired as he had been earlier, even before anything had happened. Behind him he heard their voices—ash and fire falling on the runways of the airstrip, with luck this could all be over by first light, no predicting—and he gazed out through the curtain of black onto the town, tinted brightly, streetlamps still burning feeble and dim, no shadows or figures moving on the streets, which were already covered by dark ash. He was struck by the bizarre beauty of the scene, at once sinister and terrible and yet strangely enchanted and, yes, lovely in an eerie way. The glittering eye of evil—repellent yet fascinating.

He was not really listening to their voices—should they allow volunteers to come? How to house them, feed them? Did they have the moral right to allow more lives to be risked?—and he could not throw off the impression that he was aboard a rudderless ship. These men—well intentioned, bone-weary, minds blurred by lack of sleep and inflamed by apprehension and fear, all willing to defy damnation and death itself—these men were doggedly determined to keep afloat the damaged vessel in a storm for which none of them, even the scientist, was really prepared or trained. Were they as shocked and overwhelmed as they appeared? And if so . . .

He heard Frosti Runaldsson's voice: "If that damn split goes any further southward, the airfield will be of no use. And if it extends much farther to the north, the lava will seal off the harbor entrance." He did not speak as loudly as the others, but they heard every word distinctly. The owner of one of the largest processing plants, Frosti was a tall, lean old man, gray of hair, of brow, of eye, wearing as usual a gray business suit and tie; even his rough, wrinkled skin had an ashen pallor. "That," he said, "will be the end of everything—whole damn town, the business, all of it, and then no one will be able to get off without swimming. Once a vessel can't be launched, boat or plane, whoever's here is here to stay. Then it's burn here or freeze in the sea. Ice and fire, it's our life. It's always been."

Pall wished the man had not spoken. Why had he done so? To warn the others in time—or because he himself was scarcely surviving, eruption or no? He stubbornly refused surgery to remove the kidney with the carcinoma that was killing him. Obstinate old man—facing extinction himself, was his mind filled with some perverse desire to see every-, thing go with him? Pall had observed worse, but for a moment or two he hated the man in spite of all the effort he had spent to save him.

It was the police chief who spoke, scowling again: "Frosti's right. And if Kirkjufell out there blows any higher, we'll all be marooned here with no vessels in the harbor to take us off."

The mayor glowered down the table. "If that's a reference to my order to stop all action in the harbor once the town was clear . . ."

"It is."

"I took that upon myself because someone had to."

"Had to? Why?"

"The lava is flowing to the harbor's mouth."

The chief slammed a palm onto the table. "We can't have orders issued unilaterally and in panic!"

"Panic?"

"What you did makes no sense, no sense whatsoever!"

"But . . . there are vessels waiting out there."

"With orders, from you, to stay out there. What about the frozen fish in the plants? Millions of kronur worth—how much, Frosti?"

"Fifteen million at least."

"And the machinery—that will have to be taken off!"

The mayor said, somewhat lamely, "It's only a temporary measure."

"And the household goods—furniture, appliances? How do we get all that off? And the stock from the shops."

"If this council votes to countermand my . . ."

The chief was standing, shouting: "What about currency from the bank down below, books in the library, municipal documents . . ."

The mayor stood, too, and bellowed: "Put it to a vote!"

"We can't sit up here and worry about the lava closing the harbor and then close the goddamned harbor ourselves!"

"I did what I considered . . ."

"There are fifteen hundred cars in Vestmannaeyjar!"

"We can't do everything at once!" His voice rose into frantic defiance. "I have also taken it upon myself to ask that the sheep be flown out and the cattle slaughtered. Well, we'll need food, won't we? Just as we'll need someone to prepare it. And to set up a mess hall."

"What we need is organization. I move we vote now to re-open the harbor to shipping before the lava closes it and maroons the lot of us and everything we own."

Both men were breathing hard, the chief's face swollen and red, the mayor's pale and trembling. And Pall recalled a girl, whose name he had forgotten, who had turned her pretty back on two suitors here and had married a Yank pilot thirty years ago. Pall's cynical recognition of the vagaries and mysteries of the human psyche allowed him an inward smile: the smoldering hatred unloosed now by a freak of nature, and after all those years.

In the pause—no one wished to vote against either man—a single, shattering concussion punctuated the low grumbling, and a pane of glass in one of the windows stellated. All heads turned.

Then the mayor slumped leadenly into his chair. His voice was almost a whisper: "I gave what orders I thought had to be given." He waved a soft thick hand. "I could have been wrong." Then he rapped the table sharply with his knuckles. "Is it the consensus to re-open the harbor to all ships?"

Silence again. Except for the somber rumbling outside.

The mayor rapped again. "So be it."

The chief resumed his seat. He said nothing.

Jonas stood then—somewhat unsteadily, Pall thought—and the exhaustion was in his tone: "The fire chief at Keflavik Airport is a friend of mine. They have more powerful equipment than we have, in particular a water cannon or nozzle, that could be useful if the fires continue. I'd like to ask him to bring it over."

It was not quite a question. The mayor nodded agreement.

Then Jonas said in his hoarse voice: "And since I have the floor, I have a vital problem to lay before the council. Can't we find some way to keep the water in the toilet bowls from swooshing around the way it does?" He looked very solemn indeed. "My balls hang low and they get wet every time."

Laughter then. Relief again. And a scraping of chair legs.

Frosti held up a withered hand and all action stopped. The old man looked even older now, more gray, more haggard—and, Pall knew, undoubtedly in pain despite the analgesics which he might or might not be taking as prescribed. "One thing more, gentlemen. If the electric current and the water lines from the mainland are not severed, I'll have my plant in operation within two days. *If,*" he added, "we all live that long."

Pall was again astonished: human nature indeed! Ashamed of his earlier momentary hatred when he had made his sour conjecture of the old man's motives, Pall returned to the table, saying: "Next meeting I'll be armed with tranquilizers. Be sure to remind me before we come to disorder."

He went to the door and down the stairs and out into the dust-filled street, already blackened beyond recognition. He turned on aching legs toward the empty hospital. He was struggling against a feeling that he could not quite define—a sense of chaos. As if the ferment in the atmosphere, the derangement of nature on all sides, had infected the minds of the men now charged with navigating a floundering ship. Yes, chaos.

But even as the helplessness took over, he was amazed to realize that his own weariness had dissipated. He would not sleep, he knew—by some miracle he felt no need of it now. He may as well set up the first-aid station so that it would be ready by first light when, undoubtedly, some grown man would do something childish and need help.

Karl Sveinsson heard the roar of aircraft motors all day long so his home was situated in the suburb of Keflavik most distant from the international airport. When he came there in the evening, he often said, what he wanted most was quiet. And his wife's good and solid food. And his wife. But was that enough? Could that ever be enough for a man like Karl Sveinsson?

Lilja wondered about this, but not often. Now, as the night refused to become morning she lay in bed, awake, and the question haunted her mind. And she felt alone. Their three daughters were safe and asleep in their rooms, but Karl was not here.

When the telephone had sounded, hours ago, she had known at once that the message would be a summons. Karl, a thorough lover and heavy undreaming sleeper, had not wakened. After she had whispered into the telephone, she had hesitated to do what she knew had to be done but looked musingly at him in the dimness, tempted to wait a bit. Tempted, too, to reach out, somehow to add to and not to disturb that calm that, in sleep, seemed to surround the vigorous muscular body and lusty mind. Stretched long and hard, he reminded her, again, of a well-built ship, becalmed now but stalwart, capable of beating any violent sea or wind. With the voice on the telephone echoing in her mind, she had felt fear touch her—apprehension. She placed a hand lightly on his sinewy face, ran it tenderly over his great beak of a nose, and he stirred to consciousness. With reluctance she said: *They want you. At the airport. There's been an eruption on one of the islands.* Sitting up, grumbling in a voice that betrayed his excitement and stirred her anxiety, he reassured her at once: *What do they want me to do? You can't put out a volcano with a fire hose.* And then, shamed at her own selfish uneasiness, she said: *Those people. Those poor people.* Towering sturdily above

her, dressing, Karl said: *Means they'll be coming in from all over.*
Scientists, picture takers, damn sightseers. Boys in the tower'll go
nuts trying to keep a safe traffic pattern, and I'll be there if they
don't. Go nuts: he often used American phrases because of
his day-to-day contact with U.S. personnel—she smiled. And
then he had gone, without the coffee she offered, saying *Kiss*
me, girl, and put yourself into it. What she had put into it was a
kind of desperation that puzzled her. And afterwards she
could only lie and sadly wonder again whether what she
offered here—flowers and soft passion and the comfort of
everyday friendly things—could ever be enough for a man
the like of her husband, much as he appreciated them, and
her.

Since there was more than the normal activity tonight,
she could hear the sound of engines roaring and whining in
the skies above. She threw back the *dyna* and stepped out of
the bed, shrugging into the robe of many colors that Karl
had himself bought for her. She went into the kitchen and
turned on the fire under the coffee, still bewildered by her
mood.

She was not surprised when she heard the telephone
jangling lightly again—not surprised, but filled with a stupid
premonition that held her still a long moment before she
returned to the bed chamber: he was going to go there himself. She knew.

Clutching the telephone, she listened to him explaining:
". . . friend of mine from navigational school . . . fires over
there . . . need some equipment I have . . . thought I'd
take it there myself . . ."

She could picture him in his spare but spacious office,
his fine mouth and strong teeth clenched on the stem of one
of his many pipes as he spoke. She could imagine the glitter
of excitement and anticipation in his blue, blue eyes.

"When . . . when will you come back?" she heard herself ask—knowing that already he was moving away from
her.

"Tonight at the latest," his voice assured her—but she
knew, she knew. "Telephone line went out while I was talking with them, so probably a submarine eruption has severed

the trunk line. I won't telephone, but give you-know-who each a kiss for me. And, Lilja, Lilja, listen—don't fret, hear? There's nothing to worry about."

Nothing.

"I won't fret if you'll take care. *You* hear!"

"I hear, girl."

And then he was gone.

A volcano in eruption—don't fret.

She went to the coffee, poured it. And sat, feeling the steam over her face. It did not warm her.

But her fear was not for his safety; he was a cautious man, and wise, and unafraid to be afraid, if not being so threatened the safety that had long ago become his abiding obsession on the job.

No. Her fear was deeper and more personal. She knew his restlessness, sensed it along with his tenderness. She had always known that, although she had him snared and safe, cherished by her and by the three girls, his nature was at war within itself—and he was himself only dimly aware of the buried battle. She acknowledged clearly now, sipping the coffee which she did not taste, the mysterious and furious thing within him that would never be tamed and gentled by her gentleness, and his own—or by their love. In some way still darkly obscure but nevertheless real and disturbing, she also understood that if it were not for this perverse contradiction in the man, he would not be the man she knew him to be.

And if it were not for this, she would not be the woman that she had somehow become because of him.

The thought calmed her.

Slowly, slowly, consciousness returned. He lay stretched out full-length along a curb on a strange and deserted street. And he was covered with dust, or dirt. No—he was all but buried now in black, gritty ash. He did not move at first. The cobblestones under his cheek were rounded and very hard—and slightly warm. And what was that sound? He tried to lift his head. Failed. What was he doing here? How had Arni Loftsson come to this? Someone had warned him—who? Warned him that someday . . .

His mouth was parched. His stomach twisted cruelly. And his head was a roaring muddle more terrible than the cannonade with its deafening reports cracking the night open. He remembered then. But only that Helgafell had exploded. Only that.

Over a black sea of ash he saw a bottle glittering in the strange light. He could even see the liquid inside it: was it amber, was it maroon? Then he recalled. Going into that house—no, several houses, because all doors stood ajar— going in and finally finding the bottle, unopened, and whiskey at that, American bourbon, harsh and burning. He remembered walking, too. His whole body ached from the endless walking. He had been striding, bold and strong, toward the cataclysm in the distance. It held no terror for him. Hadn't Tyr, god of war, lost a hand which he had placed as a pledge in the jaws of the wolf Fenrir? A man, or a god, has always to contend with enemies, giants and monsters, until the great Armageddon ends with death by fire! He had decided to walk to the very mouth of the furious abyss. Let the air throb. Let the pavement quiver and heave and crack. A true Norseman has only contempt for his own death. But there had not been one mouthful but many, and it had been too hot, the whiskey moving in him by then, too hot, and then he had stumbled, he remembered stumbling, falling, trying to stand, wobbling sideways and falling again, finally deciding it was not worth the effort, what he needed was sleep, and, sinking to the stones, he had been conscious of what was happening, the ultimate degradation which he had always feared, of which he had been warned, but which he seemed helpless to prevent.

Margret. She had warned him, in fury, eyes bright, lovely, Margret. Tenderness weakened him now with the thought, the memory within a memory when he could not get his mind clear, then or now, all a blur, and she had not signed her note *With love.* What note? When? He had to get it clear, the night clear, everything.

He rolled in the heavy softness, the dust on his face, in his nostrils, stinging his eyes, and he attempted to stand, could not, so sat up instead. Each fountain in the line was distinct now. Before, there had been a rampart of fire behind the rooftops, and the rooftops were all black now under the parabolic streaks of sheer gold. Then he became conscious of another sound, closer, and he saw something, streaming sparks, fall thudding to the pavement of the sidewalk only three meters from his head. What? It glowed red, flickering, and even as he stared, it seemed to lose its heat, to blacken. He managed to stand then and to step to it, legs threatening to cave. He stood above it: a misshapen rock the size of a soccer ball. Its heat rose against his face. A lava bomb—hadn't he taught his classes about them many times? Most such lumps fell back into the crater or fissure, but some shot higher, cooling and hardening and then dropped as far away as a hundred or more meters. Through cracks in the dark blue lava he could see the still-seething molten core quivering orange.

He could not stay here. Then where, where?

If he could only force his mind to remember.

He picked up the bottle. He drained it. Then, turning his back on the spewing roaring radiance, he began to walk again. As he had walked all night, aimlessly. Searching. Yes—he had been searching. First, he had spoken to his mother on the telephone. Or rather—as usual—she had spoken to him, telling him what was happening, and he had listened and then . . . then he had gone in to waken Margret, he had it now, he had it clear, Margret had not been in the bed. And he had gone sick with hate and knowing and had found the *brennivan* where he'd hidden it, and afterwards he had gone out into the streets where a tide of people was moving toward the harbor. He remembered the streets quivering under his feet, his rambling at first, she could be anywhere, with anyone, any male anywhere, the gall in his throat and blood, the air hot and oppressive and the constant drumfire and cannon blasts, the fantastic and grotesque and unreal on all sides, going to the hotel, how many times, being told, how many times, that no rooms were occupied, knowing they could lie, everyone lies, staggering, lurching to the bank corner, the clock reading 1:55 each time, impossible, impossible, time doesn't stand still, and then, spent and sagging by the window of the bookshop across Heidarvegur from the aquarium, she might have gone there, she spoke of it often enough, but when he crossed through the steady, moving tide, the door was locked. And then he had seen the boy and sheep dog huddled together on the steps, and he had been tempted to offer the boy help, but the boy, he was one of the different ones, the boy had turned back his head and looked up, and he saw on the young face a look of such holiness and bliss that he felt as if the boy might offer help to *him,* and he stumbled away, wondering, feeling strangely assaulted, and then he turned and saw a heavy giant of a man standing above the boy and dog, the boy rising and taking the man's huge hand, and then his mind had returned to Margret, to how she had spoken often of the aquarium, as if it held some splendor and enchantment that he had never understood, had he tried, had he ever tried to . . .

Margret. Hate flooded him hotly. Or was it love?

He knew where she would go. To her sister's house.

No. Not now. That was earlier—hours ago. Wondering then whether she might be on one of the boats, the ones he had watched drawing away, phantomlike, toward the narrow mouth of the harbor's snug enclosure. Was she safe then? Was she safe now? Where, where?

The torment returned. And the rage. He could feel it now, again, but as from a distance, recalling. The night past and the night present—were they one? Again he was walking. Only now his eyes were stinging, and there was dust thick on his flesh and under his clothes, grit between his teeth. Where was he going, though? Earlier, in that other time that seemed as if it were now, he had gone to Hana's house. Which was empty. He had known as soon as he stepped through the door. And the small kittens crying, he remembered, and the larger cat slinking soft against his calves and no *brennivan* anywhere. Had he ransacked the house? Pillaging, like his Viking ancestors—smashing crockery, shattering glass, ripping off cupboard doors, and hurling them at the wall. What sort of home would not have *brennivan?* And then all those blocks of streets and corners—he seemed to recall leaning against the wall of the tight-shut building and shouting curses. And then, weakly, frantic and yearning, seeing the wall of a building across the street cracking in a wild pattern, the concrete falling in chunks from the facade, crumbling . . .

Had he gone home then? He could not remember. He turned now into one of the empty houses. He moved through its shadows, light glowing and flashing outside. Certain now, certain: Margret had gone, hours ago, on one of the fish boats. By now she was asleep at his mother's house. In Reykjavik. Safe. He located the telephone. He lifted it to his ear. He dialed.

Nothing.

How could it be? He pressed it hard against his ear. Silence.

It could not be!

He would, then, find another. His ears, he decided, were adjusting to the hollow, hacking sound, the occasional explosions. The air was filled with falling blackness. Another telephone, one that was still functioning . . .

Why hadn't he thought to telephone his house instead of walking to it earlier? Stumbling through that no man's land of distance, endless rows of spectral houses where lights burned, faint and futile, corners where only dogs came running to him, cats meowing forlornly in doorways, his legs aching, as they did again now, his body stiff and empty, all the while knowing he would find no one, and then finding no one of course, only the note propped against a glass, his fingers trembling as he read through a blur: *I have gone to the mainland. Please be careful. M.*

He halted now, leaning against a wall. She had not written *Dear Arni.* She had not signed *With love* above her initial.

The rage had returned. He remembered the paroxysm of fury as it took possession of him: the sound in his throat a roar then, one hand sweeping the message away, a fist smashing the table, standing straight and tall himself, snarling, his whole being filling to the brim with a poison that had intoxicated him instantly. Remembering, his mind flashed like lightning again. He felt it *crack,* a definite sound in his head.

She could not do this to him!

Wasn't it enough that in three years she had not given him a child?

Wasn't it enough that she had betrayed him—was betraying him now, this minute? The insistent, cruel, dreamlike image returned: Margret lying faceup and darkly beautiful, sensual, eyes speaking love, softness writhing, arms groping.

He stood a long moment more, then moved, swaying, turning toward the blaze. The yellow-cored flame was a blue in his eyes. Above it, billowing black clouds massively folded in upon themselves, streaked red. He clenched his jaws. He was without fear. He alone. He spat, but his mouth was dry, swollen tongue trapped, throat closed. He walked toward the ruddy, growling menace. He spat again, the taste of gall, choking. Passing houses again. Empty, empty, deserted—the streets, the town itself, gone, forever gone? All life in the past, now it was an unholy place of ghosts and spirits when only a few hours ago . . .

But if he was going to die, he would go to Valhalla, Odin's abode, he would die in battle, not a man shut out from the joys of eternity by dying ignominiously of disease or old age. He would pass proudly by Heimdell, sentinel of the gods, who sees by night and day, who can hear grass growing and the wool of sheep. Wide shoulders set against the east wind, heavy and opaque, oppressive, his chest straining, he would find her, wherever she had gone, and whomever she was with, and after avenging his honor, he would be ready to die. Let the weak, those Christian fools, forgive, turn their cheeks—he was not one of them, he would keep his hand near the hilt, and if a man came at him with an axe he would take revenge in blood, which was the foundation of all honor, the only true justice. He had waited long enough now and afterwards he would show no shame!

Seeing the fire and smoke beyond the bank building—it meant nothing to him now—he turned into the post office. He crossed the high, empty, echoing room, went down the passageway, Jonas was not on duty. He was asleep, sitting up, in the small anteroom where coffee was brewing. Jonas blinked awake when he jostled his shoulder. He saw Jonas staring, then heard his friend mutter astonishment and annoyance.

"Have the vessels landed?" He heard the rasping in his voice and a blade turned in his throat. "Tell me."

"All of them, and safely," Jonas growled. "Long ago. What the hell are you doing here?"

"I tried to telephone."

"Trunk line's ruptured." Jonas stood up. "Arni, let me give you some coffee. You look . . ."

"No!" And then, his mind sharp, he told Jonas what he must do: call Margret at his mother's house in Reykjavik. He gave him the number. "Use the radio. I know you can do it."

"Arni, listen, if everyone asked us to . . ."

"There's no one else here."

Jonas, frowning, hesitated. Then he shook his head once, uttering a long sigh. "If you're really that worried—*and* if you'll have some coffee and sober up—I'll try. Man, you look like a black ghost."

When Jonas had gone and he was alone, he sank into a chair at the small table. Worried—was he? Yes. Because if Margret was not there, then he would know what he did not, even now, want to know as a certainty. But if it was true, then he would find her—find them both! And she would be banished, as in centuries past, every door closed to her, every face and heart set against her, and like Freydis of the saga she would weep tears of red gold.

But what if—he lowered his head slowly to the table—

what if, after all, he was wrong? What if, all along, it had
been only his mind, distorted, distorting, alcohol or madness
itself, what if he had only imagined . . .

His body went slack and empty again. And his mind
recalled the brilliance of summer on the high moor atop
Heimaklettur, flat, green heath after clambering up the
steep cliffside, yellowed with angelica, the sea and all the
world stretching in all directions under the golden sun, the
harbor far below and beyond it the village, colorful roofs and
neat, meandering streets, and Margret gathering bird feathers, calling out the names, her face radiant with discovery
and joy: the tufted duck, the herring gull, the redwing, raven, the gray falcon and the rarest of all, the gray phalarope!

Where had it all gone? What had happened to all that
wonder? It seemed long ago now. As if it had happened to
two other people altogether. Decay gnawed his mind. His
blood was a scorching fever, yet he was cold all through.

He had brought them to this. He, alone. He had driven
her away. If she was gone now, the guilt was his. And the
loss. The anguish was so overpowering and intense that he
thought for a moment that he might cry out or howl. Or
perhaps weep.

"Margret is not there." Jonas had returned. "I spoke to
your mother."

Lies. She was there. *Had* to be. Lies!

"Your mother insists you come and . . ."

"She is lying. Or you are." His tone was bleak and he was
too weak to stand. "Margret is there."

"Arni, listen now. She's gone somewhere else. To a
friend. The authorities are providing . . ." He stepped
closer. "What you have to do is to clean up and get some rest,
no more *brennivan* . . ."

Everyone was always telling him what to do. *Your mother
insists.* Everyone, always, always . . .

"Hell, man, if Margret saw you now, in this condition,
she'd hate you."

Hate! He leaped.

Jonas' neck was between his hands.

Margret would never hate him, never!

Jonas cried out. His back was on the table, eyes bulging, face reddening.

Margret could never hate him, never, never, *never* . . .

Jonas was gasping for breath.

Then it was over. First, the sensation of nothingness, then pain, and as he doubled over, hands and arms going slack and numb, grip broken, he went sick all through, and weak, and he was staggering back against a wall, the agony in his groin blanking his mind just as he realized that Jonas had brought his knee up between his legs, now he was choking, his lungs tight and empty, body sinking along the wall, drowning in excruciating pain, while Jonas stood above him now, looking furious and yet sad at the same time.

"You're possessed," Jonas growled. "Man, you are not drunk, *possessed*." Then Jonas was bending down, face close, streaked eyes baffled, lips moving. "Arni, you may not be able to help yourself. I do not know. But whatever, you are destroying that girl. And if she doesn't hate you yet, she'll come to it. Is that what you actually want?"

Then Jonas straightened and was gone.

From the floor he could hear the voices squawking on the radio apparatus, the clatter of teletypes, and outside that other evil rumble that seemed to have intensified.

But Margret was not here. Margret was safe.

And she was alone. He knew now: innocent and alone.

The pain was receding. Chest heaving, he stood. But not upright.

He would go to Margret now. Find her and explain.

But no. He could not risk her hate. He had let her go off alone. Tonight. He had not been there when she needed him.

Still bending over, he went down the passage and through the post-office room, his heels echoing faintly. The windows were shaking furiously in their frames.

Hate. It was the last thing he wanted. Or could risk. Margret was not like his mother. He knew that. When he was sober, he knew that.

He made up his mind then. He knew what he had to do. He could not let her see him now. Then . . . he would stay here. Work. He would be needed. And he would not drink. Ever again. Never. He could do it because he was strong: And the drinking was what Margret knew it to be: a weakness. Which he could conquer. *Would* conquer. Because he was Arni Loftsson, proud and a true Viking: he would prove it. And then, when he had proved himself to himself, then Margret would love him again, because he would be worth loving, and then it would all come back, everything they had once had, and they would be together again.

On the street he halted—and stared. It was as if a bombardment had begun. Glass was shattering everywhere. Windows were black, square holes. In a wild pattern of arcs cinders, trailing tails of flame, were crisscrossing high and then plummeting behind and on to rooftops in every direction. The sound now was deafening—staggering. He could not move. As he watched, a home down the street exploded into a blaze. The town was engulfed in red fury.

Was it all over then? Was this the way it all ended?

But Margret was safe. From this and from him. Somewhere, Margret was safe.

On that first morning more than five thousand people saw first light in a way they had never before greeted a new day. Not one among them knew what lay ahead, but all sensed that their own individual lives would never be the same. Long ago now the international distress signal had faded from the atmosphere, but many felt that it should continue until everyone around the world knew and paid attention to what was happening here. But, knowing, what could the world do? What could anyone do?

This thought invaded Karl Sveinsson's orderly and vigorous mind as he hovered above the conflagration and havoc in a helicopter on which, after receiving Jonas' request, he had found space from Keflavik. And he recalled what he had said to his wife: *What can a fire hose do against a volcano?* But at that time he had not yet experienced the shattering might of the thing—its wild fury and the devastation it threatened. Looking down upon it now, he was somehow reminded of certain women in the old sagas that he had read as a child— violent, utterly without mercy, diabolical hags of hell. Females gone berserk, raging, snarling, like Freydis who took the axe and killed the women the men would not slaughter. "The bitch," he heard himself mutter, as hatred filled him.

The fissure lay like a gaping wound, red-lipped, oozing blood, and as the craft tipped and made a half circle, he caught a long, clear glimpse into the depthless canyon, which gurgled a thousand colors. But now, he noted, there was only three fountains, not the forty or fifty that had been described to him, three shooting pillars of lemon yellow flame that seemed to reach up for the helicopter like the arms of some monster from the deep. In spite of the brilliance everywhere, however, he had to peer down through billowing smoke, blacker than any he had ever seen before. On the other hand, great vapor clouds, white and silver, sizzled skyward from the edges of the surface wherever the lava reached cold water. In the town now he could see other fires beneath a chaotic pattern of arcing bombs, small blistering furnaces that had once been homes, and the figures of men running and turning puny crystal spouts of water onto the tiny infernoes dwarfed by the three towers spewing flame and fiery cinders and black ash.

The havoc appalled him. And from this feeling, as the 'copter began its flat-footed descent, came something more personal and even more intense than the shock itself: a slow, strange anger. Very puzzling. Very strange for Karl Sveinsson, who had a quick temper only. The rage went deep and seemed to possess him. He climbed down from the cockpit without remembering to thank the pilot, also very

odd for Karl Sveinsson, and stood staring, seeing everything
through a blinding glare and falling sparks, hearing the
sound, which filled his head with an empty roaring sensation
now, and at once feeling the trembling underfoot. How was
it possible to hate a *thing*? How could a man be furious at
some accident or abomination of nature? He tried to shake
off the feeling as he walked through the pumice that covered
the runway to the helmeted figure already approaching
him—unmistakably Jonas Vigfusson, who had first seen The
Bitch explode. Already, he realized, as Jonas clasped him in a
bearlike embrace, thanking him in a gruff whisper for coming, already he was thinking of the thing as a *being*. How
foolhardy, stupid really, to allow himself to become enraged
by something that was not even alive.

But the thing *was* alive. Listen. Look at it. Look at *her*.
The Bitch!

Jonas drove an American jeep downhill and into the
town. They passed the church, where the lower headstones
in the graveyard seemed already threatened by extinction in
blackness. Jonas was explaining, in an unfamiliar spiritless
voice that made Karl feel like he was sitting next to a
stranger, that during the violent part of the barrage earlier
in the morning, the pumice had spurted so high that it
cooled below freezing and had then fallen white over the
blackness in places. Trucks moved, helmeted men passed
like shadows—there was action, yes, but to what effect, what
end? And Jonas lapsed into silence, as if to allow Karl to
absorb completely the awesome reality and the overwhelming savagery of their foe. The sound was everywhere, a
groaning and bellowing that shook the atmosphere so, that
Karl's eardrums began to quiver, and at the same time the
hot, dry air refused to penetrate his lungs. Hot bits and
pieces of ejecta clattered on the roof of the jeep and struck
the windshield, and on all sides the pumice swirled blindingly, as if they were passing through a storm of black snow at
night. Yet it was almost midday now. An atmosphere of futility pervaded the vehicle. It was as if the whole world shook in
fear, knowing what was to come, helpless to prevent the in-

evitable. By the time they reached the small fire station and Karl was climbing down onto the quivering pavement, he felt a fool—and even more angry. The water cannon he had brought seemed a mockery, part of some malicious joke.

Inside the empty, garagelike room the fire chief, whose name Karl did not hear, sat slumped at a bare table with a jug of coffee in his hand. He regarded Karl with tired red eyes, hooded, slightly resentful, in a face so splotched with soot that Karl could not fix his age.

The fire chief examined the nozzle that Karl placed on the table, then slowly shook his head. "It won't fit our equipment. You made the trip for nothing."

"Can't other equipment be requested?" Karl asked, feeling his ire quickening.

"From whom?"

"How do I know? I do know it's available."

"Even if we had more, we don't have enough men."

Jonas spoke: "It's true, Karl. There are new fires starting all the time. At least twenty, and it's only the first day. And then there's the air pressure—damned windows just explode."

The fire chief said, "And once one of those bombs goes through a window, there's no way to put out the fire."

"Then cover the windows from the direction of the eruption."

"With what?"

"Corrugated iron."

"There's not enough in the few stores we have here."

Karl heard himself growl. "Then get more from the mainland."

"Karl," Jonas said then, "we don't have the manpower to do a job like that."

"Then *get* the manpower."

Jonas cast a quick glance at the fire chief, who shrugged and said, "My job's to put out the fires."

"Whose job is it to prevent them?" Karl demanded, hearing in his voice the same impatient sharpness that he heard only during emergencies at the airport.

The fire chief stood up. He was, Karl realized, a very young man, and his authority had been challenged. "I have to take an hour's sleep," he said, but not apologetically. "Thank you for your offer."

When he had disappeared into the dormitory, Jonas poured more coffee and drew a chair up to the desk, motioning Karl to sit. Jonas studied the other man, who felt the appraisal and was alerted. "I should have checked out the size of our pumpers before I phoned you, Karl. No one can think of everything. That's our trouble here now."

"I know," Karl heard himself say. It was not this that annoyed or dismayed him now, but the general air of confusion, disarray, helplessness. On all sides! He could not be certain now whether his rage was directed against the damned bitch out there or against this general attitude of futility. Had they given up? He asked it.

Jonas suddenly shouted, eyes going furious, fist slamming the table. "Given up! Look around, man. The scientists give us less than a fifty-fifty chance even to survive. The whole place could blow up and go down like a sunken ship any minute. Or we could all be burned to cinders. Or if not burned by fire, then smothered by ash. It's a war, it's a war, that's what!"

"Like hell! It's a retreat in all directions."

Jonas slumped, and for a moment Karl thought that he might lower his heavy head to the table. Nevertheless, he felt a stab of satisfaction: he had struck through to outrage, anger—had he brought his friend to life? He poured coffee and waited.

Finally Jonas asked: "Where do we start?"

"Let's start with pumping and fire-fighting machinery. The larger the better. To be shipped by cargo plane as soon as fixed-wing aircraft can land again."

"*If* they can ever land again."

"I didn't say if, I said *when*. And if not, then by freighter or fishing vessel into the harbor and chalk up your losses for the delay."

He saw something like amusement come into Jonas'

eyes, behind the astonishment. "And the corrugated iron—
the same procedure, I suppose?"

Karl shook his head. "No need for any delay on that.
Start with what's available in the construction stores here." A
strange excitement had begun to throb in him. "And why
should the 'copters, meanwhile, come in empty?" When
Jonas, studying him, only shook his head, Karl asked: "What
do they take back, incidentally?"

"Whatever's waiting for them at the airstrip."

"Who decides that?"

Jonas began to grin, faintly. "That's decided, so far, by
whoever hauls *whatever* to the airstrip."

"Jesus Christ," Karl said.

Then, on a sly note, Jonas pointed out: "Much of the
destruction's done by ash. At least two roofs have caved in
already."

"Clear the damn roofs."

Jonas said: "That's being done. Here and there."

"Here and there," Karl growled and stood up.

"How else?"

"Organization. Crews detailed to do certain jobs. How
the hell else? If it's a war, treat it like one."

"I guess it would be safe to say that . . . it's a war without a general."

Karl nodded grimly. "From what I've seen, you can be
damned certain it's safe to say that."

"Only . . . where would we get the manpower?"

Before he answered, Karl thought of his wife. He remembered her not-quite-spoken hesitation. And he sensed
something in Jonas that he only now began to suspect.
Nevertheless, he said: "What about the men from here
whose houses are being burned or smothered? And there are
volunteers already landing at Keflavik: all of them didn't
come to take pictures. Then there are three thousand Yanks
stationed at the NATO base, sitting on their tails and bored
shitless."

"U.S. personnel? You know how Icelanders feel."

"I even know how U.S. personnel feel about Icelanders."

"Would the U.S. authorities be willing?"

"How the hell do I know? Has anyone asked?" But he was not going to allow to happen what he knew now could happen. He quoted the fire chief: "My job's to put out fires.".

"Biggest damned fire here I ever saw." Jonas stood up, his eyes sharp now. "Could you get permission to stay?"

There it was. Slowly Karl stood, too, shaking his head, thinking of his wife. But the excitement was kindled in him, he could feel the fibers of his mind and body straining toward action. And there was his hatred for and anger at The Bitch gnashing her teeth and muttering threats in the distance. "I don't know. Until I request it."

"Will you?"

"I don't know." What he did know was that he would be fighting, not only the depradations of The Bitch, but the benumbing shock and chaos in the minds of those under attack. He also knew—or could tell himself—it was not his fight. But if not his, whose? If these people ever gave in utterly to their weariness and stunned panic, the mood would become one of helplessness, even despair, and then, no matter how much sweat and devotion were spent, all would go down, even if The Bitch didn't go through with her threats. Then she would win anyway.

Jonas said: "I'll have a council meeting called. I'll propose you take over." And he added: "Absolute authority."

If he turned away now, if he didn't make the effort, win or lose in the end, he knew that he would never again be the man he had to believe himself to be.

"On those terms," he said, wondering whether he could ever make Lilja understand.

Jonas' familiar grin returned. "What do you say to a drink or three, to seal the bargain?"

Karl Sveinsson shook his head. "Too much work to do."

And Jonas shook hands across the table instead and said: "Aye, aye, Skipper."

FOUR

A TELEVISION CAMERA had been placed high on Heimaklettur overlooking the harbor and the town so that the people in Reykjavik could follow the eruption and its depredations by camera's eye. Some, Kristrun Egilsdottir knew, sat staring all day and into every night, mesmerized, nursing hope, fighting despair. But nothing she had seen reflected there could have prepared her for what she was gazing at now: the overwhelming, heart-staggering reality. Her bookshop on Heidarvegur and Rudolf's building-supply store around the corner, facing the harbor, were intact, although the windows of both were dark, almost opaque. But she wished she had not insisted on coming. She had told Rudolf that she had to see for herself. Now she was seeing. It was as if her whole town were slowly sinking in inky grit, drowning.

Never mind the deafening roar and grumble, the rasping thunder and whooping coughs, or the three plumes shooting red and yellow. Never mind the shaking underfoot, which she could feel as she and Rudolf had walked, or the cracked, bulging pavement beneath the crust of loose ash or the black drifts along the curbings. Or the always-present possibility, as Rudolf had admitted when she had tried to prevent his returning here to work, that the whole island might explode, sink into the uncaring sea. But he had himself decided, with his usual good cheer, that it was better to work, regardless of consequence, risk, or success. She had seen the cars being hoisted and swung onto the decks of the coastal steamers, and now she saw crews of men working to clear the rooftops and trucking household goods toward the harbor. Rudolf had, with a smile of amusement and pride, told her of this man Karl Sveinsson, a fire chief from Keflavik, and of how he had taken command, turning soldiers and volunteers and even boyscouts into thieves, ransacking all the warehouses for corrugated iron, which she could now see being hammered onto the windows to the east. But, Rudolf had said, he favored anything that would save the town. By this time one warehouse had already caved in, its roof and walls cracking and crumbling under the weight of the volcanic materials, and if it should rain now, as was normal for this time of year, if water should add its weight to the ash . . .

But, trudging the street, Rudolf holding her hand as if she were a child he really wanted to protect, Kristrun had arrived at such a state of disbelief that the idea of saving the island—can anything be saved that is already lost?—struck her as pathetic and ridiculous, although in some way admirable, even touching, but foolish, foolish, foolish. How many Sundays ago had Gudrid told them what was to happen here? Should she have believed the child, as Rudolf had done? Could she—dare she—believe that a ten-year-old girl could know? Even Gudrid, sharing with her mother the small room and narrow bed that Rudolf's brother offered in Reykjavik, had not spoken of it—was she as bewildered by her premonition of last July as her mother was?

Kristrun saw the house. Or was it her house? A lovely yellow, it was now black. Its windows were speckled dark. She stood staring, the disbelief turning to shock. She felt Rudolf's hand clutching hers, as if this were the moment he had dreaded. She knew that he had cleared it of everything he thought she might wish saved. She knew that, before reporting to the work headquarters for assignment each day, he had personally and alone worked on the roof, which was covered now with only a thin skin of the black ash that was heaped solidly on most. The roof, he had said, was the weak spot. If the fall of tephra should continue much longer, and if then it should rain . . .

She turned away. She realized that the air was hot. She was cold. It was as if she realized now, for the first time, that the thread of their lives—hers and Rudolf's and little Gudrid's—had been severed. Perhaps the old sagas told it true: that the fabric of life is woven complete at birth and that fate is all-powerful, with man at its mercy. Heathen magic, superstition, of course. Yet she saw Rudolf's face, and gratitude filled her and more confusion: all that work, all those hard hours, what if it were all for naught because the outcome had already been determined?

She said nothing. They turned away together and walked again. And as it happened so often during those long dark winters, her body as much as her mind began to yearn for those hot places under the sun—exotic places, whose pictures appeared in the books in her store, warm, with sandy beaches and glittering blue water and soft breezes and houses whose lovely pastel colors were not blighted and engulfed by evil blackness.

Here, in Vestmannaeyjar, it would always be winter now. Always hereafter.

And Kristrun, shivering so that Rudolf's grasp of her hand increased, stared at the brilliance and the blackness and knew that she would never come back.

She could not.

Ever.

She, who had always craved to shape her own destiny in spite of the beliefs around her, now made up her mind that, somehow, she would do so.

Now.

Gunnar Axelson's mind was less on the chores he was performing in and around the shed than on his family, especially on his son Josef in that strange place, with strangers. Svana would meet anyone and have her way, her say. Yes. But what of Josef? And might this be the time, the first time, that she would turn her acid tongue on the boy?

He had been working alone on the farm for—how long now? Two days, maybe three. He no longer looked up when he heard the motor of a plane. He had seen all kinds coming and going: only smaller ones at first, then huge, roaring things that would disappear, sliding down under the falling sparks and ash; and when the wind was heavy, those strange-looking ones with no wings and the propellers on top; or sometimes, for many hours, none at all. Were they still taking people off to the mainland? He couldn't go into the village to find out because his pony had never come back and Josef's dog, Odin, wasn't large enough to ride. He could walk, of course, but he really didn't have much interest in what was going on there, and there was so much to do with no one here to help.

But then a truck came to the farm driven by a man he did not know, but a farmer like himself by the look of him. The truck, the man told him, had come to fetch his cattle. His spirits lifted—so that was it, they were removing the cattle from the island, from the threat. But no. Orders had come through to slaughter the cattle and to save as many sheep as possible. It was, the man said, the sheep that were being evacuated now by the planes at the airfield. He had come for the cattle. The meat would be needed to feed the volunteers working in Vestmannaeyjar.

Gunnar, heart faint and quivering in his massive chest, helped load the cows onto the truck. How many ewes did Gunnar have here? Someone else would come for them; they would be made safe on a farm on the mainland. For however long was necessary. Then they would be returned to their owners if—but he did not need to finish that. Both men paused then and stared together at the gash that, this far south, was a low, spluttering wall of fluorescence, no fountains here, but beyond the airstrip and beyond the cone of Helgafell flames tried to scale the sky and black clouds twisted higher. Then, as if to break the spell, the man went back to work, driving the last animal up the ramp with a shout that sounded angry. Gunnar knew, though, that the man's anger was not at the cow, but at whatever was happening and whatever was about to happen.

Before he climbed into the truck, the stranger grinned at Gunnar. "Dumb Americans," he said. "One flight, they loaded thirty-seven sheep and one ram on the same plane. Ram must have had a fine flight, och? But that pilot, he must have thought he hit a storm on the way." Then, roaring with laughter, he shook Gunnar's hand and stepped up and into the cab.

Gunnar saw it all going. The family. Now the farm itself. For the first time he came to realize the ugly cruelty of that fire over there.

And then, only a few hours later, he heard a motor above and a clattering, and when he looked up he saw the plane, one of those strange ones with no wings but those propellers whirling and clacking on top, and he watched as its huge, bulbous body descended. The wind was a howl and a blast by the time it was on the ground, taking his breath, and then he saw the blades slow to a standstill, the wind abating, and then he watched as a man in a uniform climbed down. He was a Yank—Gunnar had seen a few of them—all smiles, a boy really, not much older than Josef, and like Josef he seemed to enjoy what he was doing. He spoke and he shook hands, but Gunnar understood only a few words of the Yank tongue. However, he knew why the bird was here, so he helped run the sheep aboard while the young man tried to tell him a story of some sort, counting the ewes on his fingers until he reached thirty-six, then stopping them and pointing to one of Gunnar's two rams and then roaring with laughter, while he made wide gestures indicating the rocking of the airplane. So Gunnar joined him, laughing too, because he knew then what the boy was trying to tell him and, while he didn't think it so funny because what was more natural, he

didn't want to offend this young man who was saving his
sheep for him. Then he signed some papers because the pilot
indicated that he should, and they shook hands again, and
then he made out a few Yank words—something about jolly
and green and giant—and he watched as the youngster
climbed up into the big green bird with all the sheep that
Gunnar owned.

Gunnar couldn't imagine how it could lift all that load,
but it did, roaring, and he watched it rise and then tilt against
the gray sky, circle and finally disappear out over the water.
Gunnar could not help wondering how those sheep would
feel, up there, suspended, when they had always had solid
ground beneath them. But everything was changing for
everyone. And, with an emptiness in his innards and a terrible tightness in his chest and throat, he wondered again
about Josef: would they treat him well over there, how could
they do for him what his father could, would they understand that Josef was different?

It was raining the morning that Reverend Petur Trygvasson finally arrived on Heimaey. On the transport ship
Esia, crowded with volunteer salvage workers, many of
whom spoke foreign languages, he had learned that it had
been raining steadily now for two days and nights. But as he
stared stunned, aghast, one word occurred to him:
apocalypse. Followed by another: deluge. If only God would
send a deluge from the skies to drown out the horror.

Petur felt guilty at his delay. After he had made his
decision that late night, after receiving word of what was
occurring, he had not telephoned the pilot and had not
braved the small one-way airstrip that night, but not because
of cowardice. No. Because of Veiga, his wife. When he had
told her, she had not begged him to stay, although he saw

fear in her eyes and was moved. She had asked him only to
love her. Now. Tonight. And in her father's house, with the
man slowly dying, they had made love. But as never before.
At first astonished, then appalled by himself as well as by her,
he had met her lust with his own. Seeing her desperation
turn her into a wanton, stripping off all her clothes that night
and at every opportunity thereafter, he had discovered a
deep, dark well of passion in himself—and had become its
willing, its joyous and exalted slave. He had become aware of
his maleness and had exulted in it. At times he knew that he
should leave; he was needed down there, all those frozen
miles away. And at times, too, he would wonder whether this
wildness that had brought the pale woman to glowing life,
there in the house of death, had been stirred by her knowledge of death closing in on the man in the other bedchamber—some sudden realization of the brevity of living
and the long pale nothingness of death—and also whether
she was clinging to him by every voluptuous wile and
utter abandonment, because she was afraid that he, if he
went, might perish before the two of them, for reasons
beyond their own comprehensions, had ever really lived together as man and woman. Whatever her reasons or im-
pulses, Veiga had become, for him, another woman—and
for the first time, truly a woman. But then, not exhausted,
but strong and her face filled with the healthy flow of life,
she had told him, softly, that he must do what he had intended. Even that decision she had made, sensing his guilt,
knowing his entrapment, and then, with reluctance, he had
finally telephoned the pilot, the wind had been from the west
that day, and he had left the peninsula on the far northwest
part of the country and had flown south in a state of vivid
aliveness, without fear. She would, Veiga had told him, come
whenever or if ever he needed her. He needed her now; he
would always need her. And the thought, with the memory,
brought a new kind of reverence into his soul.

   He walked through the darkened town, roaring with
machinery and the steady grumble of Kirkjufell, picturing
himself as he had been: a tall, thin wraith of a man, preoc-

cupied, nodding to the townspeople and using wrong names. Now he walked through the wet-cement pumice, nodding to all, strangers and parishioners alike, careful not to call anyone by name, his long step vigorous, his mind clear as to what he must do here, what was needed. Even the volcano had been named for the church.

When he reached it, though, he halted. It was no longer white. Its walls and arched windows were shades of gray and black, and its slanting roofs, once a soft maroon in color, were a desolate pall. The pointed spire was illuminated from behind, starkly profiled, almost as if it were itself an elongated torch of intense lemon or gold, backgrounded by a ruddy red. In the churchyard, the lower headstones were all but obliterated, others pushed their peaks above the drifts of black waves, and the statue of the Madonna, her base completely enshrouded, remained proudly erect, gray in color, still presiding over all, but somewhat mournfully. One of her hands was missing.

Then his mind went to Baldvin Einarrson. Baldvin had been wrong: Helgafell had not taken revenge. This was a new volcano altogether. Or was it really? Yes. He would not allow his mind to be drawn into questioning and doubting. What Baldvin believed was part of the paganism that Petur had tried to fight—and would continue to oppose as it existed in the minds of the people as well as in the convictions of the painter whose friendship he valued.

Baldvin. It was clear from here that the whole eastern section of town, especially the outskirts, no longer really existed. All was covered, smothered—a sea of dark cinders in which not even the rooftops could be seen. More desolation. Incredible. How Baldvin, and especially his wife Inga, had loved that fine old house. Where had they gone then? Had Baldvin been able to salvage any of his paintings? He would ask Pall. Pall would know. And Pall would be here. Yes. Of them all, Pall would stay.

He looked beyond then, to the east. The sound here, this close, filled his head to bursting. He had been told that the rift was a series of burning chimneys, but no: a single crater had formed, a huge-mouthed mound rising alongside

Helgafell, not nearly so high, two conic forms, one spewing flame and magma, the other long silent, long dead.

He turned and went into the church. Ash had seeped in and the pews were faintly dusted with it. The walls shook. He climbed the steps into the steeple. He pictured Sundays, the people filing in, in finery of serge and silk and lace, bobbing and nodding, crouching or kneeling to pray, bawling or quavering through hymns, frowning at children through the sermon, all grave, all serene, and the organ pealing. It was what they needed now. And more. Worship, yes, and prayers of thanksgiving that they had been spared, but more: the appeal to a larger comprehension, a plea for mercy and justice—and for help to understand why.

He took the bell rope into his hand. He pulled, again and again, the bell ringing out with more and more confidence. Now they would know. Now they would know where to come for peace, for solace. The bell was not tolling, it was clanging out across the town, and some would hear, stop work, look up the hill—not at their enemy, but at their friend for whom the enemy had been named. He pulled again and again, faster and faster, as if in the motion itself there was triumph, defiance.

But even as he did, he wondered again how, riddled himself by doubt, he could answer those who might question. They would ask why. They would ask: *Why us, what have we done?* And what would he answer? That God in his infinite wisdom and mercy . . .

Mercy?

That God was Himself justice . . .

But what have we done to deserve this?

Exhausted, he allowed the last peal to echo and die across the blackened fields and houses. He would find a way. Whatever he might feel himself, they needed what he had come to give them: faith, reassurance, hope. First then, the place must be cleaned. The day after tomorrow was Sunday. He did wish, though, that Veiga were here. If he had come the night he had first made the decision to come, would he feel this now? Would he feel this now? Would he have needed her now?

Did he have Kirkjufell to thank for her being a new woman, himself a different man?

When her father asked Thurbjorn to come to Reykjavik to discuss business matters, Elin knew that Thurbjorn would interpret this as a summons; but then, she knew now, Thurbjorn had resented, perhaps even hated, her father for years. And after all her father had done for Thurbjorn: had allowed him to take over the freezing plant, had given them both the house in which she had grown up in Vestmannaeyjar, so much, so much. (And now that house was gone, but she must not think about that; she didn't know how she felt about that really.) She had not told her father the details of that dreadful scene in the office overlooking the harbor that first night of the volcano: only that Thurbjorn had refused to take care of her (until her father had ordered him to do so on the telephone), but not how Thurbjorn had cursed him in such an obscene and venomous way, like a man gone berserk. (No, to tell her father would be disloyal to her husband.) Nor had she told her father, or anyone, how she had been transformed into a stranger—to herself as well as to Thurbjorn. She could not recall exactly what she had said. Had she actually screamed something about Thurbjorn never being a fraction of the man her father was? Had she?

She didn't want to think about that or any of it, the house, the cursed volcano, any of it—she wanted to put it all from her mind. Here, in her father's house—how spacious, how lovely, where the two servants did everything, and she was free to shop, to go to the cinema or theater, visit her friends, or simply to loll about in a pleasant state of euphoria—here, it was nice, so very nice, to feel safe and detached and cared for. Why, it was almost as if she were a child again.

When Thurbjorn did arrive and the three of them were

seated at the long dinner table laid with Delft atop Irish
linen, the contrast between the two men was startling and
oddly disquieting: her father with color high on his lean
cheeks, his halo of silver hair, and Thurbjorn looking so pale
and tired, even a trifle grimy, although not in any definite
way, hair thinning and pale and his head almost round. Her
father took his meal in leisurely fashion and spoke with his
usual unhurried grace. Thurbjorn ate in moody silence,
abstracted, answering questions only. He explained how the
house had been destroyed: no, not by fire or lava, but by
something to do with vapors of cooling lava penetrating the
sewerage and ventilation systems and then being drawn out
through the chimney and windows so that the heat inside
became so intense that the foundation simply cracked and
melted, and the house collapsed.

Because she did not understand or want to think about
any of that, Elin spoke of the many art exhibits she had
seen—especially the showing of that marvelous painting by
Baldvin Einarrson titled "Revenge of Helgafell." It had
caused a great stir, especially after the new volcano had
formed its own crater and cone alongside Helgafell.
Everyone had seen this on television, of course, but it had to
be a case of life matching art, not the other way round,
because Baldvin had done the picture before the eruption.
The prints of his fingers were still on the rim of the canvas
because when he had saved it the very night of the eruption
the oil was still wet. "Isn't it the most curious thing?"

"Incredible," her father said, sipping his wine.

"Baldvin's house was one of the first to go," Thurbjorn
said. "It's completely buried in lava."

"I know," Elin said, wondering why Thurbjorn had to
insist on bringing in the sour note. "I had a long coffee with
Inga at the museum. They don't know whether they'll go
back or not. Inga said it was too early to decide."

"Precisely," her father said. "Perhaps there will be no
need to decide. Possibly Vestmannaeyjar will not be there."

Thurbjorn cast her father a dark look, but briefly, and
said nothing.

Then her father stood, tall and trim, with that courtly

confidence and serenity that she had always found so reassuring. And when Thurbjorn stood, he looked more rotund
than ever. When they went into the living room, his step
seemed uncertain, even apprehensive.

Over brandy and coffee—one of her father's European
habits of which she approved because it always seemed so
civilized—Thurbjorn bluntly asked, over the cry of wintry
wind out the windows, what her father wished to discuss. He
realized, he said, that over here no one could picture what
life was like over there on Heimaey, but everyone there, he
rushed on, was busy sixteen or even twenty hours a day. Her
father smiled faintly, mildly: he wanted Thurbjorn to know
that he was aware of what a fine job he had been doing,
keeping the freezing plant open, the only one of the two
operating, and all reports were excellent, even the press had
praised what Thurbjorn and Frosti Runaldsson had done.

"But . . .?" Thurbjorn prompted, brandy glass in hand,
brandy sloshing nervously in it. He waited.

"But. Ah, there you have it. I have been doing some of
my own research. It tells me that the very earth over there
might suddenly yawn wider and the whole island, which we
all three love, might disappear under the ocean. Or, as I
understand it, new tremors could cause Kirkjufell to blow up
completely. At the very least, it seems possible everything in
the village will be engulfed, or burn."

Thurbjorn nodded heavily, his eyes shaded. "I think
everyone there is aware of that." There was an edge in his
quiet tone.

"Then, being a man of business, Thurbjorn, as you are,
there seems to be only one reasonable and businesslike procedure open to us."

"Yes?"

"Can't you guess?"

"I can. Tell me."

"To dismantle the machinery, which represents a tremendous investment on my part, and to ship it here."

After a moment, Thurbjorn took a sip of brandy. Then:
"In spite of everything, we are operating at a profit."

"I said you have done a fine job."

"Thank you, sir."

Elin straightened. Was this Thurbjorn? Was this Thurbjorn talking to her father in this ironic manner?

"There can be no profit if we lose the refrigeration machinery," her father said, his tone soft, almost detached. "Others have salvaged theirs and more is being shipped here every day. They were wise. Not as brave perhaps, or as foolhardy, but wise."

A long moment passed in the spacious room. The wind wailed mournfully. Elin sat silent, waiting, disturbed.

Finally Thurbjorn stood up. He set down his glass. "It's your plant. You have the right to do as you please. I have never felt it was mine. That, or the house. So . . ." His heavy body heaved with a single deep breath. "So if that is what you wish to do, I suggest you come out to Vestmannaeyjar and do it. Because I will not. Good night."

As Elin rose to follow, her father said: "Soft, girl. He's a tired man. Soft."

In the bedroom that had become hers now, she closed the door gently behind her. Cautiously, her tone carefully silken, she said: "Does it make a difference Thurbjorn? We can't go back anyway, can we?"

He was seated on the bed, head down. "It's too early to know that."

She stepped to sink on the floor at his feet. "We're together again," she said, struggling to feel a desire that she could not summon. "Let's forget all this tonight. Heimaey, everything there, father, work—you look so tired. Can we forget all of it together, the way we once did?"

His brown eyes stared into hers. And slowly he shook his head. Abruptly she felt pain, deep and stabbing. And also a quick anger: he did not desire her. For the first time in their life together she had suggested what she desperately wanted, to desire yet did not, and *he* did not desire *her*. Stunned she studied his face. Tired, yes, but . . .

"You'll never forgive me, will you?" she asked, knowing—hoping, because that had to be the reason, *had* to be. "For what I said that night. About you and that . . . the French woman. Oh, I know she's gone back there now. Everyone knows. But don't you see, I must have been crazy with fear. I know now why I behaved so. I know you've never been near that woman. I knew it then and I know it now."

He rose to his feet quickly and moved heavily but swiftly away.

"It's not fair to blame me for what my father does," she said, hearing the plaintive note on her voice, but knowing she was right in this, too.

He was at the window now, his broad back to her. "Yes," he said. "Yes, that would be unfair."

She stood. "What then? What?"

"Unfair, too, to blame you because no man will ever satisfy you, no man but your . . ." He stopped then, and she knew a flutter of panic as she stepped to him.

"Thurbjorn, I'm your wife. I love you."

He whirled about. "Love me?" He spoke in a low, harsh whisper of contempt, face contorted, eyes glittering, and now they had returned to that horrible night in the office above the harbor. "You don't even love him down there, except for what he can do for *you.*"

She seemed, she thought, to stagger backwards but knew she had not moved. She felt tears scalding and her world seemed to reel.

He stepped toward her. "You *were* wrong about Odette. That night you were wrong. You would not be wrong now. And you have yourself to thank for it. Yourself and *him.*"

She had begun to tremble all over.

She saw him unclench his hands and straighten his hunched shoulders. She heard him say: "I'm going back where I belong. Where I'm needed." He moved past her, and now his head was lifted, the muscles of his flabby chin hard and throbbing. "*He* can do whatever he has to do and I'll do what I have to do." At the door he turned. "And you can do whatever you imagine will make you as happy as . . . as you'll never be, Elin."

She was staring at the closed door. It took a long moment, the wind blowing even more dismally now, for her to feel the relief. Now . . . now she could stay here forever. Safe. With someone who would always take care of her.

The rain had stopped. The wind had shifted again south-southwest, five knots—so the tephra was not falling over the town. But for their house, as for many others, it was too late. How Agnar wished that he could have convinced her not to come. He had warned her at first; then he had told her the truth.

She stood staring, and then she said quietly: "You said the roof had collapsed."

And so it had. Because of the rain. Many roofs had caved in under the added weight. But, after the rain had stopped, the wind had risen, remaining easterly and gusting to fifty knots so that again the airfield had to be closed. And the ash went on a rampage, so that now the house lay almost buried, half-crushed, a forlorn and broken ship awash in a calm sea, but appearing as if lost in black wind-washed waves. One gable jutted like a stubborn prow and a glimmer of blue roof showed in patches.

"I thought to clean it," Ruth said then, her voice low and stunned, to Agnar all but unrecognizable.

His heart twisted. "Let's go home, Ruth."

"Home?" She looked up into his eyes, her own already so blank as to seem withdrawn—not her eyes at all, another's. Ruth's eyes had a light in them and joy and always the look to tomorrow. She nodded only.

He did not know whether to touch her. They walked then, together but each alone for the first time in twenty-one years, from the home that was no longer a home through a town that was no longer a town. Rather, it was an ocean of grime with storm-shattered ships, some charred, afloat but deathly still on its dark softly rolling surface. Here and there the tops of fence posts were barely distinguishable, and the electric and telephone lines were disappearing in loops beneath the inky drifts. The sky was a flat stupor, the sun a faded gilt platter, Kirkjufell fulminating in low snarls.

"Once so green," she said, and he lost a breath because she had spoken at all, until he heard again that new tone her voice had taken on. "Once so lovely. So." And no more.

She remained on the aft deck instead of joining him in the wheelhouse of the *Njord* on the return—and she did not look back, not once. It was then that he realized that she had not mentioned her piano. There was no cause, of course: it too was gone.

But she did not cry. She did not cry then or afterwards. And often; later, he was to wish that she would, that she would weep and cling to him, give herself over instead of moving away from him in her mind—as he first saw her do on that bleak Sunday afternoon aboard the *Njord* on a quiet sea.

The next day came to be known as Black Monday.

When Karl Sveinsson had assumed absolute command more than three weeks ago, it had been with the approval of the Icelandic Emergency Fund and of the town council. Almost at once, though, he had begun to doubt his own decision: was he, in fact, up to this, could he do it? His first order was to have the telephone trunk line to the mainland repaired; the facilities of the radio communications center were not adequate to the job he saw before him. He set up a general headquarters in a huge room on the ground floor of the hotel. He had radio and telephone apparatus installed so that he could be in contact at all times with the police, the fire station, which was almost directly across Heidarvegur, the

airfield tower—which by some miracle still stood—and with
the Disaster Control Center in Reykjavik and the Defense
Command Post at Keflavik. He had the town council meeting
room moved from the bank building to one of the dining
rooms in the hotel and, at the suggestion of the mayor, ordered the town documents and the bank records and cash
sent to Reykjavik. A mess hall was set up in the fish-
processing plant on the extreme west end of the harbor,
farthest from the fire and fallout. And he arranged at once
for the council to make a formal request for manpower from
the NATO base at the international airport, where, until he
had received his leave of absence, he had been working.
Volunteers also arrived from various countries, a few wom-
en, or young girls, among them. Because almost all of the
homes were vacant, housing was a problem only in the sense
that he insisted on strict billeting procedures to avoid, as
much as was possible, anyway, the occupation of houses in
what he considered danger areas and so that headquarters
would have some record of everyone's whereabouts.
Priorities had to be established so that the trucking of household and other goods to the harbor and airstrip and the
removal of cars by ship would not be done by whim and
therefore become chaotic. Every east wind was the enemy,
bringing a storm of flaming dust to start new fires or to
gather on street and roof. There were, he estimated, thirteen
thousand windows exposed to the east; the job of covering
them with corrugated sheets was begun in a pattern and
continued now. Details of men were assigned to clear the
rooftops of the deadly weight of the ash. And the streets had
to be cleared regularly. What then to do with the debris? Into
the sea. Trucks and earth-moving machines crept up and
down the potholed streets. He ordered overflights of the
area each morning, the photographs to reveal the lava lines
and any changes. At the suggestion of the scientists, he arranged for infrared photographs by American satellites to
detect and reveal any new hot spots on the island.

Then, because he wanted to consolidate control in a
single area, he requested that the first-aid station and infirm-

ary be removed from the hospital to the hotel. Doctor Pall, who had approved all other moves with a kind of sour admiration, scowled at this idea. Not because it would be a complicated move—and it damned well would be!—but because there was X ray and other diagnostic as well as therapeutic apparatus that might be needed. *If that time comes,* Karl had said at the council table, *and if the hospital is still there, we'll manage to get the patients there from the hotel.* It had been clear from Doctor Pall's expression then, as he studied Karl Sveinsson, that he had not considered the hospital to be in danger until then. He grinned, faintly, the scowl turning to amusement. *Whatever you say, General Patton.* Until then Karl had not known that someone, undoubtedly one of the U.S. military personnel, who had recently arrived, had dubbed him so. And he wasn't too damn certain that he liked the idea. But the name stayed with him—blood and guts—and in time he came to accept it as a well-intentioned compliment and sometimes, in rare moments of detachment and self-mockery, wondered whether he tried to live up to it.

Possibly, though, the concept, however intended, served to buoy up his confidence. There were days and nights of sinister quiet, tempting one to hope, and periods of such fury that the world seemed about to end. He learned, though, to live with uncertainty, to meet whatever freakish whim The Bitch indulged herself in, hour to hour, minute to minute. For she was indeed a cruel and willful tyrant, sadistic in her own power, exulting in her own hysteria, delighted by the horror and havoc she could cause. Regardless of her vagrant contrariness, though, the days and nights fell into a pattern of sorts for Karl Sveinsson. Before first light, at 0900 hours, Karl would hand out the work assignments. Then, approximately an hour after first light, he would study the aerial photographs, matching this morning's against yesterday's: advance of the lava front, encroachment into street and field, houses or other buildings burned or buried or collapsed. Each time Karl would curse The Bitch—spuming waste, malicious hellcat from the sagas, always devouring more—and would wonder, each time, how a thinking man could be so consumed by such irrational hatred. He could actually feel it boiling hot in his blood; he could taste it in his mouth even as he smoked his pipe. He would often thank the photographers for what he called their pretty pictures, good enough to be framed. *Only what the hell happened, did you get smoke in your eyes? Or maybe the developing fluid is getting weak.* While they shrugged, shook their heads, sometimes winked, or even laughed, he would trace then, with a vivid red marker, the wavering line of The Bitch's latest depradations on the huge map of the island on the wall. Then he would throw the pen to the table and thank them, cursing.

Then he would go upstairs to the daily council meeting, where he would sit, fighting impatience, biting his pipe. There was talk when there should be work, so damned much to do. When the mayor called on him, he would attack with a barrage of requests, demands: more heavy equipment, especially 'dozers and fire pumpers and trucks—what the hell was holding everything up? The representative of the Icelandic Emergency Fund did not know. Then why didn't he find out for God's sake? The fund had the money, he was told, but these things take time. The others, amused or annoyed, assured him this was true. And he would remind them that The Bitch didn't realize that, or she wouldn't be so impatient to gobble up the town, bit by bit. But he would go out and have a private chat with her, perhaps she would quiet down. At one time or another during the meeting or after it had been adjourned, old Frosti Rundaldsson never failed to place a withered gray hand on Karl's back or shoulder, and while this did not calm him, it held a certain significance. Karl knew that the tall, thin man, who looked ill, owned the fish-processing plant that was in operation again; its thin plume of smoke might be lost in the mists and vapors and clouds of the harbor, but it rose there day and night, a feeble symbol of hope. Earlier one of the freezing plants had also been in operation, but its owner, who lived on the mainland, had closed it down, and its machinery was being dismantled.

After the meeting Karl would go out into the town to see for himself. On some days it would be darkest night at mid-

day, except for that eternal fluorescence, sometimes violent
with color, at other times somber, dark clouds only. When
the wind blew, it whirled the ash and lashed it into any exposed face with such a ferocity that those working often had
to wait minutes at a time to continue to shovel or even to inch
forward in the narrow streets. The finest particles crept
under any collar or muffler and seeped down over chest and
back, and perversely into the most tightly laced boot. Karl
drove a half-ton truck, painted red, with four-wheel drive.
Bulldozers whined, groaned, clattered. As he passed, a work
crew on a roof or in a street might pause, several hands
might lift or, here and there, a helmet might be doffed in a
mock salute that denoted fondness but respect. Then, decision made here, machinery shifted there, he would return to
the command post to face whatever and inevitable new problems had developed in his absence, and to dictate new demands by letter or memo or to make them personally by
telephone to members of parliament, the defense minister's
office, the U.S. command at Keflavik—begging, threatening,
snarling, cajoling. He used friend, acquaintance, stranger,
anyone who might help pull the taut, glue-tangled strings of
bureaucracy.

And then, at night, after eighteen or sometimes twenty
hours of growling, swearing, barking orders in a voice that at
times became a hoarse whisper, eyes blurred with fatigue,
mouth desert-dry from having smoked too many pipes, he
would climb the stairs with aching muscles to the spartan
room on the fourth, or top, floor of the hotel—only to discover, more often than not, that he could not sleep. He had
had a telephone installed, and on some nights he would ring
his home, which he could picture through a screen of weariness and nostalgia. Yet, while Lilja's words were invariably of
concern, which he knew to be sincere, her voice, as time
passed, took on a quality which he found disturbing without
being able to define why. And the distance between them, he
sensed, was becoming more than physical. After replacing
the telephone, he would sometimes wish that he had not
made the call. Still, when he did not, he found himself aching

to hear her voice, and, alone in the bed, he dared not think of her warm womanly loveliness.

The tiredness in him deepened, and, looking out over the slanting roofs, all dark, he could see the glowing cinders of the growing mountain come tumbling down the slope like a mass of whirling, bouncing lights, many-colored and incredibly brilliant, even beautiful in some bizarre and terrifying way. By looking out the other window of the corner room, he could see the harbor. On some nights the water was glazed with light and looked like glittering blood; at other times it coruscated wildly; and on certain nights its surface held a deathly blue pallor. Often then the self-doubts would return, seeping like poison into his mind: was he, Karl Sveinsson, the man to do what he was foolishly trying to do here?

On one such night, slack and sleepless on the bed, wondering whether he might, after all, be getting older, he of all people, and picturing the lava moving like thick dark honey, relentlessly carrying before it and on it a wall of cooled and hardened volcanic tuff and clinkerlike scoria, he recalled the photographs that he studied every morning. And a question was churned to the surface of his mind: had he looked at something so often that he no longer really saw it?

He dressed swiftly in the chill, an excitement beginning to throb in him. Again then it came to him: that recurring impression that in the black convulsive heart of horror here, he had come quiveringly alive. No longer imprisoned behind a desk, no longer the safe and pampered husband and father, smothered by feminine softness. What he was doing here was hard-edged, it held danger, and it mattered. Win or lose, it mattered mightily.

He clumped down the narrow stairs, and in the reception area on the second floor, as he was about to descend again, he was confronted by a youngish man with a dark red beard, wearing an Irish-tweed hat with a brim, and a down parka instead of sheepskin.

"Mr. Sveinsson." It was the American way of speaking, using the last name so, but Karl was accustomed to it. "Mr.

Sveinsson, I was on my way up to see you, but I didn't want to wake you."

"Damn good idea," Karl said. Another journalist or photographer or whatever—they were everywhere now, onlookers only. "Well?"

"My name's Owen Llewellyn. I'd like to volunteer."

"For what?"

"For work."

Karl studied him: small, not too heavy, gentle of voice, of manner. "It's ball-busting work."

"I've got two of them if that's what you mean."

Karl almost grinned. "I'll put down your name. Assignments are made at 0900 hours. No cameras on the job."

Owen Llewellyn's smile was a twist of lip all but hidden in the red beard. "I already have my pictures. But I've been here for awhile and a man has to sing for his supper."

Karl hesitated a moment, then nodded. He turned and continued down the stairway. Sing for his supper—well, he'd take what help he could get, whatever the motivation and this was a decent enough one. He wished some of the other sightseers and hangers-on shared it. The main headquarters room was dim, a single young man was manning the telephones and sorting files, assigned here because he had burned his left hand somehow. He looked startled to see Karl, who threw on more lights and jotted the name "Owen L" on a notepad because he was damned if he could spell the last name. Then he spread the aerial photographs of the last few days across the long, wide table that served as his desk. He flipped on the aluminum-hooded light and stood studying the pictures.

Then he lit one of his pipes. He *had* been blind. Yes. There it was, clear on each. Along the edge of one of the lava rivers a sort of natural dike of scoria had been formed, building up day by day and blocking the flow. But since that inching movement was toward the west and the cliffs over the sea and not toward the town or harbor, no one had paid it any attention. But there it was—a dam, by God, a barricade holding back the lava!

He whirled to the map on the wall. What if . . . what if, along that irregular red line on the east and northeast edges of the lava field, where the threat was aimed at the streets and buildings of the town itself . . . what if, at the spots where the incursions were most threatening, other barricades, man-made, were constructed? Pumice and scree and tuff—The Bitch's filthy vomit—built up in barriers before the red black muck and slime reached that point. Berms ten or twenty meters high, with long slopes, so that when the lava did reach them, it would be forced to climb up and could not slither or burrow under.

He would have to have more heavy bulldozers now, he would damned well have to have them, and he would get them, somehow, somehow. Throw The Bitch's offal back at her, choke her with it!

He was no longer tired, only impatient and avid to get on with it. The decision made, and knowing he could not sleep now, did not want sleep now, he began arranging the photographs one below the other to determine the areas of greatest danger and where the movement was most swift, even though that swiftness was reflected by only centimeters on the map.

And long before 0900 hours he had the assignments ready.

The machinery worked day and night, the roar and growl and metallic clatter a feeble but satisfying counterpoint to the furnacelike whoosh and detonations of The Bitch.

Later, when the lava reached the three barricades, they held.

And they continued to hold until Black Monday.

During the night, it had turned colder and snow began to fall heavily over all the island. Gusting winds raked every street, every crevice, whipping the snow and falling ash together so that by first light the town had taken on a new, strange face: a salt-and-pepper coating everywhere. Then The Bitch, as if encouraged, exploded to fresh life. In addition to the crater's turbulence, lava fountains erupted again along the fissure, shooting over four hundred meters into the sky. It was all but impossible to work outside. All operations, except for the repairing of machinery, came to a halt. Karl ordered the airfield closed but was informed from the weaving tower, which was being abandoned, that one reconnaissance plane was already aloft and that radio contact had been lost. From the communications center Jonas reported that, because of the ash in the vapors, even radar would not function. And from various vessels offshore came inquiries: had a new eruption begun?

It was then that the first barricade gave way, first undermined, then overwhelmed, and the cinders and lava moved in a massive way, slag and flaming ooze, to ignite and then swallow seven houses.

Karl Sveinsson, his fury hotter than the lava itself, went to assess the damage, to hell with the snow and black wind. Peering at the smoke and debris through his goggles, he felt the doubts creep through him again: could any paltry effort of man have any effect? Who was he to imagine he could outwit and outflank The Bitch and push the muck back down her filthy throat, what the hell did he know about any of this, what in fact was he doing here anyway? Then his wrath turned to something else inside him—something he didn't like. He felt slack and drained, and by the time he had returned to the command post he was feeling old, very old.

In what had once been the hotel lobby, Doctor Pall and the red-haired, red-bearded Yank with the Welsh-sounding name, which Karl could not immediately recall, were waiting. The Yank's eyes were half-closed and dripping fluid which Karl took to be medication of some sort.

Without preliminaries Doctor Pall growled: "This young idiot needs a thorough eye examination by experts. Possibly therapy I'm not equipped to provide. I want him to see a man in the Reykjavik hospital. He refuses."

Karl looked from one to the other. "Why weren't you wearing goggles, Llewellyn?" The name came to his tongue as he spoke. "You know the rules."

"I do," Llewellyn said. "But I was not on duty and you can't take proper photographs with dirty goggles."

"You'll take no more pictures at all if you're blind," Doctor Pall said. Then to Karl: "Your decision."

Karl barked: "Don't I make enough decisions around here?" Then he turned to Llewellyn. "Why the hell do you want to stay? And don't give me any shit about singing for your supper."

Llewellyn took a long moment to consider that question before he said: "Professional reasons."

To which Karl grunted: "You're a liar. But you're no good to me in your condition now, so ship out, first vessel, first plane. Sooner the better. Airfield's closed now and I may have to close the harbor."

A moment, then Llewellyn said: "Aye, aye, General."

This little red-haired sonofabitch was mocking him. "Listen. We've had no casualties to date, and no serious injuries. You think I want The Bitch to blind a photographer?"

He passed on and entered the headquarters room, liking the small Yank in spite of himself and hearing Doctor Pall's voice behind: "What you have in your eyes are very tiny shards of volcanic glass. That's what this so-called ash really is."

The room was crowded with men, coffee fumes filled the air as usual, and a silence fell when Karl entered. He glanced. "Tell me."

It was Jonas who told him: "The barricade along Austervegur has collapsed."

"And . . .?"

"At least twelve houses and the row of stores at Landagata."

Karl nodded. "And the plane?"

"He's made two passes at the strip. The tower tried to send him to Reykjavik but . . ." Jonas shrugged heavily. "He's a fool. Like the rest of us. Coffee, Karl?"

"What the man needs," another voice said, "is a drink."

Karl saw Jonas turn to the other man, who was very tall and blond and handsome, and he saw the other man stiffen his wide, lean shoulders and grin, heard him say: "I was advising the general, Jonas. I haven't had a drop since old Kirkjufell started belching. Remember me?"

"Too well, Arni," Jonas said grimly. "Too well."

Karl didn't know what the hell that was all about—and didn't give a damn. He sat behind the table and tried to contact the airfield tower, until he remembered that it, swaying, had been abandoned, and then sat staring. The faces around him looked bleak and stunned. How many an angry fist was clenched hidden in those pockets? How many struggled secretly with despair, even tears? Was this it then? Had all the work been for nothing after all?

He thought of his wife, his daughters. He thought of all those others on the mainland, wondering. So far, at least, there had been no lives lost. Yet he felt a gnawing pervasive sense of defeat for the first time.

"How many on the island now?" he heard himself ask and heard a strangeness in his voice.

"Karl," Jonas said, "it wasn't your fault the barriers didn't hold."

"How many?" He spoke into a waiting stillness. "Including the volunteers from outside."

A moment passed. Glances were exchanged. He waited. Finally a voice said: "Almost three hundred by last count. But some come, some leave."

Gently then Jonas said: "It's not your fight, Karl."

"It's not that Yank pilot's fight, either. Or that photographer's. Or—how many outside volunteers from how many different countries?"

"Karl, nobody blames . . ."

"Half the people here are here because they *made* it their fight!" Karl shouted, and his voice reverberated in the high room, drowning out the rumble of The Bitch for a moment. "But comes a time, there always comes a time when. . . ."

One of the several telephones sounded. Karl snatched it up, spoke, listened. Then he set it down and, in a totally different and very quiet tone, said: "The plane's on the ground."

In a few minutes now they would have more photographs. Why? To what end?

"U.S. Navy," Karl said then, almost a whisper. "Not their fight, either. Damned fools."

After a long pause, during which those who were there wished they had not come, Jonas poured more coffee. "Listen, Karl. There's not a man here who'd blame you if you deserted."

"Deserted," Karl said, a dangerous edge in his tone. "Every man who leaves now may mean one more life saved."

"If you go," Jonas said, "it will mean many others also will. But it would not be fair for you to consider it that way."

"I was not thinking," Karl said evenly, his eyes meeting those of his friend, "I was not thinking of the word 'desert.' I was thinking of the word 'evacuate.' "

Jonas' gaze did not waver, or harden. "Some of us would stay, regardless."

Karl knew this, of course. He also knew that if he ordered total evacuation, and then The Bitch subsided after destroying the town, he would always wonder whether—somehow, in some way—it might have been saved, and he would hate himself forever. He also knew that if he did *not* order total evacuation, and three hundred lives were lost, he would hope that his would be among those destroyed.

Carefully then he said: "I am thinking, Jonas, of issuing an official order to abandon ship."

He knew, though, that Jonas was aware of this. As were the others listening. He saw Jonas shake his head. "At the point you do that, Karl, you lose the authority to enforce the order."

Karl felt a slow, warm flood of relief inside. How simple then. How easy. But . . . but doing it so, under the circumstances, would be far worse than desertion: it would be a dishonest evasion.

Another telephone sounded. Karl did not move. Jonas took it up. Then, replacing it, he said: "One of the two water lines to the mainland has been severed."

Only that.

Then a burly man whom Karl recognized as one of the younger geologists asked, in English: "May I say something?"

Karl nodded. "Join the party," he said, also in English.

"There have been surges of lava below the water. We can't determine exactly where but that doesn't matter." He cleared his throat. "They've caused the seabed of the harbor itself to rise. Unless, or until, it returns to normal, none of the larger ships can dock."

What he was telling Karl was that it would be impossible to remove three hundred people in the few small craft moored in the harbor now. "Why wasn't I told this?" Karl asked.

"I don't know sir."

"Christ," Karl snarled. "Boreholes, magnetic fields, lava temperatures, pyrometers, tiltmeters!" He stood, wishing he had not. "Island crawling with scientists, but not a one of you willing even to make a *guess* as to how long The Bitch will go on puking her filthy insides on us!" Ashamed, he could not stop himself. "I beg for information, day upon goddamned day, and then when you do have some, you keep it a secret!"

Appalled at himself, he saw the young man's face drain and stiffen—Englishman from the look of him, only a boy.

"Our job here," the young man said, "is to observe, sir. For future reference."

"Future? *What* future? If the island explodes, if things go on like this, if we all smother or choke or . . ."

Abruptly then he subsided. He looked about, abashed—incredulous. Every face was tense, waiting, and he saw sadness in eyes.

Then, in an altogether different tone, he asked: "What's your name, son?"

"Hawkins, sir. Arthur."

"Mr. Hawkins, I apologize."

"No need for that, sir. Black day for all of us." He cleared his throat again. "No offense taken." He threw a challenging glance around the room. "By any of us." And then to Karl, directly: "Hereafter I'll report personally, sir."

"If you don't stop calling me 'sir,'" Karl said, "I'll be tempted to tell you what to do with your tiltmeter. If it's pointed enough."

Arthur Hawkins grinned. There was laughter. The sound grew. Jonas clapped Karl on the back, hard.

And then two others entered, wearing flying uniforms, one a shambling bearlike man of late middle age, the other a thin, gangling boy. Both were covered with black and white and both approached the table with swaggering defiance or pride.

"The pictures are being developed upstairs," the middle-aged man said to Karl. "Nasty day, ain't it?"

"We always get a few like this during Lent." Karl sat down. "Coffee?"

"Coffee?" The pilot sounded shocked.

"*Brennivan.* Whiskey. Third drawer over there. Help yourselves."

"More like it, man!"

Karl flipped some papers, busying himself by doing nothing in particular. Imagine those two: damned idiots both. Whose fight was this anyway?

But the shadow in his mind deepened. He could ask Jonas to radio for more small vessels. If they waited too long, if they waited much longer . . .

"Excuse me, Mr. Sveinsson."

Karl looked up—into the face of a man he had seen about but had not met. A scholarly face, small and thin. He had spoken in English, but not with an American accent or even an English one.

"May I introduce myself?" He had thinning gray hair and a neat mustache. "My name is Alexei Varanin." He nodded pleasantly, and his eyes, behind thick gold-rimmed glasses, were huge ebony marbles. "I am one of your despised scientists."

To his own amazement, Karl stood and shook the man's hand, which was thin but surprisingly strong. The man was tall, with wide, spare shoulders, which looked somewhat frail. Then Karl lit his pipe. "My name's Karl Sveinsson, but they have other names for me around here."

"I must apologize for not speaking your language, Mr. Sveinsson. And even my English is not of the best." He smiled with schoolmasterly indulgence, as he said: "You, sir, demand the impossible."

Karl nodded. "It's the only way I know to get it."

"What a volcano will do is not scientifically predictable. Like the actions of a man gone mad. My business, you see, is . . . that is, I think of myself as a doctor of volcanoes."

But Karl was thinking of the photographs being developed upstairs: what could they possibly reveal that he did not already know? And how could they affect his decision? "Well, Doctor," he said, "if you have any idea how to cure that insane bitch out of here, open your kit bag."

Alexei Varanin lit a cigarette. "Cure? No. All one can do is to attempt a prognosis. At this stage, however, even that is a dangerous undertaking. But"—he shrugged—"based on instinct and a superficial diagnosis, I should say that Kirkjufell will continue to rant and rage for some extended period."

Now Karl was listening, alertly. "How extended?"

The shrug again, the professorial smile again. "You see—the impossible. But I shall venture a prediction: months at least, perhaps a year, possibly more."

Karl knew he should be grateful: it was more than any of the others had risked. But he felt a further collapse inside and wondered whether he had not come closer to the decision. Irked, he sat and knocked out the bowl of his still-burning pipe. Why the hell should he believe this man's word?

"Now if you had summoned me during the early symptoms, I should have been able to tell you yes or no whether it would erupt. That is really what I am most expert at."

"The Bitch showed no symptoms!" Karl snarled. "She went berserk and that's it!"

"Yes. A most unsatisfactory foe, this Kirkjufell." Alexei Varanin began to drift toward the door at the far end of the room. He walked with his wide, thin shoulders canted sideways, like a sailboat tacking into the wind, but with his dignity and detachment intact.

"Jesus Christ," Karl muttered.

Jonas sat in the chair beside his. "When that gentleman talks," he said, "pay heed."

"If that gentleman's correct," Karl said, "we may as well fold up our tents."

"Doctor Varanin is the world's leading volcanologist. There aren't many of them. He goes all over the world whenever a volcano begins to make noises. And he's the only one who goes down into the crater itself to predict whether it will explode."

Watching the tall frail man disappear, Karl said it again: "Jesus Christ." But beneath the shock and incredulity he felt a strange surge of something that was close to joy or hope.

"Down into the bubbling guts," Jonas went on. "Temperatures one hundred and fifty degrees Fahrenheit. Only man alive who does it. Good man to have aboard."

But the man had to be sixty-five years old. He couldn't weigh more than a hundred and fifty pounds. If that man could go down into a crater threatening to erupt . . .

The photographs arrived. Routinely, but without any expectation that they might lead him to the decision that he knew he must make soon, he compared the new photographs with the ones of the last three days. Because of the weather conditions today, the lava lines were not as distinct as on the others. He rose and turned to the map on the wall and was about to make the red mark to conform to the new pictures in his hand. But he did not make the mark.

Instead, he took the pipe from his mouth, rearranged the aluminum-hooded light and spread the fresh photographs across the table again, bending over them.

"Well?" Jonas asked.

Without speaking or even glancing at the other man, Karl now turned to the wall map again. He began drawing the red lines. They revealed the lava's slow inexorable encroachment; they showed the deep charge into the town where the two barricades had collapsed. But then, without pausing, he continued the lava line to the northeastern quadrant of the map, then stepped back and studied it.

What the red line exposed was that one of the main rivers of lava, until now moving harmlessly toward the sea in a diagonally northeastern direction, had changed course.

The river was clearly, but almost imperceptibly, turned in the direction of the harbor.

Karl turned away.

Jonas moved closer, studied the red marking, realized its significance, and then he too turned away.

They stood in silence.

Then music suddenly blared from above. Someone had placed a record on the phonograph in the recreation area. The sound throbbed through the walls. With the happy sound of wooden clogs in it, the music drowned out the steady rumble that their ears had become so accustomed to.

Both men, Karl knew, were sharing the same thought, the same knowledge: even if every building in town were destroyed, they could be rebuilt, but if that narrow mouth of harbor should be closed, there would be no reason to rebuild. Without the harbor there could be no town.

Jonas' eyes asked Karl the question which, without really thinking, Karl answered: "We'll move all equipment and build a new dam *here*." His pipestem stabbed the map at a point between the lava river and the harbor. "Every piece of machinery in town."

Jonas did not smile, even faintly, but he asked: "How can we do that and evacuate at the same time?"

"What the hell good would it be to order evacuation," Karl growled, "if no one's going to follow the order anyway? Zipper up."

Jonas did grin then. "You expect men to work in this weather?"

But Karl was already striding along the room to the door. "Zipper up, I said. There's a slight breeze out there, they tell me."

The music with the thumping sound, like that of people gaily dancing, reverberated through the entire building as they left it together and went out into the dim street and the icy blast of wind.

FIVE

AFTER THREE WEEKS on Heimaey, the day and night tumult and barrage and violence, Owen Llewellyn found it difficult to adapt himself to the tranquility of the snug, clean house twenty miles from Reykjavik to which he had returned after two days in hospital. Outside, the fields stretched away, white and uncorrupted by dark ash, the snow falling softly, and silently. Here was an island, too, but of a different sort; here, the pulse of life held no sense of desperation, or fear. Now that he was again in the house from which he had gone on the morning of the eruption, Owen was even more conscious of what it really was: an oasis of warmth and certitude and quiet joy. Why then did he continue to feel, as before, that ever-present detachment? If he had been an outsider in Vestmannaeyjar, he was even more of an outsider here.

While Todd Squier spoke, describing the disaster fund to which every Icelander contributes through taxes, his tall, slim, and fair-haired wife sat folded and relaxed on the sofa, listening and half-smiling at her husband's pride in his adopted country. In times such as this, Todd explained, the money was then available for those who could not work, those who had lost their homes or places of business. Owen half-listened, sipping the tart-sweet wine, its thin redness catching the light, the same homemade wine that he had enjoyed before, on that other night when he had sat wondering at this same sense of detachment only hours before he

had stepped from the plane into the falling sparks and dazzling fireworks, aghast yet quickened to intense life by the
sinister splendor.

And now tonight—what was happening here? It was ex-
traordinary. During the two hours since he had met her, he
found his eyes returning over and over to the other guest,
the woman—or was she a girl really?—who had been living
here since that same night, arriving by boat at about the same
time he had been flying in the opposite direction. Every time
he looked at her, he could feel a thickness in his throat.
Watch it, friend, he told himself, watch yourself now, it's only
the wine, the light, the cheer, and the incredible quiet. But
his gaze returned to her over and over.

Now Todd was boasting that Iceland was the oldest
commonwealth on earth, its parliament, called the Althing,
having been established more than a thousand years ago.
"And every year since, at Midsummer, the Althing convenes
at Thingvellir, It's like our Fourth of July, Owen, only it's
called the Midsummer Festival. There's a great celebration
there—it's a volcanic plain, really—with all sorts of festivities,
even poetry readings. But music, too and dancing. They say
more romances begin that time than any other. True, Margret?"

Owen was startled, seeing pain cut into the lovely
green-tinted blue of her deep-set eyes. Until now, he had
seen tranquility there, composure, a strange, blissful expression that seemed also to be sadness, punctuated once in a
great while by a brightening, accompanied by a wide smile or
a rich womanly laugh. And he had listened with strange
satisfaction to her voice, which seemed to have a lilt in it,
even when she spoke English. The children, now in bed, had
seemed to love her as much as Mal obviously did. Yet she
seemed to be, like himself, not wholly a part of this. Her hair
was a glimmering black and her face fine-boned, even
fragile, with skin that seemed almost translucent.

And her eyes, meeting his from time to time, were always direct but impersonal, those of a frank and innocent
child. Yet the fact of her womanliness had invaded his

senses. There was a glow about her, a vivid glow! Now, though, having caught that quick, sharp flash of pain when the Midsummer Festival was mentioned, he knew that it—or one like it, perhaps on Heimaey—held some cruelty personal to her.

Mal was speaking now—of the monies flowing in from all over the world, from the most unlikely places. "The world is most kind."

And the enchantment returned: the quiet, time in abeyance, the snow falling, this lovely child-woman sitting upright and again serene and inscrutable. All of it seemed to kindle a new and different excitement in him. But anger streamed through his entrancement too. Wariness. He knew the snares of this sweet domesticity, the cruel illusion of romantic poignance, as its radiance dimmed to bitterness, regret, even hate. He had been through it, it was not for him ever again, and to hell with it.

So he remained apart, a familiar safe stance, observing, not only her and the other two, but himself as well. They were speaking now of the calmness of the people on the first night as they boarded the rescue craft. Mal thought the Viking tradition, the warrior blood, may have bred that composure—and for some reason mysterious to Owen, he saw Margret look away. But then, as if to draw her mind off whatever was stabbing it and taking the brightness from her eyes from time to time, she spoke: could it be that they were all more or less fishermen and, so, accustomed to the possibility of disaster? There seemed to be some agreement among the refugees themselves that there had been no panic because of the time that the eruption occurred: at that hour of night all families were together, so of course there was no cause to worry. And this time Owen saw the enigmatic, beautiful woman simply close her eyes—and again he wondered.

Todd quoted an Icelandic novelist who had been interviewed by the press: this man of letters had conjectured that the Vikings who had settled Iceland had been fortunate that they had captured Irish slaves and princesses and brought them here; the Irish strain, he suggested, gave the Icelanders of today a poetic quality, and it was this fierce love for their homeland and faith in it that was now making so many of the island people, now exiled, vow to return.

Having just left the ravaged island, Owen wondered whether there would be anything to which to return, but he remained silent.

"Look at Margret!" Todd said. "An Irish princess if I ever saw one. Can you imagine *her* not going back?"

And the girl—for she could be scarcely more than that—opened her eyes. She appeared startled. And then she said: "I can imagine it, yes." There was a silence. The snow continued to fall, silent, white and soft. Without any suggestion of apology, Margret then went on: "There are many who have already decided they won't. Not many perhaps, but some I know."

"Is that because they are afraid it could happen again?" Todd asked.

Margret nodded her dark head. "For some, no matter whether they would admit that or not. But of those I've spoken with, only the few. Some believe it can never be the same there. My sister, for instance—her children keep asking, but she refuses to say yes or no, but I know she's made up her mind to stay in Reykjavik. Her husband, though he has a job here now, is determined to return. So it goes." She shrugged and a smile flashed white in her pale oval face. "Some can't make up their minds—oh, not because it's too early, although it is, but because they wait for someone else to decide, or some event." And then her face grew solemn and her blue eyes found Owen's and she said: "The town may not be there when it's over. That's what you were thinking earlier, wasn't it?"

Owen's astonishment deepened. And he found himself unable to take his gaze from hers. "And what about you?" he heard himself asking, very softly, very gently, recalling the pain and bewilderment of a few minutes ago at the mention of the festival, the Viking tradition. "*Have* you made up your mind not to go back?"

She did not answer at once. Her eyes darkened. And

held his. But even then she did not reply directly. "There will be many, I think, who will realize what they have had, but too late. Is that always so, I wonder?"

A telephone sounded in another room. Todd excused himself and disappeared. Mal poured more wine into Owen's glass.

"Well?" Margret prompted Owen. "Do you think that's true?"

His red beard twisting with his crooked grin, he said: "I mistrust all sentences with the word 'always' in them. They prove inaccurate—always."

The laugh came as he had hoped it would—deep and low and merry and oddly intoxicating—and her eyes narrowed to vivid blue slits of light. And Owen Llewellyn decided he wanted no more wine, after all: the girl herself had made him drunk, wildly, with joy in it.

The telephone, however, was for her. Margret, and Owen saw the face go soft to firm, the eyes open, going flat, and he watched her slim body rise, a sliver of grace, and then Todd uttered only, "Arni's mother in Reykjavik," and the girl was gone from the room. And the room seemed somehow to dim.

Todd and Mal spoke together in quick Icelandic and Owen watched the snow, which was now drifting thinly in the windless dark. Then Todd was apologizing in English: he was sorry but since Margret was their guest they had become concerned about her. Her husband's mother owned one of the largest and most luxurious homes in Reykjavik—and, in fact, Margret had all but decided to go there when Todd met her on the dock in Thorlakshofn.

"At first," Todd said, "I thought she was just glad to see me, but I realized on the way here that she was really only relieved not to have to go there."

Mal said: "The way Margret puts it, the woman offers too much even in a disaster. She offers her house and all that goes with it. And what goes with it is the woman herself. We have all kinds of people in Iceland, as you do elsewhere, Owen."

"What the old . . . what the woman just told me is that

Arni was there and that he was no longer drinking. Since Margret's never said, I didn't know he did. Of course the whole thing may be only a ruse to get Margret to the woman's house."

"Whatever," Mal said then, "whatever now, we can hope. Because Margret does love the boy."

Love.

"Arni?" Owen asked. "Would that be the schoolteacher?"

"You know him?"

"We were on the same crew, from time to time." One of those tall, blond Vikings, handsome, with a great charming smile. "He wasn't drinking when I saw him. But of course that may be because we were working on roofs."

What he was also remembering was that this Arni had worked so hard and steadily that some of the others had laughingly begged him not to shame them.

Love.

Did it mean that now Margret, for whom he had come so suddenly to feel this powerful and bewildering affection, this damned enchantment which he resented, resisted, did it mean that now she would go off to this man and whatever he, Owen, felt toward her would have to wither into only a nostalgic memory of these few hours and then, hopefully, die from his mind and blood?

And then she was in the room again. He saw her face and he cursed in silence. Sober now, abstracted, anxious, she refused to allow her eyes to meet his. Or did he imagine this?

"May I take your Landrover, Todd?" she asked. Then she shook her head. "No. I probably won't be coming back."

In spite of—or because of—the new poisonous defeat still and hard in him, despite the ulcerous sense of having seen a light go out and wishing to rekindle it at any cost, Owen said: "I have rented one. I'll drive you." And then, seeing her dark brows draw together in a frown over eyes that now held nothing for him or toward him, he rushed on, feeling foolish, adolescent: "I'm flying back to Vestmannaeyjar tonight anyway."

"But . . . but your eyes," she said.

His eyes. She needed an excuse for not going with him. He had told them of his two days in hospital, that the final tests indicated no permanent damage from the volcanic glass. And she knew he had driven up here himself. Well, to hell with it then: if she didn't want to ride with him, it was so. What was another hour anyway?

Todd then, with an apologetic glance toward Owen, offered to take her into the city.

Suddenly, as if dismayed and amused at herself at the same time, whatever the root of her reluctance, she laughed. "Forgive me, Mr. Llewellyn. I'm grateful to go with you."

It was Owen's turn to be reluctant then. He didn't really care for the way that laugh made him feel. Nor did he really care for the drained shot-away feeling in himself as he saw her move lithely toward the hall.

There seemed to be always a bustling in the house, comings and goings, and people of all ages, but especially children and the young folk with high color in their cheeks, and all this going on at all hours so that sometimes Hulda Palmadottir did not know day from night. And the whole place seemed abrim with sound, especially laughter, and music day and night. Hulda Palmadottir realized, of course, that she was more than eighty years old now and that it was natural that sometimes she should be somewhat confused, especially by the names of these people whom she did not know, but, nevertheless, she felt that somehow, by some miracle too overwhelming to question, she had emerged from a world of shadows and now was, again, alive. In some ways it was as if her immediate past, all those years in the resthome with the others waiting to die, it was as if all that had happened years and years ago now, even the volcano—and she knew that had

begun only a short time ago, only a few weeks, so they told
her. But had not all that really happened to someone else?
What was taking place around her day to day was now so
vivid and alive that Hulda Palmadottir simply refused to believe that she was . . . no, not eighty, but eighty-three, because she had been twelve when the first boats with motors
came to Vestmannaeyjar and that was in 1902, she could
recall certain things very clearly, yes very.

Aware that the Turks had indeed returned and of what
was still occurring on the island that she had never left until a
few weeks ago, Hulda suffered certain twinges of guilt. She
had heard, for instance, that Freydis, the poor soul who saw
strange people who were always stealing from her and who
hated her—she knew that Freydis had died in the hospital
here in Reykjavik. But then Freydis had wished aloud for her
own death, and often—might it be that the volcano had released her from a prison that she hated? And there were
others—oh yes, Lars, the man who sat beside her on the bus
on the way to the airport, the old fisherman who had the
nephew who had walked with such pleasure with the red-
haired girl and had then gone to sea—Lars, too, had died, so
she had been told, but then the paralyzed man had been
scarcely alive anyway. And she knew of the houses going and
the streets covered with black, because it was all on the television, but she no longer watched. Heimaey, her own island,
had come to seem far away, even faintly foreign. How this
had come about was a mystery, too, but not one that she
spent much time pondering. She was too busy here; there
was too much always going on here!

Arriving at the airport that night, disoriented and yet
determined, realizing that she had left her dental plates and
would probably never see them again, and feeling therefore
somewhat foolish, for Hulda Palmadottir had always been a
vain woman, and with fine cause in years past—what should
she hear on the crackling loudspeaker but her own name?
Stunned, she thought at first only of her teeth, but she was
then met by a middle-aged woman who looked not even
vaguely familiar. The woman hugged her, spoke her name,

then called her mother—and she knew. Her son's widow, her son who had been dead so long, lost at sea like his father, and now this woman trying to smile, could this be the child who had become such a young widow and had then gone to the mainland and without a word after leaving?

Yes. Och, it was an amazement.

And now, while Hulda might become confused as to names and perplexed by the activities here—although she knew, of course, that the woman had married a mainlander, and she knew, too, that some of the children and young people were, not this woman's children, but her grandchildren indeed—she often wondered whether she herself could possibly have been the same woman who, such a brief time ago, had considered walking with dignity into the sea, who had felt only useless and rootless. Impossible: she would not believe it. How many years ago—no, centuries surely—had it been since she had been kissed by a child? Now it happened all the time.

She had returned to life. She no longer had to strain to remember in order to know she was living.

Why, she scarcely ever thought of death now, and never of her own. She doubted she would ever die.

Arni Loftsson was in his mother's house again, the high apricot-colored house across the street from the lake in the center of Reykjavik, where he had spent his childhood, but where he had known only sparse happiness and little joy. He had, in spite of this, grown into a man of good cheer and smiles and a certain exuberance—the qualities that, he suspected, had caused Margret to fall in love with him. But, for a time, these qualities—which he himself also prized—had disappeared, swallowed and drowned in the black death which, he had imagined, had kept his spirit alive. When, in fact, it had been the *brennivan* that had almost killed that spirit. Now, however, bone-weary from the work on Heimaey, grit in every pore no matter how many times he bathed, stunned by the quiet so that at first he had found himself shouting at his mother, as it was usually necessary to shout on the island—now he had come to see Margret. On the night of the eruption, when he had discovered her note and had then searched wildly for her at her sister's house and then through the desolate fire-lighted streets before dropping to lie unconscious, while hell itself exploded around him—at the end of that night, finding himself in the utter degradation that he had always scorned and feared, sick then and sober, vengeance then a dry, dead memory only, he had made up his mind. And since that time, in spite of all the drinking by others during the brief nights between work and work, he had proved to himself—to himself, proudly!—that he could take his own destiny in his own hands, despite the gods' skein, he would defy them! Now, the proof solid in him, he had come to reveal it to Margret, whom he loved. Whom he had always loved. To whom he had been cruel—the memory sickened him.

Upon his arrival his mother—out of politeness he hoped, or whatever—had offered him a drink. He had refused. And, slumped and almost limp with exhaustion now that he had let go, he had looked into her face: the hook of a nose, the heavy jut of a chin, the silver hair, the dark eyes quick to ferocity. He had listened to her litany of complaints: she could not imagine, no, she could not *believe* that any intelligent woman, offered this house—look at it, look around, how many houses in Iceland, anywhere, compared to it?—offered all of this, why would a woman choose to pass her time in a primitive farmhouse in the countryside? And with strangers! He had not bothered to remind his mother that Mal, now married to the American, was Margret's cousin and that they had been friends since childhood. Listening, though, he heard another, unworded but even more familiar strain, and he had grown angry—not at Margret, but at his mother. Why had she always hated Margret so? Because he, having met Margret at Festival there, had decided to go to Vestmannaeyjar to live? To hell with it. To hell with all of it.

His mother, she informed him, had telephoned Margret once she knew he was on his way from the airport. What had she said? No knowing. No divining. For if he asked, she would lie as quickly and easily as she would tell the truth. Depending on what she wished to believe. Depending on what she wished *him* to believe.

Margret.

She would be here soon. This was all that mattered now.

"I take it then," his mother was saying, "I take it that since you're here, she decided to tell you. Finally."

"Tell me what, mother?"

"If not she, then your friend Doctor Pall must have."

"Mother, I do not know what you are talking about."

"I can't believe it."

"Then don't," he said curtly and stood to pace. Sooner or later in this house he found himself pacing up and down. "I don't believe it, either. Whatever it is."

"Don't turn your back on me. All my life people have been turning their backs on me."

"I didn't come to talk about my father. Or about you, Mother."

He was, nevertheless, remembering her tearless grief when she told him—at age eleven, because he was old enough, she said, to know—how his father had died. But he had heard the shot from his father's study. He had already known.

But to hell with all that, too—the dead burden of a dead and hated past threatening revival in his mind.

He had come here to see Margret. Only that.

"Shall we talk about you then, Arni? Possibly you should have a drink. Would you like for me to pour it?"

"I don't want a drink. I told you I . . ."

"Forgive me, I forgot. But I am proud of you, Arni. Truly. It would not do for a young father to drink as you once . . ."

"Father?" He halted. The joy left no room for shock in him. He stood quite still and let the exultancy flow sweetly through his blood. "Did Margret tell you?"

"A woman knows." Her eyes flashed dark and fierce and knowing.

His childhood returned. The lies. The evasions, the wisdom from mountaintops, unquestioned, imperious last word always. Infallible female intuition, omniscient!

"But how can you be sure of it . . ."

"Why else would she refuse my hospitality here? Unless, shamed, she was afraid I would learn?"

"Shamed? What are you talking about?"

"Why else would she not tell you?"

"What are you saying?" he growled hollow all through.

"If you don't believe me ask your Doctor Pall."

Baffled now, unmoving, Arni asked aloud: "Why would he tell you and not me?"

"Possibly he assumed you knew." The great face was lifted, cold and shrewd. "That, or Margret instructed him not to inform you."

But why? Why?

"The doctor told me only because I said I was caring for the girl and needed to know whether she was lying to me or not."

His mind was reeling. Lying. There it was again. Margret lying. His mother lying to Doctor Pall.

"Why the hell should Margret lie?"

"Possibly because she was afraid of what you might do."

More bewildered now—what could Margret imagine he would do, and why?—he shook his lean head and wandered away from his mother's chair. The joy was a dead thing in him now. A stone. Worse—a jagged rock, sharp and turning. "Why should I do anything?" He heard the bafflement echoing in his voice, almost unrecognizable to himself.

"You do look as if you need a drink now. You have always had a violent nature, Arni."

He did not want a drink. No. Well, perhaps only one. To clear his mind. But he did not move.

"There's only one reason," his mother said, her tone almost a whisper, "that I can imagine why your own wife would not tell you a thing like this . . ."

"Shut up," he said.

"One reason she should fear what you might . . ."

The room had gone blinding bright. "Shut up!" he cried. Now the room was suddenly dim. And hate choked him, he could feel it blackening his soul, it blanked his mind.

"A woman knows another woman's reasons."

"Don't speak of Margret as if she were you!" he shouted.

His mother stared at him then. Time passed. Finally she nodded. "So. So . . . you know then."

"I think I've always known," he said through tight teeth.

And it was true. Yet not true. He had never been sure. He had always been too terrified to say it. Until now. A suspicion only, shadowing his boyhood, his youth, his life. He had never been certain. Until now.

"I never really knew," he heard his low voice saying, an icy wind from the pole. He shook his head again. "Isn't that the oddest thing, damndest thing of all?"

"It proves only that I know how Margret feels. I can understand why she was afraid to tell you. You're not like your father. He was not a violent man. I hope that now you can understand, though, how I could guess her condition without being told."

In another vivid, painful instant of clarity, he said: "You could never bear to see us happy, could you?"

His mother rose. "You will not put the guilt on me."

"Happy or even together."

"I have known ever since you left your own home to go live on that island your life was a ruin. Volcano or no volcano."

He whirled about blindly and went to pour himself a brandy. She always had brandy. He drank. Deeply. It did no good whatever.

"You went there," his mother said to his back, "you went over there to be with her."

Arni spoke softly then, without turning—but no bafflement this time, only a certainty that he had not known until now. "No. I went there to get away from you."

He drained his glass. And waited for the heat that didn't come.

Then he faced her. And enjoyed what he saw. Relished it. The warmth was beginning inside him now. A deep curling warmth. So he turned to pour another. To the brim.

The rage was cold, though. The brandy did not reach it.

When he looked at her again, he saw tears in her eyes.

He had never before seen tears in her eyes.

It was a beautiful sight.

He drank.

There was no place for pity in him. A Viking warrior had to be bold, utterly ruthless, and now he must do what he had to do. To avenge his honor. He must know the man, too. He would learn the name of the man.

But a single doubt flickered in his mind, which was now becoming very sharp, very clear. "Why would Margret come here, to me, if what you say is true?"

His mother's tears were gone. She sat in the great chair again and lifted her head proudly. Her hair looked like a silver helmet, like the ones the women of the sagas wore. "I told her that if she did not come, tonight, you would go there."

He stiffened to his full square-shouldered height. It was true: If she did not come—and soon—he would go to find her. His eyes were burning. The cold, though, was sharp inside his body. The heat, intense now, was only in his head.

"Is that not what you would do?" his mother asked. "Did I not speak the truth?"

"For once," he said. "Once in your whole miserable hateful lifetime."

Then he hurled the glass, empty again, at the wall over her head. She did not flinch. He stood tall and strong, no longer weary, every muscle aching for furious action.

He was in a clean, white room with windows. There were other people, sometimes in the room, always in the halls, and most of them were pleasant enough, although he didn't know them. Most of them smiled at him, some seemed to smile from inside at their own thoughts and not really at him at all, and some who smiled one day looked angry and glared the next, and there were some who waved their arms and even shouted or laughed out loud at nothing whatever or cried tears, and some who begged him in sad little voices and called him by strange names that were not his. Then there were those in the white clothes who treated him gently enough and gave him the food that also tasted strange, most of which he could not eat, did not wish to eat, all part of this strange place that was a pale yellow building with many windows, one above the other in rows. But no one explained to him why he was here and not on the farm with the lighthouse beacon flashing and the cows and ewes and his own cave safe up in the cliff with the water far below. And where was Odin? Odin had been with him that night when he saw the new Surtsey, but since time had no meaning for him in here where he couldn't see the weather or how the sky was changing or the way the animals and birds behaved, he had no idea how long ago it had been since he had gone running toward the new Surtsey on his own island—and he remembered the fear in the eyes of the people, which had made him afraid then too, and whenever he thought of Odin, he wondered what might have happened to the dog, whom he loved, whom he ached for, and now without Odin and in this cold-looking, angular place of echoing walls and windows, he was alone.

His father had come, though, and they had sat together, and he had seen the pain in his father's broad, flat face, and watched the ridges of muscle clenching in that great jaw and had wondered at the misery in his father. But when he had asked questions—when would he see his birds again, was it time for the puffins to come back?—it seemed to deepen that awful look in his father's eyes, so he stopped asking and sat in silence until his father said it was time to go now. Joy had split his heart in that instant—to go, to leave this place, to go to where he knew the sounds and the sky and could see those lights pale and beautiful to the north! But no, and he saw his father's sadness deepen still more: no, the authorities, his father said softly, the authorities say he must stay here where he can be cared for properly. Josef again did not know what that meant because he had never felt, even that night of explosion when his father followed him and Odin to the building with the dead birds and fishes, then took them both to the boat—even that night he had never felt that anyone had to care for him. Not the way he, for instance, cared for the ewes and lambs and for Odin.

There was often snow out the windows and white on the buildings and he could see across a highway where cars traveled always, headlamps burning, and he could hear the wind howling—although not the way it snarled and bellowed when he was in his cave above the water—and he kept telling himself that when the snow was gone, then the days would be longer and perhaps there would be some sun and then, then of course, they would come and take him, and soon then he would be where he belonged, where he had been happy and never alone.

But now. His mother came often but never his three sisters who were, his mother said, working in the city now. This puzzled him, but he did not much miss his sisters. What astonished him, so that he would often think about it through the night while snug in the crisp, white sheets (he wished for his own *dyna*), was that his mother came to see him so often. Sometimes he thought that she was with him more now than when they were living in the same house by the sea and far from the village. Her dark eyes still hot with anger, they were also distant, and he knew that she was not angry at him, or at anything he had done; the fury he saw in her hard-boned face was not even the malice she had so often vented on his sisters and his father—it was a different, a deeper and more general rage. When he had dared, only once, to ask why he was there and why they were not all together again on Heimaey, her face had contorted and she had uttered such a low and terrible sound that he had felt cold and afraid. But not for himself. Was her wrath turned on the new Surtsey and what it may have done to their house and farm? Or was it, as he suspected wordlessly, directed against some broader and more pervasive power—those "authorities," as his father called them—that kept him locked in here and prevented him from leaving whenever he tried? Yes, yes—he knew why she was so furious, and he tried to comfort her with words and by taking her wrinkled hand into his, feeling its hard roughness. Once, when he did this, she smiled. It was a sad smile and seemed to come from far off somewhere, but he had never seen his mother smile before, just as he had never held her hand before.

Once, when he asked, she told him that his father had gone to Heimaey: he was getting the farm in readiness for the return of the sheep. And it was then that Josef knew that it would not be long now before he, too, would go back, even though his mother shook her head.

Yes, soon, soon. Certainly when the puffins came back and the days were long again.

The snow was wispy in the air, whirling, gusting white against the windshield but level and thick across the fields and gathered in treacherous drifts on the road itself. Owen Llewellyn drove with an alert and easy grace that seemed to Margret to be a part of his nature. Small stature—Margret was accustomed to taller, larger-framed men—he looked tight-muscled, wiry, and his red beard framed a face that

looked proportioned and that might even be handsome except for the nose, which appeared to have been broken.
Suddenly she longed to know how it had been broken; suddenly this became very important to her. And she was
amazed at herself. Again. As she had been amazed back
there in the house where she had, almost rudely, refused his
offer to drive her into the city. Had she actually been reluctant to sit here like this, alone with the man?

Yes.

But why, why?

Because she had also desired it, had almost physically
lusted for it? Confusion engulfed her, and a curious sense of
guilt. This Owen Llewellyn, about whom she knew so little,
had had a curious and upsetting effect on her. Mystifying.
And stirring. In the meantime, she sat on the high seat beside him on her way to her husband. To Arni, who loved her.
Whom she loved.

Whom she still loved.

After some vague exchange about the tradition of hospitality in Iceland stemming perhaps from that Irish strain that
Todd had mentioned—Owen told her that in ancient Ireland even a stranger entered when he liked, stayed while he
would, and left when he wished, and to refuse him was tan-
tamount to a crime—they seemed, both, to have run out of
words and had retreated into silence, staring ahead.

Could she believe, really believe, that Arni had stopped
drinking? Her sister's husband had returned to Vestmannaeyjar and, while he had found their house miraculously
intact, he had discovered that it had been ransacked, as if
some madman had searched it furiously. And Margret knew:
Arni searching first, perhaps, for her and then, realizing she
had gone, for *brennivan.* But her sister's husband had seen
Arni then: *He was his old self.* Unable to believe—to hope—
Margret had telephoned Jonas at the radio center: it was
true, yes, Arni was working harder than any two other men
and would not even have a social glass. Did she have a message for Arni? No. Not yet, not yet. Doctor Pall had telephoned her to inquire of her health and the child inside. She

had asked him, she had had to ask. And he had growled: *Your husband is behaving. Are you sure you don't want me to tell him about you?* Still, she had hesitated. In disbelief. So she had reminded Doctor Pall of his promise.

Yet Arni's mother had said, only a short time ago now, less than an hour, that Doctor Pall had told Arni of the baby. Could she believe this now? Could she ever believe the woman? Ever vengeful, ever ired by anyone who disagreed or crossed her, hating Margret always . . .

Yet it was this woman who had told her weeks ago that Arni had stopped drinking completely and would not come to see Margret until he had "slain his demon," as he put it, forever. It sounded so like Arni, that phrase. But Arni's mother had then added, on the telephone, that Arni would not come back until he could see Margret in his own home, the one in which he had grown up in Reykjavik. And Margret knew this to be a lie. Could she then believe the other?

Her mind caught in the whirlpool, or quicksand, of contradiction and confusion and trepidation—she was on her way to both of them, *both* of them, now, soon, now—Margret became conscious again, acutely aware, of the man beside her in the close and cozy warmth of the Landrover. The strange excitement returned—and an urgency, for the city's lights ahead, not yet visible, gave a pale illumination to the sky.

"How did you injure your eyes?" she asked.

He laughed. "By being a damn fool."

"Are there many injuries then?"

"Only to damn fools."

"Do they pain you?"

"If I told the truth, I'd be asking for sympathy."

"No. You'd only be telling the truth."

"Is that so valuable then?"

"It is all."

In a moment, he said: "They pain me, but I can see well and will see better."

"It's your business to see, isn't it?"

"To see, yes. But to compose what I see, too. To impose

my vision of what I see on what is there and what others might see differently."

"You say that very well."

"I've never said it before."

This seemed to strike him as even more strange, and she wondered, too.

Then, in his low gentle voice, tinged by an excitement that she had sensed in him all through the evening, he was speaking of his work: how he had already sold some of the photographs of the disaster and that he hoped to have a startling and exciting book of them in time. Then he said: "Hell of a thing, isn't it—to see beauty in something like that? But it's there. A horrible sort of beauty, and frightening. Like glorying in the Apocalypse, perhaps. Makes me feel uneasy at times. I admit it."

"Is that why you work part of the time over there?"

"How'd you know that?"

"Todd told me. But I think . . ." She broke off.

"Yes? You think . . .?"

She went on. "That tonight I might have guessed that."

A brief silence.

Then a shrug: "Well, you can't stay on board and eat the rations without taking an oar, can you?"

"No," she said. "Some people can't."

He turned to face her. She had felt his eyes on her all through the dinner and the evening: a probing caress, a sort of wonderment in his gaze. As though he were amazed at himself. As she had been. As she was now.

He was speaking again then, concentrating on the road glaring white under the headlights. He told of being jarred awake in the house to which he had been assigned, at three o'clock in the morning, by the sound of singing! "Singing, hell—*bellowing*. It went on for two hours, and we all drank and chewed dry haddock, then got up two hours later and went back to shoveling."

"And that surprises you? That they would sing at such a time?"

"Don't misunderstand: I had a fine time."

His astonishment, she realized, was that of an outsider—how different they were, the two of them, after all.
She herself, of course, was not surprised at all—why not sing
in the face of disaster? What continued to startle and perplex
her was herself—her own feelings, now, this minute.

On the outskirts of the city now, its lights glittering
through the small-flaked gossamer snowfall, there were only
the sounds of the motor and the clacking wipers and the
hum of the heater—and a silence again between them.

Until, as if he knew they were moving close to parting,
Owen Llewellyn asked: "Why did you hesitate?"

She knew at once what he was asking, and she hated
herself at once for her reply: "Hesitate to do what?"

"You know what I mean."

And so she did. Hesitate? She had almost refused to
come with him. "You," she said in a whisper, "you also know
why."

Then she realized that they were speaking as if they
were old friends. Or lovers. And they both knew that both
had silently and secretly dreaded and yet anticipated,
perhaps even hoped for, these few precious moments of
quiet intimacy. The realization was frightening.

"I'm pregnant," she said abruptly. "Did you know?"

"No."

And then only the motor, the wipers, the whir of heater,
the crunch of tires on the crusted street. The lights along the
curving approach were glowing a misty blue above. The
windows of the higher buildings were yellow and orange,
and the snow now appeared to have taken on a bluish tinge.
They passed under trees adorned with lights of many colors.

"It's like Christmas at home," she heard him say.

"It's like this always through the winter."

"It's lovely."

"Yes. It's our way of holding back the night, I think."

"Reykjavik's a beautiful city. But at night it's almost unreal. A fairyland of light and color."

"Yes."

"But you don't want to live here."

How had he known that? But she didn't ask.

He knew.

She was picturing Vestmannaeyjar before Kirkjufell: the pinks and greens and yellow and blues of the roofs and walls, the meandering clean and narrow streets, the water of the harbor tranquil and glittering with golden reflections and the sea darker and vaster on all sides. And she was also remembering the photographs she had seen, the reports from those who had gone back, the television view: houses crushed and charred, streets adrift in grit and soot, the flame shooting scarlet and yellow and black, its radiance fragmented and lurid over the water of the harbor.

"Don't go back for a while," he said. "Please."

And again she had that curious sensation, at once disturbing and satisfying, that the man had somehow divined her thought—as if the same pictures flickered through *his* mind, too.

"Will you promise me that, Margret?"

Her throat was closed. She could not speak. She removed one glove. She extended her hand. She placed it over his gloved one on the gearshift knob between them.

He did not turn. But he withdrew his hand. Only for a second or two. Only long enough to strip off his own glove. He replaced his hand, this time over hers, which she had not removed from the knob because she had known what he was doing.

Finally her voice said: "You're kind."

"Not kind," he said softly.

"Yes. And you will forgive me."

"For what, Margret?"

She did not hesitate. "I've never done anything like this before, Owen." She realized that she had spoken his name for the first time, "I don't think I even understand it."

His hand turned hers over then and his took hers into its clasp, palm to palm. The snow fell silently silkenly around the small, warm space.

"I have been wanting to touch you for hours," he said.

And she heard her own whisper. "I know," it said.

She spoke a word at a time. "Right" or "Left" or "Straight," and soon they were moving along the curving edge of the lake lying in the center of the city, a small lake, ice-encrusted now and covered with the snow, and she could see the shadows of low, lighted buildings and houses across it and the two church steeples silhouetted, all pleasantly familiar, suggesting childhood memories of skating, gliding weightless and free over its surface on visits in winter, for there were no ponds or lakes on Heimaey, and in summer when the sun shone, she remembered the water with a luster of gold, and the ducks and the geese floating placidly in family groups, content and . . .

Yes, a beautiful city, as Owen had said. But not home.

Home. Did she have a home now? Would she ever have a home again?

"Here," she said, and as she felt the Landrover slowing, she felt a terrible and almost overwhelming reluctance, not fear but a shrinking of her whole being. She looked at the house. Was it also beautiful? Across the narrow street from the very edge of the lake, it stood tall, flanked closely on each side by two other residences, one pale yellow with a lavender-colored slanting roof, the other white with a roof of turquoise blue. Distinguishing the apricot-colored house were two wide circular windowed bays rising two stories and, above each, wide dormers opening curved balconies.

She was surprised at the repugnance that she felt sour in her now. She sat, very still, unable to move—to take her hand from his, to step out into the cold from this cubicle of warmth, this temporary and illusory shelter.

Owen Llewellyn did not move, either.

She felt his hand, throbbing and firm and strong, locked warmly in hers, and she became conscious of an ache in herself, an urgency almost painful—toward what? to do what?—and from their clasped intertwined hands there came a current that filled her whole body with a strange hollowness, a sweet poignance, tender and rueful and touched by the knowledge of futility and time. And waste.

The world exploded.

She had seen nothing move. No shadow.

She had heard nothing.

Too late she knew: she should not have come with him. With any man.

She was staring, aghast, into Arni's face in the frame of open door which he had wrenched open. Feverish eyes, crazed, blue gone black with hate and fury and certainty now, at last. A rapacious, triumphant beast, not the face of a man.

She heard herself utter a sound. Her hand left Owen's.

She moved as if to descend. He slammed the door at her. She whirled away in time. The vehicle shuddered and the thunder reverberated in her head.

She saw him stalking around the front, his shadow tall and huge in the headlamps' glare. She heard herself scream now, too late, the sound locked in the compartment.

And then she saw and heard the other door opening, a metallic crunching of its hinges.

Then she saw Arni's huge plunging fist and heard the thud of the blow, a flat wooden sound of bone against bone as it smashed into Owen's face. She saw blood.

Arni's hand clutched at Owen's leather jacket, pulling the leaner, thinner body out onto the snow, where it rolled, springing to life, standing swiftly, small but supple against the other, who faced him, and Owen swung once, fast and hard, into the side of Arni's face, and then she was climbing out and down and around, moving through the double beam of yellow headlamps.

They were facing each other then, the two, both breathing hard, their breath jolting from between their lips and out their noses in steamy puffs. In the bluish light from the neon tubes of the streetlamps hanging high above, the snow and the entire nightmarish scene had a sickening pallor. Arni was crouching as if to spring, lips drawing back from gleaming teeth, jaw outthrust, simian—junglelike. Owen looked bewildered, frowning but alert, studying, his beard already matted darkly with blood.

She heard herself call Arni's name. Otherwise there was

only a waiting silence. Then Arni's shoulders lowered, one hand touching the snow-covered cobbles lightly, balancing the wide heavy torso. Owen's hands, one still gloved, were fists hanging along the sides of his slim body, which was splotched white with snow.

She was about to shout again when Arni moved. From his crouching position, with a low snarl, he hurled his great weight forward, charging so fast that Owen had time only to whirl about but not to avoid the impact entirely. Arni's shoulder caught him, he gasped as he went down, rolling again as if to rise, but this time Arni stepped close and kicked him hard, first in the ribs and then, as Owen rolled, struggling for breath, Arni kicked again, this time catching him on the side of the head, possibly on the ear. Owen's face contorted and went white.

Margret could not move. She had to move. She could not.

Arni took another long stride and lifted a heavy boot, but now Owen, on his back, reached out, caught the ankle in one hand and the woolen pants leg in the other, and twisted, wrenching the towering figure, hard, fast, so that Arni went down into the snow.

Then it came again, that wild bestial snarl. Arni struggled to stand. Owen leaped to his feet first, he closed in, he brought a fist down, from above, with quick, sharp power, clubbing the back of Arni's neck. She heard the blow and heard Arni cry out, and then she saw Owen step back and away.

He cast her a single quick glance. Was it of blame? Surprise? Or—impossible to believe, impossible!—was it apology?

"Owen!" she called.

He whirled to see what she had seen. Arni was on his feet again, charging in. But this time, panting still, Owen hunched his shoulders slightly and brought up his fists, like a boxer. But Arni, she wanted to shout to Owen, Arni knew nothing of boxing. He knew only brute force and . . .

Owen's left arm snapped out, quickly, so quickly that she

could not be sure it had struck until she saw blood spurting from Arni's nose.

Then that same lightninglike stab again, Owen's left arm snapping out and back in a series of pistonlike blows hammering Arni's face, which looked bewildered and began to puff up. He tried to move closer, but the gloved hand poked again and again, like a snake's tongue darting. It drummed with maddening rapidity, the blows so close together that they became a single continuous sound.

Arni had had enough. With a wild bellow he moved in, heedless, taking the hammerlike thumps on his face, swinging his right arm sideways, like a club, at Owen's head. But the smaller man's body bobbed to one side, the rhythm of his jabs unbroken, and Arni's massive fist slid harmlessly over Owen's head, taking with it his Irish-tweed hat.

Arni backed away.

Owen moved with him, keeping the face in range.

Now Arni's arms rose to protect his face. He could not. The gloved fist found its way through, kept up its cruel, relentless tatoo.

Arni was retreating, not turning away. He was off the pavement now, only a few steps backwards across a snowdrift and he would be on the edge of the frozen lake.

His arms covered his face now, head almost cradled in the elbow bend, hands over his head, and she could hear a faint, very faint, sound, as of a whimper.

Owen, without hesitation, his left still working, plunged his right deep into Arni's exposed stomach. Arni doubled forward, mouth gaping, eyes widening, and stumbled back onto the ice, his boots sliding under him precariously.

Was it over? She was going to be sick. Was it over?

Owen waited, too. His lithe body was quiet, poised, and she could see his ear where he had been kicked. It was already enormous, and so deeply red that it looked black in this light.

Arni sank to his knees. He was heaving with the effort to breathe. He looked finished, and helpless.

Margret took her eyes from him. She saw an impulse go

through Owen's body—saw it and understood it. This was his chance. If he stepped in now, if he used *his* boot . . .

She shouted.

And then she was running and slipping. She passed Owen. She knelt on the snow-covered ice, close to Arni, not touching him, seeing the puffing red under the flesh and the more brilliant moist red over his face.

He lifted his head. In his face there was an expression that choked off the pleas rising to her throat. His was the face of a maddened beast. His blue eyes were black and hard in swollen sockets. Feral. They looked scorched. They held no flame, only a solid nuggetlike ferocity. She had never seen such brutal, naked savagery.

Hate.

Hate for her.

She could not speak.

For *her.*

She was about to rise. She was cold. She had to warn Owen: leave, leave now.

She was on one knee, her mouth open, when the blow came, and her mind went blank.

At first she did not feel pain, only a desperate need to breathe as her body doubled forward. And then the pain came. She still could not breathe, gasping, retching. The pain was all through her but concentrated, too, hard and harrowing below her breasts. She was on her knees but curled, head down, so that she could feel the snow-covered ice supporting her forehead. And her whole body was heaving. She could taste the wine in her mouth as it rose from her stomach, sour between her lips and wet on her face, but she could not take in the thin air, and everything reeled darkly, dizzily, and behind her closed lids lightning flashed, and she longed for nothingness, which would not come. She heard a crunching on the ice, as of footsteps, and panic took over, terror such as none she had ever known, but the voice she heard at her ear was not his, not Arni's, another voice, but she could not make out the words, only her name, and she lifted her head, breathing again, and forced her eyes to open. Through a shimmering veil she saw a face. Owen. He was whispering. His hands were on her. His arm was reaching beneath her. She had to fight the darkness. Yet she longed for it. She felt herself slide to one side, felt her body go limp, her cheek against the snow now, and then when she looked into Owen's face, she saw behind it that other face, that hated face, but the gnarled knot of agony, solid in her stomach now, was drawing her into nothingness so that she couldn't warn Owen, could not yet utter more than that convulsive choking sound . . .

Then she heard a terrible thud, saw Owen's mouth open in an explosive grimace, eyes bulging, his body arching backwards and begin to pitch forward, and just before the blackness took over completely, she realized that Arni had plunged his boot into the small of Owen's back as he knelt above her. But his weight did not fall on her somehow. She saw the blur of it twist to one side and felt its fall. She tried again to scream, but she was too weak, too breathless, too flooded with pain to do more than to lie there trying to breathe.

But she could hear the blows and the grunts and curses. She could hear the slipping on ice, the crunching and grappling, and she lifted her head and tried to stare through her pain. Now she could see the two bodies, fused as one monstrous whole, thrashing about, and the fine snow rising around it, a face appearing for a hideous second, straining and tortured, furious, and an arm or leg grotesquely thrusting itself into the brutal night air. And she could see, however dimly, the greater weight bearing down on the lesser, and the black sky spun crazily, the convulsion in her became a world-shaking quake, and finally a curtain fell before her vision, then all sounds dimmed, and, finally, she drifted into a vast emptiness without sight or sound or pain.

Doctor Pall had come to reckon time by his own body. When the tiredness threatened to become too much and to invade his mind as well as his muscles and nerves, he would then try to sleep. But tonight, again, the little seaman named Olaf was waiting for him when he returned to the hospital, where he slept, from the first-aid station at command head-quarters. Pall was in no mood for compassion, but it came regardless. There was no doubt that Olaf suffered the pain he described each time he asked for the analgesics and begged for the sedatives he had to have in order to sleep. The surgeon in wherever-it-was—Olaf never seemed to recall exactly—had miraculously repaired the ulnar nerve, but the agony remained, and the cold only made it worse. Pall was aware of all this, too much aware, and this was why he gave the poor man the medicine. But invariably he wondered whether he was doing the proper thing: he suspected addic-tion. No, he was fairly certain. Then what was the ethical procedure? Doctoring, Pall had decided years ago, was a matter of making decisions all day and all night. He, too, was tired of playing god. Leave that to men like Karl Sveinsson, whom he had just left, with whom he had become friends. He gave the seaman what he needed, knowing, too, that the years of steady drinking had already caused brain damage—hadn't Olaf spoken several times of having a child here, a little girl with red hair? Olaf was so pathetically grate-ful that Pall all but pushed him out the door, muttering something about being sleepy.

While he was still listening to the seaman's footsteps echoing down the dim, empty corridor, the telephone sounded. It was the supervisor of the hospital in Reykjavik, a man with an elderly troubled voice. One of Doctor Pall's patients, a Margret Magnusdottir, had given his name as her attending physician. There had been an accident—well, a curious sort of accident. A young man, an American, had brought her in. The young woman had suffered a single blow to the abdomen, a powerful blow, which, the American said, had been delivered by her husband. He was regretful to report she had aborted. Yes, she would recover very well:

"Fortunate she was brought here at once, though. Saved her, really. We treated the American, too. Brutally damaged ear, fractured ribs, lesions almost every inch. And a badly bruised spine which X rays, revealed was not broken. Terrible. Savage. Had to shave off quite a handsome red beard to get at his face wounds. Do you know him?"

Red beard. The photographer who had insisted on joining the work brigades? Who might have been blinded? "I suggested he get treatment there himself. For his eyes."

"Yes, we have his records. He was a patient here for two days."

"Where is he?"

"He's here. Won't leave. We have refused to allow him to see her, but he refuses to go."

"And the husband?"

"That's for the police. Appears to be the usual. The husband discovers, goes berserk. What man does to man, och? Such violence." The voice sighed. "The patient hasn't asked for you to come. Know you're busy there. More violence, och? Sleep well."

Sleep?

Perplexed, Pall wondered what he should do. He had a certain fondness for the dark-haired young woman—hell, he supposed that, since his wife's death in childbirth, he had always felt tenderness toward pregnant young women. The hospital bed beckoned, but he worked on the puzzle in his mind. Told of her pregnancy, Margret had asked him not to inform her husband. Many wives wanted to do this themselves, in their own ways. But this young woman had exacted a promise and had then reiterated it on the telephone from the mainland. Had it to do with Arni Loftsson's drinking? But since the eruption, Arni had been working with the others, and, whenever Pall happened to see him, had been quite sober. Then, only a matter of hours ago now, the boy's mother had telephoned Pall from Reykjavik asking—no, demanding—that he confirm Margret's pregnancy. When he hesitated, the woman with the imperious voice reassured: Margret had told her, but Margret was really a most unreliable young woman emotionally, and for her son's sake, the mother wanted medical confirmation. Which he had then given her, somewhat curtly. He had not wondered then, but now he did: why would Margret tell her husband's mother if she had not told her husband?

He decided to go. He needed a few hours away from the conflagration and the blackness anyway. There was no serious illness here, no untreated burns or injuries at the moment. He would sleep on the plane.

It was snowing lightly and had been for some time, the white snow mingling with the fine eternally falling ash, covering the town with a pepper-and-salt blanket, giving it still another face.

But he was not to sleep on the plane. It was an enormous cargo carrier loaded with refrigerators and furniture and books and all the possessions and paraphernalia of several households. The pilot in the seat beside him was a young American with a pock-marked face who said he was "Goddamn glad to have the company. This fuckin' mission is shit. Well, I got her off again this fuckin' time, but one of these nights, wait 'n' see, wing's gonna hit rock and *pow!* Trash in here's gonna be shit on the runway, right?"

Pall sat looking down on his town. Small wonder the Icelanders stood apart from the Yanks. How long had they been here now? Since the war. More than thirty years. But they were doing a job. What would have happened to Vestmannaeyjar if they had not been here?

". . . French gal, way I hear it. Open house. That straight shit, man?"

"I'm a physician," Pall said. "I'm going into Reykjavik to perform a delicate surgery," he lied. "Now I am going to sleep."

"Jeez, is that true?"

"That," Pall said, "is straight shit." And he closed his eyes.

Odette. He knew he would not sleep now.

Odette had been the first woman to return. There had been, at first, surprise—questions, even disbelief. Had she, a woman like that, beautiful and foreign, had she come to volunteer for work? In the mess hall perhaps? French food, ooh la! Pall had found time in the chaos of those first days to drive the ambulance out of the village, over a road already obscured in dark drifts. Dusted with fine ash outside, the house, inside, was as he had known it: simple, clean, high-lighted with color, inviting. Odette had greeted him with pleasure in her dark eyes, but with hesitation—as if she anticipated his questions and dreaded them. Pall decided not to ask them. Would he care for some wine? They drank together, as had been usual. The inferno was at a distance here by the sea: a barrage with occasional detonations. Like a war being fought on some distant shore. She explained that she had begged passage on a boat named the *Njord.* Its skipper, Captain Agnar, had been kind to her on the first night. He was still kind. He did not ask questions—the questions she saw now in Pall's eyes. She shrugged. She would live. Unless the volcano—what was that strange name they had given it?—decreed otherwise. Then she would not survive. That would then not be so *tragique,* would it? She had no other place to go—except, *naturellement,* the refugee places back there. She had no money, so she could not return to France or the Netherlands. She had no other place to go. This was the only home she had. There were, he told her, no shops open, only a mess hall at the docks, but she could not walk that distance three times a day. Again she shrugged, and smiled faintly. After all, all those men in there, and without a woman. Then Pall understood and was silent. Something he could not put into words ebbed from him. She sensed this. How else could she help? She had only her body—no, more, she hoped. She had whatever tenderness she could offer. Then she stood. Had he come now because he was lonely? She, too, was lonely. But he had only kissed her smooth, firm cheek and had left the house. That same afternoon he had sent food and a bottle of the wine she loved the most, but he had not returned. He knew the rumors, of course. He had even heard that Doctor Alexei Varanin, the tall, thin one who was said to descend into volcanoes, was a regular visitor.

Among others. Including Thurbjorn Herjolfsson, who, until it had been shut down and dismantled, had operated one of the freezing plants, which was owned by his wife's father. Thurbjorn, one of the town's most respected citizens. Strangely enough, though, whenever Pall heard of Odette her name was never spoken with a male leer, even by the Yanks. And it was soon understood that she would never accept money: only food, only perhaps rum, preferably not *brennivan,* but always wine, yes. And she herself never appeared in the village.

But she was gone from him. It had been his decision, but she was gone, and he felt the loss.

It was early morning in Reykjavik, still dark overhead but the streets and angular buildings were filmed in white—a scene that, as the taxicab rolled through it, filled Pall with an odd sense of relief. There was, after all, this other world, this normal, yes, real world. And there was still beauty. And quiet. And tranquility. He felt as a pilot might when, having fought with the menace of wind and space and the unknown and having by some miracle escaped, he discovers that civilization as he knew it has remained.

In the chalk white hospital room he faced a pale drawn face with colorless lips and faded blue green eyes that seemed withdrawn and wary and did not quicken at the sight of him.

"I told you," a faint, thin voice said, "I told them not to send for you."

Doctor Pall stepped to the bed. "It was my doing entirely." He reached for her hand.

She withdrew it. "You promised you would not tell Arni," the voice said, the lips scarcely moving. He heard the strain of bitterness in its drugged tone.

"Margret," he said, "Margret, believe me. I kept my word."

Then she closed her eyes and reached for his hand. The lips moved. "I knew." The bitterness sounded mornful. "I think I knew." Her hand clutched his. "*She* did."

And then he understood. Arni's mother. Who had telephoned him on some intuition or suspicion. To whom he had confirmed it. *Then* she had told Arni. But after that, what? Was this the result? If so, why?

"Where is Arni?" he asked.

She drew away her hand, releasing his. Her eyes—which were not her eyes—opened. Blue ice. "I hope," she muttered, "I hope he's at the bottom of the sea." Her head turned; she stared at the wall. Her hair gleamed blackly.

Then he asked what any sick-room visitor might: "Is there anything I can do?" How many times had he heard this?

"Yes," he heard her say. "There is. You can find Arni . . . and you can tell him . . . when he's sober . . . you can tell him that she . . . he . . . it was his." Then she added: "*His.*"

And it all came clear. He spoke her name. She did not reply. He spoke it again.

Silence. Only muffled footsteps beyond the door. Lights sparkling cold outside the window, reflected on the snow.

The supervisor had said she would recover very well.

Doctor Pall was not so sure.

He turned and went out of the room and down the corridor.

At the end of it, facing down its length from a bench framed in windows, sat the man whose eyes he had treated only a few days ago. On the telephone the supervisor had mentioned that the red beard had been shaved. But now, too, the exposed face was completely out of shape, swollen in places, with dark angry splotches of purple where it was not bandaged, and a white cotton patch covered one eye completely. His left ear was bulbous and the color of mahogany.

The slight figure stood, with difficulty, and Doctor Pall was reminded that fractured ribs, even when taped, were as painful as any wound imaginable, and there was also the spinal injury.

Pall stopped and extended a hand. Owen Llewellyn reached with his left. God, as bad as that. Pall felt a pang of rage. Very unscientific.

"You might not remember me," the American said.

"I remember you, but I'm damned if I recognize you."

A smile twisted the already misshapen face. "How is she?"

"Physically?" He wished he hadn't said it, but waited.

"In *every* way."

Pall had the impression that the other read his fear—had perhaps known that same fear himself through the long hours of waiting. "Do you wish to go somewhere?" he asked. "Coffee?"

The head shook, once. "I'll stay till they allow me in." Then: "You've answered my question."

Astonished, Pall peered into the single brown eye. "She'll recover." But he knew he was being the omniscient, reassuring physican now. "She's . . . how do you Yanks say it so well . . . she's got what it takes." But he was not sure, not sure at all that anyone did, ever.

Nor was Owen Llewellyn, who did not nod. "I had a chance to finish the sonofabitch."

"Why didn't you take it?"

"I really don't know. I did some boxing in college. I quit because I got tired of smacking people around, even if . . ." He broke off. "I don't know, that's the truth."

"You didn't take your chance," Pall heard himself saying, "because you're not like him."

"When he hit her, I think I was, though." A slight, painful shrug. "It was too late then. I had to get to her, and once he had me on the ground, I knew I was done for. So when I got my chance, I kicked him in the balls and brought Margret here."

"You stay here," Doctor Pall said, frightened now by the picture evoked, the feeling of rage it stirred in him. Not scientific at all, very nonobjective. "Be here when they let you in."

"I should have told them I was her brother. I made the mistake of saying I was a friend and that I'd only met her last evening."

Pall considered this. If the young man knew her so slightly, then how . . .

But no more questions. "I'll have a word with the supervisor," he said.

"Thank you."

Pall went down the stairway to the supervisor's office. The man was not elderly at all, and his face was as troubled as his voice.

"I don't want her disturbed. Not yet. I'm worried about her attitude."

Suspicion confirmed. "She's a woman who's just lost a child," Pall said.

"Yes. But more. You've seen her. Don't you agree, Doctor? More."

"Yes," Pall said and went outside.

Into a white world, and cold. The taxicab was waiting.

But a figure materialized from near or behind a snow-laden shrub.

"Doctor Pall . . ."

And he knew immediately. The shadow was tall, square-shouldered. It stood upright, the face unlighted, obscure. But Pall recognized Arni Loftsson and felt the poisonous anger curling in his tired body, gall beneath his tongue.

"How is she?"

"Someone else just asked me that."

The figure took a long step. Into the light of a window. Pall could see the face now: a mask of bluish bruises, bumps, unwashed blood—anguish. "Answer me, please."

The sight gave Pall satisfaction. And the voice. He warned himself that he should be tolerant. The man was himself sick, wasn't he? Pall was a physician. He should have compassion, show restraint. But comes a time, comes a time when intoxication, obsession, narcotics, feverish irrationality, even madness—comes a time when nothing excuses. *Nothing!*

"I'll tell you how she is. I'll give you my professional opinion. She may not recover. She'll live, but she might not ever recover, and she'll carry tonight with her to the god-damn grave." His tone was ferocious but low, strangled. "She's where you put her. And her child—*your* child—is gone." He took a deep breath of the icy air. "Murdered. By you. *Your* child. She told me only minutes ago. She gave me that message for you."

In the distance, across the rooftops, a church bell chimed, clear and forlorn in the thin air.

The battered face before him was as dismal as any Pall had ever seen. And he took a terrible pleasure in this, too.

"But him," Arni Loftsson said, tone baffled. insisting. "Him. Not my child." Uncertainty in voice and eye, torment. "His."

Pall took a step then. "Yours," he growled, his own voice a total stranger's now. "She was almost three months pregnant. She met the man yesterday."

It was like delivering a blow, a near-mortal blow, and watching it reach the heart, knowing no mercy and no regret.

The distant bell sounded again.

Arni Loftsson turned and walked away, like a blind man. Pall watched the tall figure, slow now, slightly stooped. It walked with a limp. Then it disappeared, swallowed in a sudden wind-whipped swirl of snow.

Still, Pall felt no pity. None.

But he did realize how abysmally tired he was.

What man does to man, och? Yes, and even at a time like this.

SIX

It continued to snow on Heimaey. For two days and two nights the snow fell lightly and fitfully. Then it began to come down in great clouds, heavy and all but impenetrable, until it overcame the ash. The town, bleak and black, turned white. And, once again, lovely.

Kirkjufell, as if responding in some mysterious way, quieted. The near-silence after the roar and bellow, gave hope to some—was it nearly over then?—and gave only temporary respite to others, while some grew even more apprehensive. Was it gathering new force, marshalling new power to vent in fresh and even more devastating savagery? The crater, which now threatened to dwarf the ancient cone of Helgafell, took on the shape of a horseshoe with flaming driblets of molten lava splashed down its sides; there were few lava bombs, and only a thin pillar of fire and smoke stood over the whitened town.

The work load, though, was intensified. Equipment needed for barricades, especially the new one protecting the harbor, had to be diverted to keep streets clear. The level of water in the harbor, having dropped to its more normal state, was nevertheless being carefully watched, and Karl Sveinsson had a large coastal-protection vessel standing by outside the harbor at all times in the event that swift evacuation should be required—for any reason. The water line from the mainland was repaired twice, but each time underwater upheavals severed it again, so old abandoned wells were searched out, fresh water was brought in by boat: warnings were posted everywhere and orders issued that fresh water be conserved and used sparingly for essential purposes only.

But the snow, falling and also gathering, obscured the aerial photographs of the lava's progress. Then, for three days, the flights had to be suspended. Karl Sveinsson fumed and cursed. His hatred had deepened to an almost fanatical fury: The Bitch had come to represent and embody all the inscrutable malice and evil of the world. Even her brooding quiet seemed despotic—menacing and scornful. He sometimes wished she would snarl away again. And often he thought again of those ruthless hags of hell in the old sagas.

Then, abruptly, the snow stopped falling. And when Karl Sveinsson, studying the new, clear photographs, drew his red marker along the new lava line on the map, he made a discovery. He measured with great care, alone, to make certain that he was not imagining it. No. It was true. The inexorable progress had been slowed. Not by much, but slowed.

Why? Who might know? How had it come about? And if so . . .

On his way over the snow-covered road to the farmhouse by the sea where, he had learned, Alexei Varanin spent much of his time, he wondered whether a man willing to descend into the bowels of a volcano about to erupt would have the answer to the speculation, not quite hope, that his discovery had stirred in Karl's mind.

As usual, though, in spite of the excitement that he was trying to quell in himself, his thoughts drifted toward his wife. He had come to acknowledge by now that it was not the miles or the sea that separated them; it was more as if they now existed in different countries altogether. The throbbing warmth that had been an emanation of a giving, happy spirit was no longer in her voice on the telephone, and he was saddened and dismayed—was he somehow guilty of that change of spirit? Where then did his duty, his commitment, lie? His devotion if it came to that . . .

The door of the old house was opened by a slim and

lovely woman of uncertain age who invited him in. The atmosphere was as foreign and exotic, and somehow as tranquil, as the woman herself appeared to be. She served him a glass of wine before leaving the room. He had never been in a room quite like this. He had, of course, heard the rumors that a Frenchwoman had returned to the island, but he had been too busy to do more than to wonder distantly at this or at its implications. It was not his business, and he had no personal interest.

The tall thin man who joined him seemed to walk slightly sidewise, his smile on a creased and narrow face upturned and questioning. Alexei Varanin—Russian birth, Karl remembered hearing, citizen of Belgium, lecturer everywhere—sat on a chair, of a blond color, that appeared to have been designed and handworked with great care, even pride, and regarded him with the professorial indulgence that Karl recalled from their first meeting.

"An evening off," Varanin said. It was not quite a question. "You . . . what is the word . . . you owe it to yourself. But have you come to see Odette or to see me?"

Karl wasted no words. He stated his observations, asked his question, then waited.

Alexei Varanin tilted his head, ran a finger over his mustache and said: "You are inquiring, if I am not mistaken, whether the cold of the snow or the moisture or both may have retarded, however minutely, the forward motion of the lava."

"I am asking for your diagnosis . . . Doctor."

"Yes. But behind this question is, I believe, another, is there not? You have begun to wonder whether the movement of lava might be stopped, or at least slowed appreciably, by the application of cold water along its edge perhaps . . ."

Astonished, Karl Sveinsson said: "If we've got anything around here, it's cold water."

Alexei smiled again and his dark eyes darkened further. "The result of cooling molten lava by pumping cold water onto it should be, in theory, to produce at the leading edge a solidified wall of the lava itself, checking its flow. And as the wall grows higher and more dense, the deeper the water penetrates, the fluid lava behind should not be able to bypass, burrow under or climb over. Thus the magma would, in theory, be contained until it too can solidify."

"Why," Karl asked, "do you keep saying 'in theory'?"

The professor's head tilted to the other side. "Because to date the theory has not proved successful where applied."

"Do you think it *could* prove successful?"

There was no hesitation. "Yes."

Karl stood up. It was all he needed.

"Would you perhaps convey me back to the village?" the professor asked.

Taken by surprise, Karl could not say what came to his mind: that he had assumed that the professor was living here. "Of course, Professor."

"Excuse me, won't you?" He was gone only a few seconds, during which Karl realized that this tall, almost-frail man had walked out here from town. "Now," the professor said, throwing a colorful wool scarf about his somewhat scrawny neck. "You are so kind."

On the way, the truck jouncing in the direction of the inferno, the older man answered the question that Karl had not spoken: no, he did not live with Odette, no one did, but wasn't she lovely, and weren't they lucky, all of them, to have such a woman here at this time, the basic animal urges remained, did they not, even in the face of disaster, and somehow Odette made them seem not so animallike after all. "I have just come from a place called Bloomington, Indiana— you have not heard of it? Well, they have a fine university there but no such women as Odette, and believe me, they have much need of such."

But Karl was not really listening. He had made up his mind. He would put in a request—no, an order!—for heavy pipe and hose and pumping equipment, preferably one of those pumping ships the U.S. was said to have, one or several, as many as he could get! As for manpower, he'd get that, too. He'd shoot as many thousands of gallons of icy water onto The Bitch's black vomit as the sea held! What if it had not worked before? Was that any reason not to try?

If this fragile-looking man at his side could go probing into the cruel and fiery throat of volcanoes all over the world—as close to the depths of hell as a man can go—then he could do what he had to do, what he damn well would do!

If he failed, at least it would not be for want of trying.

"It should be an interesting experiment," the professor said mildly. "I shall be privileged to help if I may."

"I'll need all the help I can get," Karl said.

"You are driving terribly fast, my friend. I have a dread of motorcar accidents."

Karl heard himself laughing.

But his new friend spoke again as Karl slowed: "You have another danger of which I think you are not aware but of which you should have been warned by the ones working more closely with you. Those great drifts of magma—rock and ash and cinder—on the crater's slope. I don't think there's enough snow on them to do it, even when it melts, *but* if it should rain, rain hard, those drifts could swell into an avalanche many times their original size and weight. I have observed this. A tidal wave, but of solid matter. A veritable landslide of such proportion that it could destroy everything in its path."

Karl had stopped laughing. He was struggling, not for the first time, with despair. Always, for every glint of hope, always more darkness threatening . . .

"Can anything be done to prevent this?" he asked.

Beside him, Alexei Varanin shrugged his thin shoulders. Bleakly he said: "If you are a religious man, you can pray that it does not rain, especially while the snow is melting."

All through the evening Hulda sat in the chair that had
become her own, although by no agreement spoken, and
they were all around her, doors slamming upstairs and
down, and voices, so many voices, and laughter, including
her own, which reminded her of when she was a girl and of
the time when her son, long dead now, was married to the
kind gray-haired lady who had been a girl herself then, all
those years ago, over on Heimaey. There was singing, too,
loud and lusty in the early evening, softer, later, sweeter. She
knew she would never get all their names straight, and this
seemed to amuse them mightily, and they smiled at her but
with love, patting her hand, the small ones even climbing
onto her lap, their breath young and sweet and their voices
bright with delight.

Hulda Palmadottir had never been one to try to add up
the good and evil of life, to weigh the happiness against the
sadness and loss, and she did not do so now. She was quite
content to let the evening flow around her, almost like music
itself, and then to doze in the midst of it, and later to go to
the room they had so kindly given her, which she did not
even have to share with anyone. And even as she felt herself
drifting into sleep, she could still hear voices and the sound
of singing, all very soft now, distant, and she wondered at
her good fortune. Such a terrible thing had happened in
Vestmannaeyjar, she knew, she knew, yet . . .

The next morning she did not awaken.

Thorroblot! The festival of midwinter. A night of good
cheer, music, revelry, dancing—and a night of romancing
and lovemaking. On the fifteenth of February the winter is
half over, so let us celebrate! Tonight the crest of the dark
hill of another winter has been reached, and far off now, yet
faintly visible in the mind, the green fields and crystal light,

and the long, long days of summer. Birds and blue water and
yellow angelica blooming on the cliffsides. Tonight is *Thor-
robolt,* feast of Thor, god of sky and wind. Let us celebrate!

Kirkjufell is thundering again. The air has warmed and
the snow is melting so that the black is reappearing
everywhere. And the black ash is again being whirled and
whipped in all directions. The day has been long and tomorrow another stretches achingly from dark to dark. Who then
will have the energy, the spirit, to drink, to dance, to con-
sume the mammoth feast? All are invited, all, and all will
come.

Since his return Rolf Agnarsson had retrieved and repaired his motorcycle, but had not yet gone out to the farmhouse to see Odette. Tonight, although he did not wish it to
appear so, Rolf was searching for a certain girl, a foreign girl
with long hair the color of cinnamon, whom he had seen in
the mess hall and more often at the church services that
Reverend Petur had begun to conduct three evenings a week
now that he had returned. Rolf and this girl had never been
assigned to the same work squad and they had never spoken,
but in church, holding a candle and singing, he was always
painfully aware of her presence or absence. But she had not
come to the hall tonight for the festivities, and probably
would not; he had been foolish to imagine that Winter Festival would be the time to meet her.

But just as he gave in to that idea and its disappointment, a lusty cheer went up all around him, loud and raucous, and the men were all standing, clapping their work-
hardened hands, some stamping their heavy boots, some of
the Yanks whistling. Rolf stepped on the seat of an empty
chair—and saw her. The cheer was not for her alone. Eight
females entered together, some smiling, some solemn: the
two middle-aged townswomen who operated the mess hall,
the only nurse, three girls from town, and two foreign volunteers. The girl, wearing a poncho of many colors, moved at
once—she did not walk, she drifted—to one of the long ta-
bles occupied by the Yank servicemen, their uniforms tattered and covered with black-burnt holes, faces stubbly with

beard, faces now bright and quickened by the *brennivan* and rum and the whiskey they had brought from their base. What was a girl like that doing here? But it was an odd question for Rolf Agnarsson to ask, for hadn't he himself returned on his father's fishing boat for reasons still obscure to his own mind?

A very tall marine corporal stood and held a chair for her, mocking a grand bow, and she sat, unsmiling. By the time Rolf reached the table, everyone was speaking at once, but no one had taken the chair next to hers at the end of the table, which was a mass of heaping platters. As he sat, he felt the silence that fell along both sides of the table. He ignored it. She looked at him then: gray eyes, or black, very frank, and her skin was tawny, and the hair that fell from the bright knitted cap had an amber aliveness. She regarded him with amused curiosity. "Hello," she said. "Do you speak English?"

"Only when I'm spoken to," Rolf heard himself say in English.

She did not smile, but something very pleasant and exciting happened behind her eyes.

The tall marine was speaking: "We risk our goddamn necks, y'know how many sorties all told, one hundred and twenty-two to date, hell, we lifted out eighty-five thousand pounds of cargo *so far,* and now we're taking out the machinery from what they call fish factories, yeh and also the goddamn medical apparatus from the hospital . . ."

"Have a drink, corporal," another voice called out. "It's a party."

"I got the figures 'cause I type out the news-release shit, that's how I know. And what I really want to know . . ." He looked past the girl and into Rolf's eyes. "What hell thanks do we get? They still treat us like we're invading their goddamn country, and who'd want it?"

"You're stinkin'," another voice shouted. "Knock it off."

The girl turned from Rolf to her fellow Yank and said into his face, sweetly: "He's not only stinking, he's stupid. None of us came to be thanked."

"You tell him, Catfish!" still another Yank shouted.

"I came," the corporal growled, "'cause I was ordered." He reached for the whiskey.

"Is that your name then?" Rolf asked the girl. "Catfish?" Then he added, smiling: "I don't think I've ever heard that name before, but it's nice."

Turning to him then, she did smile, at last. "It'll do. For the duration. What's yours?"

"Rolf. I live here." Then he corrected himself: "I used to live here." He didn't care for the puzzlement this stirred in his mind so he asked: "Where are you from?"

"Boston. Most people know because my accent's like JFK's. Of course I was only eight when he—well, that's what they tell me."

"Is it? What's mine like?"

"It's like a Swede trying to speak English to make it sound like Irish."

It was his turn to smile: "Have you been all those places?"

"I've been everywhere, lad. And where I haven't been, I'm going." She pulled the poncho over her head, shook her hair. "My tan's from the south of France. Picking grapes. You should see the rest of me." Her eyes did not waver—was she teasing him, mocking? A picture went through his mind.

"I'll tell you how they show their goddamn gratitude . . ." It was the corporal again.

"*His* accent's undiluted red-neck," the girl said, pouring herself a tall glass of *brennivan* from the pitcher.

". . . feed us this here hogwash, that's how. I ain't tasted one goddamn thing tonight that wasn't sour."

"It's sour"—the girl's voice was pure music—"because it's all been pickled."

"Yeh? Whale blubber, they told me. And seal! Blood sausage. *Blood!* Christ, what I'd give for a hamburger."

"Try this," Rolf said, and handed a platter to the girl, who passed it along. "*Hakari.*"

"Soun's like suicide—what hell's that?"

"*Hakari,*" Rolf said, surprised at the irritation gnawing at him, "is sharkmeat." Laughter. "Sharkmeat that has been buried in sand for five months. It's only worth eating when it's rotten." More laughter.

The marine, scowling now, stood up. "You makin' sport a me, son?" he demanded over the girl's head. "If you wasn't such a *little* squirt, I'd take you outside."

Anger stabbed, swift and sharp. "Let's go to the kitchen instead. I want to show you the *svio*. That's a sheep's head. First, you singe off all the hair—*after* the sheep is dead—and then you boil the whole thing for hours. The important thing, though, is not to remove the eyes. They're the tastiest part."

The girl joined in the laughter. And Rolf's anger faded as her eyes, merry and pleased and inquiring, met his.

"Whole country a goddamn savages," the voice over her head muttered, and was ignored.

A boyish-looking officer in a U.S. Air Force uniform across the table from the corporal said: "I'm engaged to a girl in Keflavik. Only now I'm beginning to wonder what I'll get for breakfast."

"What you better worry about," the corporal said, slumping into his chair, "is what you get *before* breakfast."

"You," the flier said, "had better stop sounding off, or you're going to get a broken jaw."

"Fuck off," the corporal said and stared away.

What amazed Rolf was himself: what was he doing sitting here defending a way of life that he had once hated? No—hated still. He poured himself a whiskey. Hated still and intended to leave forever.

"Dance, Catfish?" A handsome square-rigged fellow in a double-breasted blue uniform, *not* burnt, stood at her shoulder.

She stood. She had a way of standing, even rising from a chair—a lithe grace. "Why not, Lieutenant?"

The music was loud and leading the group was the radio operator, Jonas Vigfusson, whacking and whanging away at a guitar, grinning, his body moving in rhythm, possibly a little drunk. Only two couples danced, but many watched, Rolf among them. The girl seemed detached and oddly alone, even when dancing, facing the lieutenant, moving her slimness in such a way that she seemed separate from the room, as well as from her partner. Her lips were open, but her smile, if it was a smile, seemed meant for no one, directed into space. Who was she really? And why had she come here, where—Rolf knew, because of the fear that he had to fight over and over in himself—she was in minute-by-minute danger of annihilation?

He poured a drink from the pitcher this time. He was remembering the evening of the Sunday that his mother had come out here on the *Njord* and had then returned to the unfamiliar rented house in Reykjavik. *Black, black, black. You wouldn't believe it, Rolf. And everywhere the smell of burning and fumes. Black everywhere. Once so green. You remember, don't you? So beautiful. And the roof so blue. You remember*—she spoke as if of a long-ago day when it had been then but two weeks. *The roof, how blue it shone in the sun and at night, at night, like a blue wave outside my bedroom window when the moon was on it.* And he had said: *I remember*—staring out of the large metal-framed windows at the flat-faced house across the street where strangers lived. *But we can have another house, Mother. I can paint the roof blue myself.* But even as he spoke, he knew: whatever his parents might have hereafter, he would not be a part of it. He knew sadness then but also a sense of freedom, and he had wondered whether, in some manner, as mysterious as the transformation that he had begun to glimpse in his mother, he had left his boyhood behind. And he had seen her shake her head. *No. There's no more blue.* And after that he had seen the stunned look in her eyes flatten even further— those eyes that had always been clear and blue and, even when leaping with delight, somehow serene and steady and reassuring. He watched and wondered: could this be the woman of good cheer, the always-hopeful mother of his childhood, ever-indomitable, stronger even than his father in her quiet way? Slowly her pain had engulfed him. In the days following, he heard her complain, though she didn't eat, that even the food here was not the same; the neat, clean woman became untidy, the rooms strewn and littered as she drifted into lethargy, and he saw anxiety and anguish seep into his father's broad, strong face, even, at first, anger at the woman, but then a compassion that seemed to drain the man, and, finally, a sense of futility, not quite despair. But, half-drunk in the city one night, Rolf had realized that if his father ever gave in to despair, he, Rolf, would himself be changed. He did not know how. And he wondered at it, but became convinced: yes, he would change. But how?

"If drinking made me gloomy, I wouldn't."

It was the girl. She had come back. She was sitting down, shaking her hair. She reached to fill her plate.

The melancholy retreated. All he could say, though, was: "That's rutabaga."

"Even I know that. But this—what's this?" She was chewing and her eyes were half-closed. "Beautiful. What, please?"

He glanced at her plate—and hesitated. He could sense the tall marine, drunker now, leaning forward. He made up his mind. "They come from a ram. They've been pickled for a long time."

"Ram?" It was the Yank again. "Catfish, I heard about those, but I didn't believe it." He laughed. "I got news for you—what you're chawin' right now is goat's balls."

Now, though, there was only his laughter; the others did not join in and a few heads turned away. Rolf himself sat tense and wordless.

"Are they?" the girl said. "May I have some more, Rolf? They're far more tasty than the bulls' balls that American cowhands cook over a campfire. Beautiful."

Serving, seeing the marine twist away in his chair, Rolf said: "I suppose you've eaten at a cowboys' campfire, too."

"Chuck, they call it. Many times. But not in Boston." She took the plate. "The reason they call me Catfish is that I was billeted in the aquarium the first night, and I woke up and looked up into the tank above my head, with a light in it, and the catfish looked like sharks. I had the wildest fit of hysterics ever heard in these parts. After that no simple little volcano could scare me in the slightest. My name's Donna Blakely and since you've been wondering all evening what I'm doing here, it's not for kicks. I simply wanted to feel useful." And then she added: "For a change." And then: "Aren't you going to eat?"

He ate then, still drinking, and then they danced. After he had watched her moving sensuously across the distance between them for a while, he stepped in and took her into his arms and felt her arm, soft, go around him and her hand, soft, gripping his, and he caught the scent of her hair and went a little weak. And after another while, when he was drunk on the warmth of her breath against his face and the firm softness of her cheek against his neck and the fragrance of her flesh and hair and the pressure of her breasts, softest of all, against his chest, he heard her say, as from a distance:

"This is the way my parents dance." The idea seemed to amuse her, dreamily. "They're sweet, really. I only wish I could bear living with them." And later, the reverie deepened: "They send me an allowance. When it doesn't come or goes to the wrong place because I've left there by then to go someplace else, I get a job."

"Like picking grapes?"

"Hmm. And other sorts, too. Do you like this place? Vestmannaeyjar, I mean."

At once he thought of himself in the small boat the night of the eruption, almost triumphant with hate—and fear—watching what had appeared then to be certain and total devastation. Yet here he was now shocked at a girl who could leave home and travel alone, and so widely, so aimlessly. Why should that disturb him, shock him, excite him?

The music stopped. The musicians drank. The noise had increased, the roistering filled the hall, there were smiles and laughter on all sides, not a scowl to be seen now, and Kirkjufell's rumble was drowned out. Mistily, as time passed, he saw the mayor, fleshy face beet red, with his arm flung in comradely fashion over the shoulders of the chief of police—but hadn't he heard these two had despised each other for years and for some reason that only a few knew?

As he drank more, Rolf recalled how he had felt those first days and nights in Reykjavik: giddy with freedom.

There he had also discovered the sweet Dutch gin that he had come to love. And that night, coming into the house late, trapped by sudden light at the entry, standing there blinking and wavering, staring into his father's face, fixed and stern and somewhat sad, and then his father's iron-muscled arms lifting him when he stumbled, carrying him up the stairs as if he were a child again, and then facing his father in the small bedchamber that was still foreign to him, hazily angry and defiant. His father's voice had been a whisper, but not harsh: *Your mother sleeps and needs it. Your sister is even later than you. Now let me help you undress.* He had allowed his father's rough hands to remove his clothes, the room reeling, his stomach faint. But then, of a sudden, he had pushed his father away. *I'll do the rest*—wondering drunkenly whether he had shouted. He had ripped off the rest of his clothing and had stood there. *See! A man, after all. Not the boy you think me!* And then, amazingly, his father shrugged: *Possibly more man than I can allow myself to think you. Someone told me that once.* Reaching for his nightclothes: *Who? Who . . . told you that?* A hint of a smile on his father's face of leather: *A friend of yours. The French lady. I've thought of it many times since.* Shame flooded him hotly then. He had promised to return for Odette if there was any danger. Instead, overcome by his own terror and hate, yes, hate, he had pushed his small boat into the harbor to save himself. And his father had brought Odette to the wharf. Had saved her. More shame. Worse because of that. As if comprehending then, his father, at the door, had said: *Rolf, my son, can I help the matter that I am taller than you? Heavier? Stronger? Is this my fault, or God's?* So he had known. Even this, his father had known all along!

There was a change in the hall now. He peered around. A silence was falling in slow waves over the crowd. And there was no longer music. Where was the girl? Where was Donna? The silence became complete and then he saw him: General Patton himself had joined the festivities—and the festivities had stopped. At Karl Sveinsson's side was the tall Russian scientist, his spare shoulders turned, as always, like a mast tacking into the wind. And with them was a boyish-looking geologist, whom Rolf thought to be English, named, he thought, Hawkins.

General Patton stood stolidly and faced the room as if he might explode into rage. But into the quiet he said: "Down the street I could hear you louder than The Bitch herself. Any man who doesn't report on time tomorrow will be rousted out and will answer to me. Now drink away and fill your guts but don't spill them on the street. We've got enough to clean up out there."

Beside him, Rolf heard: "Beautiful." She had come back.

Then the applause began, scattered at first—no voices, no shouts or whistles, a dignified clapping of hands that rose in volume until the sound filled every centimeter of space under the high vaulted ceiling. But Karl Sveinsson only grinned, once, and then he turned and joined the mayor and the chief of police, both of whom by now looked drowsy and disheveled.

When the sound died, Donna asked: "He's the one, isn't he, the professor-type with the gold glasses, he's the one who goes down into the crater, isn't he?" And then, when Rolf nodded, "Rolf. I want to look down inside."

The idea, even in his present state of bemused detachment, filled him with a slow and awful dread: "Can't. They won't let you get that close. Forbidden."

"What isn't?" His vision cleared: the girl meant it! *"They* won't let you do anything that's worth doing." Her face was bright, her tone breathless. "Anything that you can really enjoy." And then, the uproar in the hall returning, she sat and lowered her head, then lifted it and spoke directly into his face: "Do you know that the mountains of Killarney are of volcanic origin? And Yellowstone Park in my country is really a crater? And in India, imagine, in India the Deccan Flats are really a lava field, more than two hundred and fifty square miles. Do you know this?"

No. Her face fascinated him. And her solemnity. "How do *you* come to know so much about volcanoes?"

"Do you think," she demanded, "that I'd come all this

way to fight one without finding out something about
them?"

No. He did not think anything. He did not know what
to think about this strange, lovely creature whose throat
throbbed when she talked. And who, like Rosa, believed that
they will never let you do anything that you really enjoy.

Rosa.

"How about a dance, Catfish?"

Rolf did not look up to see the Yank's face. Another one.
Another one of many. All around the whole goddamn world.

Now what? Was he jealous? How could he be jealous of a
girl he had met only two hours, or three, ago?

Rosa. Donna was like his sister. Like the new Rosa who
had changed beyond knowing. What had happened to the
tall composed girl with the plain features and the radiance of
golden hair and the once-quiet, once-docile brown eyes?
Even her appearance had changed in Reykjavik. And when
her father asked questions, she gave flippant, evasive replies,
while her mother, sagging in a chair with glazed eyes, hair
askew, face haggard, seemed not even to hear. And when
her father roared at Rosa, as he had once roared at Rolf, she
became playful, all tantalizing smiles and allure, almost
seductive. Rolf had spoken to her, once, only once, his
father's face haunting his mind; she had left a boisterous
group at the fashionable bar atop the Hotel Borg and joined
him at a table overlooking the many-colored tranquil rooftops of the city. He was thinking, he had told her, of going
back to Vestmannaeyjar to help—why didn't she come
along? She had hooted, holding her cigarette for him to
light: wasn't he the one who wanted to escape the place, why
didn't he take his opportunity? As for herself—blowing
smoke coolly—she had a job here with Icelandic Airlines now
and even a chance to train as a stewardess; she really did not
care what was happening out there. A chance, she said, to do
something she really wanted to do instead of what she was
told to do.

They won't let you do anything that's worth doing—who had
said that, Donna or his sister Rosa?

He had by now lost all sense of time. Dancing, he heard Donna whisper: "You are holding me very tight."

He knew. He held her tighter still. She was very close. *My tan's from the south of France. You should see the rest of me.*

Later a Hollywood film was unreeled. In the flickering color from the screen he could see the fine line of her neck and chin and nose and forehead. The horses thumped, chased, and the Yanks hooted and howled around them, and once when the outlaws were squatting around a campfire on the screen, the voice of the tall corporal shouted: "Deelicious, Catfish. *Beautiful!*" Donna only smiled.

When the lights came on, *Thorroblot* was ended. The lights went on, went off, flickered, and at once singing broke out. Icelanders sang with Yanks, Yanks left the hall with arms over the shoulders of Icelanders, and the tall marine corporal, passing them in the entry, called back: "Ne'er had better goddamn time whole life. G'night, Catfish. Hang in their, squirt."

"If I wasn't such a little . . . what'd he say I was, little what?"

"Squirt," Donna Blakeley said, looping her arm through his.

"Well, if I wasn't, I'd cut his balls off and pickle them."

The wind had tapered off and it was not so cold on the street now. Donna's head was back, she was laughing, music, and she pulled the cap down over her ears and went on laughing, music, as they walked through the slush. Lit by the pale streetlamps and the sinister flare of Kirkjufell beyond the rooftops, the streets echoed with shouts of farewell, in English and Icelandic, and with singing, Yank twang and Icelandic boom and buoyancy. Some ash was falling still, but drifting. And in only a few hours now the new day would begin.

"I like you, Rolf. I think."

"You don't have to decide tonight," he said.

The figure of a man, shoulders straight, hurried past them. *"Bless,"* he said without turning his head.

"I love that word," Donna said. "I'm trying to learn the

others, but I'll always love that one. Good night, good-bye, good cheer. Beautiful."

Another figure—smaller, rushing, head jutting forward, hands shoved into the pockets of his pea coat—stepped off the curb and passed, not speaking.

"Bless," she called after him as Rolf recognized the man: the seaman with the blurred and feverish eyes whom he had been forced to strike with the oar on that night that, in shame, he did not want to remember now. "Oh, *bless, bless, bless!"* She took her arm from his and threw both outwards, as if balancing, and spun around. Then she fell against him, suddenly holding him to her, her face close and happy. "I can't ask you to stay with me," she whispered. "Too many *they* in the house. They with the rules. Forbidden, verboten." She laughed again, softly this time, and leaned away. "Your face. You should see your face. Well, what's a bacchanal for if you don't bacchanal a bit?"

Somehow he could not find his voice. His mind, still hazy, was also stiff with shock. Childish, hateful, stupid shock. "And I do want to thank you, Rolf."

"Thank me?"

"For agreeing to take me to the crater. So we can really *see.*" She brushed her lips against his. *"Bless."* And then she was gone, alone, a slim figure, gliding with only slight uncertainty along the street a thousand miles from home.

Halldor Danielsson had not enjoyed himself at the festival; he had missed Juliana and would miss her even more now when he arrived at the house where he had been billeted with five other volunteers. The *brennivan* loosened the brain, that was the trouble, so that now he would have to spend at least the first hour—and he had only four before he was scheduled to report for work—fighting that loneliness and the picture in his mind of her face, fair and freckled, on the pillow next to his, her red hair sprayed out over it. He had been hurrying as he passed the couple, the young Icelander and the girl from the States, and he hurried still along the street that was thick with gray slush: the melting snow mixing with the ash. He had promised himself he would not stay at the festival till the end, and he had not enjoyed the film because the seat next to him was not occupied by Juliana. What a strange festival this year. Like everything else. But he had done what he felt he must do, even though Juliana did not fully understand: he had stayed on the island from the beginning. Juliana wrote, over and over, that she and little Jakobina had found a new life in New York and that both were waiting for him to join them. But Halldor was not certain when this would be. Her letters, though, were so full of joy—as she was, and as little Jakobina was, too—that at times he was tempted to go to the mainland and to take the next flight out of Kaflavik for New York. At such times he would tell himself that what they were doing here was futile anyway. But something in him held him here.

Because of Kirkjufell's familiar groaning and belching and the sludge on the cobblestones, he did not hear footsteps behind him before he felt a hand on his shoulder, swinging him about. Then he was looking into the eyes of a man about his age whom he had once known, although only slightly, and whom Juliana had known and much more intimately. But all that was in the past now and no business of his. He had seen the man many times in the weeks just past, too, and at first he had nodded to him politely, but when Olaf Jonsson only passed him by, ignoring him or glaring at him, he had stopped nodding and had made every effort to avoid him. Now he could not.

"Yes?" he asked. "Yes, Olaf?"

"Where have you taken her?" Olaf's eyes looked sick, as if with fever of some sort, and bleakly menacing. His voice was clouded: "Where have you taken my daughter?"

Halldor Danielsson was not certain at first that he had heard. "Who?" he asked. "I have taken no one anywhere."

"Where is Juliana and where is my daughter?"

"Juliana is in New York, Olaf. With . . ."

"You know my name then!"

"I do. Let me help you, Olaf. You are ill, I think, or perhaps only . . ."

The smaller man shouted: "Where is my daughter?" Then he cried, as if in anguish: "What is her name?"

The little seaman was either drunk or mad or both. So in spite of his own tiredness and his own somewhat blurred mind, Halldor said: "I'll take you to Doctor Pall if you'll let me."

Olaf stepped back and away, blinking. "If you do not tell me where I will find my daughter . . ."

"I know nothing of your daughter." Incredulity mingled with annoyance in him now. "*My* daughter—whose name is Jakobina—is with my wife in New York City. Now if you'll . . ." But he could not finish.

"Lies! You have taken them both!"

The blow was a wild one, and from below, so he could shift easily from it, but the kick, that was almost simultaneous, directed at his groin, caught him in the flesh of the leg above the knee, and his whole body shuddered with sudden pain. The man had turned into a raging animal, face gone savage, wolflike, eyes ugly and flaring, and he kicked again, his boot plunging out and up, and Halldor swung his body to one side, knowing now that he would have to act, his mind still hesitating, the anger coming but not there yet, and then the blow, which he even saw, slammed him on the side of his head, which filled with pain, and he crouched, still reluctant but knowing the man intended murder, the fool, the little damn fool, and then the anger did come, hard and swift, but sadness too, and he struck out, his face crashing into Olaf's face, blood spurted from Olaf's nose, and then maddened, Olaf moved in recklessly and fast, and plunged a fist into Haldor's stomach and as Haldor bent forward, Olaf brought up his knee into Haldor's face, and at the same time brought his hand, held flat and stiff, down hard on the back of Haldor's neck and the larger man went down to the cold muck on the cobbles, gasping for breath, he saw shadows running, heard shouts, but he was lost in blazing, blinding pain, and then he saw, through streaks of livid red, the other man stooping, picking up something, but what, a lava bomb, cold but heavy as stone, and, helpless, he saw it lifted above his head, he tried to roll, tried to summon strength, but the voices were close now, and uniforms appeared, Yanks, two or three, in a blur, and then he heard the lava rock thud onto the stones alongside his head and heard a scuffle, grunts and curses and growls, and his mind cleared slightly so that he could see two of the uniformed figures struggling to hold the wild animal of a man who was Olaf, but failing, and then he heard the sickening flat sounding crack of bone against bone, and he saw the small figure crumbling and then curling into a small knot of unconsciousness in the wet, gray mire.

A Yank voice said: "I had da, I had da. The li'l bastard was gonna kill him. He'd a killed him!"

"Yeh. Now what we gonna do?"

"Get 'em both to first aid."

"This time a night?"

An unshaven face was over him, hovering, speaking: "Y'all right, pal?"

He managed to sit. He was able to see now. "What about him?"

"The li'l guy? What hell you care?"

And another, standing: "What hell did he have against you?"

Halldor stood. He used a Yank phrase that he had learned: "Search me."

But he knew and, gazing down at the fallen man folded fetally, he was sad. For, thinking of Juliana, he knew what Olaf had lost. And it was then that Halldor Danielsson decided that he would leave Vestmannaeyjar. Probably forever. He decided in that moment that it was hopeless here anyway, hopeless, and had been so from the beginning. Juliana needed him and he needed Juliana.

It was then that it began to rain. It did not begin faintly

or as a shower. Torrents fell, of a sudden, and filled the world.

Jonas Vigfusson, normally high-spirited, was depressed and weary but not despondent. It had been raining now, sporadically but heavily, for more than thirty-six hours. The thaw was all but complete, and on an island without streams or rivers, the streets themselves were flowing like shallow creeks of black water. Jonas often wondered whether his wife was as lonely as he was, and he often thought also of her nightmare that had preceded the eruption. It seemed long ago now. He also wondered whether his four sons, who praised it when he spoke with them, really liked the school in Reykjavik—and whether they missed him as bitterly as he missed them.

Sometimes it rained so torrentially for hours on end that he indulged himself in the foolish fantasy that the water falling into the crater had to dampen or extinguish the flame. Instead, what it had done so far was to undermine the barricade between the lava river and the harbor, which had been so painstakingly constructed and which was not yet completed when it gave way, leaving the lava an open path again to the harbor entrance. The lava edge was also approaching the masts supporting the high-tension cables. If those two towers were to be overwhelmed or even toppled, they would be inaccessible for repair and then, whether electric current from the mainland continued to reach the island in the underwater cables or not, it could not be distributed. And, Jonas knew, there was not sufficient generating equipment to supply the electricity that they had to have if the work were to continue. Accordingly, but somewhat hopelessly, as a long-range precaution, he put in a request for additional generators from the mainland. But would they be sent? And if so, would they arrive in time? Jonas had begun to share his friend Karl's frustration, but not his impatience or anger. And Karl's impassioned, even obsessive, hatred of Kirkjufell bewildered Jonas—even disturbed him at times.

At one of the daily meetings of the council, deep in the debilitating detachment of fatigue, Jonas slouched, eyes half-closed, and listened to a familiar dissonance. The chief of police had complied with Karl Sveinsson's suggestion to cordon off a large section of town, allowing no access whatever, but he thought the council should have an explanation. Wearily Karl explained: there was danger of an avalanche of magma because of the thaw and continuing rain, and the greatest accumulation threatened that area; he hoped, however, that it would prove to be an unnecessary precaution. The chief nodded and the two geologists present agreed, one admitting that although he considered such an event most unlikely, he should have thought of it himself. Again Jonas was amazed that in the throes of fighting fire, it should be water that added to the threat—as it had been rain which, earlier, had caused the collapse of so many roofs covered with ash.

Ironically, though, it was also water which stirred the most virulent controversy that morning. Karl had commandeered the larger of the two fire pumpers, and the young fire chief, who, Jonas knew, would never forgive Karl for coming or for taking over, demanded to know why. Karl, who was more tired than any man at the table, explained that he had given orders for the pumper to spray water on the edge of the encroaching lava, heavily and steadily, day and night, and for a detail of men to lay pipe and hose, the largest available, from the sea to the apparatus.

The fire chief was scowling. "My department needs all the equipment we have. There are still fires every day."

"Houses!" Karl said. "If we don't stop that lava from reaching the harbor somehow, there'll be no need for houses here!"

While everyone waited, Frosti Runaldsson nodding his

gray head, the fire chief considered this, then he nodded, too, and growled: "Then try it. Try anything."

Karl grinned at him across the table then spoke to the group. What he needed was all the pumping apparatus he could obtain. He knew, for instance, that the U.S. had huge pumping ships, ships that could operate from the sea and from the harbor, and he believed that, on official request, they would supply one or possibly more; meanwhile, the council should requisition whatever was available on the mainland.

But the young geologist from the University of Reykjavik cleared his throat, shaking his head. This maneuver had been tried during the Surtsey eruption. "With no success whatever."

Then Karl's anger ignited and his eyes hardened. A failure in one instance was no reason not to try again. Perhaps "this maneuver" on Surtsey had not been on a massive enough scale.

The scientist stood his ground. "It will not work," he said with pedantic precision and certainty.

Karl stood. His face was taut and his eyes glinted like blue ice. "I'm making a formal motion that we attempt to get enough equipment to make a try. You have my vote. Now I've other things to do."

He turned and walked out.

A long moment passed. Then Doctor Pall said: "My vote's with Karl."

But the mayor rapped the table with his knuckles, a habit he had fallen into during the crisis. "I believe," he said, "that in all fairness to everyone, the motion should be tabled until we can explore the matter more thoroughly—and more calmly."

It was Jonas then, to his own astonishment, who was on his feet. "Gratitude!" he heard himself shouting. "Is this the gratitude the man gets for all he's done here?"

"Jonas," the mayor said gently, "we are all bone-tired."

"I vote with Karl! With Pall's, that's three in favor."

"We are not voting, Jonas. At least not today." Then the

gentleness left his tone. "This is a council and, helpful as
your friend has been, he is not a dictator, even if he sometimes behaves as if we have granted him that authority."

"We agreed to give him complete control."

"I'm sorry, Jonas. We do not operate that way here."

Jonas uttered a single obscenity and went out, hearing
the geologist saying: "I'll provide all the research you'll need.
The cold-water maneuver, while theoretically correct, has
never been used successfully."

Jonas returned to the communications center and then,
less than three hours later, it happened. It began as a sound,
a rumble turning into a roar, all quite distinct from
Kirkjufell's booming and growling. And Jonas knew at once
what it was.

The great drifts of dust and slag on the side of the cone
had swollen into the avalanche that Karl had feared, and
now it was roaring down the mountainside, gaining strength
and size and speed as it picked up more scoria in its path. Its
sound drowned out that of the volcano now, and by the time
it reached the first buildings, it had become an irresistible
torrent of solid matter. Hurling clinkerlike cinders in all directions, it roared along three streets, crushing and pushing
everything, houses and stores, before it, turning into a battering ram more than thirty feet high. It cut a swath three
blocks wide from one end of town to the other, and in less
than seven minutes after the first sound it crashed against
the high cliffs on the west side of the island which stood
between the town and the sea. It was like an explosion, debris
hurled up the cliffside and skyward. In those brief moments,
at least, the violence of its death was more overwhelming and
shattering than the eruption in the east. When the sound
subsided, Kirkjufell's familiar splutter and roar seemed like
silence itself.

At the meeting of the council the following morning, the
faces around the table looked haggard, ridged, and grim, as
if, Jonas thought, they had been stunned. Old Frosti
Runaldsson was not present, but no one asked why. There
were two outsiders: Doctor Alexei Varanin, who came with

Karl, and a short rotund man wearing the uniform of a commander in the U.S. Navy, who did not speak Icelandic and therefore often appeared bewildered. There was an assessment of the damage: thirty-seven houses had disappeared, including that of the mayor, and seven stores had been obliterated, along with the school and the resthome for the elderly. Feeling the depression around the table, Jonas reported that the masts bearing the high-tension cables remained standing, and the water line from the mainland was still in order. Doctor Pall then pointed out, in his sour tone, that there had, after all, been no loss of human life, causing the chief of police to remind them that this had been due to Karl's foresight. But Karl, who looked more crestfallen and dispirited than Jonas had ever seen him, shook his head. He then introduced Doctor Alexei Varanin. "He is the one, not I, who foresaw the danger."

But the question that was in most minds, Jonas knew, was whether the time had not come to abandon altogether, even though no one put it into words. Many volunteer workers were leaving and it was the mayor who said that if anyone on the council felt that he should leave, there would be no blame attached. There was a note of futility in the man's voice and a bleakness in his eyes, that Jonas had not seen until now.

In reply, Karl said: "Leave, hell. What I want is a vote on my motion to requisition pumping apparatus." To which there was nervous but pleased laughter and grins.

Even the mayor managed a small tolerant smile and said that such a vote might not be necessary. Then, in English, he introduced the U.S. Navy commander who, with a self-deprecating smile, said that he had come with a suggestion, and a suggestion only, which had no formal Washington sanction as yet: the idea of careful and selective bombing in order to divert the lava flow from what he called the "village" and from the harbor. If they agreed to the experiment, he would request further research quickly, and the States would provide the bombers, which were in fact available at Kaflavik. Then he paused and looked around.

After a somewhat startled silence, the bearded young geologist from the university said: "Yes. Such a tactic was used in Hawaii. The bombing actually did deflect the flow from its course and out to sea. The settlement was saved. Yes."

The commander nodded agreement, but the others were silent until Doctor Alexei Varanin spoke in his gentle tone: "The Hawaiian-type eruption is quite different from the ones in Iceland. Most different. It is even a different kind of lava there."

"You'd oppose it," Karl said, not a question but a flat demand.

The older man inclined his head, lifting his brows. "I am not, after all, a member of this . . . committee."

Karl ignored this. *"Why* would you oppose it?"

The volcanologist shrugged. "We know so little of those forces down below. But in my . . . considered opinion, a single bomb could trigger a fresh eruption, open a new fissure, or possibly blow up the entire island." He paused and then added: "There is one thing else . . . more. So far you have not had to contend with gases. But they are down there, and lethal. If they should be released . . ."

He did not finish; he did not have to finish.

Karl said: "I'd vote to bomb The Bitch if it would destroy her, but I can't see blowing up the island in order to save it."

The young fire chief said promptly: "I agree with Karl."

The mayor rapped with his knuckles. "I doubt there's any reason to vote." Then he stood and extended his hand to the commander. "But we are all grateful, sir."

"As we say in my country, no hard feelings."

When the commander had gone, Karl said: *"Now* what about my motion? I invited Doctor Varanin here today to explain the theory behind my idea, with which he agrees."

The young scientist asked: "Hasn't that also been tried, Doctor Varanin? I have records of failure . . ."

"If you agree with the theory, young man, then many failures mean nothing. Unless the theory is wrong, and therefore you were wrong also."

Subdued and, Jonas thought, somewhat awed by Varanin's reputation and presence, the younger man said: "I'll
vote in favor, but I still believe it a waste of time."

Karl's fury erupted again, but his tone remained low,
controlled. "A small indentation has already appeared where
the water has been steadily directed. Slight but I have the
photographs to . . ."

The mayor rapped again. "I doubt we need to vote on
this matter. I'll put through the requisitions whenever you
have them ready, Karl."

Karl reached into his pocket. "Here they are." He placed
a sheaf of papers on the table. "In specifics."

More laughter. More smiles.

"But this is only the beginning, and we have to move
fast!"

As Karl strode out, Jonas wondered what would have
happened if he had not thought to ask Karl to bring that
nozzle out to the island, the nozzle that wouldn't fit.

In all of his experience with volcanoes around the world,
Alexei Varanin had never heard of a lava party. Yet here he
was crunching up a hill of cinders at the base of the cone. He
saw Jonas Vigfusson, the radio operator, stoop down, pick
up a lava bomb in his gloved hand, hold it to light his cigar,
then hurl it, as if in defiance, toward the flaming crater
above. Another of the group, another of these huge Vikings,
scooped away two feet of ash, baring a bed of red-hot coals,
onto which others dropped thick steaks. Then there was a
whanging guitar, the *brennivan* flowed down dry throats, including his own, there was much laughter, and then singing,
the bellowing of boisterous Icelandic ballads, which Alexei
Varanin found himself enjoying, even though he could not
interpret the words. The mood was buoyant, even
exultant—and to Alexei Varanin, under the circumstances,

unreal, almost incredible, yet strangely exhilarating. By the time the steaks were charred, Alexei, who normally had no taste or desire for alcohol, decided that he must be quite drunk—for the third time in his sixty-five years. But he couldn't decide whether this was due to the odd-tasting potato liquor or to the sense of camaraderie and high spirits that he, normally a solitary man, was privileged tonight to share. Or whether it was due to the opportunity to observe the defiance and courage of men who seemed now doomed to failure. He knew the pumpers had not arrived; a valley of waste, the path of the avalanche, ran through the town, and much of the town was still afloat in a sea of black, and the work force had thinned to fewer than two hundred men. Astounded, he felt very much alive, almost exultant.

Then he found himself staring at the expression on the face of Karl Sveinsson, who, smoking his pipe, stood to one side, detached, his eyes fixed on the frenzied top of the cone in the distance. That expression, grave, held something deep and inscrutable. More than anger—an implacable fixed loathing. Directed, strangely, toward an original, elemental action that no man could control or pacify or destroy. Phrases rose in Alexei's blurred mind: *Satan's Pyre, Wotan's Brazier, Forge of Cyclops, Vulcan's Furnace.* And he thought, too, of Saint George and the dragon and of Ahab and the white whale.

He longed to join his new friend and to say: *All your passion is as nothing.* Or what he often told his students: *We know more about the stars millions of miles away than we do of the earth beneath our feet.* But he was not drunk enough. He wished he could say: *Spare yourself, my friend.* But he was not a man who could say such things to another. And he was also aware that Karl Sveinsson, under that dark spell, obsessed, would not listen.

What amazed Doctor Pall was that, as time passed, there were so few injuries and so little illness. By some miracle no one had been struck by a lava bomb; there were minor burns, wrenched muscles, two fractured arms and one fractured collarbone, both due to falls from rooftops; there was much fatigue, often masking itself in other symptoms. (Pall sometimes wondered about the Yank photographer, Llewellyn, whose eyes had been injured and who later had been badly beaten; he had not returned to Vestmannaeyjar.) And then there was the operator of the bulldozer who, while clearing the roof of one of the processing plants, had driven too close to the edge; the machine had fallen off the roof, making a complete turn in the air and had landed upright, its driver still seated. In the midst of all the merriment, no one, but the operator and Pall, knew of the pain the man suffered in his testicles for days. The most serious accident, near-fatal, was a case of hypothermia—when one of the foreign volunteers fell off the dock and was pulled out of the icy water with a body temperature of ninety degrees. If it had dropped four more degrees, he would have lost consciousness, and if it slid to eighty, he most certainly would have died.

Frosti Runaldsson's gray countenance still presided over his processing plant, and his gray eyes reflected, not only the deepening pain, but the hard-bitten pride of an old man who took satisfaction in what he certainly knew was his final act: one of stubborn defiance. Recognizing the futility of words, Doctor Pall no longer bothered to recommend surgery, only strengthened the doses to ease the pain. But the thin spiral of smoke continued to rise from the plant's chimney to become lost in the vaster steam and greater vapors over the harbor.

The only other medical problem was more complex—and so much more perplexing. When Doctor Pall had examined Olaf Jonsson's arm on which some surgeon in Europe had done a fine job of reconnecting the severed ulnar nerve, he had had no doubt that the arm gave the boy steady and, at times, excruciating pain. But as the young man had continued to demand more and more pain-killing drugs or barbiturates, Pall's suspicions were, in his own mind at least, confirmed: the pain was real, but the seaman was addicted. Then when Olaf committed violence on the night of *Thorroblot,* Pall had decided—and had thereafter refused further pills, suggesting that Olaf go to a mainland hospital for treatment. And Olaf had gone, but for only a few days. After that, he would appear and reappear, and Pall suspected that he had found some source over there. But why did he continue to return? What stirred in Pall a compassion that he tried to resist was the expression of anguish and loss in the little seaman's eyes. But Pall had done what he believed had to be done, again hating to play the role of some god or other.

One wall of the hospital had been damaged by the avalanche, but it had been repaired. Pall had continued to sleep there and, once in a while, use his old office as a retreat from the action at command headquarters. Everyone knew where he would be in the event of an emergency. So when Baldvin Einarsson came back to Heimaey for the first time, it was here that the three old friends met: Pall and Baldvin and Reverend Petur Trygvasson.

It was one of those rare nights when the monster seemed to sleep, not quietly, ever, but with only a low snore punctuated by belches and groans—one of those nights when, listening, some took hope.

When Pall had first seen the parson after his return from the far north, he had been puzzled by the expression in Petur's eyes. Normally timid and withdrawn, they now seemed stunned and bewildered. Pall had taken it for shock—after all, the parsonage had been one of the first houses to be swallowed up. But as the days passed, he had come to wonder: was Petur suffering some inner conflict that he would probably never speak of? And if so, what?

Tonight, when Pall saw Baldvin for the first time since the eruption, he was again startled: the heavy man with the bald head, whose own house, at the foot of Helgafell, had also been one of the first to go (the lava field bubbled there now, black and scarlet), seemed more than cheerful—actually exuberant. He and his Danish wife, Inga, were going to Europe, he said. But Pall sensed there was more behind Baldvin's exultancy.

Petur did not drink: religious scruples. Baldvin could not, because of his blood pressure. And Pall drank only on rare occasions—such as when he had been with Odette in her house by the sea, to which he had not returned. The three men drank coffee. They talked. But for reasons that puzzled him, nothing seemed quite as it had once been, and Pall found himself fighting down a sense of disappointment that threatened to turn into melancholy.

Finally Baldvin said: "I came because I had to see for myself!" There was a sly satisfaction in his face. "I had to see the two cones standing side by side. Just as I painted them! I painted them *before* it happened!" His excitement rose and he stood to pace. "I *knew*. Helgafell's revenge—I knew, I tried to warn. Holy Mount acted."

Listening, seated behind his desk with his heels on it, Pall glanced at Petur on the couch. His lean face had begun to darken into a scowl. Lightly, Pall said: "Don't forget your blood pressure, Baldvin."

And Baldvin swung about to face him, eyes bright with his victory. "You can still believe that the gods, *our* gods, have not spoken?"

"Did you know," Pall asked, "that the word 'volcano' comes from the little island of Vulcano in the Mediterranean where, centuries ago, the people believed that Vulcano was the chimney of Vulcan, who was the blacksmith of the Roman gods? What came out of that chimney, they believed, were thunderbolts for Jupiter and Mars."

Baldvin did not grin as he had always grinned. "You still think it's all mythology and superstition."

To Pall, the difference between the beliefs of his two friends was so small as to be insignificant. What does it really matter what a man believes about such things? He shrugged and said, "What difference?"

"It makes a difference," Petur said, his tone almost a whisper, as if he were speaking to himself, and his face was dark.

Then Pall recalled the story of the child named Gudrid who had predicted the eruption to her parents in July. And he recalled Jonas Vigfusson telling a group of fellow drinkers of his wife's nightmare. And then Pall remembered his own dream: his dead wife helplessly and wordlessly trying, in anguish, to warn him of some dread disaster. And now Baldvin's painting, which was going to be shown in Europe.

"How," Pall asked, "can one know?"

"Heathenism," Petur said. "Country of pagans. Even the gunboats are named for the ancient gods. Hopeless, hopeless."

"Well," Pall said then, irritated that the atmosphere of friendly discussion, as of old, had taken on a quality of bitterness, "well, the country's been Christian only since the year 1000. That's about when the Vikings stopped hacking each other with swords and started bashing each other with crosses."

Petur leaped up and made a sharp gesture. "There is only one question. Why?" His voice became shrill. "Why this town? If God is merciful? If he is really *just?*"

And then, without saying *bless,* he stalked from the room. Baldvin and Pall stood quiet and stunned, hearing Petur's footsteps along the dim deserted corridor. And now Pall knew. Because of what had happened, Petur was suffering—yes, it was the only word—some philosophical or spiritual crisis, that went beyond Pall's comprehension and was deep and real. Was it possible that Petur had begun to doubt the beliefs by which he had always lived?

Then Baldvin turned to him, somewhat stiffly and extended his hand. But his heavy face was solemn except for that sly triumph and certainty. And then the evening was over.

Pall knew that something had gone from their friendship forever. It was as if, because of what had happened to the town, differences, previously subject of pleasant and often bantering dispute, had now been altered in spirit. He wondered at this. By popular belief and accepted myth, shouldn't people be brought more closely together by mutual affliction? He had certainly observed this among strangers here. Then, if friends before, shouldn't they become locked in an even tighter, warmer bond? Now, whether the town became a town again or not, whatever had been between these three would never be the same.

Alone in the dark and empty building, he wished he could, as he would once have done, go to Odette.

But no.

That, too, was of the past.

And for a moment he, to his own quiet astonishment, knew a long moment of loss and desolation. Nothing would ever be the same. He had felt so when his wife had died—and he had been right. Now it came upon him again: the forlorn certainty that whatever lay ahead would have some emptiness at its core that had not been there before.

For Rolf it was a night, a long night, of fear.

Lying in his sleeping bag but far from sleep, Rolf knew that Donna, in the house across town where she was billeted, was also conscious of the lull. Many times she had said: *You promised, lad. You promised on the night of Thorroblot.* And each time he had said: *The first day the sea and Kirkjufell are calm at the same time.* Hoping that the day would never come. But the harbor was smooth tonight and the town was quiet. Which meant that tomorrow . . .

It was a stupid idea and he had not actually promised! Awake now, quiveringly awake, he recalled that terror that had sent him out into the harbor that first night, and the shame that had followed, the shame that still haunted him. He also remembered coming into that strange house in Reykjavik late one night and finding his father sitting alone in the dimness, his voice a whisper: *Rolf? Why do you avoid me? Is it that you suspect I know why you took out your little boat that night?* Rolf's silence was his answer. *Any man,* his father had said then, *any man who is not afraid at some time is a fool. And a fool has no fear to overcome.* He had had to ask his father then: *Weren't you frightened at all?* The man, who in this unfamiliar house seemed himself unfamiliar, and older, shook his head: *Not then, no. But I have been. And I am.* At once Rolf knew: the man's wife, beloved and cherished, becoming another woman, floating off, already beyond reach, and his daughter, also beloved, also cherished, turning into a stranger as well; and his son celebrating his freedom in drink and almost adrift, without the manliness to so much as apply for a job on one of the cargo vessels such as the one on which his school-teacher, Arni Loftsson, had shipped out. Ashamed, Rolf was tempted to step to his father that chill late night, to reach a hand to that years-scarred leather face that he had not touched in years, the face that had faced storms and ship-wrecks and floating icebergs but that now seemed vulnerable and bewildered. *Are you taking the* Njord *out to Vestmannaeyjar in the morning?* His father said: *I take it every morning.* And the following morning Rolf, for reasons still obscure and troubling, had been aboard.

Through the night now he could hear the others singing and drinking in the kitchen below. While, having imagined that he had made friends with his guilt and fear, he lay here in frigid dread. He considered rising and joining them— were they singing against their own fears? And had Arni been afraid, the tall strong Viking with the bright grin and square chin—was that why he had gone?

Damn Donna Blakeley of Boston, U.S.A. Teasing, smiling her enigmatic smile. Challenging. He had warned her of the danger of what she demanded, and she had laughed. Well, if that's what she had to have, she would have it. At first light. If the weather held and if Kirkjufell still slumbered.

In the morning the harbor was busy. It was a place of steam, whiter than fog, and even more dense where the hot lava met the frigid water. Vessels were leaving and entering through the narrow aperture that he knew was threatened more each hour. The warehouses appeared ghostlike, deserted except for the one plant now operating, all dreamlike and unreal in the overwhelming mists. At the stern of his own boat, now rigged with an outboard motor, he was sick with even greater dread than he had felt on that first night.

The girl sat with her back to him, looking forward. Her hair was gathered under her red helmet and her slim body was stiff with a hungry anticipation and joy, that he could not share or even comprehend. All she had said was: *We'll go AWOL for a day,* and he had understood her meaning only by the childlike delight that lit her face.

Out of the harbor and beyond the wakes of the larger vessels, the sea was almost waveless, and he steered well clear of the narrow streams of lava, gold streaked with livid red until they reached the water and then, paler but still burning, even beneath the surface. He took the boat well beyond the subterranean lava field, the outline of which the Russian scientist had drawn on a map for him a few days ago. He had approached the scholarly looking man with the mild manner and gold-rimmed glasses with some misgivings, and even now he wondered whether the man had guessed his intent. *What one must forever bear in mind is that a volcano is like a man gone mad.* Had Doctor Varanin been trying to warn him? *Its every action is . . . what word shall I use . . . beyond prediction. Capricious—yes!*

They rounded the island on the northeast and bore south, a hundred meters off the craggy shoreline. Rolf could not see the cone above the high cliffs but only a spiral of dark cloud with a suggestion of glare from beneath it. He chose a ledge that would allow them to disembark and steered toward shore and saw Donna pull up her gas mask and adjust the two thin cylinders on her back. No ash fell here today, but the dark gray cliffsides were darkened by it and on the purple brown terraces were rough square blocks of tuff that had been thrown up or had tumbled down to lodge there, and there were shining perpendicular ridges of black lava in an irregular pattern that, he knew, would make the climbing even more treacherous. But it was too late to think about that now. He was conscious of the cold rising from the water yet also of the warmth, not yet heat, against the flesh of his face. He lifted his own mask. He saw her holding the prow off the rock, and then he saw her leap onto the ledge, her movements surprisingly graceful in spite of the fiberglass moonman suit that she had somehow been able to obtain. After cutting off the motor, hearing only a low rumble as if it came, not from above, but through the cliffside itself, he followed her onto the flat terrace. She faced him—a creature from outer space. Then she turned and began to clamber up, ledge to ledge, avoiding the slick looking strips of black. He looked up the harsh-featured face of stone, wrinkled and pitted, and in that instant, recalled other times here, summer days, and the rapid whirring of the wingbeats of the puffins, flooding from their nests in the cliff caves and out over the ocean by the thousands. But there were no birds now, only that craggy precipice leading up to the flat lava field. He looped the roll of rope over one shoulder—descending would be more difficult, he knew—and then he too began to climb, looking always up and ahead for the next handgrasp, the next foothold, not thinking of anything else, not thinking of what lay beyond that brink they were slowly approaching. In spite of the awkwardness of her space suit, Donna moved with a secure agility that surprised him. He forced his mind to concentrate on each ash-smooth treacherous outthrust of rock, his gloves slipping more often than his rubber-cleated boots.

The sound of the volcano, slight in town, was more definite here—not deafening but a slow rolling thunder, steady and filled with the whooshing of wind. The air, though, was free of fallout, but it grew hotter as they reached the crest. He joined her, out of breath in spite of the oxygen which was thin in his chest and a trifle dizzying behind his eyes. And then he reached the summit and stood and stared—as a still and quiet terror took over.

They looked across a plain of cinderlike rock, littered with chunks ranging in size from small pellets to huge blocks as large as houses, and below the cooled crust an underlayer of still-hot lava glowed orange. Heat wavered visibly in the air, and through its pinkish haze they could see the cone. It had taken on the shape of a horseshoe and, from this side, it would be possible to look into the vent without climbing more than, possibly, twenty meters. Above the crater heavy vapors rose and thick gray clouds tumbled upwards, but there was no flame to be seen, only an eerie intense glow from below that appeared as if it might ignite the clouds themselves.

Together they stumbled across the surface. The terror was quiet in him now, solid, like an extra weight that, trudging, he must carry, but he realized then that they were walking on the newest land on the face of earth itself, recently delivered, not yet cooled. As they approached the open side of the horseshoe, he wondered at the girl: was it courage that she possessed or a reckless unawareness of where they were?

The heat penetrated his boots and, before they reached the base of the cone, his feet began to feel as if they were actually burning in the hot contracting leather, swelling painfully, and the heavy crepe-soled boots seemed to be melting as if they were being consumed, his feet trapped and blistering in them. But he went on. He had come this far. He placed one painful step before the other and became conscious then of a quivering underfoot, as if the earth itself were shaking beneath the torrid floor of uncertain stone.

He felt himself go weak and his whole being filled with horror. He fought down the impulse to turn away. The heat had risen all through his body now, his blood slowly igniting into streams of fire, so that he became feeble with a fever so intense that he was certain, although he staggered forward, that at any second he might go slack and drop to the scorching rock. The lava field looked vast, not measurable by space or distance. It was as if they had stumbled onto some new undiscovered planet where heat and time had gone still and meaningless. Appalled, he knew that he would never escape.

He drew deeply on the oxygen, struggling with a temptation to throw off the mask, his lungs would not fill, and in a blinding panic he wondered again about the girl, a shadow in a trembling-edged halo, unreal: what was she feeling as she climbed the hill of loose scoria and arrived at the rim before him? She was standing straight and looking down.

Then, his will gritting in pain, he was beside her. And he looked. And was overcome. Blinded.

Then he was staring into the mouth of an unimaginable hell, down its raw red quivering throat, at the seething heart of chaos itself. At the unknowable madness of an unknowable world. At the secret menacing mystery of life itself.

The burning pain was forgotten. Gone. He was without breath, not as if he had been struck a blow, but as if breathing, in this place, was not even necessary. He forgot the girl beside him. He forgot the town beyond and the sea behind. The moment was whole in itself, and his, and even he was not important now.

Below, the surface foamed, surged, splashed; it spurted geysers of gold and scarlet and intense yellow, and there was a bubbling everywhere. While on the edges, against the red walls, blacks and purples gurgled and congealed into a slow breathing rhythm, and the whole incredible cauldron heaved. Smoking incandescent rocks shot from below through the surface, tumbling only a few feet into the scorched air, splashed back, disappeared, and there was no low thunder here but a cacophony of sound so overpowering that the human body shudders, cowers within, as if to ward off certain annihilation, doom itself. The brilliance was painful, enveloping.

Either he felt no fear or the terror was so overpowering and profound that it devoured even his sense of it. The moment took on an intensity that defied time, space, reality itself.

This could not be.

This was.

The splendor and glory became too much. Joy burst in him—a shock of pleasure that stunned his mind as it invaded his spirit.

He did not know why. Or care.

The limitless moment became eternity. He was in the presence of powers beyond comprehension or definition. He gave himself over to magnificence without and awe within.

Even when it became too much to bear, he still did not turn away.

Then, dead center in the seething lake there suddenly rose a pyramid of liquid that seemed to turn to flame in an instant, blinding, and there was an explosion so deafening and overpowering that he felt locked in the center of all sound. The flame shot higher, red and yellow, and he had to turn away. He saw the girl's figure stumbling in panic down the side of the cone, then running across the rock plateau. He took no final backward glance, but, with reluctance more than fright, half-slid and half-clambered down onto the hot floor of cinders and rock. The strange moon-walk figure ahead ran with outflung arms toward the edge of the cliff.

The blast behind him turned into a crackling roar, and he felt himself shuddering, while below him the lava floor was quaking crazily as if at any moment it might open. He saw her nearing the precipice, the world filled with smoke, and she disappeared, there was a hail of stone on his helmet, his burning feet seemed to crumble, sparks fell on all sides, flames were bursting everywhere, he remembered what the scientist had warned, he ran blindly, his head bursting with sound, he stumbled, he almost fell, his gloves touched the cinders and were scorched, his palms caught fire, he could not see the girl, the universe was burning, and then he saw her, she was on the brink, and she had turned around, her arm came up across her goggles, he tried to shout, a blade turned in his throat, and he saw her turn away from the inferno, his heart stopped completely, there was a bellowing on all sides, he was stumbling through a cave of fire and smoke and falling projectiles and sparks; and then he realized what she was considering, he tried to yell again, he tried to hurry, he was too late, she had leaped, he tried to run faster, waves of fiery stone lifted under him, the floor threatened to open and devour him, but he ran, and when he reached the edge of the cliff, stopped only long enough, tearing off mask and goggles, to see her form far below, but in the water, thrashing, the arctic water, but she had cleared the ledges and crags, and without thought, knowing only by memory in his veins how many had died of shock in that sea, he judged the outthrust of the widest terrace and then hurled his body as far out as he could spring, and then he was falling, falling rigid, legs held firm, straight, his hot body longing by instinct for the cold and wetness even before his boots cut the surface.

Nothingness.

He froze and his mind went blank.

Then he was moving, arms climbing, legs kicking, cold, cold, and then the surface, with rocks sizzling on all sides, and the sea itself going wild, churning, and then he had her, he had hold of her, the boat was there, he was lifting her into it, she was conscious, shaking all over, she was falling over the gunwale, he climbed to the ledge, he could see her in the livid glow, she was curled up, he felt the heat reach the cold in him, he tore the rope loose, leaped aboard, ignored her then, started the motor, and as he steered toward the open sea, in the din and glare, he crouched against the downfall; he looked down on her, her body was quaking convulsively, he felt icy water in his own lungs, what of her, what of her, he knew that he should place his body over hers for the warmth she needed, but he dared not leave the motor in the stern, and then the pain returned to his feet, and his boots seemed to throb as if they would burst, but he had to ignore that, had to ignore everything, had to get her to warmth and help and safety, had to, would.

SEVEN

THE VOLCANO SPLIT asunder during the evening of that same day, producing a phenomenon that no geologist had ever before witnessed or heard of: the *Wanderer,* as it came to be called, a huge heap or hill of pumice estimated at millions of tons which floated on the lava field like an iceberg in the sea, its movements, not constant, but erratic, so astonishing in fact that, instead of going northeast with the main lava flow, it took a course across the crater gap to the northwest—and toward the harbor.

Would *Flakkari,* or the *Wanderer,* do what Kirkjufell had, at least so far, failed to do?

Word of this astonishing spectacle, and new threat, did not reach Karl Sveinsson, who was in his home in Keflavik overnight, until very early the following morning when the strange nature of *Flakkari* had been determined. When the telephone sounded in the bedroom, Karl had been asleep, but his wife had not been. She had been thinking how lovely it was, how truly lovely, to be in the warm bed with his warmth beside her again, finally beside her again, and the snow falling in the darkness outside, swirling and white, and everything misty beyond. She no longer felt deserted and alone. She remembered with a shiver of pleasure the lovemaking, the unbearable excitement and excruciating release; and she remembered how, before that, he had come in, had simply appeared, without warning, filling the door-frame, filling the house with his presence, his eyes streaked

263

red with tiredness and a pallor behind the ruddiness of his broad face, a small smile twisting his lips and his eyes on her, blue, blue, while she went weak, the hard core inside thawing, dissolving, a flash of intense heat everywhere in her of a sudden, and then into his arms, wordless, engulfed, his great thick muscle-ridged arms sweeping her up, and into the bedchamber then, a sweet exultancy all through her. She had not asked, had not dared ask, how long he would stay.

And now, while he listened, after saying, "Yes, Jonas, yes?" she fought down apprehension, threw back the *dyna* and stood. Karl was asking quick, curt questions, paying her presence no heed; resentful and ashamed of herself, she did not want to hear. She drew on her robe and went into the kitchen.

There she stood undecided. She would prepare what he loved most—oh, this man, he had a taste for food. She went to work. How could he know what it had been like here? At night, alone, imagining him out there, the risk, what might happen, what the newspapers said *could* happen. And the long dull days of being alone, really alone, the girls off to school and the knowledge always that, at a certain hour, he would not come in as usual. There had been times when the heart shriveled. And always the shame, too: against a catastrophe of such dreadful proportions, to feel personally deserted or ignored, forsaken, what a trivial unfeeling woman she must really be!

Last evening, after the first lovemaking and before the second but after the girls had gone to bed, his mind had seemed to return over and over to that island. How emergency generators, requisitioned weeks ago, had not yet arrived. What great spirit the volunteers and U.S. servicemen revealed. How frustrating at times. He had become, she knew, some sort of almost mythical, almost godlike creature, who commanded the troops, who worked miracles. And whenever neighbors or relatives spoke to her of him, she had suffered a terrible and harrowing confusion—pride and love and that ever-present resentment, that she so despised. General Patton. Blood and guts. But the man she knew was tenderness, and those hardened hands at the controls of his small army over there were the ones that had given caresses and had lingered on her breast, stirring tumult deep within, had touched her face with reverence, transfiguring it, and her, his electric vitality flowing through those hands, that body, and into her, eradicating the years, returning her to youth. She knew the miracles of those hands—and needed those miracles herself.

He had told her of an old man who had kept his plant open when all others were closed. And he told her of a scientist who actually descended into volcanoes—an older man who had confessed to him his strange dream: that a day would come when all that power would be, not only curbed, but controlled—harnessed to man's use instead of his destruction. Fertile soil, underground water supplies, cheap and abundant energy without pollution. Karl had laughed but with bitterness. He himself could see nothing in The Bitch but evil. Karl's absorption and intensity had frightened her somewhat. And listening to him last evening she had remembered the day he had left: she had known even then that she could not really hold or tame such a man.

And now, in the kitchen, the smell of tobacco smoke reached her, sharply fragrant and familiar, and she turned. He stood in the doorway, fully dressed. Something in her collapsed.

She asked the question that she had not asked last evening: "When are you leaving?" But she knew.

"Three of the freezing plants are burning. Not, thank God, the only one that's functioning. And there's more, something very strange." He stepped closer. His blue eyes were intense now, almost wild. He took the pipe from between his lips. "They need me," he said softly.

"*They* need you?" She heard her own voice with astonishment. She seemed to have no control over it or over the words: "You need *them*. General Patton!" She heard contempt low and not shrill in her tone. "You need them, Karl. Or what's happened there anyway—you need it all. But don't fool yourself, please don't. You're doing what you're doing for yourself."

"Is that what you think, Lilja? Is it?"

She whirled away.

"Lilja, listen now. There may be some truth in what you're trying to say. I've even wondered about that myself. But today I have appointments with the minister of defense and with the Emergency Council in Reykjavik. I need more machinery to pump water, ships if possible. We've made official requests, nothing happens. I'm going to try to cut through the red tape. I'm going to the prime minister himself if necessary. I can't give up now when my theory's working. Can you understand that?"

Her head went down. She understood. She did not face him. It was worse than she had thought. His coming here, coming home for one night—it was only a mission. He had not come to be with her. "I think," she heard herself saying in a whisper: "I think I do understand." And then she added: "Perhaps too well."

She heard him utter what she knew to be an oath, although the word was not clear. Then, in a reasonable tone, he said: "It's snowing there, too. But the airstrip's open. By the time I get to Reykjavik, see those men and get back to the airfield here . . ."

"Go!" She did face him then. She felt the tears, struggled against them, gave in fully to her anger. "Then go, why don't you go, what are you waiting for? What you need is not here! Please go, will you, please!" She turned away.

He hesitated a long moment, his face fixed but his eyes uncertain, then hardening, quickening into a brightness that startled and almost frightened her. He took a step toward her.

And in a moment or so she heard the door open and close. And he was gone. Again.

Had she driven him away?

What was the drum he heard in the distance that she could not hear?

And his eyes: what was the tempest she had glimpsed there, elation and eagerness and yet hate, fury? An intensity that she had seen before only in their most intimate moments.

Was it possible that a volcano had in some mysterious way become her rival?

She felt as if she might laugh. But she wept.

And heard the sound of the girls' voices in the passageway.

He had not stayed long enough to say good-bye to his daughters.

He was a stranger.

Who was this man and what was it that drove him, possessed him?

She fled to the bedchamber. She could not let the girls see her tears.

After the snow, it had turned cold. Nevertheless, walking, he could feel the heat inside his clothes, damp against his flesh.

He had told himself that he had come back to take more photographs, and he had taken them. But he no longer had the illusion that they could catch and hold moments of time; nothing held back time.

The sky, as he walked, was the color of wet cement with a pale disc suspended in it, glowing silver like the moon, but actually it was the sun showing its first faint light in days: no harbinger of good things to Owen Llewellyn. Nothing was, or could be. It only reminded him of a day of golden sunlight that he had now to forget.

He had come back to Heimaey, he admitted to himself, because he could not face returning to New York and Connecticut. Even the thought of his refuge in the woods repelled him. And what he had found in Vestmannaeyjar had appalled him. True, there were pipes and pulsing hoses everywhere and the steady sound of pumping twenty-four hours a day and silver arches of water turned steadily against the enemy. But now he knew it was hopeless. The devastation while he had been away had been so much worse that he hesitated to record it on film. And he also hated filming that wandering hill of pumice inching its way in all directions like a lost ship on the lava field. He came to the conclusion that the whole project was like Sisyphus pushing that damned rock up the mountain over and over, only to have it come tumbling down each time through all eternity. Hopeless.

He was walking away from the village in the direction, if he had been told correctly, of an old farmhouse where a lovely, willing, and alluring siren sang her songs. No questions asked, no enveloping, smothering personal entanglements—and no abrupt rages and retreats. Freedom. As he had known it for years. As he now knew it again. How the hell had he allowed himself to become involved again—when he had held himself aloof and detached for years?

Perhaps it would have been better, for Margret even more than for himself, if he had not waited at the hospital that night, if he had taken his pain and his wounds and had boarded the next flight to New York. Then he would not have always hovering in his mind the picture of her stretched out beneath the sheets, the room twilit with the creeping morning outside, her face wan and drawn, her eyes baffled, questions unspoken when she saw him. And anguish in those eyes, more loss than physical pain.

What was it she had said when they first allowed him into the hospital room? *I would have known you without the beard but now I can't see you for the bandages.* And he had said: *If I'd had to wait much longer, it would have grown out again.* And then she had smiled, and joy rushed through him, and then the faint smile faded. He had known then that he had to make her smile again. He had somehow to make her laugh. In time.

But in the time that followed there had been only a few smiles, and always evanescent. He would walk from the hotel to the hospital in the cold dark of morning, and he would ask about her night, and she would say she had slept well, and he would wonder whether she told the truth. Fine and frail, her black hair vivid against the white pillow, her translucent skin looking almost transparent now—he would sit and allow a sweet tenderness to engulf him slowly, wondering at it, and at himself, amazed. Once she had whispered out of nowhere: *I'm so sorry, Owen.* And he had said: *Oh, I don't know. I've always sort of wanted a cauliflower ear.* And she had smiled then, with only a suggestion of tears in her eyes. Hours of silence might pass. Or she might speak of some incident of her childhood, which, he came to realize, had been a happy one. Once in a while she would ask of Vestmannaeyjar; he would tell her what he knew. One evening, as he was leaving, she had said: *You must not . . . you must not feel obliged, Owen.* What had he answered? He could not recall—something about all the shops having sold out the Japanese film that he used, so he couldn't work anyway. Had she smiled then? How he came to hold his breath for every faint suggestion of pleasure, of life—of caring. He would bring books and magazines; she would read, or pretend to, while he was there, and sometimes she dozed. When he came to recognize from her breathing whether she actually slept or not, he would get up softly and go out and walk the streets of the city, past the shops and restaurants and the odd-shaped buildings that he took to be government offices, sometimes to the docks, often along the lakeside, trying not to recall the violence and especially the bile of murderous rage with which he had struggled on the blood-stained ice with the thrashing weight always returning to hold him down, while he fought only to get to her, to Margret, who was in pain, who needed him. He would eat the delicious open-face sandwiches with the exotic-tasting fish and then he would go to one of the hotels, not always the one in which he had taken a room, to have a whiskey before breasting the wind to return to the small white room where Margret lay. During this time he had struggled to reassure himself: she had had a shock, time would pass, would heal, and then the trauma would fade, and she would be herself again. But who would she then be? Who was herself? He had never had time to learn before she had withdrawn from all self, and from him, from everything.

They've told me I can go home tomorrow.

I still have the Landrover.

Still? Do you mean you have been paying rental all these days?

For a second he had the impression of hearing a wife's amused rebuke, and he then told her of the publishing contract. The photographs were to be gathered together into a book, and the publisher in New York wanted them as soon as possible because the event on Heimaey was international news now.

I am pleased. Only that, and without a suggestion of pleasure, really, her spirit, quickly glimpsed, retreating again. *Home,* she said, and her mind was over the water in Vestmannaeyjar, he knew, but what was it picturing?

Todd and Malfrour expect you to go there.

Yes, I shall go.

But in the seat the next day, she said: *I do not really wish to go there, you know.* Her voice had taken on a soft trancelike quality: *Home, they said. I don't know where home is. Or even whether I have one.*

On the country road the wind grew stronger, flailing at the snow. He looked at her again. He had the insane impression that he had known her for a long time, yet did not know her at all.

Walking now, on the narrow ash-flecked road, where the bulldozers had piled the snow and the powdered volcanic pumice along the edges, Owen was remembering the days that followed. He had no idea how many. *Everyone is so kind,* she had said. The paleness remained in her face, on her delicate brow. She seemed to be going through motions: playing chess with the children or with Owen or Todd; listening to music hour after hour, refusing to look at the television coverage of the village, often shut away in her room reading or brooding or simply staring. His room was next to hers, and at night he would hear her turning in the bed, could hear the snap of the light switch at all hours. Until, finally, Owen asked her to go into Reykjavik with him. He had seen them skating on the lake—did she skate? No—there was much ice but no pond or lake on Heimaey. Then what of the art galleries or the theater or the cinema? She smiled. *You are kind. But I told you in the hospital: you are not obliged.*

Hearing the anger in his voice, surprised himself at it, he said: *I do what I want to do. I always do what I want to do, Margret. And now I am going to kiss you.*

The smile vanished. She frowned. Then, uncertainly, she said: *Very well.*

But when he did it was no good. Her body was stiff and her lips were firm and cool and closed.

They had not gone into the city together.

Nevertheless, he had stayed. While his restlessness tugged at him. He had to go—but where? He could not stay here. But he stayed. Why? He had glimpsed another Margret on the night they had met; he had seen the woman she had been, could be. And the woman that she was now stirred such feverish compassion in him that he ached to will that brightness back into those eyes, which seemed more green than blue now, and always withdrawn.

He had heard the telephone. It was late evening and he was in his room. There were voices. Then he heard a shriek that was almost inhuman, a cry of such rage and anguish that he felt a shiver go down his body.

Then a voice—it could not be her voice, not Margret's!—raised, shouting, screaming in Icelandic, hysterical, echoing sharp and hard and violent through the quiet house. Shattering.

And then, as abruptly as it had risen, it fell into silence.

Now there was a mumble of other voices: Todd's, Malfrour's, speaking in urgent whispers, words he could not comprehend. And then he heard sobbing.

Almost a wail.

And footsteps in the passage.

The door opened.

Her face was streaming tears. Her eyes burned. Her hair fell wildly over her shoulders. She was trembling. Her face was contorted.

His heart twisted cruelly.

She had never been more beautiful.

She stared at him. Pleading.

He stopped, unable to do anything else, and took her body against his. And then she was clinging to him, weeping softly, her hair soft against his face, her body quivering against his.

Arni? he whispered.

Her head shook. *His mother.*

He would have led her to the bed, but she seemed too weak to move now. He picked her up in his arms—as he had intended to do on the ice of the lake that night—and carried her gently to the bed and lowered her onto it. She lay staring up at him, as she had done in the hospital.

Helplessly he stood looking down.

He's in Beirut. She wanted me to know he's in . . . Her voice rose again, shrilly: *I don't care, can't she, won't she, why won't she understand, I don't care, hate him, her, him. She's had a postcard* . . . Margret began to laugh. There was no mirth in the sound. The laugh reached every nerve in him. *Postcard, he's in Beirut, Beirut, why isn't he dead?*

She rolled away and drew up her legs. Her body continued to shudder. Her breath came in short spurts, as if she were gasping for air.

He could think of nothing to do. To say. He sat on the edge of the bed.

When his hand touched her shoulder, she flinched.

Then her own hand reached and found his and placed it on the back of her cold, shivering neck, under her hair.

He kept it there for many minutes.

There were whispers in the passage. The sound of footsteps. Then silence.

There was no wind. The house, except for her shallow gulping as she breathed, was very still.

He lowered himself to the bed, he folded his body against hers, his arms over her, and for a small eternity even the sound of her breathing stopped.

He held her like that, very quietly, unmoving.

Another eternity and he realized that she was asleep.

He remembered waking later and realizing that she was still there, close and warm, breathing lightly and regularly. He reached and switched off the light and saw the sky out the window, hard and sharp with stars. He kissed the back of her head, the fine womanly scent of her hair stirring him. But she did not move. And soon he was slipping steeply down into sleep again.

He did not wake till dawn then, and she was lying facing him in the gray light, her eyes grave but childlike on his face. *It's late.* Her tone was quiet, very soft. Like her eyes now. *I could have gone to my room.*

He kissed her. This time her lips opened softly and her arms went around him. But there was no desperation in her now. Only softness and warmth and a desire that brought her closer, then closer, joy exploding in him.

Remembering, he felt his steps slowing on the road. And then he was remembering the cottage on the edge of the white-crusted fjord, surrounded by trees. The cottage was brown with a green steeply slanted roof, the edges of its gable decorated with a scalloped frieze of white. It had been Todd's idea. He did not want Margret to feel any sense of rejection; she knew, as Owen knew, that they were both welcome, but he did have this place and in summer the fishing was good and the children sometimes swam; it might seem primitive to Owen, but it was there. And, Owen surmised, the children had begun to ask questions about himself and Margret: her nightly sharing of his room would not have gone unnoticed. When, in bed that night, he mentioned it to Margret, she rolled close against him and it was a long moment before she said, *Yes, I think so, Yes.* But behind the excitement that he heard, or perhaps only hoped or imagined he heard, there was hesitation, uncertainty.

They had moved through open country, vast plains of nothingness where the eye travels unendingly over the bare bones of the land; between vertical cliffs, where glaciers aeons ago had scoured the valley into chasms; through sheer-sided river gorges. In time the journey became dreamlike and, even with no sun, the whiteness sometimes shimmered blindingly. And Margret's mood remained, puzzlingly, as desolate as the landscape.

Finally into the silence she asked: *Why are you doing this?* There it was again. *I told you before: I'm doing it because I want to.* Silence, and then: *But why? Is it pity?* Even more startled, he said: *Can't one be kind without pitying?* He had sensed the word "love" on his lips but had not uttered it. She leaned against his shoulder then and her hand, bare, covered his on the gear knob, as it had that night as they approached Reykjavik. He wondered whether she was thinking of that now— and of what followed. *Be kind to me, Owen,* she whispered. *I like the way you're kind to me. It's only a few miles now. Then you can be kind to me again.* Her hand tightened over his, and he peered into the gathering twilight and bore down on the fuel pedal.

It was almost dark when they arrived, and leaving the Landrover, they trudged through the snow toward the shadow of the cottage. They could see the far end of the fjord on an outwash plain, probably once a glacier, now water-washed gravel with mossy bog and a scattering of low green mounds, dimly visible in the fading light and, surprisingly, not snow-covered. At the fjord's opposite end, he knew, lay the sea. And on the far side he could see silver water tumbling into the bay as from under a roof of white ice, but they could not hear it. The stillness of the beginning of the world seemed to surround them. Owen felt her eyes on him. He turned to her, placed an arm around her lithe back, and they went inside.

Margret went to work as if she had lived here all her life. The generator began to hum, warm light filled the single room, reached the small balcony bedroom above, and in a few moments there was a flame on the butane cookstove and in the furnace beneath the floor. Margret appeared before him, face aglow, eyes brilliant. *In a few minutes, in a very few minutes now, you can be kind to me.*

He was kind to her, and she was even kinder to him, and during the night, in the strangeness of the room, after they had eaten from the larder that they had brought and which would last for at least ten days, they had been kind to each other again, exciting in the comfortable balcony bunk and then sleeping and waking warm in the night and feeling no longer alone, lying close, with the night cold outside and strange, not hostile, but closed out, her head touching his cheek, his own body curved into hers. He had been alone for years now and often most alone when with women and even more alone those last few months of the marriage that he must not think about now.

He woke in the morning and went down the narrow ladderlike stairway and looked out the window, surprised at the snow-hung trees, the spruces green, forming a cave for the house, and he looked across the bay, its green water visible only at the foot of the waterfall on the other side of the flat snowy surface that he knew to be ice. Yet, already, none of it seemed strange. It was almost as though they had been living here together for a long time. He decided to prepare breakfast himself.

When Margret appeared, she was wrapped in a deep-fleeced blue robe that matched her eyes. *The coffee smells beautiful,* she said. *I'm sorry.* He placed the food on the table, which he had moved to the window overlooking the bay. *Why sorry? I've cooked many a breakfast, and for a long time.* He moved to her. But a doelike flicker appeared in her eyes and she turned her head, as if evading his kiss. *Owen,* she said softly, *I'm frightened.* He felt a frown on his face. *Frightened?* She nodded, lowering her eyes and moving off vaguely. *Not of you. Of us. Myself, really.* He did not speak; he did not understand; he waited. Her whisper reached him across the room: *I'm ashamed.* Then hastily: *No, not ashamed. What is the word in English? Abashed. At myself. How I . . . the way I . . . I can't say it.* She faced him. *It shatters me. The way we . . . last night. Us, all along. I feel . . . brazen.* There was an expression of defiance on her face. *It was never like that . . . before. With him. Or anyone. Not like that, and I am frightened.* When he stepped to her then, she came into his arms, and she was trembling, and he was excited again, but troubled, too, because in her intensity was something that perhaps—but why, why?—she feared or hated or mistrusted. *Pay no heed,* she said, twisting her head against him. *Bear with me, Owen, and pay my stupidities no heed, please, please.*

They walked in all directions—the fjord became their private lake—but at least once a day they would walk down to the beach. It was always wild and lonely, waves pounding in, twenty or thirty feet high when breaking, their curling edges grayed by sand. The sand was black, and the beach was scattered with huge gray stones scoured and rounded by centuries of water. Off the shore were three grotesque monoliths, close together, of weird shape, rising from the water, creatures of erosion. *Giants turned to stone,* Margret called them. Then: *My giants.* Then: *Our giants.*

On one such walk, they saw the clouds darken ominously, swiftly, and she said in a childish rush: *We had better go home now.* She had reached for his hand as she spoke, but then she let her arm drop, and he saw the sullen and glowering sky reflected in her features. And he saw bafflement there, too. She turned and walked briskly away along the ebony beach, its wet edge as shining and lustrous as her falling hair. Should he allow her to go alone? Go where? Home? For that was the word on her tongue that had startled or disturbed her.

When he arrived at the cottage, she was at the cookstove, stiff back to the room, and she was moving with her usual swift grace but noisily. By now he knew the storm-signals— but never the exact nature of the storm. *Well,* she demanded in a sharp bitter voice without turning, *well, Owen, is this my home?* Again he heard that echo of loss and pain, and again he felt that familiar shot-away sensation all through, and he longed to find the word, the right word, the comforting gesture. *I'm not a married woman, you know. I'm a widow. My husband's dead.* She whirled. Her eyes were bright, sharp points of blue. *Arni is dead.* This frightened Owen, who said: *Margret, listen. Your husband is not really dead. Only, perhaps, to you.* He took a step. *It's important, Margret, for you, important to keep reality separate from what you want to believe.* Did she comprehend? Had he reached her? He saw her give way then.

Her slim body sagged, shoulders going slack, eyes lowering. But that hated spirit still hovered in her mind, he knew, haunting her always, and at times like this, even he could feel its presence palpable in the atmosphere between them. Her hate could not exorcise that ghost—her hate of it or his love for her. Love? She lifted her head and cast him a little hooded, hunted glance. *Come here,* she said, in a different voice altogether. So he went to her, not touching. She lifted her head and the loveliness of her face struck its familiar blow. *I'll be good, I promise.* Her raven hair shook and tumbled. *I don't know what happens. Don't hate me, darling. Sometimes I feel like the kind of person I've always hated. Don't hate me.* He did not hate her. He would never hate her. *Be kind to me. Now. It's so warm now, be kind to me.* And then it was as it should always be, her whisper *No, please, no, please, Owen, no—oh yes, yes, yes, yes . . .*

It did not snow that night, after all, but there was a great howl of wind that shook the cottage. The northern lights were dim and silver and seemed far away. Lying beside her, half-asleep himself, he heard her weeping. In her sleep? Should he waken her? Or was she awake? He decided not to move, and in time the animallike whimpering sound stopped. He did not sleep then, could not, but lay there helpless in the grip of tenderness and compassion—and hate for the man who had done this to her.

In the morning with that too-bright smile that suggested inner gloom, she told him that she had decided not to walk and suggested that he go alone. The walk had not been the same and his mind had been on the cottage. Their three friendly giants in the sea appeared menacing.

When he returned, they played chess at the table, her mood grave but not melancholy. She looked pale and the luster had gone from her eyes. And then, slowly, they became aware of the sun. It came very slowly and flowed through the windows. It was the first time it had appeared. And gradually the room and the scene of snow and ice beyond the window were transformed. Outside, there came into being a rich and almost tropical profusion, full of color, conjured out of pure, blinding sunlight, and everything seemed alive and incessantly changing. They gazed in silent wonder at the fjofd, their lake, through a dazzling latticework of ice-encrusted boughs, whose twigs appeared to be many-colored blossoms, all illusion, of course, conspiracy of light and frozen snow. It was as though they could not speak, or would not, for fear of shattering the delicate chimerical world that had come miraculously into being. Across the fjord, glazed and resplendent, the waterfall glittered gold and above it the cliffs had a tawny hue that softened them, and the higher range beyond was now bathed in the incredible yellow richness of an unmoving cloud. Finally Margret took in a breath. He looked across the table. Her face now, itself transfigured, was lifted, a chalice of gold holding quiet wonder, and Owen felt a renewing surge of hope. *My eyes are dizzy,* she said. *Are yours, darling? Are your eyes dizzy, too?* The radiance filled the room as well. He saw her rise. He did not, at first, realize what she was doing. She moved slowly, but in only a moment the heavy robe fell to the floor. For one intense and almost unbearable instant he felt the immense quiet power of beauty and knew, in that same instant, that they were indeed alone in the world together, as if she were the first woman, as if creation were only beginning. He knew, too, that the blood surging and scalding through him was life itself and that, no matter what cruel future tricks time held, he would never fully recover this splendor. In the pulsating stillness, with the unlikely glory of sun shimmering on her womanly whiteness, burnishing it, he believed again in miracles, in hope, in tomorrow. He hesitated to move, as if the fragile gossamer web might unravel and the brilliance dim and darken. But, aching with hollowness and afire with need, he stood, mind reeling with the room.

Afterwards, with the sweet taste of her mouth and body on his lips, in all his senses, he lay on the soft sheepskin and gazed at the vaulted ceiling. She was stretched full-length on her back beside him, her splendid body quiet now, her eyes closed. Hanging above were intricate designs in white rope which, when he had asked, she had said had some religious significance, that she herself did not understand. The designs were beautiful in themselves, and mysterious—symbols of what? *Don't,* her voice, clouded as if drugged, said, *don't try to decipher it, darling. Or anything.* Again he had that always-startling impression that, even without opening her eyes, she had probed his mind. *There's really no way, is there? If only . . . if only we could all accept that. Accident, chance . . .*

In bed, hours later, listening tonight to her tranquil, quiet breathing, he could not sleep. He was aware of the vast mysteries extending on all sides—the sea, the mountains, rock and plains stretching away and, farther off, the volcano and the small menaced island, and farther still, the cities teeming with life and joy and misery. The northern lights flickered clearly and vividly tonight, many colors, also mysterious. But was anything, anything, as incalculable and unfathomable as the human soul? His own, and hers, especially hers. The exaltation of the afternoon had become an overpowering awareness of this woman, this child, this *person* beside him here. What had been compassion for her turned to torment: her world had gone out of focus, wrenched awry, and here she was, sometimes weeping in her sleep, defenseless, lost, and alone. Except for him. And how had he hoped to help? Had he really thought of her, or had he been too blinded by his own desire and enchantment? How could he, himself as uprooted, as lost, hope to help her to return to a state of health in which the awesome cruelty and haphazardness of living—what she termed accident, chance—could be accepted, made sense of, reconciled with the necessity in all of us to *know* that there is certainty, continuity, meaning? He thought of all the other refugees from Heimaey, scattered, waiting. And he thought of the child that would never be, the child that she had wanted, needed. He felt hopelessness settle through his mind, a heavy bleak sense of helplessness. What the hell had he hoped to accomplish for *her* by bringing her here? Or had he come to gratify his own sensual needs and hungers, to assuage his own loneliness?

The night stretched endlessly ahead. And now he recalled, with bittersweet nostalgia, the glory of the sunlit day as if it had happened long ago, to another self. As if, perhaps, it had not happened at all but had been dreamed.

It was always dark at breakfast and the gray light usually came while they were still at table. It was always slightly chilly, too, and each morning Owen wished there was a wood-burning fireplace, as there would have been in such a cottage at home. (Home, there was that word again. Where was home?) He remembered the spitting sparks, the crackling, and the fine sharp smell of smoke from cedar or apple-tree. But here there was no wood to burn. This morning she was quiet again, withdrawn, her eyes evading his.

Until she said: *Take me back, Owen.*

At first he could not believe what he had heard. He did not reply.

She leaped from the table, violently, and she looked at him with hysterical rage, crying: *It's too much, it's too much, it's too much!*

Baffled, he was astonished at his own quick anger, did not ask what she meant. It didn't matter now. *If that's what you want, Margret . . .*

I don't know what I want. I'm not me anymore! Her voice was shrill and he remembered her shrieking at the woman, Arni's mother, on the telephone the night she came to his room. *I don't know anything!* The anguish behind the rage sounded clear, and his own anger lost itself in a sudden familiar writhing of his heart. Then, as if she sensed his feeling, she screamed, wildly: *I don't want your pity, I told you, I told you, I don't want pity!*

He did not answer. He was not sure how to answer that. *Do you want to go today?*

Yes, yes, yes, now!

He stood up. Was this the golden girl in the sunlight of only a few hours ago? Could this be the same person? *We can make it to Reykjavik before dark, I think,* he heard himself say.

And then he saw tears in her baffled, furious eyes. He felt a cracking in his chest and a choking breathlessness. And then she swooped and was against him, trembling, soft and vulnerable and fragile, and he felt her cheek cool against his, and tears. She was shivering all over.

Be kind to me, Owen. One more time. Don't hate me, be kind to me. Once more.

They made love then, again, but it was no good. There was not even desperation in it. She seemed to have gone away. And she did not murmur no or yes or anything else. And there was no quiet moan of contentment at the end. Later, driving, he wished they had both come away with the memory of yesterday instead of the taste of ashes.

The countryside looked bleak and harsh, its starkness ugly. They did not speak for many miles and then she said: *Would you take me to a hotel?*

If that's what you want.

I think I'd prefer to be with strangers.

He tried to understand. He failed. Again. He drove the distance with the feeling inside that he had failed in many ways. But he said nothing.

In Reykjavik it was sleeting. The streets were coated with shining ice, and the wheels slipped, and the people on the streets looked abstracted and cold and, for the first time, seemed to be hurrying. In the dim wintry light he took her to the small hotel where he had stayed while she was in the hospital. In the tiny entrance foyer, he did not wait for her to go to the reception desk. He did not kiss her. She said: *Thank you, Owen.* And he said: *For what?* And nevertheless, she leaned and kissed him lightly on the mouth, but her lips were cold, and it was no good. It was like being kissed by a polite stranger.

He drove to Keflavik then, where the runways had iced, and a wind was blowing, and he had to wait three hours for space on a plane to Heimaey.

On the narrow road on Heimaey now, he wondered whether any of it had really happened. It was unreal, like a dream remembered. Ahead now he could see the lonely farmhouse silhouetted against the iron gray sky over the Atlantic and he could picture the cliffs and crags dropping beyond it to the sea. He halted. What the hell, exactly and precisely what the hell, was he doing? Did he imagine that by taking a woman, any woman, he could purge himself of the memory of her? His love of her—yes, love.

Christ, what an idiot, what a damn-fool, adolescent idiot.

Sooner or later he would have to go home—although now his cottage in the woods, which he had loved, did not seem like home at all. He would take a few more pictures of the desolation of violence here and then return to the desolation of loneliness in Connecticut.

The sound of a motor reached him from behind. He turned to see an ambulance approaching along the road. He stepped onto the crusted ridge of snow to allow it to pass. But it did not. It came to a stop and he recognized the driver now.

Doctor Pall rolled down the window and asked: "May I . . . what is the Yank phrase . . . may I offer you a lift?"

"No, thanks," Owen said, for he had decided.

"How is she?"

It was the question he had asked the doctor that morning in the hospital—a lifetime ago. What could he answer? The truth: "She had not recovered." His eyes met those of the other man, which looked sad and knowing beneath bushy silver brows. "I have tried," he heard himself say, answering the unspoken questions.

"Have you?"

How could he explain to this man, here in the open cold, that her affliction, the canker of her soul, her despair withering her womanhood, were all beyond his fumbling, feeble ministrations?

Only a fool could believe that love can cure all.

"*Have* you tried, Mr. Llewellyn?"

Rage took over, and bitterness. "Damn right I've tried! Goddamnit, there's only so much a man can do. *He* did it to her, that bastard, and if I knew where he was, I'd kill him!"

And hearing his own harsh shout, he was suddenly terrified that he would burst into tears. Here, standing on this road, cold all through, he fought the tears that he had needed to shed with every stupid futile photograph he had taken since leaving her at the hotel.

The doctor smiled. "I recognized your ear a mile down the road. How are your ribs? How's your back?"

"Fine." Except when making love. "I'm fine." A lie. He would never be fine again.

In the distance the low, hollow rumbling of the volcano exploded in a series of ferocious blasts. Perhaps the whole world would never be fine again.

Doctor Pall said: "Killing her husband—would that help *her*?"

"No. To her he's dead already. I think, in some strange way, she believes it." His voice rose again: "That's how confused she is."

"Hell of a time to desert then, isn't it?"

Startled, he said: "I didn't desert. I was thrown overboard!"

He watched the doctor light a cigar. "If she's so confused, who's going to straighten her out?"

"I'm out of my depths," Owen admitted, the awful sense of futility streaming through him again.

"Then swim harder," Doctor Pall growled. "You think this town here has a chance?"

"No."

"Nor do I. But they're still fighting."

Owen turned and looked at the fire and smoke shooting into the sky in the distance.

"Get in," Doctor Pall said. "I'll take you where you're going."

But Owen shook his head. "I've changed my mind."

"Then get in anyway. I'll be going back to the village in a short while." And then, when Owen did not answer, the doctor spoke in an altogether different, milder tone: "There's never as much time as we imagine there is. And when it's gone, all we can do is wonder what we were doing while we had it."

And Owen recalled something he had heard in town—something about Doctor Pall's wife dying in childbirth years ago. Odd he should remember that now. Owen turned to face the other man.

Doctor Pall's face was expressionless. As if he were waiting.

"Thanks," Owen heard himself say, urgency pulling at his muscles and his mind now. "I'll walk, thanks!" He had already wasted enough time. *"Bless,"* he said.

"Bless."

In the rearview mirror outside the window of the ambulance Doctor Pall could see the figure of Owen Llewellyn diminishing in the distance behind—first walking, then breaking into a trot, in the direction of the village. Doctor Pall had observed the uncertainty and anguish and self-blame in the younger man's face. The red beard was growing out again, and the bruises appeared to have healed, but Doctor Pall sensed deeper, less visible wounds. What a mystery the world was, really. He should have asked where Margret was staying now. After the night of the violence in Reykjavik, her husband's mother had telephoned him again, several times, her knifelike voice frantic and demanding: had Arni returned to Heimaey? When Pall had said no, she had all but accused him of lying. The chief of police, at one of the council meetings, had told Pall that the Reykjavik authorities were also making inquiries about the schoolteacher. Then, later, Jonas had received a postcard from Ireland. Pall recalled the dark morning when he had shouted furious accusations at the young man outside the hospital. Had his own outrage played a part in or been responsible for what young Arni had decided to do? He would never know, but he had become acutely conscious of the infinite intricacy of that tapestry sometimes foolishly referred to as life. His friend, Baldvin, who was in Europe now, would probably call it fate. And Petur would call it the will of God. Was there any knowing?

Odette's farmhouse was a hundred meters away now. A young Marine corporal had, somewhat abashedly, delivered a message, written in French:

Please come, chéri. I may need you. So here he was. More mystery.

She greeted him with a smile. As usual. Offered wine, black eyes shimmering as usual. But when she poured, the carafe clattered against the glass.

Was this a professional visit?

In a way—yes.

She said she might need him—was she then ill?

She could not be certain.

Perhaps if she described her symptoms.

He examined her, professionally unaware of her loveliness. What he discovered was ugly. Yes, she needed him.

"It is true, *n'est-ce pas?*" she asked.

"What you fear is true," he told her.

"And?"

"And now you must have treatment. And I must know the names of the men who have visited you."

She laughed her husky laugh, self-mocking, and her black eyes glinted. "I do not know names. I prefer not to know names."

"They should all be examined," Doctor Pall said gently but with firmness, wondering at the anger stirring in himself. "We have enough trouble here, we don't need more."

"Because of me. That is what you mean, yes?"

"We don't need it because of anyone! I'll make arrangements to have you flown to the hospital in Reykjavik, but meanwhile I shall require names, as many as you do know or can recall."

"Would that not be a betrayal?"

The word struck a cruel and sour note. He said: "If you do not, it would be criminal."

She sobered. The dark glitter went from her eyes. Her brows came together above the fine narrow nose. "I shall try."

"Now."

"Now?"

"The boy, Rolf Agnarsson, who came here often before?"

She smiled then: the faint smile he had known well. "No. Rolf, they tell me, has a girl in town. An American girl, I think. No. Rolf will not forgive himself for leaving me here alone that night of the first explosion."

"Thurbjorn Herjolfsson?"

"Ah, there is whispering then in the village. Prattle about me. *Bavardage*."

"Thurbjorn?"

"If you know, why do you ask?" She was, as in the past, teasing. She lay back on the couch, throwing her head back as well. "Poor Thurbjorn. His wife accused him of seeing me when he had not, so he did."

"Odette," Doctor Pall said then, "Odette, I don't think you realize how serious this can be. You were probably infected by some foreigner who perhaps didn't even know it himself. But I must insist you see no one else, you will make up as complete a list as possible, and if you do not know the names, give me descriptions."

"It will be a long list, Pall."

"You have till morning. And will have nothing else to do."

She straightened and her face was grave and troubled. "I have hurt you, no? I have hurt *you*."

"I'll come for you in the morning."

She shook her head. *"Non."*

"Odette—do you want to die?"

"Mon chéri, I do not wish to die. I do not wish to live. It is of small matter to me."

The simple truth and sincerity in that stabbed at some deep-rooted conviction or emotion in him. He had spent a life working for life. "You have no choice," he said, somewhat harshly.

"I will see no one, as you say, as you command. But I will not leave this house." Her tone softened. "I am sorry, my darling."

"I am sorry, too," Doctor Pall said. "I shall come for you in the morning."

"I shall be joyed to see you," she said softly. "As I have always been. I have missed you. But I will not leave this house."

"In the morning, Odette," Doctor Pall said and went to the door and out to the ambulance without looking back, and he drove back into the village, making his plan.

At whatever cost, of whatever kind, he could not allow the contagion to spread. There were not sufficient antibiotics on the island to fight an epidemic. Didn't he have enough to contend with, damn it? The mention of Rolf Agnarsson made him angry in itself. Damn fool—fortunate he hadn't been crippled for life with feet burned that brutally. And even in his pain the boy had seemed to take a certain pride in what he had done. There had been, even as Pall cut away the scorched boots, a look of joy in his eyes in spite of the contortions of suffering in his face. And both he and that American girl could have died of hypothermia in the water, and no one would ever have known what had happened to them. Youth—a time of idiocy.

If he hurried a bit, Pall would be in time for the funeral of Frosti Runaldsson. Did Pall regret what he had done? Perhaps he would never know what he himself felt. The old man had collapsed at his desk, and Pall had had him taken, not to the first-aid center, but to the hospital. There, he took it upon himself to give an injection that could not possibly relieve the man's pain, but by increasing the dose, it had. As sleep closed over him and the lined gray face went slack at last, Pall hoped it was a final slumber. And it had been. But even then, knowing, the old man's used voice, still crackling, had said: *Now I will never know what happens, will I?* No, old friend, no. But you are out of misery forever. Doctor Pall has played god again. Meting out mercy. What god was there to forgive *him?*

In Reykjavik she walked the streets, dreamlike, until she was aching with tiredness. Then she went back to the small barren room at the hotel and slept. Or drowsed. She ate little. She came to know the window of every shop. She went to the historical museum and stared at the past: altars, weapons, armor, clothes, utensils. She went to the art museums and stared at pictures that seemed unreal. She had vaguely hoped to see Baldvin Einarsson's painting of the two cones, but it was now being exhibited in Europe; it was of no consequence really. She tried to avoid the lake but could not. Across it was the high apricot-colored house. She blanked her mind to the violence on the ice. She did not even re- member her own pain. She watched the skaters and took a faint, distant pleasure in their rhythms, their flushed faces, the joy in their eyes. She tried to read: the page became a blur. She went to the cinema and could not recall the film afterwards. She felt as if she were dead. The illness, she sensed, was worse than death; it was not of the body or even of the mind, but of the spirit. There was only emptiness in her.

She went to visit her sister in the rented house in the suburbs. Her sister had grown fatter; she now walked more ponderously and her self-indulgent eyes seemed angry. She would never go back there to live because she would not give the gods a second chance. Her husband stood up and left the room. Margret telephoned for a taxi and knew she would not return. On the way to the hotel she realized dimly that she had not waited for the children to come home from school. The boy and girl she had loved. Once. Reminded of her own childhood, she looked into the mirror in her room and saw a face she did not recognize. She wondered where that eager girl, once herself, had gone. And what of that soft and happy young woman in Vestmannaeyjar?

Todd and Malfrour came. They insisted she go to lunch. She looked, Mal said, as if she had not eaten for years. She ate little, said less. Arni's mother telephoned often, they said. She insisted they tell her where Margret had gone. She sounded pathetic, Mal said. For a brief moment Margret came to life: she felt a pang of bitter pleasure at the thought

of the woman's suffering. Todd spoke of Owen. He hoped
Owen had not hurt her. He should have warned her about
Owen. She shook her head. Since his divorce, Todd said,
Owen had become what Americans called a loner. She shook
her head again. Todd did not know Owen, really; he
doubted anyone did. She wished he would stop speaking the
name. He did not know Owen, well enough; neither did she.
Nor would she now, ever.

And it was of her own doing. Alone in the room again,
she tried not to remember, but did. The cottage with the
lovely green roof. The demons in her. The sullen and
morose withdrawals. The gnawing guilts: was she using him,
was she avenging herself on Arni? The hot shame in her.
Owen's bruised face and bandaged ribs. The terror of her
own feelings: the snarled fevers and the wild giving of herself in passions that had never been unleashed in her before.
In the end, that day of sunlit splendor, the demons had won.
Too much, too much!

And here she was, alone, really alone for the first time.
Her life a total loss. All waste. She did not even weep. She
had not wept once. She was not even sure it mattered.

Two days later—or perhaps it was three, for she had lost
all sense of time—there was a knock on the door. She rose
from the bed, tossing aside the magazine that she had not
really been reading, and then she was facing him. He carried
the dufflebag, and his camera gear was strung over his
shoulders, and now he had a very short stubble of red beard.
His brown eyes studied her. Then he said: "Doctor Pall asked
how you were."

She could not speak.

Owen said: "Look at you, girl. God, I'd hate to have to
tell him."

Then, when she still could not speak, he brushed past
her and into the room, dropping the bag and beginning to
untangle the straps of the camera cases. She finally felt astonishment overtake her. He turned to face her. "I'm here,"
he said, almost defiantly, "because I couldn't bear to think of
you alone." His voice was firm and excited. He waited.

For what? For her to say what she had said before? She

couldn't remember exactly what that was. She managed to say: "I . . . I thought you were in New York."

He shook his head. "I've been on Heimaey." Then in a different tone, that tender tone that she knew: "I couldn't leave."

Confusion descended on her mind. But only that.

And then, as if he had been thinking about it and knew precisely what he was going to say: "Yes, Margret—pity." She felt herself stiffen. He rushed on: "What the hell's the matter with pity? It can even be part of love. Why not?"

Love?

She retreated. She leaned back against the closed door. She met his gaze. "I cannot . . . I cannot love anyone, Owen." Then not knowing herself what she was going to say, she added: "I am too . . . filled with hate."

"Why not?" he demanded, but in that same soft tone. "You've every reason to hate, every right. So do it." He took a single step. "Only . . . don't confuse him with all men. Or with me."

Had she? Unfair, unfair—had she done that? She felt a stinging behind her eyes. "I will not," she said. "I will try."

"Go on and cry," he said, his voice hardening slightly. "Any woman who's had her child killed inside her—and by the man who planted the seed—has bought herself the right to shock and a flood of tears."

She felt them scalding in her eyes then and on her cheeks. And then she was sobbing.

But she felt a quickening of life somewhere inside.

Head down, she said: "Owen . . . I do not want to love anyone. I cannot. Ever again."

A long moment passed. She lifted her head and he was a blur beyond the blinding tears.

Then she heard him say, very gently: "You don't have to love me, Margret. It's enough that I love you."

The sobbing stopped. Her vision cleared. But her throat was locked, her breath gone.

"Margret . . . I swore I'd never say that to anyone." He came closer. "You've been lonely for weeks. I've been lonely

for years—and didn't know it or maybe didn't have the guts
to admit it. So the time we had together—it was not for you
only, you see."

She heard herself utter a strangled sound and then,
without volition, she moved, stepping to him. His arms went
around her, and her head was against his chest, and she was
crying softly: "Oh God, oh my God, Owen, Owen, Owen."

His voice was close to her ear. "I've a rented van below,
with a heater. I'm going north to take one last set of pictures
for the book."

She leaned back and looked into his face. "Even if I
cannot love you?"

"Aren't you sick of this room?"

She nodded, feeling its ugliness and bareness around
them. But if she had learned anything, it was that she could
not use him again because of her own needs. "Yes," she
admitted, "but . . . I cannot, Owen. You're doing this for
me, I know, and I am grateful, but I cannot."

He released her and stepped back and away. "I've two
separate sleeping bags."

And then the life that she had felt as only tentative and
quivering in her before burst fully through her, body and
mind. "We shall need only one," she said softly.

Doctor Pall's plan was devious but, he felt, necessary in
view of Odette's intransigence. He arrived at the house just
after first light the next morning. Now in March the light
came a half hour earlier than it had the month before. He
asked for the list, which Odette gave him with a half smile.
He looked it over. It contained names he had expected, such
as Thurbjorn Herjolfsson, and many that surprised him,
such as Doctor Alexei Varanin. He placed it in his pocket,
then informed Odette that he had changed his mind: he

understood her reluctance to leave and therefore he would take it upon himself to treat her here. He would come every morning, bringing food and wine and medicines, and the treatment would begin today. He prepared a hypodermic and, as he injected it, he silently asked her forgiveness. When she was quite unconscious, he folded her slim body into a heavy blanket and carried her to the ambulance. At the airstrip the Icelandic Airlines plane, as arranged, was waiting. She was carried aboard on a stretcher. When the plane was in the air, he went to the command post and telephoned the Reykjavik hospital, as prearranged, and they dispatched an ambulance to the airport. Then he took a lonely walk through the havoc of hoses and action and noise and blackness and wondered whether he would ever see her again. He needed this time to himself before beginning the arduous—and embarrassing—job that lay ahead.

The transport ship *Esja,* returning to the mainland with volunteer workers—some of whom, Thurbjorn Herjolfsson suspected, were leaving for the same reason that he was—with newspapermen and photographers, with plant machinery and other salvaged valuables stowed in the enormous hold below, was bombarded, as it churned through the harbor opening, with coarse black ash that pinged off the helmets of the passengers on deck. Thurbjorn was accustomed to it. And he was too brimful of anger to notice. It was a quiet anger, and it had not begun when he had stood staring at the gutted, black and smoking shell of the freezing plant—no, there had been a certain odd satisfaction in that sight, as there had been when he telephoned Elin's father to report the loss. But Elin's father had said: *I have already heard. Now, I trust, you realize what I might have lost if I had allowed you to continue operating. The machinery, at least, is safely stored here in Reykjavik.* Elin's father was always right. Had to be. *That* was when Thurbjorn's simmering rage had really begun.

The island, low and, from this distance, seemingly on

fire, was receding in a mizzling rain. He turned from the view. He—now he, too—was an exile. Following orders— why was it that he was always following someone else's orders? Doctor Pall's this time. After the examination in the privacy of the empty hospital, with a sigh: *You are not the only one, unfortunately.* No. But he was the only one who, having had one function taken from him, had found another so fortuitously. Chance, ill chance perhaps. No one wanted old Frosti Runaldsson to die, but many knew he had been dying for some time now. Even Frosti himself. Or else why would he have sent for Thurbjorn, and why would he have asked him whether, having lost his position when the freezing plant closed, he would be willing to take over the operation of the processing factory, the only one now still functioning? *I had mine going again in the first week. The only one till you started up yours—well, perhaps not yours, but you know what I mean.* The lean, gray leather face was lined with furrows of age and panic. *Now I want you to help me. And when I'm gone, keep it going, hear me, keep it going!*

But Thurbjorn had not even had the opportunity to begin when, damn him, Doctor Pall had intervened. And now Thurbjorn° had reason to regret those hours with Odette, during which he had always been aware, even in the intensity of his pleasure, of the vengeful malice behind his more immediate physical need. Ever since Elin had turned herself into that raging demon, that violent accusing harridan out of the sagas themselves, and especially since that last visit to the mainland, when he had become completely convinced that she really preferred her father to her husband—all along a volcano of his own had been seething inside. Now, very soon now, that volcano would erupt. He would allow it to erupt. And in a way that only he would realize.

The rain had become a thumping, clattering hailstorm by the time Elin herself opened the front door of her father's house. She was wearing a bright silken robe and smoking one of the long, brown-paper, Havana cigarettes that her father favored. Her small face looked drowsy and, yes, even happy.

Without him. Her floating contentment added fuel to his wrath but, facing her over coffee and brandy, he warned himself that he must, if he were to succeed, be careful not to reveal what he was actually feeling. So he told her how much he had missed her, a lie, and how sorry he was that the freezing plant had burned, another lie, and that he hoped her father was well, the most satisfying lie of all. Her father, she said, would be disappointed that he missed Thurbjorn's visit—this, too, a lie, hers in retaliation, and with a question lurking in it: was this a visit only?

He ignored that. "I have missed you in many ways," he told her again, but with a difference.

She seemed less surprised than pleased at this and knew his meaning at once. Her lids lowered. "What of the servants?"

"You answered my ring yourself." He knew the game, all its intricacies and feints and tricks familiar. If she did not protest, refrain, play the coquette, resist his blandishments, now expected, before granting the privilege, succumbing for his sake, not her own, why then, her pleasure would not be complete. "Do we have time then for another brandy?"

"Before what?"

He ignored this, too, as she would expect. "It's a champagne occasion, really, isn't it?"

"You're in a very jolly mood, aren't you? The last time you were here . . ."

"This is today. The way I spoke that night was unforgivable. But you will forgive me, won't you, Elin?"

He felt like an actor on a stage. He was standing off and observing his performance, judging his words before he spoke them—a mockery of the games that he had always been forced to play. Orders again, but of a different sort. And it came to him, as he poured another brandy, that everything was really a game to Elin. And he had always thought her childishly charming. Perhaps that was one of the reasons.

She lay back now, her arms along the back of the couch. The gown fell open to her waist. "I forgive you, yes. But that is not why you have come, is it?"

"You know why I have come, Elin."

"For a visit only?"

"That is for you to decide," he said, suddenly hating himself for the whole charade. And when she did not answer, her pale eyes steady and contemplative, weighing her reply, he warned himself again to contain his fury. But he said: "You would prefer it be only a visit, wouldn't you? As well, as well. So then it will be." But his anger was not because he wished it otherwise, but because he knew now that she was really content here. Without him.

"We have," she said softly, "less than an hour, I think. Certainly no more."

He knew then that he had triumphed. Her father could not, by the rules, give her the one satisfaction that she needed and that he, her husband still, offered. His success burned bitterly in his mouth. They would need less than an hour. Much less.

He set down his glass and as they mounted the stairs, he felt no sensual excitement whatever—but a deeper, uglier anticipation. His revenge would soon be complete. He would soon lose his anger within her. And more.

But he knew, too, and did not now care, that he would never forgive himself yet at the same time would never regret doing what he was now about to do.

Flakkari, the *Wanderer*, continued to traverse the lava field in all directions, its path capricious, even freakish, but closely observed and recorded because of its unique nature. Whenever it drifted toward the town, and especially toward the harbor, alarm prevailed: would Flakkari do what, so far, Kirkjufell had failed to accomplish? Then on a night of blinding high flame, unobserved behind it, the Wanderer disappeared into the sea on the east.

The thin plume of smoke no longer rose from the chimney of the processing plant. Now all the fish-processing factories were dim, dead shadows along the wharf. Vessels loaded with fish no longer entered the harbor.

Then, to the astonishment of all, and without previous warning, a powerful pumping system, dissembled and shipped by air, arrived from the United States. It consisted of forty pumps with diagrams and spare parts. Twelve-inch plastic pipes carried water from the sea and, overnight, thirty-five hundred metric tons of cold seawater were being discharged into the encroaching lava. How many buildings might have been saved if the equipment had arrived earlier? Photographs had established, to the surprise of some and to the satisfaction of all, that the river of lava moving toward the harbor entrance had been slowed considerably, but it continued on its inexorable way nonetheless. Had the equipment arrived in time? And would it be sufficient?

Seven more houses were shattered, two of them bursting into flame. And a power line came down, plunging a third of the town into darkness.

Then, on a bleak March afternoon, the skies already darkening to night, two vessels, awkward hulks, enormous, entered the narrow passageway into the harbor: the *Sandey* and the *Loosin,* dredging ships from the States, equipped with huge pumping systems. Word spread fast and soon the dim docks were lined with men. There were no cheers, but a waving from the waterfront and from the decks—and on land solemn, wondering faces. Did they dare hope?

They had had their midday meal together, Captain Agnar and his son Rolf, and now they were walking along Strandvegur and past the charred ruins of the three processing plants, and when they were in front of the building-supply store where Rolf had worked, its owner, Rudolf Haroldsson, came out. He halted briefly, a lean man, taller than Rolf, but not as tall as the captain, and inquired of Rolf's burns. This embarrassed the boy, who was on crutches, so Rudolf grinned at the father and moved on, carrying a huge tool box. Agnar knew the meaning of that grin, and his son also knew. Well, was it not to be expected? The whole town—what was left of it—had heard of that foolish escapade with the American girl. And while shaking their heads, some at least there were who admitted a grudging admiration for such courage or foolhardiness. Would the boy never be done with childish things? He would soon be eighteen. Yes, imagine. And what could be made of the fact, of which the town was also aware, that Rolf was now living with that same girl in the bookshop where he had worked for Rudolf's wife, Kristrun? Was that more adolescent foolishness? Or . . . or was that another way for Rolf to prove to himself that he was now a man? Just as looking into the volcano's crater had possibly been his way of proving that he was not a coward. Rolf, in spite of his limping and his pain, had revealed no regret, at least not to his father. Perhaps he was even proud of the reckless folly that might have crippled him for life or killed him. But Agnar, shocked at himself, could understand in his own way. Certainly Rolf seemed more confident of himself now—and more easy in the presence of his father, who towered above him as they walked.

"Does it hurt, to walk, I mean?" Agnar realized that he had asked the same question several times since he had arrived. But he could feel the pain in his own feet, as if it were actually his.

Instead of answering, Rolf asked: "Is Mother better now?"

"Much better," Agnar said. Untrue, though, most untrue. "I bought her a new piano."

"She must love that."

"Yes." Also untrue. For since she had first thanked him—a flash of her old bright self for a moment only—she had not touched the keys. Instead, she drifted wraithlike around the unfamiliar house, which by now had become such a shambles that he often wished, disloyally, that he could stay alone on the *Njord*—and she always a woman of casual tidiness in the past, a woman who had taken delight in order. Often, when he came in, he had the impression that she was surprised to see him there, as if he were a stranger intruding. Two or three times she had asked: *Is the winter over?*

"And what of Rosa?" Rolf inquired, perhaps sensing his father's thoughts and the aching distress in him always these days and nights.

"Your sister has a room in the city center now." It was all he said, or cared to say. Agnar suffered again that impression that lately something seemed about to overwhelm him, feeling with certainty that all about him everything was changing, and everyone. Including himself.

He hoped Rolf would not ask about Axel Sitfusson. Seeing Rolf on crutches had reminded him over and over of his old friend and crew member who had walked for years on one wooden leg, when he walked at all. Axel was dead. Agnar still had trouble accepting that or even believing it. Imagine an old sea hand like Axel dying of pneumonia, and on land.

Not wishing to think of this, he said: "Rosa has her own life," and he hoped it would be a happy one, much as he missed her presence. Her visits were few and, during them, her mind was always elsewhere.

The volcano, on this day, was quiet again—only sleeping, as he had heard the workers say in the mess hall. Agnar was aware that whenever the turbulence abated for several hours on end, the townspeople on the mainland, and presumably the men here, would reach longingly for a hope that, they had learned, would prove to be unjustified, as on many occasions in the past—a hope that they dared not embrace. Just as he personally had learned that there was an invisible frontier in his own mind which he dared not cross because on the far side lay a tundra of hopelessness.

Where Ruth now lived.

Turning the corner at Barugata, Agnar sensed rather than saw a movement at his side. Then, halting and turning,

he heard Rolf coughing, gasping for breath, saw his head
shoot forward, eyes bulging and as, aghast, Agnar watched,
the boy's smaller, shorter body doubled, and he was choking.
The crutches clattered to the cobbles and Rolf's head was
down now, body heaving, and he dropped to one knee. Agnar, who had seen men drown, threw his pipe aside and
stepped, tall bulk bending as Rolf collapsed completely, and
in that instant, head lower, Agnar felt his own chest contract
with a suffocating heaviness, an iron band tightened around
his skull, his vision reeled, then blurred, and he felt that he
also would go down. But he knew he could not, could not, so
he gathered his son's body into his arms and straightened
with an angry effort. Standing, he could breathe again. His
vision cleared. The iron band loosened. And then, the boy's
body cradled in his huge arms and the strength returning to
him, he climbed the incline of Barugata, his thick legs pumping in long strides that became faster and then faster still.
The boy was still coughing convulsively, his body writhing
and jerking in his father's arms, his eyes wide and glazed.
When he reached the corner of Vestmannabraut, he turned
right in the direction of the hotel and command headquarters, moving faster now on level ground. Fleetingly, he recalled the many times he had held Rolf so, but the terror in
him propelled him into a near-run and he charged on.

By the time they arrived at the first-aid station, Rolf's
gasps had become a wheezing only, his body had stilled, his
eyes had cleared, and he seemed weak and drained and content to lie so in his father's arms.

Jonas Vigfusson was having coffee with Karl Sveinsson
behind Karl's huge cluttered table-desk at headquarters
when Doctor Pall reported the incident. The boy had already
recovered with the aid of only a little oxygen, but they would

need more now, much more, because Rolf Agnarsson had been overcome by gas.

"Where?" was all that Karl asked.

Doctor Pall told him and he reached for one of the telephones, spoke sharply into it. He dispatched the U.S. Medical Corps toxicologist, who had been on the scene for two weeks because of Doctor Alexei Varanin's warning to the area of Strandvegur and Barugata. Karl's face was set and his voice was strained. What a few, knowing, had feared the most, had happened.

Then Doctor Pall was explaining. The gases are heavy and close to the ground and seek out low places. That's why the boy had been overcome and the father, being taller, had not. Where the gas gains access to closed cellars or houses, it can build up and saturate the air and become explosive. And the gases are, not just toxic, but lethal. "The boy was fortunate," Doctor Pall said. "The gases can kill within seconds."

Then Karl was in action. He was speaking quietly and tensely into another telephone ordering the mess hall moved at once from the processing plant near the east end of the docks to the secondary school which was on higher ground. Doctor Pall was warning that he did not have sufficient oxygen. Karl was cursing: he had put in a requisition more than two weeks ago! Doctor Pall was also suggesting gas masks. Karl was demanding on the telephone to know how many masks were available, and when he heard the answer he didn't even bother to curse. He growled: "Get them here by air, now, today, as many as you can, and if that's not enough, we'll find another source!" He slammed his fist on the table.

Doctor Pall retreated. Karl rose and stepped to the wall, ripped down the latest reconnaissance map with the red lava lines and replaced it with a large street map of the town. As he drew, from memory, a rough line indicating the encroachment, thus eliminating that area from consideration, he was snarling: "Where are the precious scientist boys now? Why didn't we have a warning of some sort?"

"Easy, Karl," Jonas said.

Karl studied the map a moment, then made a red X at

the corner of Strandvegur and Barugata, and circled it. Then he pressed a button on his desk. "Science," he muttered.

Almost immediately, from other posts on the ground floor, two men appeared. One was the bearded geologist from the university who served on the council, whose name Jonas had learned was Geir Helgi.

Karl spoke to the other, a middle-aged man with faded, tired eyes: "I want signs, at least fifteen to start with, and fast. Reading 'Off Limits—Danger of Gas.'"

The older man only nodded and turned away and left the large room, showing no surprise and moving swiftly.

Karl did not sit down. He pointed to the map and barked: "Why weren't we warned?"

"You were not warned," Geir Helgi said stiffly, "because we could not get close enough to the eruption vents to take readings. Because of the fallout and especially because of the lava bombs. Do you imagine we haven't been trying?"

Outwardly unmollified but, Jonas suspected, inwardly chagrined at himself, Karl said: "Let's get readings all over town. Bring them here, and we'll mark off the danger areas and I'll have the police post them and cordon them off. Begin at the harbor and work south."

Then Geir Helgi said, somewhat gently: "We knew it had to come, Karl. We have twenty-seven masks now."

"I've ordered more," Karl said wearily and quietly. "Not requisitioned, that gets you nowhere—*ordered.*" He did sit then. And his eyes met the gaze of the younger man. "Let's keep in touch now, Geir. Close touch."

"Certainly, Karl." There was more than reassurance in his tone—concern. Not, Jonas knew, for the new hazard they now faced, but for Karl Sveinsson. "We're all in it."

And he nodded to Jonas and then hurried down the length of the room. When he was gone, without glancing at Jonas, Karl said: "We get the pumpers, we even get the ships, *Flakkari* commits suicide in the sea overnight—but there's always something more."

Jonas felt a solid jolt of fear. Ever since Karl had returned from the night and day on the mainland, Jonas had sensed a change—could it be a faltering of spirit? Or something too personal and subtle to put into words? Or some combination of both, one feeding on the other?

Karl relit his pipe for perhaps the tenth time and stared gloomily at nothing. Finally he asked: "Do you know what the Yanks mean when they say 'ego trip,' Jonas?"

"I've a fair idea, yes."

"Maybe that's all this really is. For me."

Jonas had no idea how to answer this. But he said: "Whatever it is to you, it's something else to us." And when Karl did not respond by so much as an eye flicker, he said: "Do you want to see Doctor Varanin before he goes?"

Karl stood at once, frowning, puzzled, as if amazed that he could have forgotten. "Let's move."

They went. Out of the hotel and down to the waterfront. In a cold stillness without wind, they could hear the sound of pumping, which Jonas had come to think of as the heartthrob of the town, and they could hear Kirkjufell's low but steady barrage, although by now this seemed only a part of the atmosphere.

Jonas was silent, the apprehension expanding in him, but Karl spoke: "A man could win here, although I doubt it, and lose something a hell of a lot more precious to him somewhere else. To the man personally."

Jonas could only conjecture what Karl might mean, and if his conjecture was correct, Jonas would be the one responsible for Karl's loss. What was vital now, though, was that the clouds of depression which threatened all of them from time to time had now attacked Karl's sharp and vigorous mind on which everything and everyone had come to depend. If Karl Sveinsson ever gave in to despair . . .

One of the U.S. dredging ships was at the eastern end of the harbor, shooting great powerful arcs of water onto the edge of the lava bed, its sound competing with Kirkjufell's.

Doctor Varanin was already on the deck of the fishing vessel that was to carry him to the mainland. "Back to the dull lectures," he said when they came aboard. "Back to the classroom and spring in Indiana and the quiet and the youth with such bright eyes and such dull minds." He was smiling, as if at himself, and behind his gold-rimmed glasses his dark eyes mocked. "Be certain, please, to give Doctor Pall my regards. I'm sure that, as one scientist to another, he knows I understand the necessity of my . . . banishment. But convey also to him, please, that I would not have given up the pleasure for the punishment."

"Some volcano will be kind enough to start gurgling somewhere, Alexei," Karl said, "and you'll be rescued."

"I have observed men with masks," Doctor Varanin said then, glancing along Strandvegur to the east. "Usually, but not invariably," he went on, "as a loose, general rule, though, when gas is discovered in the close proximity to an erupting volcano, it is an indication that the eruption is on the wane."

Karl gazed at the man steadily. "You're a liar."

The tall man smiled and shrugged his thin shoulders. "I have been called worse. And by men who know me better than you do." He turned to Jonas and extended his hand. They shook, Jonas surprised at the other's wiry strength.

When Karl was shaking Doctor Varanin's hand, a curious thing occurred. The two men, on simultaneous impulse, stepped into a clumsy bearlike hug, each slamming his hands hard on the other's back. Then Karl turned sharply away, hurtled his weight over the rail, dropped to the dock and began to walk fast, not glancing back.

Jonas did not follow. He disembarked, and the whistle hooted twice, the engine began to throb, and he stood to wave to Doctor Varanin, who was staring off over the rooftops toward the flame and smoke. Jonas moved along the wharf and saw Karl's figure as he strode up the incline of Heidarvegur, himself again, swift and vigorous, in the direction of headquarters as if eager once more to return to the battle.

Jonas watched the vessel chug out of the harbor and disappear. Then he walked to the communications center. There he learned that a house located on the westernmost edge of town, far from the lava front and farther from

Kirkjufell itself, had exploded for no apparent reason. As if a bomb had gone off inside.

Recalling Doctor Pall's warning earlier, he could no longer take comfort in Doctor Varanin's prophecy.

At night Josef would often hear the husky chuckling of hundreds of fulmars, and he could see them flapping, then soaring, free and beautiful to watch. But then he would waken, and they would be gone, and the emptiness inside would be there. And the large white room and the rows of beds and no sky.

Then he would decide to try again. He had to get outside, he had to find a door that would open onto the cold and snow that he loved, and he would try, over and over, but after a few doors that would open there was always that one that would not. And always, sooner or later, he came to that door. No matter what direction he took, which passage he walked along, he always reached that door, and it was always locked.

His mother, visiting, would warn him, but not in her usual rage, as at his father or sisters: there were rules here, do not keep causing trouble, they are losing patience, Josef. But his mother, herself a wild creature, had to understand.

Josef's body had begun to ache just the way his mind had been aching. The sick overpowering longing was worse than pain, oh much worse. But he would bear it. He would fill his mind with pictures of the puffins. He would remember every smallest detail. The black-and-white body and the head that always seemed too large for it, its enormous bill like a false nose painted with brilliant stripes of red and blue, its fat cheeks and bulging white chest with the black collar around its neck and its white webbed feet. Even the thought or memory filled Josef with a sad sort of joy, but he no longer smiled at the bird's antics and the craving stayed in him, as did the desolate loneliness of being in pain here when he could be in joy in his own place.

The windows were all small but large enough for his lean body—which, as time went on, became leaner still—to pass through if he could ever find one, just one, that was not locked like that final door that he always reached. Then they told him: if he persisted in roaming about, especially at night, they would be forced to put him in a room by himself with only one door, and that one locked; he would not like that, would he?

He could sometimes hear the whimbrels—were they in his mind only? It was becoming hard, very hard now, to know. The whimbrels uttered delightful airs, trills, and lilts with an unearthly quality, sweet and hurtful at the same time.

He was not aware that he was not eating. He had not decided not to eat. His mother told him that he would waste away to nothing. And she begged him. So he tried. But he forgot. And in his mind the golden plover cried, and the sandpiper sounded, sorrowful yet comforting. And gulls wheeled incessantly, raucous and gracefully gliding, making patterns against the sky.

He gave up on the doors. There was always that last one. Finally, he became frantic, wild, and cried and did not sleep, then slept and cried in his sleep, but he gave up, there was no way, there was no way. He knew that this was what people meant when they spoke of sickness. He had seen his sisters sick, and animals, but he had never been sick before. And, strangest of all, he had not been sick when they brought him to this place.

But now he decided that he was going to die. He knew what dying was, too. He had seen dead sheep and cats and birds, and once he had seen an old cow die in great misery giving birth. He felt that his blood was drying up. His heart was shriveling in his chest. And his skin had begun to sag and was going gray.

He had never before thought of himself, or of any human, as dying. But he knew. It might take a long time. He did wish he could see Odin again. And his cave. And the auks perched on the rocks jutting up out of the sea. And especially the puffins, especially . . .

The city of Oslo, Inga knew, was almost exactly a thousand miles east of Heimaey, but to Inga it may as well have been ten thousand miles or light years away. The impossible had happened: her dream that Baldvin would someday receive worldwide recognition for the work that he loved doing and Baldvin's unspoken hope of someday being able to travel and to see the great art works of the world, by some accident or miracle springing from tragedy and loss, both her dream and his hope had been fulfilled. The house, their lovely, comfortable old house, was gone, gone forever, buried deep beneath pumice and lava and ash that had by now become solid tuff. Gone. But Baldvin's painting, "Revenge of Holy Mount," had been saved: Baldvin himself had grabbed it up, the paint still wet, that night of her terror when she was not certain she could get him to leave at all, and the imprint of his fingers remained on the upper edge of the canvas.

The painting had then been put on display in a museum in Reykjavik, where, as much because of its subject matter, she suspected, as because of its merit and sinister beauty, it had become the object of much interest and discussion and curiosity. An American named Todd Squier, whose wife was Icelandic, had become so fascinated and excited by the picture that he had taken it upon himself to inform one of the two or three most important private art collectors in the States. A curator had flown to Reykjavik, had studied the painting, had made an offer for its purchase. After a European tour accompanied by its artist it would hang in a famous gallery in Washington, D.C. Amazingly, Baldvin had been, at first, reluctant to part with it. But when he realized the freedom that the money would provide, he agreed, still with some regret.

They had flown to New York, to Washington, where they had been royally feted, to London, to Paris, to Amsterdam where they had spent more than ten days. She had visited her aging parents and brothers and sisters in Copenhagen—what a joyous time, joyous! And through all of it Baldvin had lived at such a pitch of excitement that Inga's only concern had been for his blood pressure.

Then, in Oslo, they received a surprise visitor at their hotel: Arni Loftsson, the schoolteacher in Vestmannaeyjar. He had read of their arrival in the newspaper. He was now a seaman on a Norwegian oil tanker, he said, without mentioning his wife, whose name, Inga knew, was Margret, although they were only acquaintances. Inga and Baldvin, out of some shared silent reluctance, did not inquire. It was an uncomfortable visit, unfortunate: Arni appeared to be suffering, his face, that had always been full-blooded, appeared wan, withered even, and there was in his eyes an unaccountable expression of sadness and pain. He seemed years older. Even his enormous height and wide shoulders seemed to have shrunk. He asked them about themselves, their house in Vestmannaeyjar, the painting. But his tone was flat and his attitude disinterested. Out of courtesy they offered a drink. He accepted quickly, and Inga recalled the stories about his missing days at school because of his drinking, and she regretted the suggestion. He ordered rum. It was brought to the sitting room of the hotel suite. He drank. He talked. Had they visited the historical museum? Had they seen the Viking longships that the Norsemen had used a thousand years ago? They had gone to Iceland on such ships! And near Fredrikstad there were rock carvings of the earliest Norse ships, strange, long vessels with curves and decorations dating back, imagine, dating back to 500 B.C.! While today, in today's ugly mechanical world, he worked on a long, flat, metal ship, over a thousand feet long, that carried more than two hundred thousand tons of oil. A prison really, he said, a smelly prison till you come to port. But in the end he seemed to be speaking, not to them, but to himself, or to some demon of torment inside himself. He left them saddened, depressed: the poor boy seemed lost, and so far from home.

But did he have a home now?

Did they?

Baldvin had told her several times, as if it were a shadow on his mind, of his visit with Doctor Pall and Petur Tryggvasson in the hospital office. He spoke with a bitterness that puzzled her. And she came to wonder whether this was rooted in what had actually occurred or been said or in a more pervasive and perhaps frightening realization: that that life, all of it, lay behind them now.

And Inga realized that she could never think of going back there. It came to her swiftly, a sharp and cutting knowledge, and gave her a certain odd relief. They had found a new life, a broader one, with more grace, more satisfaction. Did Baldvin agree?

They were strolling the curving cobble-stoned streets between medieval buildings in the dusk when she asked.

Baldvin stopped, turned, stared, shock naked on his broad face. "What are you saying, Inga?"

But he knew. It was the beginning of April now, and the volcano was still active; the destruction was continuing. Was there anything to which to return? They both loved Paris— what an exciting, gracious life they could make there. She spoke sufficient French, and he would soon learn. He could work there—some of the finest painting in the world had been done there, had it not?

But she had always been so content in Vestmannaeyjar, he said. It was a thing that had always surprised and pleased him.

Vestmannaeyjar was not the same. He should know that better than she; he had been there, he had seen.

But someday it *would* be the same.

Very well then—someday. Meanwhile, they had money now, enough, and he had recognition and would sell more pictures. Hadn't they asked for more paintings in the States? Wasn't this his opportunity?

No.

But why?

Because he was an Icelander. He was not a Parisian, not an American, he would be an exile. No.

They walked, some distance apart, no longer strolling. The darkness was closing in. Lights were coming on in the buildings, along the street.

Again she tried to reason. Didn't he understand? There *was* no Vestmannaeyjar. In another month or two it would be only an ancient ruin.

Under an arc light he stopped and turned to her. His fleshy face was suffused in color, a livid dark red. His eyes were brilliant. His lips moved but he said nothing. His heavy shoulders heaved.

Terror struck. In the instant she recalled all of Doctor Pall's warnings.

Then she saw his heavy body collapse to the stones, and heard someone screaming and realized it had to be herself, and when she paused, she heard running footsteps, and then she was screaming again and could not stop until she dropped to her knees and placed her face against his, promising him in a whisper yes, yes, yes, anything, they would go back, oh yes, please, they would go back, the town would be the same someday, just the same as it had always been, please . . .

The stars had come back. Every once in a while now, turned away from the continuous glare and the billowing dark clouds that obscured the sky above the cone and the still-smoking fissure, Rolf and Donna could glimpse a star or two. And during some days, but not often, there was a hint of gold, and on several evenings they caught a view of the sun as it disappeared along the western rim. But the convulsive upheaval was always there to the east.

While still on crutches, Rolf had worked in the repair shops, because General Patton had given orders that no one stayed who did not work. But now he was back on the streets and the rooftops, and at night, weary to the marrow, he would return to the small bookshop, where he had once worked, and which he and Donna had converted into a small snug home. There was no electricity in that area so they lived by candlelight: Donna had produced candles as mysteriously as she had obtained the linen tablecloth, the single iron skillet, the coffee urn and burner, and the champagne on the night of his eighteenth birthday. *Now,* she had said gaily, *we are both eighteen!* The familiar shop, transformed, became a refuge, a place of escape and enchantment, the tinkle of the bell above the door an overture to delight and passion.

He would walk with this girl from the States, who remained strange and exciting, walk the bleak, dark streets as if they were lanes of blossoms. And the hail of cinders would sometimes ping off their helmets, sometimes they would hear singing, and always there was the pulsing of the hoses and the thumping of the machinery and the roaring of the trucks, and less often now they would see a lava bomb like a red star trailing sparks of gold in a high arc.

Even the acrid smell of sulphur took on a fragrance of unknown exotic flowers as they strolled. Once, at water's edge, she had said: *Those birds. They're beautiful sounds when you can really hear them, but do they never stop, day or night?* And he had answered: *Never.*

Soon they were assigned to the same work crews day after day, and Rolf came to suspect that General Patton knew of their makeshift home together. Since Rolf had been overcome, gas masks were required now in certain areas, and on the job Donna was as featureless and anonymous and sexless as any other volunteer—goggles, mask, helmet—but at night in the bedroll on the floor of the shop, the softness of her was always a glory of amazement, warmth beyond belief, with an overwhelming scent, flesh, her flesh, while her cinnamon-colored hair cascaded around both their heads. All their nights were magic now. And Rolf began to realize that you need find only one woman, and your searchings and questionings are over. In one woman you will find all. The rest of the world, even the raw threat of Kirkjufell, softened and blurred, became distant and phantom.

But there was more between them, too, alive and quivering and usually unspoken. His feelings, contradictory and bewildering, continued to disturb him—and made him curse himself for a fool, a child. He could not yet get a full picture of her wanderings, which he knew were mysteriously idealistic, yet she seemed detached from the tragedy here, that she had come a thousand miles to fight.

Have you been like this with many others?

A few. Yes, a few. She often spoke Icelandic now, if the sentences were simple. *Many—no. And you?*

Only a few, he lied—and had the impression she knew it. One, one only—Odette. But it had not been like this.

Nothing had ever been.

And in this unlikeliest of time and place he had realized that he was happy, and if this was all they were to have . . .

During some nights, when Kirkjufell would sound with a single shattering blast or a series of spasmodic explosions, she would waken and roll close, clinging and trembling, and he would hold her, remembering that small terrified figure cowering in the inferno of sparks and rocks and flames, then disappearing in panic off the edge of the cliff and into the cold sea below. He would recall then Doctor Pall's angry face and gentle hands, as he cut off the boots and growled at the seared, swollen flesh of Rolf's feet and advised that he go to Reykjavik where he could get more help than the infirmary here could offer. And Donna's insistence, in Icelandic, that she could do it, she knew first aid, and she could learn what she didn't know. Some of the fury had left the doctor's face then: *I believe you could, little lady, but you look as if you might need more help than he does. I'm pleased that it frightened you. We have enough to deal with here without you two going out of your way to get yourselves killed.* And Rolf had learned that Doctor Pall had spoken true: her wound, being inner and of the soul, was more grave than his physical injuries. Just as the un-

speakable exaltation that he had known at the sight of the
latent, dark powers of the universe and their splendor had
never left him, her terror had become a part of her. And he
wondered, again, whether that fear would not bring an end
to the sharing and love that he had known since they had
begun to live together that night.

Karl Sveinsson had ordered notices posted and had
barked orders morning after morning: anyone venturing
near the cone would be asked to leave, much as every hand
was needed. But Donna did not ever again say a word about
rules preventing one from doing what could be really enjoyed. And for his part, Rolf came to question whether any
order could be achieved, rules or no, against the chaotic
power he had experienced on the crater's edge that day.

When *Flakkari* had come into mysterious existence, they
had strolled together close to the lava tract and, like the
others, stared at it in awe and apprehension. But then she
had turned and had run, had run wildly, and on still-sore
soles he had followed. He found her huddled in the shop,
and she began to chatter in panic: did he know that *Flakkari*
had already traveled almost a hundred and fifty meters in
two days, that while they couldn't actually see it move, it was
now slowing, and no one could predict what direction it
might take next, did he know this?

The soul-deep fright was in her always now, would always be, and he knew that sooner or later, she would try to
escape it. Then what? The idea filled him with longing and
with an elegiac sadness—a sense of inevitability and loss.

Over and over, too, she would thank him. *You saved my
life, didn't you?* He insisted that he had not, knowing otherwise and knowing pride as well. Yet there was more. While
he knew that he had, through the experience, conquered the
cowardice of the boy that he had been, he knew, too, that he
had been weak and foolish to have given in to her careless,
reckless whim. That, too, was cowardice of a sort. Regardless
of which, he was, contradictorily, grateful for an experience
more profound than any he could ever hope to have. But he
was also aware that she had not slept with him until *after* he

had taken her to the crater. Had he then been paid? Or had he made payment for her love? Was love a thing of paying? Such conjectures and doubts brought a rueful wretchedness that even the intensity—and sometimes desperation—of her passion could not dispel.

Now in April nightfall came later, and the work periods were longer. They returned to the bookshop in a cold drizzle—the streetlights were again burning—to find Kristrun waiting for them. She stood up, tall and slender, her flaxen hair twisted as always atop her head, and she smiled.

But there was a strain in her tone: "Don't look so startled. Rudolf told me you were here. And that he had given you permission. Which surprised me much, as it would you, Miss Blakeley, if you knew my husband." She extended a hand. "My name is Kristrun. And you are lovely, as Rudolf said."

"Thank you," Donna said. "Would you like coffee?"

"Yes. Oh no, I do not think now—yes, thank you, child, it may help." She sat again in the office chair and looked at Rolf. "You seem older, Rolf. In such a brief time. Well, we do change, do we not? To think that I once spent hours here dreaming of tropical islands where the sun shines always. Now, all I can think of is: how soon can I reopen the shop? Possibly being separated from what one really loves makes one . . ."

But she did not finish the thought, and did not need to. And Rolf knew what the visit portended: it would all end, it had to end, he had known it all along. There was more, though, now. "Do you bring a message, Kristrun?" he asked, but knowing.

The woman's blue eyes met his. "I do." She no longer spoke in English. "Your father came to me. He has fears. He has fears the sea has taken your mother, Rolf."

The sea.

He did not believe it. He turned to Donna. "I must go to my father."

"I know," Donna said. "I understood."

But she did not offer to go with him, so he walked in the

rain to the airstrip alone. He remembered that he had not thanked Kristrun. He inquired about space. He did not mention his mother because he did not believe it. A U.S. naval aircraft was about to take off. It was crowded with tired and tattered Yanks, some sleeping, some in an uproarious mood of release. He looked down. Kirkjufell flared and smoked. The sea was there. Deep and cold and impassive with its own secrets.

He would not think of that. Or of her.

His father then. The skipper often slept on his boat now—in order, he said, to go out early in the mornings. *Thirty-one tons between here and Thorlakshofn day before yesterday! And only a one-man crew aboard.* But there had been a hollowness in his tone, no zest in the report or in his eyes. And what had his father tried to tell him? In the vessel moored at dockside and rocking—something about a dream he had once had, years ago when he was in navigational school, a nightmare about a flood in Holland, water twenty feet deep in the streets; something about having the same feeling these many years later the night of the eruption, imagine it, the impression that he had lived through all of it before, remarkable, very baffling. *Déjà vu,* someone had told him. Had Rolf listened? Had the man been trying, in his own faltering way, to make contact? Had he been doing so, in other ways, all along?

Finally though, that night, his father had said: *You must go see your mother, Rolf. She asks.* And so, on a day of rolling seas and dun-colored sky, he had gone, himself at the wheel of the *Njord* at his father's suggestion. And on the way: *Be prepared, son. She has suffered a shock.*

But nothing, no words, could have prepared him. His mother's face had been a mask. Her hair was matted and dangling—and almost white. And a starvation of light in her eyes until, briefly, they flashed recognition and relief, a second's pleasure even, but went flat as quickly again. The stiff, alien room had become more cluttered, more littered than when Rolf had been living here. Was this really his mother? The vigorous, happy woman had become limp, lost in a lassitude that seemed to Rolf more desolate than all the vast black ruination he had left on the island. So strange, so unbelievable—a woman who only two months ago had been so sure, so full of joy and laughter and the love of living each day or minute. He had to take his eyes away. He asked about Rosa. Her voice was dry, not so much bitter as bewildered: *Rosa is going to have a baby. Yes, Rosa, of all the girls in the whole world, Rosa. She does not even know whose baby. Rosa herself does not know.*

And then, in a harsh savage tone that he had never heard from her before: *What has happened? Do you know? Tell me, Rolf, tell me, do you know what has happened?*

He had not had the words. And had known that words were of no use here.

Out of nowhere then, in a different voice: *There are always sounds here. Creakings and such, Rolf. In the walls. And water tapping. And always the smell of burning. Do you smell it, can you?*

Not here, Mother, he said gently. *There. Not here.*

But she did not hear this because, abruptly, she demanded: *Has he sold it?*

Sold it, Mother? The house?

Her faint voice sharpened: *There is no house. The boat. Has your father sold the* Njord?

Rolf had known then why his father spent so many nights on the boat, looking into his wife's old and ravaged face stirred too much compassion and anguish in him. Rolf knew—but how did he know? When had he come to know his father?

I'm tired now, his mother had said. *I shall sleep now. I sleep much. Yes, I sleep much now.*

Rolf had been ashamed of the relief that flowed through him as he rose. He stooped to kiss her cheek: the flesh had the roughness of dry leather. The cheek that had always been flushed and soft and warm.

Come back, Rolf. I miss you. Her eyes were closed. *I miss . . . everything.*

As the plane began to bank for the landing at Keflavik, Rolf wondered: were those to be the last words she would ever speak to him?

When he arrived at the house in Reykjavik and saw his

father's strong and kindly face gone pale and old, he knew. "Two days now, Rolf. Two days and two nights. She walked into the sea."

Yes.

And later: "I should not have left her here alone, Rolf."

"No one is to blame, Father."

No one and everyone. And Kirkjufell most.

He went to see Rosa. He walked along the lake. A low wind bit hostilely into his flesh, through his clothes. He did not weep. Around the lake lay the city: the gabled roofs of many colors, the two high-reaching church spires in the distance. Red-cheeked youngsters, shouting, swept by on the blue ice, which spluttered under their skate blades. It was not raining here; he had not noticed. The geese and ducks honked and circled and dipped overhead. He thought of her as she had been, and he thought of the vaguely demented creature she had become, floundering about in rooms she could not recognize, bleakness in her withering face. Still, he did not weep. The core of her despair had been greater and deeper than he or his father or Rosa could realize—or perhaps accept.

Rosa wept. Bitterly. Her yellow hair was no longer neat but fell into her brown and dismal eyes, which were smoky with anguish. It was her fault—hers, she said, and his and their father's. Yes. They had not heard. No one of them had heard deeply enough. Does anyone ever really hear?

And what of Rosa now? She was training to be an airline stewardess; but the dream of faraway places was no longer in her eyes. Didn't he know? She was to have a child. Didn't he know? Yes, he knew. Now, she had no idea what she would do, could do. What was it like in Vestmannaeyjar now? He told her. She tilted her fine narrow head: she had thought of going back, true, but only because her life was finished now, her dreams gone. Now there was only growing to be an old woman, and alone. She wept. For herself, her mother, those dreams, the past or the future?

He left her small room and walked the streets of the city. It was beginning to rain here now.

Had his mother found the peace she had once known in Vestmannaeyjar? Was there peace now where she was—or nothingness? No more steps to scrub with pleasure, no more meals to cook with joy or clothes to launder or music to play or to hear. No more warm bed with her man beside her. Or the voices of children from the street or from the next room or across the table. Immune now for all eternity from the beauty and sweet content, the sadness and beauty and mystery that was living. And, yes, the horror.

Ruth Helgadottir was dead.

He walked to the wharf to wait for his father. He saw the *Njord* docked there.

The joy and hope and love that were Ruth Helgadottir's were gone forever.

Let the rain fall into the sea that holds her. Let the sun return soon. Let the moon show once again on the water. She would not see it.

The winter had become too long, too endless, too dark. She would not know that it would soon be over.

Returning to Heimaey, he took the wheel and set the course while his father stood on the deck below in the block of light from the wheelhouse. He smoked his pipe and stared over the cold, dark water. Was his mind filled with his own silent final requiem? No bell would toll. Except in their minds, their souls.

Rolf saw the low crimson flame on the rim of the sea glowing like a ruddy midnight sunset, and then he saw the steam and clouds. He thought of all those people facing death and fighting worse. And he thought of himself at the crater's edge trying to prove his manhood and of Donna, waiting now, and he knew as certainty at last that he would have proved that manhood more by having refused Donna than by taking her to the cone and risking both their lives. He would then have missed seeing the awesome magnificence, but he would have shown greater courage, and of a different sort. What he had placed in jeopardy was what man really has for only a brief and uncertain time. He knew now. He knew what death was.

He smelled the strong tobacco smoke before he realized that his father was beside him.

"What now, Father?" he asked. "Will you live on the boat?"

"I think I'll find a room somewhere. Not here." There was a distant regret in his heavy tone, acceptance. "In Reykjavik perhaps."

"And what of the *Njord?*"

"There are those in Norway who would buy it. It's a fine vessel."

"I know."

His father worked the radio dials, calling Vestmannaeyjar to give position. Jonas Vigfusson answered and, after thanking the skipper, reported: "Agnar. We're not certain. Can't be certain yet. But we think the lava's been stopped."

Rolf pictured the town center: bank, town hall, post office, telephone exchange, hotel, aquarium. Saved?

"What of the harbor, Jonas?" Rolf heard himself ask.

"No one is positive," Jonas replied, his voice excited as it crackled over the airwaves. "But we think, we think, yes."

Agnar had not spoken. It was as if he did not care.

Did Rolf care? If the fight was almost over, then what of Donna?

After docking the *Njord,* he ran under the burning streetlamps to the bookshop with a sense of inevitability, like a hand gripping his heart. He opened the door—and discovered what he had always known he would someday find.

The room looked unfamiliar. It looked deserted. But her pack was on the floor. She emerged from the stockroom.

They regarded each other a long moment.

Then she asked: "Come with me?"

Again he recalled the night of the eruption—his small boat in the harbor, the hate in him, the fear and anger.

Slowly he shook his head.

"I knew you wouldn't," she said with a small shrug. "I understand, though."

Did she? How could she when he couldn't?

"The lava's been stopped," she said. "Did you know?"

He nodded. He also knew this was not her reason.

She smiled, sadly. "It's not over, though. Kirkjufell was awful last night." She took a step. "Please, Rolf—understand. I'm spooked."

"I know."

"I've been that way ever since you . . . ever since we went up to look in." And when he only nodded again: "I can't stand it any more. Last night, when you weren't here . . ." She shook her head, and her amber hair whooshed about her pale, troubled, childlike face. "Old Kirkjufell really raised hell, Rolf. I thought I'd go crazy." She moved closer. "Now do you understand?"

He did. But also he knew that her fear of Kirkjufell was only part of it. Hers was a fear of a different kind as well—of her own feelings, of his perhaps, or of what those feelings portended. He could not sort it out now. He would have time, too much lonely time, to try to fit the pieces together.

"When?" he asked.

"Now. If we . . . if I hurry. I had to see you, though."

He stooped and picked up the pack and threw the straps over his shoulders. How could a frail girl handle it in all the thousands of miles she traveled?

On the street, she turned toward the docks, not toward the airfield. "He said they'd wait until the hour."

He? Rolf did not ask.

But she answered: "I met him last night. I had to talk to somebody. I couldn't stay in there alone. I told you I was . . ."

"Spooked. Yes, you did."

But his anger was strangely muted.

"He was very nice. And sweet."

The two of them together in the shop. He was surprised at the cool calm inside himself. The sense of betrayal also held a certain inevitability. Had he expected this, too, without being able to focus it? Or to face it?

On the wharf, the waves lapped lazily at the pilings below, and he heard the ever-present sound of pumps from the ships and, farther off Kirkjufell, as always, as perhaps forever. No, she was not leaving because of the volcano or her fear alone, but because of something in her that even she

could not comprehend, the same restlessness and rootless-
ness that had brought her here. She took the pack. The crew
was already on the vessel and it was lighted, its engine spluttering with guttural impatience. A whistle blasted shrilly.

"He's sweet," she said, "but he's not beautiful. You, lad,
are beautiful." She leaned and kissed him on the lips and the
loss deepened in him, a shot-away feeling, as if he were hollow and sick inside. The hand that had been gripping his
heart tightened. She leaned against him. "Remember me,
Rolf."

He would.

But he could not say it.

"Au revoir, Rolf."

"Bless."

"Yes!" The familiar merriment came into her voice, into
her darkened eyes. "Yes—*bless, bless!"*

He saw her turn and go up the narrow plank. Shadows
pulled it aboard. Voices sounded. The lines were lifted. The
boat moved away. She stood at the rail.

He did not move. She stood at the rail, a shadow, until
he could no longer distinguish her outline. He stayed,
though, until the vessel, diminishing in dimness, its lights
reflected pale on the water, passed between the stone cliffs
protecting the harbor.

He was thinking of the night of *Thorroblot,* how long ago
it seemed now, and of how she had reminded him then of his
sister Rosa. Yes, they were alike, and the thought made him
sadder still. How many more like them all around the world?
Would Donna ever find what she was seeking? Did she even
know what that was?

He turned to face the town. The streetlamps glowed and
they seemed brighter now, now that Kirkjufell no longer
filled the sky with its mile-high brilliance. No, that was not it.
By some miracle or other, the electric power had been restored.

But he did not move. He could not go back to the bookshop. He could not go alone, and he could not go with the
bitter knowledge of last night. He could never go again.

Bless, Donna Blakeley of Boston, Mass., U.S. of A.

She was on the water that covered Ruth Helgadottir of Vestmannaeyjar, Island of Heimaey, Iceland.

Both gone now. *Bless.*

He walked along the dockside until he came to the *Njord.* There was no light on board. The smells of salt and fish and wet metal were as familiar as the harbor that, except for the dimly lighted pumping ship at the far end, now looked deserted and dark.

It came to him that, somehow, by stranger paths than he could ever have imagined, he had come home. And that he now knew where home was. And he felt a sorrow for the girl. And was thankful, too, for what they had shared: not only a brief life together, but an experience that only a few could even dream of having: a glimpse into the depths that would always fill her with terror and him with a reverence, awe, and exaltation that would forever be a part of him.

She would look back in terror, and he would stand forever astonished at the chaotic splendor and mysterious menace lying always beneath the tread of every foot on the uncertain crust of an uncertain earth. Which he now accepted.

The hand released his heart and lifted away.

He decided to find his father somewhere in the town and have a drink with the man. For they were both lonely tonight. He passed the bookshop on his left and the aquarium on his right and went to the hotel, where lights were showing again through the windows.

It was an uneasy peace between the earth-shaping processes of the universe and the small town that refused to die. The battle was not over; neither side had yet won. And indications, according to some geologists, were that the war would continue for some long time, perhaps as long as a year or more.

Think of Hekla. Remember Surtsey. Others agreed with Doctor Alexei Varanin that it would soon be over.

Had the flow of lava toward the harbor been arrested and diverted? If so, it would be the first time in history that man had been able to accomplish it by the use of cold water. Day and night forty-five hundred tons an hour were being poured onto the molten rock at a thousand degrees Celsius, causing it to cool and congeal. But, while the action was not spasmodic, if the volcano should erupt again with its original power and savagery . . .

Flame no longer towered above the town. There were whole days and nights when what rose from the cone was a low, at times almost invisible fire, itself more lemon yellow than scarlet, hugging the crater's edge, low and jagged; but almost always above it great billows—turbulent and twisting, steam and smoke of every shade of gray and black, sometimes even soft white—surged skyward or, depending on the wind, would swell and heave horizontally, covering the sea and the town with a breathless blanket that seemed, at times, to threaten to smother all life that was left. And in this time there was always the sullen growl, the sinister reminder that the beast was only half-asleep, far from dead. And in the crater and over the lava field, there was always the cauldron simmering and bubbling, a seething menace. Then, after a day or night of ominous quiet, when a timorous few would begin to wonder whether the holocaust might possibly be over, *POOM,* a ferocious plume of fire would shoot thousands of feet into the air, the town would again be shattered with a blast, and ash and sparks and pumice would fall over it again. On one such day a lava bomb crashed through a roof and another home burned.

The days continued, imperceptibly, to lengthen: a few more minutes more light each day. Always dull gray at dawn and dusk. And every once in a while the sun could be seen as sun, not as the pallid, somber slate-colored disc that had occasionally hovered above in the last month. Now, but not often, there was even a glint of gold in it. The promise of summer glimmered in the sky.

Four of the remaining waterfront plants resumed operations, and fishing vessels again came and went in the harbor. Had the harbor actually been saved?

The arctic terns returned. Since the beginning of winter they had flown nine thousand miles to the Antarctic and then another nine thousand on their way north—as they did every year.

Was it possible then that the ordeal was coming to an end—and without the loss of a single life?

He had to have the medicine. Something. *Anything.* He couldn't go on, he couldn't bear the pain without the medicine. Damn Doctor Pall. It was not the pain only. No. The trembling, and the sweating—he was wet all over and it was cold on the street. It was night, it was always night here.

Under the swaying yellow lamps, the streets lay glistening black, heaving like waves. The fever was in him, all through him, a core of heat in his chest, especially in his arm. It flamed also in his head. And there was that snarling presence always, to the east, he still knew his directions, you couldn't fool Olaf Jonsson as to direction—he was a man of the sea—but the light over the town was dimmer now, it had to be midnight, past midnight. He had wandered this street before, the night that the world had exploded, the night he had been struck over the head by the oar, how long ago had that been now, so much had happened in between, so much and nothing, nothing at all of any importance. He had been looking for Juliana that night, Juliana and his daughter, both with the red hair, but they had already gone—where, where had they gone? Someone had told him, later, much later, he knew, but with the agony in his arm now he couldn't think, with the quaking emptiness in him, the craving, he couldn't recall. Where had Juliana gone and where had she taken his daughter? He could remember the bar-room fight—was it Marseilles, was it Bombay?—and his arm crushed, stomped, the heavy boots over and over, shattering it. He could remember that, but not what had happened to Juliana and his daughter here.

Juliana, where are you?

Doctor Pall didn't know. *Said* he didn't know. Doctor Pall, liar. Doctor Pall knew. Just as Doctor Pall could have given him the medicine if he had wanted to, if he had the pity in him to do it. He had had the pity before, he had been a friend before. The medicine would bring, first, relief that you couldn't believe and then, then that pleasant, blurred swimming in the head and calm all through you. But no. Even Doctor Pall had deserted him. Never again, he had said. Doctor Pall had suggested he go to Reykjavik—to experts who could cure him. Cure him of what? His arm had healed, it was only the pain. But he had gone to Reykjavik and on the docks he had obtained what he needed. Then he had run out of money.

A red and yellow light somewhere and the eternal low thunder and smoke. He had nothing, not even *brennivan,* nothing, and his lungs ached, his head a ball of fire, his arm a thing apart, excruciating. Was there no pity, did no one care, ever?

And those many other nights came back: thousands of miles from here, nights of despair when he wished to see his own *fylgja,* he wished to be death-doomed, as his Uncle Lars had warned years ago—Uncle Lars who was now himself dead, blessedly dead, lucky man. Uncle Lars who could not hear or speak and could only sit and stare at him—a terrible, terrible thing. Uncle Lars, the only one who had ever been kind to him, really kind. Except Juliana.

Juliana, where are you?

He arrived at the hospital. No light burned. Doctor Pall slept here. He knew—oh, he knew. But he was careful. He would be silent.

He entered. The building resounded with emptiness. He walked in dimness, room to room, he smelled the medicines, the odors of death, but there was nothing, nothing, nothing, the building was empty, a cave, dark, dark, dark.

He emerged onto the street. Which was empty, too. Nothing moved. Only that flicker in the sky, and that sound.

Juliana, where are you?

But he was not searching for Juliana now. He knew where she was now. He had forced the truth from her husband, Halldor Danielsson, whom he hated, whom he had almost killed, night of *Thorroblot,* yes, would have killed if those cursed Yanks hadn't come running. Halldor—hate, hate, hate—he had taken Juliana, and now he had taken the child, Olaf's child, Jakobina, what a beautiful name; and now even Halldor was gone, had disappeared so completely that sometimes Olaf, drinking or with the medicine in him or both, wondered whether he might actually have killed him after all.

Jakobina. His child.

No.

He was walking. His legs throbbed. His body otherwise felt dead. Except for the arm: twisting, a live tortured thing apart from him. Flaming. And his mind was alive, his memory, more agony, the worst.

He knew where he was going. The pharmacy. Yes, yes, yes, it had been evacuated, but they must have left something there, anything, something to lift himself off and away, to detach himself, from arm and memory and now.

He knew what he had to do: go to the United States himself. He had been there. Key West. New York. San Francisco. He would go again.

His daughter. Jakobina. He knew her name now!

And Juliana.

Damn Reverend Petur! Liar. Another liar.

But he, Olaf, he had seen the church records himself. He had compared the dates—the marriage, the birth, the christening.

Liar. All liars.

The child had been born more than a year after he had left the island.

Fifteen months.

His child. She *had* to be his child!

Reverend Petur had been soft-spoken, kindly. Liar. Was there something he could do? Could he help?

No. There was nothing anyone could do.

No help. None.

Except the medicine. If he could get the medicine that Doctor Pall refused him . . .

The door of the pharmacy was ajar. He pushed it inward. There was a smell. A strange smell.

He struck matches. The shelves were empty. A fine dark soot was everywhere. Ghostly room with counter, cabinets. All empty.

But there was the cellar. That's what they had done: they had hidden the medicines in the cellar.

He found the stairway behind a door. The smell now was heavier. Familiar, but he could not name it. Not now. Not in this pain, with the *brennivan* also in him, inflaming the fever, deepening the torture in his arm.

He descended the steps.

His head reeled with dizziness. His chest was being crushed in a vise and his breath came in short quick spasms. Darkness lay ahead, down below.

He felt himself plunging into it.

And then he was on a street white with snow and there was laughter in him, and more, excitement, there was a girl beside him, holding his hand in hers, her face radiant, her red hair luminous about her face, eyes bright and warm in spite of the cold; and then it changed, it all changed, it was the same girl, it was Juliana, but it was summer and they were beside the sea, and he saw her through golden glory, flooded in light, in a halo of summer under the wide blue sky with the white line of foam behind as well, and he knew again the immense bright power of beauty and knew, too, that he would never die.

Two days later, on a routine patrol to take readings of low-lying areas and cellars, Geir Helgi, the geologist, discovered the body of Olaf Jonsson. At once he summoned Doctor Pall and the police, advising them to bring masks. The chief of police arrived first. By this time he was very tired; no, he was exhausted. He often told himself that it had gone on too long. Doctor Pall brought along in the ambulance two medical orderlies of the U. S. Navy. There was nothing to be done except to convey the body to the hospital and to summon, as he had done when Frosti Runaldsson had died, a mortician from Reykjavik and to arrange for burial with Reverend Petur.

Doctor Pall decided that, rather than accompany the body in the ambulance, he would walk to the hospital. He had the energy. Curious: at the beginning he had been so weary that he had had to force himself to rise in the morning; but now he seemed indefatigable, always fired with physical energy even when his mind was filled, as now, with sadness. Sadness and remorse. But why should he feel remorseful? Or guilty? Because, again, he had played god. But he couldn't go on feeding the boy drugs, could he? Why not? What difference could it have made, really? If the tormented little seaman, in mental anguish as well as in physical pain, chose to relieve both and to retreat into a dreamworld, a half world—what harm?

Pall had no doubt as to why he was in the pharmacy. Now he was dead. Now he had no world at all. Was that mercy?

Was that more merciful or less? And who was to decide?

Doctor Pall, mounting the steps of the deserted hospital, had come to realize that, unlike Baldvin and Petur, he would live out his life without even an illusion of certainty, of discovering an answer to the myriad mysteries swirling around him on all sides.

The chief of police was a very tired man. And he was, he knew, becoming irascible. Or had he become so already? He could not shake off a feeling of apprehension, which had been haunting him from the beginning. He had never really believed that this handful of people could win, and now that some indications at least were favorable, he still could not believe it. And perhaps because of this he worked all the more intensely and drove his subordinates all the more relentlessly—always, however, in his quiet, sometimes gruff but fatherly way.

The threat of disease or general infection had been averted, thanks to Doctor Pall. The chief had participated in what he assumed was an illegal procedure: ridding the island of that foreign woman in that furtive way Doctor Pall had devised. And then other faces disappeared as well. He had had to use threats against only two or three stubborn fools. But in that small area of the battle, apparently he and Pall and Karl Sveinsson had all won; the chief felt that, somehow, they had scored another point against fate.

The young officer who had been on duty the first night of the eruption—for whom the chief had developed an odd affection and to whom he had found himself delegating more and more responsibility and authority—had maintained a youthfully hopeful attitude from the start, one that the chief found admirable and irritating. He had learned from his scientist friends, the young man told the chief, that the emission of gases normally indicates that the strength of the eruption is on the decrease. All very well, all probably very accurate. But now that the force was diminishing—the chief had learned from *his* scientist friends—the upward surge of heat was no longer enough to drive the gases high, so that now they only cleared the crater rim and rolled down the side of the mound. He did not, however, point out the high yellowish gas flames with black smoke clouds rising from them or the bluish haze hanging over the lower area of the town in calm weather, sometimes so low that snow buntings were killed by it, while pigeons and gulls, flying higher, survived. Nor did he make the observation that more dead cats and rats were being cleared from the streets every day and that the birds would now settle only on the highest parts of the cliffs. What encouraged the young officer and what, in his opinion, would prevent the tragedy that the chief feared, was the presence of sulphur in the volcanic vapors which, although in so minute a quantity as to be unmeasurable, gave them a smell that should serve as a warning for those not equipped with masks.

Well, no fumes had warned one Olaf Jonsson, formerly of Vestmannaeyjar. After viewing the body, the chief drove the police van—he walked no more than necessary now— back to the small once-white one-story police station, went into his office, spread the young seaman's belongings, such as they were, across his desk, and took up the telephone to report to Karl Sveinsson at the command post, which by now had been moved from the hotel to the secondary school which was on high ground.

When he replaced the instrument, fatigue like a poison in his blood, he sat a moment without moving, and the young officer, who had first received word of the eruption from Jonas Vigfusson, entered. He had heard.

"What did the general say?" he asked.

"Nothing. Not even thank you. Absolutely nothing."

"Well," the young man said, "one casualty. Only one."

The chief regarded him with hooded eyes. Only one human life. Only one. He had not known a man could be so weary; it was an ache in every fiber. He admitted it then, looking at the ruddy-faced youth before him, admitted to himself in silence the feeling that had been gnawing at him for weeks: he was too old for this job. He had been certain only a short while ago when he had gazed through his goggles of his mask at the pale, lifeless body in the cellar. And now he was more certain still.

"If this is ever over," he said, and then he corrected himself, but without conviction: "*When* this is over, but not until, I'm going to retire. And recommend to the council that you take my place."

The young officer, visibly startled, said: "You're only tired now, sir. You'll feel differently after a while."

The chief did not reply. He liked this boy. Working

closely with him, coming to depend on him in this time, he almost loved him as 'a son. Shoving the seaman's wallet, handkerchief, papers and cigarettes together, he said: "List these. And study whatever's in the wallet. Try to locate a next of kin, if any."

"Yes, sir. I was in school with Olaf. His only kin was an uncle, and I understand he has died on the mainland. But I'll do what I can, sir."

When his subordinate had gone, softly and considerately closing the door, the chief lowered his head to his folded arms on the surface of the desk. No man likes growing old. No man likes admitting it. How much longer would it go on?

He could not brush off the swarm of somber thoughts that the exhaustion had brought or the bleak and lonely sense of dread and foreboding. If the emission of the gases increased, would it matter then whether the eruption itself died or that the harbor had been saved? If those vents and the still-open fissure continued to exude that poison, wouldn't the entire island then become uninhabitable?

After dinner, over brandy and coffee in the living room, her father asked, casually: "Why didn't you tell me. Elin?"

"Tell you?"

"I have been aware, of course, that something was amiss. So, during my annual medical examination this afternoon, I gambled. I asked Dr. Indridi how you were getting along."

"Oh?" Her hand holding the coffee cup had begun to tremble slightly, so she set it on the low marble-top table. "And . . .?"

"And . . . he told me. Precisely. He said the antibiotics are slowly clearing the infection. As a matter of course, he assumed I knew."

Elin, tense and alert now, had to decide quickly. She
picked up the snifter and sipped the brandy, then said: "I
doubt Thurbjorn knew—about himself, I mean—or he
would not . . ." But, seeing the expression on her father's
thin patrician face, she broke off, her heart beginning to
hammer violently. "Yes, Father—Thurbjorn. Naturally."

"But Thurbjorn has not been here for many weeks
now." His tone was gentle, even tender—and, she realized
with a quivering in her midsection, dangerous.

"He . . . Thurbjorn came one afternoon while you were
at your club."

"And you forgot to tell me . . ."

"He asked me . . . it was his idea not to tell you." Then,
to buttress the lie: "It was after the plant burned and you had
been so . . ."

"Yes . . .?"

The quivering became a quaking and threatened to
spread. "You had been so . . . cruel to him on the telephone
when he rang to tell you of the fire."

"Cruel? As I recall, I reminded him only that, against his
judgment, I had saved the machinery. More coffee?"

Elin took a gulp of brandy and stood. She moved away.
She had telephoned Thurbjorn, who was again in Vestmannaeyjar, as soon as she had discovered . . .

"Elin," her father said, "Thurbjorn was not here, was
he?"

Now what was he saying? She moved to the full-length,
small-paned windows and looked out—at nothing. Why had
she not told her father of Thurbjorn's visit? It had been her
idea, not Thurbjorn's. Why? Now she was trapped. The riot
in her mind was becoming a tempest. She had to concentrate.
"Why should you doubt me, Father?" She had not told her
father because life here was so peaceful, so easy and lazy and
fine; she had not wished to stir her father's disapproval or
resentment. Yes. But other questions stabbed: how had
Thurbjorn been infected, by whom, that French whore out
there?

"Did the servants see him?" her father asked.

"They were not here that afternoon." She had telephoned Thurbjorn, to warn him, to inform him, but he had not telephoned her—why?

"How convenient," her father said.

She whirled about. She did not understand. "What . . . what are you thinking?" She heard a shrillness in her tone that reminded her of the first night of the eruption, her panic in Thurbjorn's office. "What do you mean?" she demanded. *"What?"*

"Precisely what I said. We cannot blame everything on poor Thurbjorn, can we?"

And then, her whole body beginning to shake, she knew. "You think I've been seeing other men."

"All those afternoons at the cinema. The galleries. Shopping." He stood, tall and stiff. "I suspected all along."

Suspected? Why should he . . .

"Elin . . . how could you do this to me?"

The shock then was a hot blade plunged through her. She stared at her father—the handsome man with silver hair, the gentleman. He was speaking as if he were her husband—or lover.

He was jealous.

She could not believe it. Would not. But had to. Yes. Was this why he had been so pleased to have her here? Was this why he had always hated Thurbjorn?

"Elin, if you are going to indulge in such things, I think you should find a place of your own."

She did not hear those words. She refused to hear those words, they had not been spoken. What was happening? Wasn't it enough that she was ill? Full of poison, full of medicine—wasn't that enough?

She went to him, swiftly, and stood before him, struggling to remain calm, to control her voice and the shuddering that had taken over her body. "You don't mean that, Father."

It was then that he changed. His eyes went wild, his face became set, his shoulders stiffened, and he spoke through tight but quivering lips. "Yes, yes, yes! A place of your own. Thurbjorn has money now. He's operating Frosti's plant. If he can't provide enough, I'll help. But you cannot stay here!"

He turned away and strode from the room and up the stairs.

Stunned, her whole being inundated with fury, she stood, racked by violent paroxysms that she could no longer control, in the center of the handsome room. Alone. Quite alone. Knowing. What was it Thurbjorn had said when she telephoned to tell him, to warn him? *Yes. I know, Elin. But I've been cured.* He had not asked about her. He had not warned her, once he knew. Or had he known before?

No. Thurbjorn wouldn't. Couldn't. No matter how hurt, how furious, at her, at her father—he was not capable of that! No, no, no!

Yes. I'm cured, he had said, *that's why they have allowed me to come back.*

So he had known when he came to Reykjavik. That was why he had come.

Revenge. Knowing that her father loved her.

Loved her, yes, but in a way she had never imagined.

And now. She could not go to Thurbjorn. Unless to kill him.

She could not stay here.

She placed her knuckles in her mouth and screamed. It was a silent scream, which only she heard, but all the more deafening and horrendous for being so.

EIGHT

SPRING COMES EARLIER TO the Vestmann Islands than to other parts of Iceland. On Good Friday the work force, which in recent weeks had swelled to nearly four hundred, wakened to a hush. Silence. For the first time. The quiet was eerie, uneasy. The volunteers and the few women who had by now returned to clean their homes, all began to speak in normal tones. But they did not talk of the change, as if afraid of disturbing it or unable to believe it. They spoke of it only with their eyes.

Kristrun was painting the interior of the bookshop. If she stayed, she would paint the exterior later; the dark stain of ash would have to be removed first. And while she worked, a cloth wrapped around her piled-high fair hair, she began to develop an idea. There would be tourists now, many of them, thousands—if. What if each store had souvenirs of the disaster for sale? Photographs, samples of pumice, even lava lumps? The profits could be used to help finance the vast cleanup that lay ahead—if.

The word lurked always in her mind.

If.

She discovered that she was shivering. What was she doing here? What had become of that resolve when she had first returned to see the yellow house, intact, which Rudolf had kept clear of ash? And then, when she had come again, the night she brought the message to Rolf of his mother's death, seeing then the further depradations, the resolve had been intensified. Still, here she was. And now, in the quiet, which Rudolf had said was so unfamiliar that it was frightening in itself, she realized that it was not her sickening revulsion at the appalling black ugliness that she was trying to conquer by work, but something else, something new in her: fear. It could happen again, any day or night, at any moment. And next time . . .

She had heard of the death, and when Rudolf had suggested walking through the town with Gudrid, Kristrun had protested. It must have been then that the fear set in. But Rudolf had assured her that the gases were no longer a threat aboveground. The soil and tephra were dense enough to hold the greater part of them down. They rose now only through houses whose foundations extended below to the bedrock of porous Helgafell lava. These houses, he explained, acted as vents. No masks were being worn now, he had told her.

Nevertheless, she continued to shudder as she worked, and she worked feverishly in the hope of ridding herself of trepidation and apprehension about the future. Today, only yellowish gas flames with black smoke clouds rising from them like smoking candles could be seen above the silent crater. The eruption was subsiding. But for how long? She had made the proper decision almost three months ago: she would never live here again. She would not stay even through Easter Sunday as they had planned. She could not.

The bell over the door tinkled, and then Rudolf was beside her, looking pleased. She had not mentioned her decision to him—had he guessed then, and did he take her painting to be capitulation? She longed to tell him; it had to be. But he leaned and placed his cheek against hers, and then he turned, murmuring something about work to be done, the bell sounded again, and he was gone.

Gudrid stood at the murky ash-stained plate-glass window staring out on Heidarvegur or across it to the front of the aquarium, on which the mural of birds and fish was obscured, like everything else, with the black dust. Gudrid's face, in profile, was solemn. Troubled. And at once her mother remembered the child's prophecy of last July—which had proved to be more than premonition, a certainty, and accurate. But Kristrun refused to believe in such; sooth-saying, sorcery—she still could not accept. Then why did the fear congeal in her now, and why did she put down the brush and move to where the girl stood, impassive, her forehead furrowed, and her pale flaxen eyebrows drawn together?

"Gudrid . . . what is it, child?"

Without moving, Gudrid asked: "Will they open the school?"

"I imagine so," Kristrun said. If.

"I saw our house."

"It can be cleaned."

Then Gudrid faced her. Looked up into her face. And the girl's expression became one of disbelief, almost derisive, almost apprehensive. "Will we live here?"

No. But Kristrun said: "That must be decided, dear, when this is really over." If.

"I don't want to stay here."

For a moment only, Kristrun was certain she had been correct: the girl had had another premonition and she was frightened. "Tell me, Gudrid."

Gudrid's blue eyes did not flicker. "It's . . . it's too ug-ly."

And relieved, in spite of herself, her rational nature, and her doubts, Kristrun said: "It can be changed."

Gudrid shook her fair head. "It will not be the same. Ever."

Gently Kristrun said: "It will take time. It *could* be the same." If.

Gudrid moved away. She moved into a corner and stood with her back to Kristrun. "I saw the volcano," she mumbled. "Close." She took a breath. "It . . . it scared me." Then, eyes blazing and blurred by tears, she whirled about. "I don't want to, I won't, don't make me, please, I hate it, I hate it!"

Nonplussed, utterly disconcerted by this torrent of emo-tion from a child who rarely gave vent to her feelings, Kristrun stepped across the shop. "Gudrid," she heard herself saying, "Gudrid dear, even on that awful night we left here, you were not afraid."

"I didn't know then. I didn't *realize*. And we were going *away* from it." Her eyes were steady but her lip was trembling. "Now you want to come back. To stay. And it's still on fire."

Kristrun understood then. "Gudrid, everyone lives in danger. Everywhere. In the cities there's the danger of accidents and in most, crime, murder. In the country there are blizzards, tornadoes, forest fires." Her mind seemed clear enough; she sounded confident and certain enough. "In some places, wild animals, tigers invading a native village. And wars, kidnappings, terrorists, hostages, rapists. All over the world." She took a deep breath. "Danger, Gudrid, is a condition of living. And we have been safer here, until now, than most places—than almost any place on earth."

Gudrid nodded, but there was no scoffing hostility in her eye or tone: "Until now." It was almost a whisper. "Until now."

"Until now!" Kristrun's own voice rose, to her own astonishment. "For five thousand years! There's been no eruption here on Heimaey since the one that formed the island! Five thousand years ago."

Silence then. Until Gudrid again shook her head. "I won't live here. I won't."

Something rare and strange flared in Kristrun: quick anger. "You will live where your father and I live, Gudrid. You will do what everyone else has to do, has always done. You will make friends with danger."

Now Gudrid's face reflected bewilderment but not rebellion. Puzzlement only as she stared at her mother.

And, seeing this, Kristrun softened. "No one was killed," she said, gently.

"One . . . one man," Gudrid said, but in a different tone. "Father told me."

"It was his own doing," Kristrun said. "The volcano didn't kill him. He had been warned." She stepped closer still. "There's been no death in Iceland from a volcano in more than a hundred years."

"But," Gudrid said softly, "but it's all so dirty. So ugly."

"Then we'll clean it up. Take a brush and help me finish painting."

And as she saw Gudrid move to do so, Kristrun realized that somehow she had been purged of her own fear.

"I'll try," Gudrid said. "If . . . if you can, I can."

Could she? Could Kristrun live forever faced with that *If*?

Yes. And would.

If.

Whether she had convinced Gudrid or not, Kristrun realized, she had convinced herself. And a burden was lifted.

She did not have occasion to speak English often, so when the pilot, who was no more than a boy with longish black hair and a winning, ingenuous grin, asked her if she would like to join him in the cockpit in the otherwise empty plane, she hesitated. But then she moved in and sat before the instrument panel and enjoyed the takeoff from Keflavik Airport. Although Karl worked at the air base, she had, for no reason in particular, not flown often. During the twenty-minute flight the pilot told her that he would soon be going home—he named a town in Iowa—and would he be glad to get out of this godforsaken place. Then he apologized at once, and she smiled and said she understood, although she did not.

She saw the smoke first, great black, gray, and white billows rising and writhing, folding in upon themselves. But no flame. Then she saw the town and incredulity struck. The images on television could not encompass or convey what she looked down upon: houses emerging, often roofs only, from the waves of blackness, and the ribbons of cleared streets and, also, row upon row of houses upright and intact.

Staring down, she heard the pilot say: "Over four hundred buildings in all." Then he added: "Christ." Then, abashed, he said: "Sorry, m'am." And when she only smiled, he banked the plane, into the rising black cloud, and she knew a moment of panic, but the pilot handled the controls casually, and then they were in the clear again, in the sunless afternoon, and looking down, she could make out a ruddy glow but still no flame.

"Yessir," the pilot said, "over four hundred. More than thirty percent, way I heard it, and another twenty percent damaged. But it could have been worse. Hell, it would have been worse if it hadn't been for our fire chief. He's the one did it, you know. Man named Sveinsson. Ever hear of him?"

Yes. Shame and guilt assaulted her, and she was gazing down at the south end of the island now. Grass was beginning to sprout and the faint green of the fields contrasted to the black desert to the north. The ash must not have been carried south, she decided, trying not to excuse herself by telling herself, even though it was the truth, or part of the truth, that she had behaved as she had because of her concern for Karl. Was that why she was on her way to him? Was that why she had not told him she was coming? Engulfed by a familiar and hateful confusion—why can't anything be simple, anything?—she asked the pilot whether it was likely that the volcano would erupt again.

"Any damn time," he said, "Any time. Catch me living in a place like this. They must be nuts." Then hastily, without glancing, eyes forward: "Sorry. Do you live . . . did you live in . . . I never can pronounce the name."

"In Vestmannaeyjar? No. I live in Keflavik."

Relieved, the pilot said, heading the plane into what appeared to be a crevice between two upthrusts of rock: "If you ask me, this whole island's like a ship on the ocean with a load of dynamite on board and a typhoon liable to come up any old time."

The plane shot between the crags and she was amazed that, once it cleared them, it was already on the runway.

The pilot whistled. Once. "I flew into Hong Kong once. This is worse. But we're here, like it or not."

When she had thanked him and stepped out, expecting cold, she discovered warmth. Here, closer to the cone than the town was, she could feel a trembling beneath her feet, more of a throb than a quavering, and she could hear a strange sound, a low, spluttering rumble, but faraway. It unnerved her and she called herself a fool.

In the very small ash-covered concrete building, a young man in the uniform of Icelandic Airlines seemed distinctly displeased to see any new arrival, and he inquired where she wished to go.

"To wherever Karl Sveinsson is," she said. "He is my husband."

An American Jeep was provided at once, with a middle-aged Icelandic driver. It rocked downhill on the pockmarked and rutted road, black on both sides, until she had a full view of the two cones, one dead, one smoking. Smoke, white and gray and blue and streaked with yellow, was drifting over the entire area, rising from long fissures invisible to the eye. Somehow, though, in spite of the ravages that she soon observed, a sense of adventure came to her, a prickling, odd sensation of excitement. And she was again astonished. Was this the way Karl felt? Reckless and young again, with a foe worth fighting? Nevertheless, seeing the remains of havoc, she had to struggle against dismay, shock. These poor people, these poor uprooted people . . .

In Icelandic, the driver spoke: "You are Karl Sveinsson's wife, they told me?"

"Yes."

"Have you been to Vestmannaeyjar before?"

"Years ago only."

"Your husband saved the harbor. You knew that, of course. Saving the harbor saved the town."

"Is the town saved then?" she asked.

"No one knows. But if so, there should be a statue of your husband."

The turmoil in her held anticipation now, hot and urgent, but a terrible ravishing contrition as well. In the bare hallway of the school building, with faded crayon drawings still on the walls and a huge bulletin board with printed instructions and a map of the town, there was much activity, comings and goings, but there was a casualness about it that surprised her, until she realized that, with the volcano all but silent now, there had been a relaxation in attitude. How blessed that must be for all of them.

Including Karl? She heard his voice before she saw him, and she halted, stood listening. It came from a room off the square entryway, and she heard the exuberance, the confidence and certainty in it, although it was not loud. The words did not matter to her: something about steam damage, timbers in houses warping, the hot steam beginning now to penetrate further west into houses that had escaped the lava and most of the ashfall—well then, wasn't there a way to release the steam from the new lava? Another voice answered: she could not hear the words. Then Karl: "Why can't holes be bored to release it? Or what about a trench along the eastern edge of the lava field? Damned steam can't do any more damage there than's already been done there."

She hadn't realized that the voice was approaching. Then she saw him. He emerged with a younger man, bearded, who was carrying a roll of large-size papers or blueprints and nodding. And then they started toward the outside doors.

But he halted, his back to her.

She was not breathing.

And then he turned, slowly and the astonishment, the shock, and disbelief on his face sent such a jolt of pleasure and satisfaction through her—sheer joy—that she laughed aloud. And, laughing, she ran to him and against him, and his arms went around her—she saw the bearded young man looking at them from the door, it didn't matter—she kissed him, she kissed him on the lips, still laughing, and then the laughter turned to tears, and she was crying and laughing at the same time, and Karl was holding her. Over his shoulder she saw the younger man, grinning now, go outside.

"Not here, for God's sake," Karl said, and then her tears were gone and she was laughing again.

"It's all right," she told him, "it's allowable. I'm *Mrs.* Patton!"

Walking, her arm looped through his, the laughter silent and inside her now, they passed the white church, the maroon-colored roof cleared, the Madonna and the arched entryway also white and there were people going through the doors, mostly men, but more women than she had expected to see now—were they beginning to return then?—and she remembered that it was Good Friday, the day of mourning and penitence before the coming Sunday of joy and resurrection. But she was not saddened: all of that seemed part of the distant alien world of childhood.

From here she had a full view of a new volcano: no flame, only smoke and steam. "Is it really over?" she asked.

Karl growled: "Who can say? How can you trust The Bitch? She's a hag from hell." The bitter anger in his tone surprised her, as it had before. "The she-devil may be only mocking us, biding her time." But in his voice, too, was a throb of triumph, an exultation that no harshness of tone could conceal. "Yes, my girl, I think we've won! I don't dare think it but I do. She's surly now, sullen—she knows she's lost." Karl's exuberance was infectious and she clutched his arm. It was as if he were shaking his fist at the smoking cone—as if the volcano were a living thing.

Puzzled, she asked: "Why do you think of her as a woman?"

They were stepping over and around intricate tangles of hoses and pipes, which seemed to be everywhere. There was the grating raucous sound of bulldozers working.

"Because," Karl said, "because she reminds me of those women in the Eddas. More cruel, more ruthless, more bloodthirsty than any man. Wills of iron."

"A shrew," she said, her mood darkening.

"Exactly!" Karl said.

They did not speak again—she could not—until they reached the hotel and climbed the three flights of stairs to the room on the top floor. It was, to her, a sad room, feature-less, spare and lonely, without comfort. And he had slept here, alone, for three months now.

"Like me," she said at last.

"Who's like you?"

"The Bitch," she said. "The shrew."

Their eyes held. Neither of them moved.

Finally Karl said: "No."

"Yes!" she cried. "I *was* worried. It was as if you had gone off to a war and I might never see you again. But . . ." and this was what she had come to say, this was what had to be said—"but I've been a grasping, selfish child, not a woman at all. Except that I've loved." She was surprised at the calm-ness in her voice; there was a stillness through her whole being. "And I love you more, not less, for what you've done. No—for being as you are."

"There hasn't been an hour," he said quietly, "when I was not conscious of what I was doing to you. A man never knows whether his choices are correct or fair. I often doubt whether a man actually makes choices."

She nodded. She had come to that, too. "He is as he is. Yes."

Then the calm was gone; it shattered in her like glass breaking. "I'm so *sorry!*" she cried.

And Karl stepped to her, smiling faintly now. "Here, here, girl. It may be a day of repentance, but there's no atonement called for." His voice was gentle, his blue eyes gentler still. "You've come—that's enough."

She lowered her head. "How much longer?"

"A month perhaps. To get the cleanup organized."

She lifted her head. "I'll stay," she said.

A long moment. He moved slowly to the window. He gazed out—toward the volcano in the distance. Then he said: "No. I have my job. You have yours. And yours is elsewhere."

"I'll stay," she persisted. "The girls can spend the time with their grandparents."

His back rigid to her, he said it again: "No."

Once again rejected, she sensed a return of the hateful
emotions that had tormented her all this long time, the irrational but withering impression that he had chosen a rival,
deserting her. Fighting, but helplessly, against feelings that
she thought she had conquered, she said nothing.

He turned to face her then. "I told you, Lilja, I don't
trust The Bitch," he said.

And then she knew—not rejection, concern. Love. She
recalled in the instant what the pilot had said: *Any damn time.
Any time.*

"What's a month?" she asked. "We're young. You've
never seemed more so. And I've never felt younger." She
rushed to him then. "Oh Karl, I'm proud. I'm so *proud!*"

He did not kiss her. He bent slightly and, before she
realized, he had swooped her up into his arms and had
stepped to the bed and had placed her on it, full length. "If
you knew," he said, "how many times I've dreamed this.
Asleep and awake. And right here!"

The old familiar exhilaration. The old familiar elation.
The vitality of the man. All overwhelmed her and a raptur-
ous gladness flooded her.

And she laughed. "It's not even night," she said.

"I know," he said. "That's coming. And it's very long."

"I'll be large soon, they tell me, and then I wouldn't. I
couldn't let anyone there see me like that."

Agnar heard his daughter's voice as from a distance.
More and more of late voices, sounds, scenes, everything
seemed to reach him across vast, dim spaces. And he said:
"Ask Rolf. Rolf will come on the *Njord* and he will take you."

The disarray was gone now; order prevailed in the alien
house in Reykjavik. Rosa's doing. Since she had come to live
with him, all reminders of Ruth's foundering last madness

had been removed. But Ruth's spirit hovered. And would, always.

"Only for Easter Sunday," Rosa was saying. "Only that."

"No, Rosa. No." For if he went now, when he could no longer believe, it would be a mockery. In its own way, hypocrisy. Worse—sacrilege. But how could a man believe after what had happened to Ruth?

"Are you never going back then?"

Had he decided that? Yes. He must have decided without knowing. He thought of the kitchen and Ruth; the parlor and Ruth; and the bedroom and Ruth. The house was gone. But it was in his mind, etched clear, its blue roof blindingly beautiful, how Ruth had loved it. And Ruth was gone. But not from his mind. In his mind she would always be quick with life. Not the strange woman who had wandered these rooms here in blind dismay, like a demented ghost. A bird blown out of its latitude. No. The Ruth alive in his mind was that other woman, content and smiling and always busy, that girl he had married, that child . . .

Rosa sat opposite him, across the glass-topped coffee table. "Is it true then—never?"

He did not move. "It's true," he said, knowing.

"I'll ask Rolf then. I thought . . . only for Easter, mind. To go to church again, there, as I did when I was a child. Happy . . . and a child . . ."

Easter Sunday. The confident churchbell ringing out, chaos in the kitchen, all scrubbed and shining, eyes on the clock, rush and hurry, Ruth presiding merrily but sternly over all, even himself; then to the church, the congregation—serge, satins under the heavy coats, neckties and lacy hats and bows—all filing into the pews, bobbing and nodding with hints of smiles, the children solemn but restless and searching for mischief, parents frowning; then the hymns, some bawling through them loudly, others faintly murmuring or only mouthing the words, and the prayers, heads down, and then the sermon. Reverend Petur quavering and uncertain and apologetic behind the pulpit, Bible quotes and words to make a man doze . . .

"What do you do all day while I'm at work?" she asked.

Rosa. The present. Rosa grown up now, and with child.

"I walk. Or I read sometimes." Not often, no. "I go down to the docks. I watch them load. I wonder where they are going."

But mostly . . . he remembered. Only the past was really alive. For something had gone from his life. He knew, he knew. As something, something vital, had gone from Ruth's. She had been pulled up by the roots and tossed carelessly aside. By whom? By God? Small matter. There was, he had learned, no recapture. Something had gone from life and time and the world.

Rosa said: "I don't want to go because I believe in God. Because I'm not sure about that now."

"Rosa," Agnar said then, "believing or not believing in God is of no importance. Believing in life is."

"Do *you* believe in life?"

No.

"Yes," he said. "And if I were your age . . . and carried life in me . . . if I were your age and beginning again, I would believe in it all the more. Yes."

But now it was no. For him.

"How can I talk with Rolf if he's on the *Njord?*" Rosa asked.

"Jonas," her father told her. "He can connect you by radio if the *Njord* is out today. And if not, he can have Rolf ring you back."

Rosa stood, a tall, fair girl, no more than a child herself really. "Are you sure you . . ." But she broke off, her thin shoulders shrugging. She left the room.

Agnar was stiff and empty. There were times when he grew angry: that a disturbance miles below the surface of the earth could wreak this havoc. And more shamefully, guiltily angry—at Ruth. Ruth, how could you do this to us, all of us, how could you? For, walking or lying sleepless, he would never understand.

Never.

No.

Inga could not bear to look at Baldvin's right arm or right hand. Whenever she did, she felt a ghastly shrivelling deep inside. Tomorrow morning Baldvin would be released from the hospital in Oslo, and tomorrow they would board the plane for Reykjavik. After that?

For the endless time—less than three weeks in actuality—that Baldvin had been in the hospital, both had carefully, as if by silent mutual agreement, avoided any reference to his work. Baldvin, at least when with her, had been sober and thoughtful, but never despondent, no hint or suggestion of despair. The small stroke he had suffered that night on the street—she would never forget it, or her terror—had left his right side partly paralyzed. He could walk, but with a slight limp, and he could not even lift his right arm, let alone use his right hand. Inga, forever recalling the conversation—for it had not been an argument—that had precipitated it, suffered an acute and appalling sense of guilt that she could not throw off. No thought of living in Paris now. She struggled against tears in the days with him and gave into them utterly during the nights alone in the hotel room.

Today, his last day of confinement, was different from all other days. It began when she entered his room. He was sitting in a chair and holding, in his left hand, a large-format book of Gauguin reproductions which she had, with misgivings, bought for him. After returning her kiss, studying her red-rimmed eyes and describing, with some gusto, his delicious breakfast, Baldvin lifted his slippered feet to the bed and leaned back, an odd smile on his broad, heavy face, a sly triumph in his dark eyes. What was he thinking?

"Do you still want to live in Paris?" he asked.

Inga sat in the other chair, her legs weak. "I want to live wherever you want to live, Baldvin." And it was true, now.

"You know where I want to live," Baldvin said. "That may not be possible."

Inga realized this was a variation of the dialogue that had triggered the attack. She said, very softly: "If it is possible, ever, I shall love Vestmannaeyjar, no matter." The tears were close. She had to be careful, very careful, no emotion here, none.

"If not Vestmannaeyjar, Paris then, if that's what you wish." His voice was charged with excitement, as in the days when he was working well, and with enthusiasm. "I have been experimenting," he said. "It may take time—no, it will take time. But I am going to learn. I am going to teach myself to paint with my left hand."

The tears came then. She was helpless. She was weeping, she was sobbing, but there was the echo of relief in the sound, too, and then she was on her knees on the floor beside his chair, and he was holding her with his left arm, and her head was against his great throbbing alive chest, and then she was, of all things, kissing his inert right hand and spilling her foolish tears all over it.

"If there are any planes flying from the mainland to Heimaey," Baldvin said, "we could be there in time for Easter."

Easter? Too dumbfounded to speak, she did not lift her head.

"Since you cannot believe in my gods," Baldvin went on, "and I cannot believe in your god, and since you are so foolish as to blame yourself for *my* infirmity, possibly your god could release you from your guilt. Even if you have no good reason to feel it."

She did lift her head then. He smiled at her. He knew; he had known all along.

"Yes," she said, softly. "And also—I have to thank *someone* that you are still alive."

Now, in the latter part of April, the air was not so frigid as it had been on that night when she had left the island three months ago, but it was cold on the deck of the fishing vessel. Margret's confusion was still with her: dread yet a contradictory anticipation, excitement. Three months— during which her whole life had changed. But in what way? How, and to what would it lead?

The boat cut through the dense fog, all lights burning but pale, the bow light penetrating only a few meters into the dense murkiness. Fog—spring. At intervals the skipper—she knew the boy's name now: Rolf—would give a precautionary double blast on the whistle. But Margret was not concerned: collisions at sea were rare in these waters. She did wonder, though, whether she would be able to see the volcano when they came close to Heimaey.

Beside her on the deck, Owen was silent, as if waiting for her to speak, as he had waited for her to make the decision to go back. Owen, she had learned, was a man who could re- spect silences. His face, which, although it was still morning, she could see only dimly, was clean-shaven now, wounds healed, but below the Irish-tweed hat which covered his red hair, his gentle face seemed troubled, alert but vaguely ap- prehensive. Staring ahead, he avoided her glance. She knew his concern: had he been wise to suggest this? was she ready to see the town, had she healed sufficiently inside herself to be exposed to—what? His concern was for her; it was always there. But if he was anxious for her, she also wondered whether she should not have come alone. For wasn't this— whatever lay in front of her—an experience that she had to move through alone, without assistance or outside aid of any sort, even sympathy? Because, sooner or later, she would be alone.

Over the engine's steady churning, she heard a sound: a dull, menacing concussion at first, ugly, intensifying into a low crackling thunder as the boat came closer—the sound that she remembered, but muted, not so horrendous and deafening as the roar and boom of that night when she had fled with the others. Then, through the haze she saw a high narrow column of glitter which, as the *Njord* approached the harbor entry, became a pillar of gold and crimson, wavering and phantomlike, almost a hallucination. Her throat locked, the anticipation turning to dismay, dread, and the cold of the harbor penetrated her flesh, her marrow. She was conscious of Owen's nearness and silence, but even his presence did not reassure her. Hadn't the young skipper said, on the dock in Reykjavik, that the volcano had lost strength, that it was quiet now? But, staring, she realized that he had probably spent the night on the mainland—perhaps the volcano had exploded into new life during the night. What did this portend—more months, possibly years, of devastation and havoc?

For havoc was what she found ashore. She was overwhelmed; she felt she was drowning in a dusty blackness that clogged her head, every pore of her body, took her breath. The bulldozed paths of streets were unrecognizable, wakes of darkness between waves of deeper hue, ebony dunes in which houses stood, some at angles, half-revealed, while others, shattered, lay like wrecks of ships, ribs and spars exposed. Walking, she began to shudder.

She felt Owen's hand tighten on hers. When had he reached to take it?

Devastation wherever the eye moved. Hopelessness settled through her. A second's panic: why had she come? She walked stupefied, dazed. Murk on all sides. Even the sky was heavy, low, the color of iron. The fog was thinner on land. She could see and did not wish to see. As they passed, she recognized the bookshop and the aquarium—she had a wild impulse to run inside, to hide.

After passing the hotel, they arrived at the corner of Kirkjuvegur, and then she could see the two cones clearly: old Helgafell, its green sides black now, dead itself, and the new cone, slightly lower, spouting fire of gold and yellow in a straight, upright plume, spewing black clouds above. And all around it was smoke from invisible crevices and rifts in the high slag heap floating westward over the rooftops. The shuddering was inside, deeper now; otherwise, she was numb.

Her footsteps carried her west, as if without volition, to her own house. To what had been her house. Her home. Once. In another time, another age. It stood upright, soot-covered but intact. Even its tawny-colored roof had been cleared of ash.

It was not hers, though. It belonged to someone else entirely. Someone she may have known once. The door was closed. She had no inclination to go inside. This should have surprised her and did not. She had no home.

Owen, beside her still, said nothing. He had told her that the house was intact. She had not been able, quite, to believe him. And she had been shocked at herself when she realized that she had been, in fact, disappointed. Why couldn't it have been engulfed or shattered like the others? She turned away.

Along streets that she had known all her life but recognized now in only a trancelike way, she went to her sister's house. The yellow roof had been cleared. But too late: an entire corner of the structure had collapsed when the roof caved in. And everywhere was grime. She recalled her sister telling her that someone, most likely Arni, had ransacked it. Ripping off cabinet doors, smashing crockery. Damn Arni, damn him to the deepest depths of hell! Violence, violence.

There it was: the sick, sour hatred was still there. Was she doomed to live with it forever? Owen, in one of his rare moments of impatience or anger, had said she could not live *with* it. *It destroys,* he had said. *It corrodes, it corrodes you, Margret.*

Reaching the corner, she saw a man she knew. Not his name, but the man himself: that great giant of a farmer who had the stern and furious-faced wife and the gentle, half-smiling son who had been on the boat with her the night of the evacuation. Alongside the man's thick solid legs now was a large dog, which had been with Josef whenever she had seen him. Yes, Josef—that was the boy's name. His father walked in a blind, plodding way, his square jaw fixed. She stepped into his path. It was not like her to do such. She was not herself. The huge face above her frowned. How was Josef? The head shook and the pale eyes seemed to recede.

Seeing the anguish there, she regretted her impulse. And something in her winced: she did not want to know.

"Josef," the man said, "is dead." He said it as if he did not believe it. Then he nodded. "Yes. He died in hospital. Over there. They said it was a hospital. They said they would care for him." The forlorn misery and loneliness in his eyes and voice choked her to silence, when she longed to speak, to reach out a hand. "Maybe as well," the man said then. "They did not understand Josef in that place." Then she felt her hand go out. It touched the worn wool over the steellike muscle of the man's upper arm. Tears burned under her lids. The man's enormous head shook once, again. "Yes. Josef may be better now. *Bless.*" Stolidly, the man moved down the street, the dog at his side.

She felt Owen's hand on her arm. But his presence did not reassure her. Nothing could. The boy had been different from other people. Yes. But in the city: *They did not understand in that place.* No. But here, here in Vestmannaeyjar, they had understood. *Was* this her home, then, after all?

They passed the school that she had attended and where Arni had taught. Damn, damn him, may he rot. They passed the church, which looked, miraculously, as it always had. She had seen Owen's photographs of the cemetery alongside awash in black ash; now the gravestones were upright and exposed, and the stone Madonna, one hand missing, was virginal white again. They again crossed the three-block-wide flat chasm where the blazing avalanche had razed every building to the ground. Again appalled, she hurried to move on, but Owen's hand halted her.

As if again sensing her feelings and thoughts, he spoke at last: "From here you can see all the houses that escaped."

And she looked to the west. Row upon row, street after street of dwellings and stores intact, roofs cleared, their many colors a tapestry of solidity. And hope? She had already walked along streets where there had been little or no damage—but she had not seen. And she recalled that only one-third of the structures had been damaged or destroyed. In her shock she had been blind to all but the ruination.

She moved on, knowing she should thank Owen but unable to speak. The hospital was on their left, alongside the flattened avalanche path, its wounded side repaired, its roof in place, its windows to the east covered with sheets of steel. It remained. And she realized that some of the numbness had left her.

They reached the bank corner. The clock, of which Owen had told her, no longer read 1:55. It was running again.

When they turned onto Vestmannabraut, the street-lamps came on, and she realized that it was nightfall. The post office, with the communications center in the rear, was on their right. And the pharmacy, its windows black. She recalled the newspaper accounts of the man who had died. The only human casualty in the disaster, the papers had reported. Then what of Josef? What of the captain's wife, the mother of the boy now skippering the *Njord,* who had decided, Margret had been told, to walk into the sea? How many others of whom she did not know?

And what of the living casualties? Like Margret Magnusdottir?

This time, aware of her concentration on the pharmacy, Owen misread her thoughts. He spoke as softly as he could against the other sound, to which she had already become somewhat accustomed: "The danger of gas is more or less past. Except in closed houses and cellars. Otherwise, we'd be wearing masks."

She only nodded. But, again, she was inwardly moved: how kind, how really gentle and caring was this man. Had he not revealed to her that a man, to be a man, need not be demanding, utterly overwhelming, and cruelly possessive, that lovemaking was a mutual thing, not an assault—had he not taught her that a man can be even more a man for being tender, compassionate? If nothing else, she had learned what manhood was. Thank you, Owen.

They reached Heidarvegur again, at the hotel corner, and turning it, they looked down the incline toward the harbor, which was swathed in steam and smoke and fog.

Everywhere a steady pulsing sound filled the air—from the huge hoses and from the pumping vessels and from the fire trucks. The frigid arctic water was still being discharged onto the hardening ramparts of lava.

Across the street, on the left, beyond the fire station, the aquarium again beckoned—a low, square building, dusted with grit, the mural on its face discolored. She crossed the street. The door was not locked. The interior—she breathed again, more of the numbness retreating—was as she had always known it. There was even a hush here, as in the past, a quietude, that other new strange sound shut out. Beyond the entry hall, a room with stuffed birds and animals in cases, looking alive and looking as they had always looked, in the same places. In the larger main room beyond, the fish in their glass tanks, alive, still gliding, feeding, very much alive. Only here, only in this place, did she feel her Vestmannaeyjar; only here was she at home again. Strolling from tank to tank, she recalled a story that she had heard in Reykjavik: that the keeper of the aquarium, as the showers of pumice and lava lumps rained down, had taken his seals and his fish from the tanks down to the ocean and had released them. Untrue, untrue. For here they were. Just as she had remembered them; just as she had dared not remember them in the three months past.

She sank to a bench. And stared at the ugly-mouthed catfish. And was conscious that Owen had left her. How like Owen—to sense, to know. Had there ever been a man like Owen before?

To come had been his idea. Why? Aware of the horror and the consuming anguish and erosive hate that remained alive in her, had he believed that, facing and seeing this greater desolation and the fight being carried on against it, she might be able to accept her own or to fight it? Did he believe that she was strong enough now? If he had no doubts, she did. And many.

Had he doubted when he returned to Reykjavik and charged into her hotel room and confessed his love? *You don't have to love me, Margret. It's enough that I love you.* His mind fixed then, his purpose clear. And she had agreed to go to the north with him again, and during the night there had been a renewal of passion. In the early morning darkness and cold they had left the city in the rented van, and soon they were traveling the treacherous deserted roads of winter through a bare and pristine world, covered with its thin sheet of snow, the two of them warm and isolated once again in intimacy. She had refused to give in to the superstition and myth that she, all her life, had been surrounded by, but, nevertheless, in time, she stopped trying to shake off the overpowering feeling that, in some way beyond reasonable comprehension, she had known this man beside her from some earlier life, perhaps in some other time centuries ago. And in her a healing, of which she became slowly and gratefully conscious, began.

On those roads, almost impassable from time to time, it had been a day's journey to their destination. That night they spent in one sleeping bag in the rear of the van, making love urgently and intensely, with abandon, and then later, more quietly, lengthily and with infinite gentleness, and afterwards they lay close, bodies entwined, and in half-slumbering contentment they could hear a faint sound on all sides, the primordial stillness crackling with only the faintest suggestion or promise of spring.

In the gray morning, while he clambered about taking photographs with infinite patience, she explored the chasm, jaggedly defined by low cliffs, and, along its floor, a crack in the earth, very narrow, like a fault left by an earthquake. Over lunch, with wine, he explained: that long opening in the crust of the surface was the Mid-Atlantic Rift. It ran, he said, along the longest range of mountains in the world, twenty-eight thousand miles long, volcanically formed, and all undersea. And the floor of the sea itself continued to split apart at about the rate that a fingernail grows! She became aware of the banked-up intensity of his wonder. Here—and only here—was the one place on the face of the planet where the mid-ocean ridge was visible above sea level! His excitement became a part of her. And it was along this rift that all

of the many volcanoes of Iceland occurred! So . . . so this
journey was vital to his coverage of the eruption on Heimaey.
And what an excuse to kidnap her!

His vitality and gaiety were transmitted to her like an
electrical current, and in the overwhelming aliveness that his
exultancy imparted, her own grief and loss paled somewhat,
receded—had he plotted this antidote to the poisons still
roiling in her veins?

When he had used all his film, she discovered that she
was reluctant to return to Reykjavik. What then? On the way
she told him. And miles later, passing a lonely, wild beach far
below, orange in color, it had been Owen who had asked: *If
not Reykjavik, then Vestmannaeyjar?* Startled, feeling his eyes on
her, she had only nodded.

What did he imagine? That she had freed herself from
the long dark night of anguish and loss and wrath? She
wished it were so. But it was not. With the image of Arni
quivering in her mind, there came the inevitable taste of bile
on her tongue, and the hate flooding her whole body. And
with it the cool certainty that to hazard total giving ever again
would be to hazard disaster. She could never again say *I love.*

When they reached the suburbs of the city, she said:
Owen . . . I think I would like to see Arni's mother. She hoped he
would not ask why, for she herself did not know.

But, unsurprised, possibly satisfied, Owen said: *I know
the way.* His tone was wry, self-mocking. *If you think not, look at
my ear.*

She looked. *Poor Owen.* She reached to touch it. *It is the
most beautiful ear I have ever seen.* Then, on an impulse free of
guilt or even regret yet intensifying the turmoil in her, she
leaned to kiss it.

In the high apricot-colored house on the lake Arni's
mother herself appeared at the door: the great big-boned
face with the beaklike nose was cold. She ushered Margret
in—no puzzlement, not even surprise—and then she whirled
on her with a ferocious accusation: *You are the reason he has
gone!* Margret's compassion, already uncertain and tentative,
withered, and she heard the knife-edged voice continuing:

had Margret not been an untrue wife, dare she say otherwise, even now there was a man outside waiting for her, was there not! But, staring, Margret glimpsed the pain behind the savagery in the old woman's eyes, loss and bleak loneliness. Still, she refused to allay that misery by confessing to an untruth that, while it might relieve and exonerate the woman, would render her, Margret, less than she knew herself to be. Nor, stubbornly, would she give the woman the satisfaction of a denial. She turned to leave, but the other woman reached a hand and took her arm in a clawlike grip. *Please, no. Have coffee, please.* The naked plea, the depth of her need reached Margret. She stayed. She had coffee. She wondered silently why she had come—what had she expected to accomplish? And for whom? *Where could he be?* Arni's mother asked. *If you know, Margret, tell me.* But she did not know, and said it. *Do you wonder, Margret? Sometimes, yes. Do you still love him?* Margret took a deep breath but she did not hesitate: she shook her head. Abruptly then the woman demanded: *Do you think he hates me?* Startled then, Margret replied: *I do not know, Arni had . . . has much hate in him.* The woman nodded, eyes dull now: *I am the one. I am the one he hates. He was not my husband. My husband died, too. In this house. He died when he learned about Arni. About me. Arni heard the shot. Is it any wonder Arni hates me? I never told him about himself. But somehow he knew.* She blinked her eyes as if realizing where she was. *Why do I tell you now?* She stopped speaking. Her eyes were withdrawn, bleak, her strong jaw slack.

Stiff with shock and cold, Margret could not move. Behind cruelty—suffering. Her impulse was to stand and flee.

Margret, can you forgive me? I'm the one who told the lie. Can you?

Could she? *Yes,* she lied. For she could not. Compassion, yes, pity, but not forgiveness. It was not in her, even now. Too much devastation lay behind.

She stood. She stepped and placed a hand on the woman's heavy shoulder, which was quivering. Their eyes met.

I'll come again. She saw Arni's mother smile; she had never seen her smile before. *No. You say it, but no. It's as well.*

And perhaps it was. Margret went to the hall, sobered and
sad yet strangely relieved. *Bless,* she said before opening the
door. And Arni's mother asked: *Why Margret? Why did I lie? I
wonder how many years I will have to ponder that. Not many, I trust.
Bless.* And as Margret fled to the waiting van parked along
the curb, she wondered whether she herself might become
such a pathetic, bitter creature.

In the seat she wept openly, and without shame. Owen
asked nothing. But she told him, through sobs, for now at
last she knew. She had torn up the roots. She knew why Arni
drank. Why he could not trust any woman. His cruelty. Was
knowing enough? Had it severed any bond, brought any
light? She placed her hand over Owen's. Was she free?

Because of the weather no planes had been flying to
Heimaey. They drove to the docks and there, learning that
no commercial vessels were scheduled to go to Vestmannaeyjar, they had decided to go to the hotel and wait until
tomorrow, Easter Sunday. And it had been then that Margret had recognized a boat moored against one of the piers.
And when she saw the name on its hull—*Njord*—she was
certain. Its skipper was a very young man, no more than a
boy, whom she had seen about the town, often on a motorcycle, but whose name she could not recall. He walked with a
slight limp, which she did not remember, and he was small,
like Owen. He wore a captain's cap, tilted at a jaunty angle,
he smoked a pipe, and his eyes were almost merry. Welcome
aboard. It was a large vessel and only one passenger—his
sister, if she ever came.

In her days in Reykjavik recently, Margret had heard a
rumor from one of the other evacuees whom she had met on
the street in her endless walking: the wife of the captain of
the *Njord* had disappeared, and it was assumed, because of
her state of mind, that she walked into the sea. Was this then
the woman's son? Boarding with Owen, Margret wondered
how many others had given in to despair in such a way. And
she recognized something else about herself then: not once
had that way of deliverance from grief and anguish even
entered her mind.

The sister arrived, a tall, slender girl with fair hair and troubled eyes. Laughing, the skipper chided her for being late, but took her hand tenderly to help her aboard. And after he had introduced Margret, whose name for some odd reason he remembered, and after she had introduced Owen, whom Rolf said he knew, although not by name, because they had worked together in Vestmannaeyjar, Rolf went up the steps and into the wheelhouse, limping but whistling. And on the journey the sister sat alone, staring at the sea, silent and brooding. Why? No knowing what tragedies lie behind any face, every face. Was she thinking of her mother? Of their home on the island as it once had been? Or of some even more personal anguish or fear? Tempted, Margret did not try to speak to her. One must respect another's sadness, pain.

As Owen respected hers. How long now had she been sitting here alone in the aquarium in Vestmannaeyjar, where she had so often retreated to find solitude and tranquility, or the illusion of it? Here, everything was familiar and in place. There may be chaos elsewhere, even outside the doors, but here order prevailed. And it was a comfort, always had been. She stood up from the bench and strolled again from tank to tank. The familiar fish—sleek and silver, black, speckled, golden—were gliding as always behind the glass. She could not hear the earth-moving machinery or the trucks or the pumping; even Kirkjufell's detonation was muted, distant. Here, the only place, it was as if she had never left the island.

She heard her name and twisted her head to look over her shoulder, wishing she could do as he hoped her to do, smile, but she could not. But it was not Owen. His name was Jonas and he was Arni's friend, the radio operator who, the newspapers had reported, had first discovered the eruption. With him, but three tanks away, were three boys who were whispering and tittering, fingers tentatively touching the glass as if to make contact with the fish.

The man's open, friendly face was smiling, almost apologetically, for the intrusion. "Have you come back then, Margret?"

"Only for Easter. Only to see. And you?"

"We have come, yes. My wife. Three of my four sons. The oldest will complete the school term in Reykjavik." He shrugged his thick shoulders. "He wishes to stay, but he is too young. My wife tells me there are many like him, especially the young." He shook his head as if he could not imagine such. "Your house still stands."

"Yes. I saw. And yours?"

"It burned. But we have another. We are cleaning it now. It belonged to Frosti Runaldsson. The old man who owned the fish factory."

She recalled him only vaguely: tall, dignified, gray. "He had no family left, so . . ." He did not finish.

"Is it over then?" she asked. "If you have brought your family . . ."

"No one will say. No one *can* say. It is sporadic. Yesterday—quiet. Last night, without warning—you saw, you heard. Today, you see, you hear. The lava flow is less and less. But . . . there is a risk. Yes."

Yes. Risks everywhere, outside and inside, and only a few strong enough, brave enough, whole enough to . . .

"But then," Jonas said, "if there was no hazard, it would not be living. Old Kirkjufell taught me that the last thirteen weeks." He was not smiling now. Even his tone had changed: "I heard you were here, Margret. Word has always traveled fast here, but with so few of us now . . ." He reached into the pocket of his heavy coat. "I have been holding a letter for you."

She did not want it. She would not read it. No! Tear it up, please, only tear it to shreds, please!

"I had thought to give it to you next time I was in Reykjavik, but then no one seemed to know where you . . ."

She was staring at the envelope. Please tear it up, to shreds, please.

"It is from Istanbul, Turkey. He asked me to see that you received it."

She saw his heavy, dark, hairy hand and the envelope extended. Owen, Owen, where are you?

She took it between her fingers. "Thank you." Her fingers were trembling.

Jonas hesitated only a moment. It seemed an eternity. Then he said: "I wasn't certain what to do. But Arni was . . . Arni is my friend."

He spoke as she had spoken to Arni's mother: Arni was . . . Arni is. Then Arni was alive.

"Boys!" he said, and then to her, *"Bless,"* and she was alone again.

She sat stiffly on a bench and decided: the letter, whatever it contained, did not concern her now. Arni *was* dead. If not actually dead, then dead to her. Or was he? Could he be since she was shaking all over?

She tore open the envelope and read the precise schoolmasterly handwriting. *Dear Margret: They will now permit me to write for the first time. One letter. Turkish jails are not the most comfortable but I must accommodate myself for the next five years. I deserve the vermin, human and others.*

You do, yes. And worse.

It would be a foolish and useless thing to write that I am sorry.

Yes, it would. *Be* sorry, *be* sorry!

I wish I were Christian in my beliefs, because then I could believe that my life here, or living death here in this stone and filth and brutality could expiate my guilt.

Nothing could, ever, nothing.

Know this, Margret: I shall do whatever you wish me to do to free you in every way.

I am free. I am *becoming* free!

The one unbearable torture that burns in me day and night is this: did Doctor Pall tell the truth? If you can find it in your heart, would you answer? Did I kill my own child? Arni.

Yes, yes, yes.

But her head went down. She did not weep. Five years, a man like Arni, proud, fettered, in filth, not the hero of dreams, not slain honorably in battle and about to enter Valhalla, the hall of immortality for heroes, but degraded, an ignominy beyond imagining. She recalled what Owen had said about pity: that it could be a part of love, why not? Yes.

It can be—she knew that now. But she also knew that one can pity and *not* love. As she no longer loved Arni. Or even hated him. For pity can also obliterate hatred, Owen. She knew. Now.

She realized what she had to do. She would write to Arni the lie that would give him freedom from at least some of his torment: Doctor Pall was only trying to punish you for what you did to me. Your mother lied. There was no child in me.

But something in her rebelled. She lifted her head. The act *had* been committed. For whatever reasons. Arni was as he was—for whatever reasons. But she also was as she had become—for whatever reasons. She could pity, but she could not forgive. And to lie now would make her party to the act itself.

"What is it, Margret?" She had not heard him approaching. He stood in front of her, looking down. "You're pale."

She gazed upwards into his eyes—how anxious, how unutterably concerned. "Expiation," she said. She smiled faintly. "It's that time of year." Another bond broken. Another small faltering step toward freedom.

It was so like Owen not to ask an explanation. The solicitude on his face became simple gravity—hesitation perhaps. What had he come to tell her?

"And what," she asked, rising, hearing an unfamiliar, or almost forgotten, throb in her voice, "what have you been doing all this while?"

"Riding in an ambulance with Doctor Pall. He showed me a house. It's out of the village, an old farmhouse on a cliff over the sea. Inside, the walls are white and . . . it's charming."

Something in her, wary, retreated. Not in panic—a slow cautious withdrawal that caused her smile to fade. "The one where the Dutch writer lived. And his French wife."

"She's gone now." He spoke in a low level whisper, as if to banish the excitement that she knew he felt and that frightened her—or possibly to conceal his apprehension. "Doctor Pall bought the house from her. I suspect he did it to provide money so that she could go back to France."

She knew what he was saying. What he was trying to say. Please, do not, Owen. Please do not say it.

If there was no hazard, it would not be living.

Then Owen said: "I'm not afraid of the volcano if you're not."

But he knew. He knew well. It was not the volcano that terrified her. It was another risk altogether. The danger of ever giving yourself over completely. He knew. People change. Arni had been kind once, and gentle. And loving.

Owen waited in silence.

She could not bear to go on looking into his eyes.

She turned and fled.

She had not recovered. She would never recover.

Outside, it was dark. Only the streetlamps and, through her tears, that thin wavering tower of fire beyond the roof-tops.

NINE

IT WAS SO QUIET on Sunday morning that the bell in the church tower could be heard distinctly all through the town. It rang with solemnity, but did not toll a knell. There had been a church on this spot since the coming of Christianity almost a thousand years ago. The first church, of timber, had burned centuries ago, possibly in 1627, the year of the Turks, a year of thirteen moons. There was no plume of flame today, only a shimmering radiance along the crater's edge and above it a tower of smoke, almost white, with a zigzag vein of scarlet in it, like a red-hot wire spiraling up and dying out in the circular clouds which, higher, were darker. Although only the vigilant scientists were aware of it, lava was bubbling up at the eastern side of the crater gap and was running south along the base of the cone, then down and through a cave and harmlessly out to sea.

When the bell was silent, the organ took over. Reverend Petur Trygvasson was in the vestry, alone, waiting for his wife, at the keyboard, to bring the music to a crescendo to inform him that at least most of the congregation were seated. He had no idea how many would be here today. More of the islanders were returning every day now and on a Sunday such as this relatives on the mainland would come to spend the day with the workers here—and to view the depradation with their own eyes.

Petur was always nervous before a service, any service,

but this morning his disquiet was of a different sort. He was not even sure that he should conduct the service. He had been living in a turmoil of doubt ever since his arrival weeks ago. He had rewritten his sermon at least nine times: what had occurred here is the will of God, and if our finite minds cannot comprehend, we must have faith and accept; everything has meaning; we are all sinners deserving punishment. *Vengeance is mine, I will repay, saith the Lord.* Vengeance for what, punishment for what crime, what sin? There are Sodoms everywhere; Gomorrahs dot the map of the world. *Whom the Lord loveth, he chasteneth.* Petur could, try as he might, perceive no justice in this. But had not his father, the bishop, always said that if you doubt God's justice, you doubt God?

Did he doubt God then? For once one does, there lies across that line a vast desert of nothingness—a wasteland in which there can be no meaning whatever in anything. Feeling thus, could he deliver the sermon that he held, in rolled sheets, in his hand?

The music swelled mightily, then softened and continued. He nervously adjusted his heavy vestments, maroon and gold, and breathing shallowly, he opened the door to the chancel, and then he was facing the nave that was almost filled. The faces this morning did not wear that haggard work-worn expression that flickered above the hand-held candles at the night assemblies; gone were the bleak and weary eyes. They rose together from the stiff wooden pew-benches; they stood with a quiet dignity and, in surprise, he felt a sense of reverence in himself. If not for God, of whose very existence he was no longer certain, then for what, for whom? Looking out over the gathering, he was suffused with a sense of oneness with them, a unity that, until he had come back and had cleaned and painted the church himself, he had never known and, until this moment, had not quite realized.

There were strangers, too, and many familiar faces not present—how many would never return? The two rear pews were occupied by U.S. servicemen in uniform. Petur knew that many were here because of nostalgia rather than faith—a human need, not religious, but he understood. Not present in the first row was Frosti Runaldsson, whose thin, gray, withering face had become a part of the Sunday service. Old Frosti, free of pain at last, was now at rest in the churchyard outside the arched windows of stained glass. Thurbjorn Herjolfsson, who had always been a faithful deacon, occupied Frosti's place, here as well as at the plant on the edge of the harbor. Thurbjorn's pretty young wife was not with him, but then most of the women had not returned.

When the music came to a halt, his wife turned on the seat and regarded him. Tenderness swept through him. Her father remained ill, nearer to death than ever, yet she had come. To be with him on Easter she had said. But now she had decided to stay. *It's where I should be,* she had said. Her face was somber now and her back was stiff; her primness stirred desire in him. He thought of her naked and writhing with passion, eyes soft and luminous and pleading.

Then, instead of lifting his hand in a gesture for all to be seated, he took a step toward them and, to his own surprise for he had not planned this, he quoted from the Psalms: *"We went through fire and through water."* And after a pause, picturing Noah on the deck of the boat with only the flood to every horizon: *"In her mouth was an olive leaf."* Was he offering hope then, a promise? And was it possible that Noah and his family were the only good people on earth, the only ones worthy of escaping God's wrath?

To escape such thoughts, he announced the hymn and the organ began to peal again. During the singing, he gazed over the gathering and was startled: Baldvin and Inga were standing off the center aisle toward the rear, only Inga singing. Baldvin in a Christian church! But why had he not come to visit? Were they no longer friends? A sense of waste and sadness settled through him—imagine sacrificing human friendship because you did not agree with the friend's convictions about matters metaphysical. And then Petur thought of Baldvin's painting—and his bafflement deepened.

Her voice lifted in thanksgiving, Inga was conscious of

Baldvin's left hand on the back of the seat in front of them. It seemed always to be in motion now. Every waking hour, on the two planes and since their arrival here this morning, he exercised and limbered it constantly.

His eyes wandering, Petur was even more shocked to catch sight of Doctor Pall off to the side, alone. Since his wife's death in childbirth years ago, Pall had never come to church except for a wedding or a funeral. Their eyes met, held. Instead of condemning Pall for his skepticism—atheism perhaps—Petur now envied him the simplicity of his view: the easy acceptance of a vast accidentality, chance, chaos. Once Petur had thought it warped arrogance. Now . . . he did not know. If denying his Lord, like his namesake in the New Testament, led down the path to eternal damnation, Petur was already condemned. He had been in a hell of his own for weeks now. And he could live so.

Doctor Pall had sensed his old friend's spiritual or philosophical dilemma that night in his old office in the hospital, and today, observing, he wondered to what depths it had carried the man. How stupid, how utterly childish and foolish, to imagine that you must be a part of some grand design that encompasses the universe. Pall had decided to attend the Easter service, not out of any religious impulse, but because of a new-found awareness of a fellowship with the people he had known and served most of his life. A solidarity. Unless, of course, that feeling was really religious, in a different sort of way.

As the voices rose to a climax on the last verse, Petur, quivering and in sudden panic, felt lonely, isolated here in the presence of so many people, alone. He dare not, ever, express his misgivings, the harrowing rebellion in his spirit, even to his wife. Perhaps, though, Pall would comprehend. Weren't they still friends?

The music stopped and the mingled echo of voices and organ died away. He lifted two arms and the congregation sat. This was, by custom, the time for announcements: wedding bans, social functions, dates. Today he had only one announcement. He spoke hesitantly, as always, hearing the hated wavering in his tone: "It is my sad . . . my somewhat awkward . . . task . . . to inform you that our name for the volcano . . . our volcano . . . has been officially named by the Icelandic-place-name commission. The name Kirkjufell, I have been informed, is reserved for mountains whose shape resembles that of a church. Henceforth, therefore, Kirkjufell will be known as Eldfell." He was conscious of the dismay in the faces before him, a few reflecting outrage. And then, thinking of the servicemen volunteers in the rear, he repeated what he had just said in English, adding: "The volcano is officially named Fire Mountain." Turning then to the pulpit, Petur realized, knowing the people, his people, that for them the new volcano, 240 meters or 800 feet, high now, would always be Kirkjufell.

He mounted the steps and, in the pulpit, he waited a long moment. Then he began his sermon as written, quoting: ". . . *and in the earth, blood, and fire, and pillars of smoke.*" Looking down on the faces of his townspeople, expectant now, flushed with anticipation and victory, he was strangely moved. Their expressions, their presence, seemed to touch something in him—to quicken and arouse him. He thought of all they had done, all they had still to do, all that he knew would be done!

And he decided: he could not deliver the sermon that he held in his hand. He placed it aside. His voice, when he began to speak, took on a firmer, more certain pitch. From memory he quoted again: *"While the earth remaineth, seedtime and harvest, and cold and heat, and summer and winter, and day and night shall not cease!"*

Then, without faltering, he began to speak, conscious of their silence, their fixed attention: "Man is forever at the mercy of nature." He had not said God. "And nature remains a mystery . . ."

He went on speaking, with fewer and fewer pauses, without weighing each phrase before it was uttered, and he caught sight of Kristrun Egilsdottir and her husband and their daughter, whose name he could not remember, said to be a sibyl, said to have predicted the disaster. Could he be certain that she had not? Were there not prophets in the Old Testament? Why was foretelling in the Bible God's word and today superstitious soothsaying?

He was continuing, listening to his own voice, hearing it firm and clear: "What is the measure of a man? Is it how he meets adversity? Is it his inborn determination to survive whatever terror or desolation is visited upon him?"

He saw Jonas Vigfusson, his wife at his side, three of his sons—and recalled Jonas singing one night in the mess hall and afterwards describing a nightmare his wife had had shortly before the eruption. Another heathen augury? Who was he to say, who was he to deny?

". . . have come through. Not unscathed, but you have *survived.*" What of God—his mercy, his uncaring detachment? "There had been only one casualty—when there might have been thousands." Whom were they to thank? Or was it only happenstance after all, a matter of the wind blowing east instead of west?

In a pew midway to the rear Rolf Agnarsson sat beside his sister Rosa. Hearing the word casualty, Rolf felt a piercing stab of loss, a quick moment of grief. What then of his mother? Was she not a casualty? Yes. But Rolf was not his father. It was not over for him. It was only beginning. And soon now other girls would be returning and one of them, at some future time, would purge the memory of Donna Blakeley from his mind: the plunge into the sea, the nights in the bookshop, her betrayal. But nothing, nothing could ever blot from his memory that awesome spectacle—the abyss, the mysterious and horrible lower depths lying forever beneath us. He did not wish to forget that glimpse of primal chaos because it had its own terrible and appalling beauty.

Hearing his own voice, which did not sound like his voice, Petur was saying: ". . . only a few. We shall never know how many. Only a few succumbed to despair. They are to be pitied, not condemned. They are to be remembered with love and compassion."

And then another face, one which he had never seen here in church before, emerged from the others: the man

known as Patton. "We should be proud." Petur heard that
new confident voice rising and filling the church. "We
should be proud of what has been accomplished here." Then
he found himself quoting again: *"Pride goeth before destruction
. . ."* And, startlingly, his tone deepened and grew louder:
"Untrue. Man has a *right* to pride!" Patton was seated beside
a woman with a radiant face which reflected his words.
"What has been done here—by you, and with the aid of
strangers who had compassion and courage—if we are to be
grateful to anyone, we should be grateful to them and to
ourselves." He included himself for he was one of them now.
He went on: he pictured the future, it might take months,
possibly years, but Heimaey would be as it once was: "We
shall dig out; the tephra will be used for new roads and old,
for the airfield runways, for foundations in the new houses
to be constructed; the molten lava underground will serve as
fuel, piped to heat homes and greenhouses; the fish plants,
those not already destroyed, will operate again, the others
will be rebuilt; schools will reopen; seeds of grass will be
planted, possibly by plane from the air; turf will be brought
in to cover the ashy, salty soil around homes; flowers will
bloom!" His ardor reached a crescendo: "The earth destroys
itself and regenerates itself over and over!" He ceased speaking. There was a long vibrating silence. What he saw on their
faces suffused him with a satisfaction that he had never before experienced. Eyes were bright. Heads were lifted. Tears
glistened. And there were smiles. Then he concluded quietly: "Our only enemy is fear. To live in fear is not to live."
How had he come to this?

He turned and stepped down from the pulpit. He saw
his wife's eyes on him: what a strange expression. He faced
the nave again—his people, his friends, whom he loved—
whom he had come, miraculously, to love. He knew a moment's intoxicating triumph; he saw hope kindled or for-
tified in every countenance.

"Let us pray."

As he turned his back to them, he saw them rising, some
kneeling. He bowed his head, but he did not lead them in

prayer. He was not certain that he knew how—or to whom he would pray. He had not thanked the Almighty, who had spared most of the town and its vital artery, the harbor. Because *they* had done the saving. He was shaken by what he had said and what he was feeling, thinking. Heretical? The blood was coursing hotly through him. Every nerve and fiber was trembling with life.

In the hush there was a sound, outside, up the hill, to the east. A single monstrous gasp. A dying gasp? Or a warning?

Owen Llewellyn, unable to translate the words, could not mistake the zeal behind them. He took the man's fervor to be a paean of gratitude to his particular god. Margret, beside him, leaned close and whispered, "Owen . . . will you always be kind to me? Will you be kind to me forever?" Because Margret now knew, had perhaps always known, that she could not spend her life fleeing. The risks, after all, *were* everywhere, inside and without. Owen, at first frowning his astonishment, then smiled—and she realized what she had said. She brought the back of her hand to her mouth, recalling that time in the green-roofed cottage by the fjord and the meaning of those words there. Her eyes glittered with abashed merriment. She cupped her hand around her lips and leaned closer still. "Take it that way, too," she whispered.

In the stillness Petur had reached a decision: he could not go on here now. Doubting himself, how could he preach faith, belief? Because, he knew, most of those behind him *had* to believe in pattern, meaning, a greater order, an ultimate significance—whether that belief was illusion or not.

He turned slowly to face them again. Those who were kneeling stood now. And, seeing their hopeful, trusting faces again, he was engulfed by rapture. He had come, he realized in a stunned instant, to know love. For the first time. Love for them . . . and for her, his wife, who was staring at him with eyes unnaturally brilliant . . . love for all of humankind. He had, then, the overpowering impression that he was experiencing religion for the first time. The kind that Christ, if there had ever been a Christ in reality, and whether he was God or man, would have understood.

He announced the closing hymn.

Taken by surprise, about to strike the first chord of "Hallelujah"—Praise Ye, the Lord—his wife quickly flipped the pages of the hymnal in front of her, took a deep breath, and began to play. "I'm full of joy like a river." The voices, a few at first and then the others joining, amplified into great waves of sound. "I'm full of peace like a river."

She had been, at first, startled by the sermon. Was it really a sermon? And then, he had become more eloquent, more persuasive, more exciting, she had been stirred in a different way. Her carnal nature, only recently discovered, had brought heat to her face, a tingling desire through her whole being. She had thought of that time on the northwest peninsula, in her father's house, when she had held him there by a passion made desperate by the certainty that, when he left, she would never see him again—and the realization that her natural lust, and his, had never been satisfied. Now, playing the organ in church, she was experiencing the same physical craving, aroused by his mounting strength and confidence and the depth and resonance in his voice. He had seemed, in the pulpit, not the tall wraithlike man in black clothing who, uncertain, walked the streets shyly nodding; he had seemed a knowing giant of a man, throbbing with vigor, dauntless, and assured of what he was saying, inspired and inspiring.

Only now did she realize that, on this holiest of days, not once had he said: *I am the resurrection and the light*. In fact, he had not mentioned God. Or Christ risen. He had not referred, even one time, to the resurrection they had gathered here to celebrate. Yet . . . yet what had he described if not a resurrection. Not of a man, or of the son of God, but of a town.

The hearty voices, in unison, filled the vaulted church: ". . . joy like a river!" And, further amazed, she knew she had never sensed, in any church, at any service, the aura of peace and hope and religious fervency that surrounded her now. The voices soared and lifted together: *"I'm full of peace like a river, joy like a river, love like a river."*

And the music came to a triumphant climax. Knowing

renewal herself—discovery—she struck the final chord and held it. Then there was its echo and then silence again.

When, for a long space of time, Petur did not move or speak, her own secret personal rejoicing returned. She would tell him as soon as they were alone together in the house that now served as the parsonage. After he had performed the christening of the infant born on the fishing vessel en route to the mainland the first night of the eruption. The child was to be named Oceana. She had no idea, yet, what she and Petur would name theirs.

Petur took a long single stride forward. He did not make a gesture of dismissal. He simply said: *"Because I live, ye shall live also."*

During the singing Petur had reached a decision—another and quite different decision from the one he had arrived at only a few minutes ago. If *he* could live without certainty, *they* could not. If his reverence was now for them, for man, not God, they must never know. No one, except possibly Pall, could ever know or even guess. He was one of them at last. He had found a new faith for the old. They were his brothers and he loved them. And he would stay. If they needed reassurance of a God in whom he could no longer believe, he would give them what they needed. He lifted his arms and spread them wide. Who was he to say as a certainty that what they wished to believe was myth and illusion? In that vibrant voice that he had now, gratefully, come to recognize as his own, he quoted from the Book of Job: *"The morning stars sang together and all the sons of God shouted for joy!"*

Then the organ began to sound and he smiled at his wife's back: *she* had decided on what to play. "Hallelujah!"

And the bell in the tower began to ring with a swift and furious gladness, and there was a shuffling and a shaking of hands, nodding and embraces, and the music swelled.

The triumphant clanging of the church bell, defiant and rejoicing, could be heard as far away as the harbor, where the sound echoed over the water and up and around the cliffs and faded out over the arctic waters.

Walking the two blocks along Kirkjuvegur, they heard

the bell behind them. Arriving at Heidarvegur, Margret broke away from him and, instead of turning right toward the town center, she turned left. Still incredulous at what she had whispered during the prayer, Owen knew at once where she was going. He followed. She was running now along the narrow road of red lava gravel, graceful and abandoned as a child. She *was* a child! He watched with mounting delight as she stopped, swung about and came back to take his arm, hugging it in both of hers as she fell into step beside him.

"See the green," she said. "The farther you go, the greener. The tephra fall must have been light out here."

Meadows flowed on both sides, lightly flecked with new growth. They had left the blackness behind. But they could still hear the bell, distant now, and muted. The sky was high, no sun, only white clouds drifting, and the call of birds overhead.

"Soon," she said, "soon the daisies will be in flower, and the beach pea, buttercups, and dandelions! And on the cliffsides, yellow angelica. Soon, Owen, *soon*!" She stopped and held his arm more tightly, bringing him to a halt. "I forgot. You did not understand, did you?" Her face, a child's, looked stricken and guilty. "You did not understand a word of the sermon or the songs!"

He was amused. "I understood without knowing the words."

She smiled then, not the faint sad smile he had seen so often, but a smile of dazzling incandescence, a smile that transformed her face, her whole being. "Do you know what Heimaey means, Owen—in your language?"

He knew. But he said: "What does it mean, Margret?"

"It means . . . Island of Home." The smile became a deep-throated laugh. "That's where we are!"

She released his arm then and began to run again along the road in the direction of the house on the cliff above the sea. No longer unbelieving, he watched. If she had come home, he had discovered his. At last.